WILDERNESS OF MIRRORS

Lost in a Labyrinth of Lies

A Novel

By, Barry L. Jones

Copyright © 2017

Dedication

***

Wilderness of Mirrors is for those with gnawing suspicions....

For the parents, who continually feel pressured by the health care system to pump their children full of vaccines, regardless of misgivings they might have about terrible side effects.

For the skeptics who do not believe Lee Harvey Oswald murdered President Kennedy. For the doubters who question whether crazed, lone gunmen also killed Dr. Martin Luther King, Jr. and Senator Robert Kennedy. The official versions just do not ring true.

For the survivors who wonder how cancer became such a uniquely American epidemic and why, after all these years, we still do not have a cure. Could it be there are too many people sucking off the treatment teat?

For the Americans who are just starting to realize the sad truth – our government lies to us.

***

Table of Contents

***

***

Introduction

***

***"The road to hell is paved with good intentions*" –
St. Bernard of Clairvaux

An antibiotic is supposed to fight infection, NOT cause an epidemic. Likewise, a vaccination is supposed to prevent disease, NOT create a new one. It is certainly NOT supposed to be the prototype for a bio-weapon or worse, a weapon of mass destruction.

The research that gave the world its first antibiotic WAS well intentioned. There's no debating penicillin DID work – as Allied soldiers on the World War II battlefields of Europe would testify. Likewise, polio vaccinations DID eliminate the scourge of its time – one that disproportionately affected the world's children.

So how did successful, well-intentioned medical breakthroughs boomerang and put us on the path to hell?

***

"***Most of the evil in this world is done by people with good intentions***" –T.S. Eliot

Wilderness of Mirrors is the story of good intentions going awry. Terribly awry. In the field of medicine, unintended consequences can be deadly. They are mistakes. If acknowledged, the problems can be fixed and the mistake forgiven. Lesson learned.

However, if no one acknowledges the unintended consequences, it ceases to be a mistake. By definition, the consequences become intentional – requiring a cover-up.

***

"***A lie travels around the world six times before the truth gets out of town***" –Mark Twain

Cover-ups begin with one lie. Then another. Over time, the lies multiply and the cover-up is less about the original mistake than it is the subsequent lies. A new cover-up guards the old one and newer lies compound the older ones. Moreover, they ALL must be taken to the grave.

When the lies and cover-ups result in human life becoming an expendable commodity – collateral damage – they are beyond human forgiveness. When the past portends the future of humanity, they are markers, forgotten at our own peril.

Wilderness of Mirrors is a tangled drama of mistakes and deceptions. Of lies protected by covert operations. Of "black-ops" supported by assassinations. Of assassinations followed by contrived inquiries resulting in diversionary – and fictional – reports. Of faux investigations and diversionary cover stories controlled by an unaccountable shadow government. Of a bullying corporate media and an intellectually dishonest education system conspiring together, creating a multigenerational doom loop with their collection of regurgitated lies.

***

"***Desperate times call for desperate measures***" – Ancient Proverb

The stakes could not have been much higher. Concluding the Great War, beginning WW II, and lasting through the end of the Cold War, *Wilderness of Mirrors* takes place during some of the world's most desperate times.

On June 22, 1941, Germany invaded Russia,

triggering Operation Barbarossa against a very-surprised Soviet Union. The Nazis were blitzing the Soviets – winning victories, occupying territory, and inflicting heavy casualties on their way to Moscow. Times were very desperate in Mother Russia that summer.

Six months later, the Japanese attacked Pearl Harbor, launching Operation Z against an inattentive America, almost wiping out the US Navy's Pacific Fleet. Four days later, the Germans joined in the festivities, declaring war on the United States. Quite suddenly, times became desperate in America too. Such was the beginning of an unlikely alliance.

***

"***The enemy of my enemy is my friend***" –Ancient Proverb

Washington D.C. and Moscow – hemispheres apart, economically and politically. Adam Smith and George Washington vs. Karl Marx and Vladimir Lenin. Capitalism vs. communism. Both countries birthed in revolutionary fervor – one replacing tyranny with democracy and the other trading one oligarchy for another.

No question, the coupling of the United States and the Soviet Union was an arranged marriage – a passionless betrothal. No love, just a desperate need by both to survive. Thrust together by a common enemy, they united behind a common purpose – to rid the world of Adolf Hitler.

As long as there were Nazis to kill in Eastern Europe, the Soviet Union tolerated its new partner. As long as there were Germans to defeat in Western Europe, America bore with its unlikely ally. Together, as long as Hitler was still alive, the two powers coexisted in the uneasy, long-distance relationship.

Their incompatibility did not sever their affair until they finally met face-to-face in Germany's capital at the end of the war. Soviet troops had just discovered the Fuhrer's still-smoldering remains near his Berlin bunker. Hitler was finished. The common enemy was gone. Alas, also gone were the ties tenuously binding the hemispheres together. Quite suddenly, the Soviets and Americans became irreconcilable.

***

"***History is on our side. We will bury you***" –Nikita Khrushchev

In the post-war world, two antagonistic superpowers emerged – the Soviet Union in the east and the United States in the west. An icy rivalry between the two sides resulted in a decades-long Cold War between Soviet-style totalitarianism and American-style democracy, with Europe caught squarely in the middle. In the post-war reorganization, the two behemoths carved the continent into opposing east vs. west confederations. Separate alliances within these two blocs created a very bipolar Europe.

Though the US initially had the nuclear advantage, the Soviets soon caught up, raising the stakes in a direct military confrontation. The two superpowers raced to build delivery systems for their growing stockpiles of nuclear warheads, both adopting the strategy of complete and total annihilation. This insanity, called Mutual Assured Destruction – or MAD – for easy-to-understand reasons acted as kind of a perverse deterrent for almost fifty years. World War II had been appalling but a World War III would be Armageddon.

***

"***The CIA and KGB, like God and Satan, fought Miltonic battles across five continents***" –Paul Johnson

To prevent such an ending, both sides birthed massive spy enterprises to gather information about each other. Initially, that is ALL they were, faceless intelligence-gatherers. Over time however, secret missions soon crept into their job descriptions. Many of these covert operations or "black-ops" resulted in proxy wars, political subversion, assassinations, sabotage, and propaganda – the list is long. The goal of both intelligence communities was straightforward – to anonymously advance the interests of their side without turning the Cold War hot.

Joseph Stalin founded the People's Commissariat for Internal Affairs – NKVD – in 1934. Twenty years later, the Soviet spy agency dissolved, reconstituting itself in 1954 as the Committee for State Security – the KGB. Likewise, Franklin D. Roosevelt created the Office of Strategic Services – OSS – in 1942, reorganized in 1945 as the Central Intelligence Agency – the CIA.

Sneaking spies into the United States became somewhat of a Soviet specialty after World War II. In fact, the NKVD, and later the KGB, became masters at it – aided tremendously by America's sympathetic refugee and generous immigrant policies. Scores of Soviet agents strategically infiltrated refugee populations fleeing the ruthless Stalin and his Red Army. Some pretended to be dissidents or defectors. A few were legitimate immigrants.

Once in America, they blended into America's melting pot, enjoying the same freedoms of movement and occupation that natural-born American citizens enjoyed, and protected – ironically – by the same Constitution they came to undermine.

The most successful KGB tactic, however, was its recruitment of native-born American citizens. The Soviets proved clever at targeting potential assets and "turning them." The recruiters operated primarily on college campuses, incubators of America's future political, social, scientific, and military leaders. There, they exploited the American version of capitalism for their own purposes, drafting cash-strapped college students intrigued by the prospect of earning extra income into Soviet intelligence as KGB moles.

The Americans had a much tougher time sneaking its spies into Communist territory. The Soviet Union was a closed country after the war. In a speech to forty-thousand people at Westminster College in 1946, Winston Churchill characterized Eastern Europe as a "world separated from the west by an invisible iron curtain." In 1961, Soviets began constructing a REAL wall in Berlin, this one made of actual steel and concrete. Consequently, while the Soviets employed mostly human assets, the Americans had to rely more heavily on technological assets for its clandestine services.

***

"***I didn't shoot anybody, no sir…I'm just a patsy***" – Lee Harvey Oswald

Often in the byzantine world of intelligence, dishonest entities with sinister motives intentionally compromise those assets, both human and technological. An example of this occurred in 1959 when the CIA sent a human asset to the Soviet Union as a fake defector. His assignment was to give up classified information on one of the most important technological assets the US intelligence community had in its tool kit. One year later – as planned – the asset crashed to the earth, felled by a Soviet missile. Three years later, the CIA set up the same agent to be the patsy in America's Crime of the Century. In both cases, CIA assets –

technological and human – perished as a means to a very important end.

When shadowy forces exert more power than the people's elected representatives do and personal agendas trump the United States Constitution, we have reached a precipice. When we do not care anymore, we are in an abyss of our own making.

***

"***Then you will know the truth, and the truth will set you free***" –Jesus Christ

Wilderness of Mirrors takes place in such an abyss. The reader will begin to question what is real and what is not. A parallel universe of mirage and illusion. So many lies. What is truth? Is the truth really a lie? Is the lie actually the truth? Does truth even exist or is everything a lie?

Wilderness of Mirrors is the story of medical breakthroughs and their unintended consequences, followed by a willful perversion of medical science for political purposes at first and illegal CIA covert operations later.

Wilderness of Mirrors is also the story of unexpected truth, witnessed firsthand by America's Cold War enemy, the story's unlikely truth-teller. It is the story of freedom. Freedom from the bondage of some of the biggest lies ever forced on the American people.

***

"***When we hang the capitalists, they will sell us the rope we use***" –Joseph Stalin

Finally, *Wilderness of Mirrors* is a story of astonishing irony, with unexpected results and unpredictable endings. Scientific discoveries offering hope but causing epidemics. Medical research promising a cure – corrupted and misused instead as a weapon. Assassination plots that boomerang, targeting the conspirators. A very surprising end to the Cold War – one side ruined ultimately by its own hand.

***

Chapter One

***

Three Acts; One Play

Washington D.C.

March 26, 1983

"The President's favorite candy..." Kennedy says, handing Beasley an ornamented package of gourmet jellybeans. "...for your lunch with him next Tuesday."

Beasley carefully examines the colorful candy. "You can't even tell..."

"...That's the whole point," Kennedy interrupts. "The serum is odorless, tasteless, and colorless – it's undetectable."

"Jellybeans..." Beasley sniffs as he shakes his head, amused. "Pure genius."

Kennedy nods. "It so happens they're goddamn indestructible," he says, pointing at the small bag Beasley is holding. "Plus, they are his biggest and ONLY vice that we know of. People give them to him as gifts all the time. The Secret Service won't suspect a thing, especially coming from you."

"He DOES pop these things like pills," Beasley agrees, chuckling. "It's funny to watch him. He will pick through all the other colors in his jar searching for black, like a little kid. Most people hate the black licorice, but Reagan loves it. Everybody knows to save the black beans for him."

"That's exactly why Arrowhead only loaded the black ones," Kennedy replies. "We are hoping to keep the collateral damage to a minimum."

Beasley pauses, gaming out the scenario in his mind while he stares at the fancy package. "If I know him, he'll open it right away and grab a quick handful. In fact, he'll probably offer ME some too."

"Not a problem," Kennedy replies. "If he does, take a couple – just don't take any of the black ones."

"Don't worry. The President knows I only like orange," Beasley says, a wry smile coming across his face.

Walking away afterwards, Kennedy understands why Sasha was so tense yesterday. Operation Reciprocity was just one more covert operation in a career full of them until he made the pick-up at the loaded dead drop two days ago. Now that he has delivered the package for Sasha, the world will never be the same. *The mother of ALL black-ops*, Kennedy is thinking.

In this line of work, the spymaster is always the most confident when the mission is depending solely on him. For the first time, Operation Reciprocity is completely out of Sasha's hands.

FIVE DECADES EARLIER...

***

London, England

September 28, 1928

The elderly doctor is taking the familiar path to work. Aided by a cane, his gait is halting and slow, deteriorated by age. It is a rainy Westminster morning. Again. *Damn London drizzle*, Dr. Fleming mutters to himself, pausing as he fumbles with his ever-present umbrella.

He has the sidewalk mostly to himself. A few early-bird patrons are scurrying around preparing for another business day, paying him no mind. For years, they have watched scores of lab-coated gentlemen strolling by the Praed Street storefronts on their way to work. St. Mary's Hospital is only few blocks away.

The inner London borough of Westminster is world-famous for a several reasons. First, it is home to Britain's royal family and the historic palaces of Buckingham, St. James, and Westminster. It also serves as the epicenter of British politics, the home base of both Houses of Parliament and Ten Downing Street. Bordering the aristocratic boroughs of Kensington and Chelsea, it is where England's finest citizens, the elites of London, assemble.

One of its most impressive institutions is the elegant and luxurious St. Mary's Hospital, located in the toney Paddington section. A massive sign with the words "St. Mary's Hospital, Est. 1851", hangs above the grand entrance in front. The entryway is actually an atrium, spectacularly enclosed by glass. On a sunny day – a rare occurrence in London – the hospital lobby is flooded with healing rays of light. White marble columns peer down imperiously on the buffed and polished mahogany floors, mirroring their reflections like a crystal-clear mountain lake. An energetic fountain sprays good cheer amongst a phalanx of well-manicured greenery. Elegant arches resting on top of the massive columns support a towering rotunda. St.

Mary's Hospital boasts all the frivolous trappings of a magisterial palace. It has to. Its pretentious clientele will not settle for anything less. Like angels of mercy flitting about, scores of beautiful nurses also adorn the scene, perfecting the image. Even a dreary day like today cannot prevent St. Mary's from brightening the most miserable person's day.

Though he is wearing the requisite "St. Mary's Hospital Staff" lab coat, Dr. Fleming does not enter through the front door of the hospital. Instead, he hobbles past the grand entryway to another building, one hiding bashfully behind the magnificent hospital on a lonely, overgrown alleyway. It has no fancy sign above its door, just some worn-out lettering on a dirty front window that reads generically, "Laboratory". One look at the lab and it is no wonder St. Mary's does not claim it.

The St. Mary's Laboratory droops and sags like a tired old man, visibly battered and worn out by the failures and disappointments of a lifetime spent working to no apparent end. Not unlike a wrinkled face testifying to the effects of age, the building's weary façade, its cracked windows and patched-up roof seem to symbolize a cause hopelessly past its prime – an effort devoid of any lingering hope.

Deep inside the bowels of his dreary lab, Dr. Fleming conducts experiments in absolute stillness. The silence is ear splitting. It has not always been this way. He vaguely remembers a time the lab and its labyrinth of adjoining offices practically hummed with activity. If he listens hard enough, he can still hear the cacophony of sound generated by high-spirited and high-priority busyness.

Now he finds himself carrying on entire conversations with himself, responding tartly to his self-loathing quips and answering his own satirical questions. When the self-talk first started a few years ago, he worried he might be losing his mind. Not anymore. Who would care anyway? There's no one left to notice. With the exception of his ne'er-do-well part-time assistant, Dr. Fleming now works by himself – though not by choice. Like a claustrophobia-induced anxiety, the loneliness he feels is suffocating. *Maybe it is the constant failure,* He considers. Whichever it is, he cannot escape the depressing heaviness. Like a threadbare overcoat, he wears his soul's barrenness openly, symbolizing a lifetime now well into its unforgiving winter season.

Decades ago, the project started with so much promise. The then-young doctor had high expectations. That was many years ago – many long, frustrating years. He knows that his repeated efforts to grow a substance with antibiotic properties have failed. Worse, everyone else knows too. Now, after thousands of experiments, he is stymied – and alone.

Yet again, it has not always been this way. Years earlier, the hallways were teeming with eager faces. Teammates were standing shoulder-to-shoulder with him, energized by a shared vision. They were respected doctors, accomplished researchers, credentialed government officials – professionals of stature and gravitas – whose very presence betrayed the national import of the lab's research.

Especially during the Great War when the need was so great. Britain and the entire Triple Entente Alliance hung by a thread. The Allies desperately needed British medicine to come through – and soon! Germany's terrible newly engineered weapons were wreaking havoc. The Maschinengewehr 08 machine gun could fire an astounding four-hundred rounds-per-minute. Even more impressive, the German's "Paris Gun" and its one-hundred-and-eighteen-foot-long barrel was lobbing artillery shells twenty-five miles high, hitting targets as far away as seventy-five miles. Most frightening was the odorless, invisible, silent killer – chlorine gas. Once a soldier realized he had inhaled even the smallest whiff, it was too late. His skin would turn a pale, greenish yellow as his body convulsed with violent retching and vomiting, slowly suffocating him to death.

The trenches were nothing more than open sewers, distilling their toxic brew of bodily fluids, stagnant rainwater, human waste, mud, and death. Injured soldiers, treated in such filth had little hope of surviving. Even uninjured soldiers did not stay healthy long in these conditions. It is no wonder battlefield infections were proving to be more lethal than bullets and shells. Trench warfare was not much better for Germany and the Central Powers either. Whichever side first produced an antibiotic might just win the war.

Vladimir Lenin severely damaged the Allied cause when he withdrew Russia from the war. As a result, the need for American reinforcements to break the stalemate was urgent. While it surprised no one that the United States was dragging its feet as long as it could in an effort to avoid combat, England was already IN the war. Everyone kept wondering – *what in bloody hell are those damn doctors doing in that London lab anyway? What is taking them so long?*

That was a decade ago. When it counted, American doughboys DID come through; British medicine, however, did not. When the war ended in 1919, the national urgency behind Dr. Fleming's project ended with it. The funding dried up and his entourage all but disappeared. Now his failure has rendered him an orphan.

This morning, Dr. Fleming is busying himself in the lab's catacombs, shuffling around slowly in the maze of decrepit workstations that is his home away-from-home. His appearance is almost ghost-like. Silver-white uncombed hair, dingy-white lab coat, light grey slacks, and dirty white socks, no shoes. His shirt is a wrinkled approximation of white. Though it is early in the day, his tie is already a casualty, hanging loosely from his lab coat's right front pocket – he is convinced a woman invented the necktie as a curse on men. His overworked left pocket is partially torn. Stuffed down inside it are cigarettes, lab reports, spectacles, writing utensils, and neatly folded handkerchiefs. From the smeared residue on his coat sleeves, it is not hard to figure out why the handkerchiefs still look brand-new.

Not surprisingly, the lab resembles its occupant. Hidden beneath all the clutter was once a state-of-the-art research laboratory. However, thirty years of work has left its mark. At the beginning, the British government outfitted the lab with the latest technology. As years went by, newer technology replaced the old. Yet, Dr. Fleming and his staff never discarded anything. Younger generations of microscopes sit perched next to the older ones, which look like hulking antique dinosaurs.

Petri dishes and meaningless reports litter every available countertop. Long-forgotten test tubes and beakers have unknown liquids fermenting in them. There are spills everywhere – on the counters, on the floors, and even on Dr. Fleming's desk. Piles of unwashed pieces of lab equipment pose like plastic sculptures in the sinks and hundreds of old medical journals are stacked randomly throughout the lab like pylons marking an obstacle course.

The lighting is abysmal. Shadows abound as broken light fixtures with burned-out light bulbs dangle precariously from the ceiling. For every working light, there are at least five that are not. There is an obnoxious smell wafting about. Thankfully, two open windows provide small and welcome whiffs of fresh air to combat the foul odor. During the daylight hours, they also provide some semblance of light.

One corner of the lab is particularly dark, not due to poor lighting but the result of a fire. The charred remains serve as another reminder of the labs' ineptitude. The corner now serves as storage for an unused mop bucket and old discarded boxes of unopened cleaning supplies. At one time, there was a fully staffed maintenance department charged with keeping the lab in good working order. Since the war ended however, the responsibility of maintaining the lab fell to Dr. Fleming. It is obvious how that arrangement is working out.

"I wonder why...," The old doctor mutters curiously, as he inspects a Petri dish left open carelessly. "...Probably that old duffer Breckenridge," he says aloud with mild contempt for his absent-minded assistant. Then something makes Dr. Fleming take a closer look.

There is a blue-green mold contaminating the dish – most likely from the open window directly above the workstation – and forming a visible growth. *Normal,* he thinks. He notes the halo of bacterial growth surrounding the mold. Again, that is normal. However, the inhibited nature of the growth is what catches Dr. Fleming's attention. That is NOT normal. He stares at it in wide-eyed curiosity, fumbling excitedly for his spectacles.

Upon closer inspection, the old doctor realizes that this is no ordinary mold. Whatever it is, it is releasing a substance that is repressing the growth, breaking down the bacteria. “Bugger me!” He exclaims in disbelief, sitting down hard in his chair, stunned.

He may not look the part, but Dr. Alexander Fleming is an experienced, highly trained professional. A 1906 graduate “with distinction” from the St. Mary’s Hospital Medical School, Dr. Fleming later earned the prestigious Gold Medal in Bacteriology from St. Mary’s. Elected Professor of Bacteriology at the University of London earlier this year, this is a learned man. Maybe that is why it is inconceivable to him that human neglect could produce in one night what decades of controlled experiments have not, especially something so important...

...Finally! The world’s first antibiotic!

***

New Orleans, Louisiana

October 18, 1939

There is not much “happy” in THIS birthday.

There are no balloons. No flowers. No noisemakers. There is no congratulatory cigar for dad. No claps of joy from family members. There is no backslapping, no hugging, and no pictures of mom with her new baby.

Even Mother Nature appears unhappy. There is no bright cheery sunshine, no gentle summer breeze, no sweet-sounding birds, and seemingly, no life. Instead, one look at the thick condensation on the hospital room window reveals a steady, drizzling rain, Nimbus clouds parked low in the sky, and a humidity-induced steamy New Orleans fog.

No, this birth is NOT a celebration; it is more like a cruel reminder. The father is not present to light a cigar because he died tragically of a heart attack two months ago. There are not any family members here because the dysfunctional young woman has left behind a trail of broken relationships like litter on the lonely highway of her life. There are not any backslaps or hugs and there will not be any pictures taken because they are alone – the troublesome, indigent mother and her newborn son – all alone.

Marguerite Claverie is poor, uneducated, Crescent City white trash. The kind that has known, ever since HER mother told her when she was a little girl, what she is. It surely explains the bitterness she wears like a Halloween mask. It definitely accounts for her wicked-sharp tongue.

Not surprisingly, her young life has been a series of bitter disappointments. She is obsessed with people, not for who they are but what they can do for her. Her exploitive callousness is making her notorious in New Orleans. She manages to chase away anyone who cannot put a glass slipper on her foot. She is no peach – that is for sure.

Still young and attractive enough, Marguerite is devoting all of her remaining female charms toward achieving the lifestyle she craves. Men with means are her targets. Like a parasite, the money-grubbing shrew has attached herself to Carlos Marcello's New Orleans crime syndicate, hoping he or an unlucky associate will succumb to her witchery and be her sugar daddy. The result has been a series of ill-fated relationships with mobbed-up wise guys, a few of which have unfortunately led to marriage. Predictably, none of the marriages ends very well.

In one eventful divorce proceeding, the less-than-sympathetic judge ruled Marguerite to be "guilty of excesses, cruel treatment, and outrages" toward her husband – a mob hitman – poor bastard! A few years later, a seemingly healthy husband died on her. After she discovered she was pregnant – presumably by this now-deceased partner – Marguerite cursed him. Some folks around town still believe divine intervention caused his sudden heart problems. "He is in a much better place now," they say, nodding at each other with knowing looks. To hear her tell it, she is now "stuck" with his kid. Quite a woman, this Marguerite.

The hospital paperwork left behind by the attending nurse requires she choose a name for the newborn. Marguerite thinks about it awhile before shrugging and settling on "Lee" – in memory of a father her son will never know. Sadly, if today serves as an oracle for her son's future, it has all the makings of a Greek tragedy – not that anyone cares or is paying special attention.

There is nothing remarkable or even unremarkable about Lee's birth. Charity Hospital is witness to beginnings like his every day. Some hospitals specialize in medical research, others specialty care. Charity Hospital's identity is a drive-thru baby factory for the poor people of New Orleans. Labor, delivery, and recovery – all in less than twenty-four hours. The hospital staff is extremely efficient. It has to be. Most patients do not have insurance and there is always another hapless idiot waiting downstairs in the lobby for the room.

Of course, efficiency does have a human price tag. First thing tomorrow morning, like a newly minted car rolling off an assembly line, Marguerite and her newborn son will be ushered coldly out the front door of the hospital. And since there won't be a ride waiting to pick her up, she will carry her baby ten blocks in the sweltering humidity of a southern Louisiana morning heat – even in October – to her dilapidated little home in the upper Ninth Ward.

Neither mother nor child will get too comfortable.

***

Berlin, Germany

April 25, 1945 – "Elbe Day"

"The Americans want to party? Then let those sons-of-bitches drink and dance!" Soviet Premier Joseph Stalin thunders. When Stalin is angry, his face glows red like a hot burning coal. His eyes even turn crimson.

Contrasted against his panther-black hair, his appearance is as unearthly evil as Satan's most villainous demon. Furious, he pounds his fist on the desk.

"Do NOT let your men engage with the Americans!" he rages. "I better not hear any more god-damn reports of fraternization! The next picture I see in the newspapers of our troops and theirs in a group hug, your treasonous ass will be in Vorkuta! It's a propaganda bonanza for the west!"

"Yes sir," Marshal Georgy Zhukov, the frightened Soviet general stammers.

The general has good reason to fear. Joseph Stalin has only one play in his playbook. Ever since Lenin's communist revolution in 1917 – when he was just one of seven members of the original Soviet Politburo – anyone or anything that has stood in Stalin's way is gone. Dead. Murdered by the most spiteful, cold-blooded man in the Soviet Union.

After Lenin's death, Stalin set impossibly high quotas during his inaugural Five-Year Plan to industrialize Russia. Workers who fell short of the goals ended up in Siberian gulags, never heard from again. Peasants who sabotaged Stalin's collective farm policy –

protesting the loss of their land – starved to death or found themselves impaled on the business end of a bayonet. Ukrainians who dared declare their independence from the Soviet Union became victims of The Holodomor, an apocalyptic famine deliberately engineered by Stalin. The notoriously paranoid Stalin executed thousands of prominent Red Army and Communist Party members during the Great Purge, labeling them "enemies of the working class" – thereby eliminating all potential threats to his unchecked power.

The general knows, better than most, what happens to the poor unfortunates who disappoint the Soviet Premier. Now in his twenty-third year in power, Stalin has already caused the deaths of at least twenty-million Soviet citizens. The west likes to propagandize him as the paternal, kind-hearted "Uncle Joe" but the Soviet people know the terrible truth.

Stalin is not finished. "Secure the eastern side of the Elbe and stay there!" His face is swollen and still blood red. "Don't fucking move! That is a direct order!" Tirade complete, Stalin storms out, slamming the door behind him.

Zhukov swallows hard as he stands to leave. He grabs

the edge of the desk, steadying himself, wondering if he will even make it out of the building. Before he can muster his courage to walk out, the door swings open viciously, hitting the wall behind it. A hanging portrait crashes noisily to the floor.

The premier storms back in, this time with his deputy in tow. General Zhukov is standing frozen in his spot, unsure if he should leave or stay. Then a thought occurs to him. *NOBODY walks out on Joseph Stalin!* The general quietly stands in the corner, trying hard to be invisible.

"Where were the chicken-shit Americans in 1942 when we needed them in Stalingrad?" Stalin shouts, contempt oozing from his every word. "Western Europe, that's where! Holding hands with de Gaulle and Churchill! SOVIET blood purchased every goddamned mile between Moscow and Berlin! Now the Americans and their European eunuchs want us to promise free elections in our own backyard. Hell no! We would be cutting our own throats! HELL NO! Eastern Europe IS part of the Soviet Union now! Let them TRY and take it from us!"

Stalin's deputy nods his head. "Everything HAS changed," he agrees calmly. It is a meaningless act on his part because no one has EVER disagreed with Stalin and lived to tell about it. "It's a new world order. Germany is finished. Great Britain and France are second-rate. If it were not for us, Eastern Europe would be speaking German today. If it was not for the United States, France and England would be doing the Nazi goose-step. It's just us and the Americans now."

He speaks! General Zhukov thinks to himself. *I have never heard the man talk before...*

"The man" is Lavrentiy Beria. Beria is Stalin's most trusted right-hand man, which is saying something because Stalin does not trust ANYBODY. To look at Beria, one might underestimate him, which would be a terrible mistake. Small in stature and bespectacled with neatly combed-over, black hair, he could pass as a neighborhood librarian but Lavrentiy Beria is no collector of books.

Marshall of the Soviet Union, Beria is in charge of all state security. He commands the feared NKVD, the direct descendant of Lenin's original secret police – the Cheka. Before the war, Beria mercilessly carried out Stalin's Great Purge. In two of the most horrifying years, Beria ordered eight-million Russians arrested and another one-million executed. During the war, he administered the infamous network of Gulag labor camps. All Russians with a pulse are terrified of Lavrentiy Beria.

"This will be a new kind of war," Stalin says forcefully. "Not of generals and armies," he nods in Zhukov's direction, "but of spymasters and agents."

Above everything else, Joseph Stalin is a survivor – a necessary skill for any Soviet leader. He is not looking for a head-to-head fight with the Americans, at least not in the conventional sense. He knows that nobody would survive that kind of war. Not anymore. No, his sights are set on world domination through intelligence superiority. His strategy is to best the Americans in a series of confrontations by translating sophisticated human assets into actionable intelligence.

Over the next few hours, General Zhukov listens in amazement as the puppet masters plot the next war – *while my men and I are still finishing up the current one*, he thinks, the irony not lost on him.

Together, they change Beria's job description. Safeguarding the Soviet Union against internal subversion will be somebody else's responsibility now. His new task will be counterintelligence. Instead of focusing on the citizenry of the Soviet Union, Beria will infiltrate the United States with NKVD agents who will gather intelligence, spread propaganda, and use disinformation – the most potent weapon ever devised – to subvert American democracy, Stalin's new adversary.

"It's your war now," Stalin instructs Beria.

***

Chapter Two

***

Fifth Column

New York City, New York

April 16, 1953

"Do you know why you're here?" the pretty woman asks as she discreetly adjusts her sharply creased dress slacks. Her manicured hands speak of a life without hardship. Her white blouse and black pinstripe pants accentuate her feminine daintiness. While her looks are not lost on him, they do her no favors either.

Lee looks away without answering. *Another do-gooder with a note-pad,* he thinks, disgusted.

"Do you know what truancy is?" she presses him.

Still no answer.

Besides being stubbornly quiet, she observes Lee to be skinny, almost frail. He is a physically unimpressive thirteen-year-old boy and eye contact is not his thing.

Definitely not the fighter type, she thinks, more accustomed to working with confrontational boys.

Unfazed by his stoic silence, she begins. "Lee, my name is Evelyn Siegel. I am a social worker for the city of New York. The same court that remanded you to Youth House because you refuse to go to school has assigned me to be your caseworker. You may not know this – I realize you just moved here from Texas – but the law requires children under age sixteen to be in school. It's state law."

A long pause. "I know," he murmurs defensively. "The officer told me that too the last time he picked me up."

Yes...a small breakthrough...finally! "That was at the zoo, was it not?" she asks calmly, already knowing the answer.

"Yes, I was at the zoo. I like to study the animals," he replies sarcastically, rolling his eyes and smirking.

"Okay, let's talk about WHY you don't want to go to school," she continues, ignoring his antics. "What else do you like to do when you skip...BESIDES studying animals?"

Lee sighs. "Oh, just things," he answers vaguely, shrugging.

"Like what?" she asks, sipping warmed-over coffee from a plastic cup. "We've got all afternoon," she says, looking up at the clock, "take your time."

"Important stuff. More important than school anyway."

"Okay, fine. Tell me then, what's so important?"

It is evident Lee does not want to say so Miss Siegel waits. This is not her first time interviewing a recalcitrant teenager. Finally, after a few awkward moments of silence, he relents, clearing his throat. "TV mostly," he croaks, a little embarrassed. "I like watching TV and reading magazines. Sometimes I sleep."

"Important stuff, eh?" she teases him with a slight grin.

"The other kids make fun of my clothes," he blurts out bitterly. "I don't dress like they do. I talk different too. I guess I have an accent."

"A rather interesting one too, I might add," she says, impressed. "I like it. It kind of reminds me of my father – he was from New Orleans."

Lee's head jerks up abruptly, a look of surprise and familiarity in his eyes. "Well, THEY sure don't," he tells her. “I really hate it here. I wish we never left Texas,” he says, grimacing and shaking his head wistfully.

Let’s talk about your move,” she changes the subject. “Why DID you move to New York?”

Lee sets his jaw. “Because that’s what mom and I do. We move.”

“Oh? So you’ve moved a lot?”

“Too many times to count,” Lee says wearily.

“Any particular reason?”

“Mostly men,” he replies quickly. “My mom gets married a lot. In between, she has boyfriends. Jobs – lots of jobs too. It never ends.”

Miss Siegel pauses briefly. “I see. Lee, have you ever been in trouble for truancy before?”

“No. Never.”

“So...” she continues, scanning her notes. “...It says here you are in the seventh grade. How many schools have you attended? Can you remember?”

“At least nine, I think,” he says after a pause. “Five in Texas – we lived in different places. One in Louisiana, and three here in New York since we moved last year, and before all that, I was in an orphans' home for two years."

Miss Siegel nods as she writes in her notebook. "Lee, what do you know about your father? Do you know where he is?"

"He's dead," Lee responds quickly. "Died before I was born. Heart attack. Mom has nothing but bad things to say about him. I don't have a dad." His answers have a machine-gun-like staccato rhythm to them, as if he has rehearsed the answers to these questions many times before.

"How about the rest of your family, any sisters?" she asks, watching the aggravation in his body language.

He shakes his head.

"Brothers?"

Lee nods. "Two. They're both older than I am. John is in the Coast Guard. He has a different dad. I don't know him very good. Robert is in the Marines. We have the same dad. We hang out when he's home."

"So mostly you live alone with your mom?"

"I guess so," he replies, shrugging. "If you want to call

it that. She works all the time. She has gone every morning and every night. I hardly ever see her."

Miss Siegel continues pressing him. "Friends? Do you hang out with anybody? Classmates maybe?"

Lee says nothing. He stares down at the floor as he shuffles his feet, trying to distract himself.

"It's okay Lee," she reassures him. "I certainly understand if you don't."

He looks up finally and shakes his head. "I don't have any friends here," his voice now barely a whisper.

"What about back in Texas?"

"Not really," he replies. "But at least nobody made fun of me there."

Miss Siegel stops writing and takes a deep breath. "Okay, that's enough for today," she says softly, patting Lee on the knee. "I know it's been a long day."

"What else do I have to do?" he asks, worn out.

"Nothing. You're finished." She looks at the file on her lap. "You completed your exam with Dr. Hartogs this morning and that's it for me. We'll speak with your mother soon, but you're done for now."

Lee stands awkwardly to his feet. “Thanks,” he says, barely audible.

Miss Siegel watches him exit the room. Her heart aches for him. Like all social workers, she has a busy caseload and hears many heart-rending stories. So many of them end up being untrue it is hard NOT to become cynical. However, every now and then, one of her “kids” – as she calls them – stands out from the hard-hearted crowd and grabs at her heartstrings. Lee is looking like he will be one of those. “Damaged goods,” she writes in her notebook, “but not irredeemable. In spite of his wounds, a kind spirit if you can get past the bluster.” She takes a deep breath and opens the file with Lee’s psychological report, confident she already knows what it will say.

> *This thirteen-year-old boy has superior mental resources and functions only slightly below his capacity level in spite of chronic truancy from school, which brought him into Youth House. There is no finding of neurological impairment or psychotic mental changes. His diagnosis is ‘personality pattern disturbance with schizoid features and passive-aggressive tendencies.’ He has to be seen as an emotionally, quite disturbed youngster who suffers under the impact of really*

> *existing emotional isolation and deprivation, lack of affection, absence of family life and rejection by a self-involved and conflicted mother.*

The report is signed by Youth House' chief psychologist – Dr. Renatus Hartogs.

***

Washington D.C.

February 23, 1954

"Like we thought, this Vice President is going to be problematic," David Beasley begins his report matter-of-factly. "Ambitious type – will most definitely make his own run for the White House in '60. He has meticulously cultivated his anti-communist bona fides. His prosecution of Alger Hiss during the Hearings on Un-American Activities (HUAC) in '48 firmly established his reputation with the American people as a trustworthy Cold Warrior. It's not a matter of IF but WHEN he becomes President..."

Recruited by the NKVD in 1945, Jakub Berman – codenamed "David Beasley" – is a KGB agent, working since then for the Soviets – the ones who liberated his country from the hated Nazis. Before Hitler invaded Poland in 1939, Jakub's father called in every favor he could, trying to get visas for his family to migrate to America as refugees. He failed. Instead, Jakub and his family joined thousands of other Polish Jews forcibly removed from their homes by the Schutzstaffel (SS) and relocated via railroad boxcars to Auschwitz. Every day he spent at the Nazi death camp, young Jakub hoped and prayed that the Americans would arrive and save his family. Every night, he went to bed disappointed. One by one, his family around him died. Some in the gas chambers, some in the stone quarry – worked to death. One of the guards shot his older sister right in front of him. All ended up in the ovens.

With each extermination, Jakub's hope faded a little more. With each passing day, he prayed a little less. Devoutly Orthodox, the Berman family entered Auschwitz clinging to their faith. After six long years, Jakub's faith dissolved like a solute in Hitler's Final Solution. On that terrible day SS officers marched his emaciated father naked to the gas chamber, he finally cursed Yahweh. In Jakub's view, God and an anti-Semitic US immigrant policy had killed his family.

Liberation day did eventually come – the Red Army emancipating young Jakub Berman, not the

Americans. After the war, the Soviets began training Jews like Jakub Berman in the craft of espionage. When America changed its policy and began admitting Jewish refugees, the Soviets simply inserted scores of their newly minted spies into the refugee population. That is how virtually overnight, hundreds of NKVD agents including Jakub Berman infiltrated the United States.

His (and the NKVD's) lucky break happened in 1947 during the height of the Red Scare. In an effort to contain the spread of communism, Congress formed the House Un-American Activities Committee (HUAC) to investigate disloyal and subversive activities by private citizens, public employees, and any organization suspected of having communist ties. Senator Richard Nixon's office, while busily deposing witnesses in preparation for the upcoming hearings, hired Jakub as an interpreter. During the hearings, the NKVD fed its agent just enough valuable information to make for must-read material. It was not very long before the freshman Senator was using Jakub's sensational chicken feed to flush out accused communist subversives and springboard himself to national prominence.

After the hearings, Nixon rewarded Jakub with a full-time post on his staff. That is how a prominent United States Senator, widely known for his anti-communist crusade, unwittingly hired a Soviet spy to work in his office. Then in 1951, the NKVD and Jakub Berman REALLY hit the mother lode. Senator Richard Nixon became Vice President Richard Nixon. Suddenly, Soviet intelligence had its mole one heartbeat away from the Oval Office.

"...He is convinced it's his mission to save the American people from polio," Beasley continues his report. "All across the country, people are freaking out, especially since it's mostly children getting the disease now. When parents hear the word 'polio,' they picture their kids entombed in iron lungs with little shriveled-up, crippled legs sticking out. But not Nixon. For him, it is HUAC all over again. He views it as another opportunity to make a name for himself."

Beasley stops reading and looks up. "Nixon's ambition to cure polio doesn't concern me so much, though. It's the Cuba thing I'm most worried about."

There is a long pause. "What Cuba thing?" the other man asks finally.

"He's planning an invasion," Beasley answers without hesitation. "The government is consorting with mafia,

Cuban exiles – a lot of crazy types. They are already training in Miami, stockpiling guns everywhere. It is all off the books, of course. He wants to invade Cuba, kill Castro, cure polio, and run for President – in that order. If he does the first three before the campaign in '60, he figures he'll win easily."

"He would indeed. Think of all the interested parties..." the other man begins before being interrupted.

"...Sugar companies, big business, entertainment, organized crime, Cuban refugees, and all the anti-Castroites in the CIA and the Pentagon – the list is never-ending," Beasley interjects forcefully.

The other man nods as he casually sorts books in his bookstore that is otherwise deserted. He is no ordinary bookseller. The KGB's Second Chief Directorate, he is in charge of Soviet counter-intelligence in America – codenamed "Sasha". None of his agents even knows his REAL name. In the recent reorganization of Soviet state security, many NKVD officers were quietly retired in favor of a younger, more cosmopolitan KGB. Sasha is a beneficiary of that youth movement.

A Rhodes scholar, Sasha received his post-graduate education in England at the University of Oxford, confirming his intellect. During those years in the United Kingdom, he gained a uniquely global perspective – especially for a Soviet citizen – by travelling and exploring the democracies in Western Europe and eventually, the United States. Experienced at communicating in western countries, his English-language skills are superb. The NKVD recruited him upon his return to Moscow – training him under its top intelligence operatives. With a resume like that, Sasha's abilities have NEVER been in question.

For some communist hard-liners, Sasha's western education disqualifies him from high Soviet command. Stalin cultivates that kind of paranoia and distrust – which is why Sasha was surprised, even after his years of dues-paying, to be Lavrentiy Beria's hand-picked spymaster in the United States, especially considering Beria's close relationship with the Soviet Union's "Man of Steel".

The new KGB values Sasha's western sensibilities though. It needs front-line spies who know the enemy – how it thinks, what it values, and most important, where its vulnerabilities are. In the field of foreign intelligence, Beria knows the hard-liners will stick out. Sasha will blend in. It is Sasha's carefully constructed roster of spies and his concealed radio transmitter –

hidden in the attic of his dilapidated storefront – that will enable the Soviets to win this new kind of intelligence war.

Again, Sasha pauses before speaking. "I'm definitely curious about the polio thing," he begins. "I'll speak with Caleb and Joshua and see what they know about it – maybe nothing yet." Then he points at Beasley. "But your assignment going forward is Cuba. We need specifics. If it is an invasion, we need to know when and where. Will they use Cubans? If so, will they be exiles in Miami or dissidents in Cuba – or both? All those weapons will cost money. How much money? From whose budget? Training requires military advisers. Will the Pentagon be involved? Front end, back end, or both? Just find out. Be quick about it. Moscow needed this yesterday."

***

Washington D.C.

February 24, 1954

The doctor answers the ringing telephone, which is unusual. "Dr. Cherry's office," he barks loudly, looking at his watch annoyed. The click on the other end signals for him to hang up. Dr. Cherry instantly recognizes Sasha's code. Five minutes earlier, another doctor in Washington DC received the same clandestine message at his office. Something is up. Tonight, they will both find out what it is.

Nickolas Cherry and Alexander Duncan are real American doctors. They are also real Soviet KGB agents. Dr. Cherry – codenamed "Caleb" – works for the government at the Food and Drug Administration (FDA) in the Center for Biologics Evaluation and Research. He is part of a division that is directly responsible for the regulation of vaccines and related biological products. Caleb's best source is not a doctor but a paper-pushing administrator at the National Institutes of Health (NIH) named Ken Rudolph – codenamed "Razor". More importantly, Razor is best friends with NIH Director Dr. William H. Sebrell – or "Wild Bill" – as Razor affectionately calls him. Of course, Wild Bill has nary a clue that his best friend is exploiting their relationship as a means of prying highly classified information from him. Naturally, Razor would like to keep it that way. Sasha calls this threesome his "triad of truth". Dr. Duncan – codenamed "Joshua" – is Dr. Cherry's counterpart at the Center for Disease Control and Prevention (CDC). He works in the Office of Infectious Diseases as a team member of the National Center for Immunization and Respiratory Diseases.

If Beasley is right and Vice President Nixon is obsessing over polio, the KGB wants to know why. With this roster of spies ensconced inside the most advanced medical institutions America has to offer, it should not be too hard to find out.

Sasha instinctively knows what Beasley is overlooking. When a politician takes ownership of a cause, there is the motive for public consumption and there is the hidden one. In his experience, the hidden one is the only one that matters. *Beasley's information means the Americans must be nearing a cure for polio,* Sasha reasons to himself. *Why else would Nixon be interested? Time to take all the credit...*

Since the superpowers do not make a habit of sharing medical discoveries, the doctors must steal the vaccine. It is a matter of national urgency. The American people think the polio epidemic is bad in their country but Sasha knows it is far worse in his. After they succeed, Caleb and Joshua will be superstars in the international spy galaxy – at least in the Soviet hemisphere.

Both are skilled at their dual professions – being doctors and spies. They were recruited into the old NKVD during their undergraduate days at Dartmouth after they were witnessed marching in a campus demonstration supporting maintenance and food service union employees. Both are Midwestern farm boys – Cherry, a Hawkeye from Iowa and Duncan, a Buckeye from Ohio. Both are also former college athletes. Crew teammates on the Big Green rowing team, Alex was the coxswain and Nick occupied the bow seat. Friends, the doctors-to-be lived together in the same dorm room until the middle of their sophomore year after which, they split a lease on an off-campus apartment. After Dartmouth, they both traveled south – relatively speaking – for medical school. Cherry studied at Yale in nearby Connecticut while Duncan ended up at Johns Hopkins University in Maryland.

The NKVD steered Cherry and Duncan's careers separately for seven years until reuniting them in their new positions at the Center for Disease Control and Prevention (CDC) and the Food and Drug Administration (FDA). After Soviet intelligence underwent its massive reorganization, Sasha assembled his own team of assets in America, re-recruiting both doctors into the new-and-improved KGB.

It is already dark by the time Caleb enters Sasha's bookstore, arriving before his counterpart. Sasha locks the door behind Joshua a few minutes later and they all meet in the small room next to Sasha's office at the back of the store. Each man takes a seat around a folding table in the center of the room. "Talk to me about polio," Sasha says flatly, opening the evening confab.

"When penicillin was first introduced to the Allied soldiers in World War II, the only thing most people knew about polio was that it had crippled President Roosevelt," Caleb begins. "It wasn't completely unheard of but it was still pretty rare. Now it's spreading like wildfire."

"HOW bad?" Sasha asks, wanting specifics.

"It's bad enough the boys down at FDA are worried," replies Joshua, nodding. "The '53 numbers I'm hearing are almost sixty-thousand per year and climbing fast – mostly children too. Those are epidemic numbers."

"How do America's numbers compare with those of the

Soviet Union?" Sasha asks, preparing his agents for their next assignment.

"Not even close," answers Caleb quickly. "The Soviets have double the numbers, at least. Russia alone had over seventy-five thousand cases of polio reported last year. That is the official report and we all know how the Politburo fudges bad news. Regardless, that number DOESN'T include ANY of the satellites."

"Jesus," Sasha blurts out. "Multiply seventy-five thousand times fifteen." Both doctors nod their heads in unison.

"You mentioned penicillin, what's its connection to polio?" asks Sasha.

"Penicillin is an antibiotic," Joshua explains. "Antibiotics kill bacteria – both good and bad. Some of the good bacteria are in the intestines. Ninety-nine percent of the time, the poliovirus enters the body by way of the mouth. It passes through the digestive track, causing no problem. However, if the antibiotic destroys the good bacteria – compromising the intestinal wall – the virus passes straight through the wall and into the blood stream. From there, it's on to the brain..."

"...Once it reaches the brain," Caleb interrupts, "it eats the brain stem, causing severe damage to the nervous system. In other words, penicillin cures infections but also creates favorable conditions for the polio virus."

"Why wasn't it introduced until World War II? I thought it was discovered in the late 1920's..." Sasha begins asking.

"...1928 to be exact. In England," interrupts Caleb, again. "The British invented it but it was the Americans who finally mass-produced it when Hitler's Blitz made it impossible to manufacture in England. It made its world debut at Normandy on D-Day. After the war, penicillin became an important element in the public health care menu on both sides of the pond..."

"...Which is how polio has become a world-wide epidemic today," Joshua adds, not waiting for Caleb to finish. Sasha rubs his chin as his enthusiastic agents continue their seminar.

"The Center for Disease Control and Prevention (CDC) believes it's on the brink of solving the problem," Joshua says. "We have a doctor working on a polio vaccine in Pittsburgh..."

"...Who?" This time, it is Sasha's turn to interrupt.

"His name is Salk. Jonas Salk," Joshua replies.

"Razor has confirmed this," Caleb adds. "According to him, the National Institutes of Health (NIH) is working with CDC and Dr. Salk. He said somebody high up the food chain must think this is a big damn deal because he has never seen people so tight-lipped – even Wild Bill."

"He's right," agrees Sasha, nodding his head. "It IS a big damn deal. Where is it right now?"

"In testing," replies Joshua. "But it's not going very well. Last I heard, Salk's vaccine is either killing or paralyzing the marmosets," he says, referring to the South American monkeys. "The higher-ups must be confident though. They've scheduled a major press conference next spring to announce the new vaccine..."

"...Where?" Sasha asks.

"Ann Arbor, Michigan, at the University," Joshua says.

"Who will be there?"

"Everybody who matters," Joshua answers Sasha. "Of course, Dr. Salk will be there, the Vice President, CDC, NIH, the Food and Drug Administration (FDA), lots of kids for the photo-op – it should be quite the spectacle."

"Nixon huh?" Sasha notes. "Interesting..."

Joshua and Caleb exchange puzzled looks. "So what are our instructions?" Caleb finally asks with a shrug.

"Get it," Sasha instructs them. "Get the samples. I want the science in Moscow before DC can have its little party in Michigan." With that, Sasha rises and disappears into his office, closing the door behind him. Meeting adjourned.

***

Chapter Three

***

Inconvenient Truth – Part I

Washington D.C.

November 23, 1954

“Another one?” asks Dr. Eddy, her brow furrowing.

The distressed assistant shakes her head anxiously, pointing at the cage behind her where three marmosets lay dead in a tangled heap.

“THREE?” Dr. Eddy exclaims, incredulous.

“Yes. And UNLIKE the others, these three skipped the paralysis stage and died overnight,” the assistant reports, swallowing hard. “It happened so fast this time. They were fine when we checked them last night.”

“This is NOT good news,” Dr. Eddy sighs, turning to leave. She takes a deep breath and reaches for the door handle. An entourage of self-important suits is waiting in the next room to hear her report. None of these stuffed shirts will be pleased.

All heads turn and conversation ceases mid-sentence as the unsmiling Dr. Bernice Eddy enters the laboratory's conference room. She nods and clears her throat huskily. "As you know, two weeks ago we started testing with a roster of eighteen monkeys," Dr. Eddy begins, coming right to the point. "At first, they were split evenly – the control group had nine and the experimental group had nine..."

"...And?" Dr. Sebrell interjects eagerly, wearing an impatient look on his face.

"And right away, we started getting paralyzed monkeys," Dr. Eddy responds bluntly, one hand on her hip. "And that's not all. Eleven of the marmosets are now dead – three more died last night. Here, you can read all about it in my report," she declares, thrusting a thick binder into Dr. Sebrell's chest. The busyness in the adjoining lab hushes as he takes a step back, startled.

"PLEASE tell me you aren't going to inject this abomination into children," Dr. Eddy says loudly, confronting her boss.

Nobody dares move or make a sound. The Director of the National Institutes of Health came to hear GOOD news today. It was HIS decision to put Dr. Eddy in charge of testing the new polio vaccine, assuming the female doctor would be more compliant than her male counterparts would. "She doesn't have a political bone in her body – she'll be an easy mark," he argued then to his superiors, setting her up to be the scapegoat if something went wrong – a convincing argument in political circles.

Dr. Sebrell hands the binder to his assistant and straightens his tie awkwardly, taking care to avoid eye contact with Dr. Eddy. Then he clears his throat and announces in his most official-sounding voice. "The Salk vaccine is in very short supply. I am here today on behalf of the Vice President of the United States who wishes to offer you a small token of his AND the nation's gratitude." He pauses for effect but the assembly is not impressed. "We are offering you," he continues, nodding stiffly at Dr. Eddy, "your co-workers, and all of your children a chance to go to the front of the line and be immunized today, before it's offered to the general public." When he finishes speaking, the crowd turns and looks at Dr. Eddy.

"Why all the cameras?" she points behind him. "Are

you expecting us to be your props?"

"Certainly not," Dr. Sebrell defends himself testily, taken back by her directness. *I'll be goddamned if this woman is going to make me look bad,* he thinks angrily, already regretting his decision to involve the pesky doctor in a project with so many important eyes on it. *This broad is sure NOT cooperating.* He takes a deep breath, composing himself. "It's helpful to include images with the public announcement. I'm sure you understand – to inspire confidence in the procedure..."

"...Thank you. No," Dr. Eddy interjects firmly. "I'll wait until the vaccine is fixed. My children are already healthy. I prefer they stay that way. But that's just me, I don't speak for my staff," she says, gesturing at the gathering of people behind her.

Dr. Sebrell looks around, searching in vain for volunteers. Nobody budges. "None of you want your children immunized either?" he asks with raised voice, irritated. Again, nobody moves.

The heavy breathing of Dr. Sebrell is the only sound. After a few uncomfortable moments, the furious Director turns on his heels and storms out of the room, followed closely by his small army of flummoxed sycophants. With them goes the evidence nobody seems anxious to see. Today was supposed to be a celebration. What is he to make of this apolitical Dr. Eddy now?

Born fifty-one years ago in the small coal town of Glendale, West Virginia, Bernice Eddy's childhood experience in the testosterone-filled Appalachian mining culture prepared her well for the medical field's locker-room masculinity. After earning her Ph.D. in 1927 from the University of Cincinnati, she came to Washington D.C. to work as a virologist and an epidemiologist at the National Institutes of Health (NIH). For the last twenty-seven years, she has been testing the safety of vaccines at the Hygienic Laboratory. She takes her job very seriously. She HAS to – it is not easy being a woman in a man's world.

Earlier this year, she and her staff received the first samples of the inactivated polio vaccine (IPV) to certify with a "due yesterday" deadline. The rush was on. Aware it was a time-sensitive project, Dr. Eddy made the Salk vaccine her number-one priority. The severity of the polio crisis motivated her – she knew the numbers better than most. In 1953, there were sixty-thousand people diagnosed with polio – an epidemic – with 1954 promising a lot more.

If the vaccine had worked as intended, Dr. Eddy would have gladly certified it – but it didn't. There were only three outcomes during her testing. All of the marmosets injected with the Salk IPV polio vaccine came down with polio – some ending up paralyzed and others dead – not promising. According to her report, not only does the Salk vaccine do harm, it is lethal!

Dr. Eddy has dreaded this day for weeks. She knows how badly everyone wanted Salk's vaccine to cure polio and end the epidemic. She is merely the messenger of disappointing news. It is out of her hands now. For whatever its worth, Dr. Sebrell now has her report. She has done her job. As disheartening as it might be, the government will HAVE to put on the brakes now, right? Lives depend on it!

***

Washington D.C.

November 24, 1954

The Vice President angrily hurls the report across his desk. "God-dammit!" He screams at no one in particular. "Who the fuck is Bernice Eddy?"

“She’s our doc in the lab,” Dr. Sebrell responds hesitantly.

“I know WHO she is!” Nixon interjects loudly, standing to his feet. “I want to know why someone thought it was a good idea to put her in charge of all the testing! Who in the hell hired this woman?”

“I did,” the National Institutes of Health (NIH) Director admits after a long pause. “I hired her. I thought...”

“...You thought what, that you could control her?” Nixon interrupts again. “Jesus Christ! This report...” he pauses, searching for the right words, “...it’s a fucking nightmare!” He glances over at his senior staffer, quietly trying to collect and reassemble the scattered file. Jakub Berman is unaffected, used to his boss’s profane tirades. However, making their retreat in the direction of the door, Dr. Sebrell and HIS assistant are quite taken aback, having never witnessed the Vice President this red-faced irate before. Both faces are ashen as they watch Nixon pacing back and forth, shaking his head and muttering to himself.

Finally, he plops down in a seat next to his desk, exhausted. “I don’t understand this shit,” he grumbles, pointing at the reshuffled report lying on his desktop. "What exactly went wrong in there? What is the problem with the vaccine? Wasn't the testing just supposed to be a formality?" It was as if he had flipped a switch, going from rage to reason in a matter of seconds.

Now it is Dr. Sebrell's turn again. With a deep breath, the NIH Director begins...cautiously. "The doses are too strong, too potent. The vaccination's live poliovirus is overwhelming the immune systems of the monkeys. They are ALL infected...every one of them. They are ALL ending up paralyzed or dead. It's like getting a booster shot AND a polio steroid shot all at once," he adds for good measure.

"Well, can't the doses be made LESS strong?" Nixon questions him calmly.

"It's not that simple," Dr. Sebrell responds. "It will take some time..."

"...Son-of-a-bitch. I knew it. More fucking time," the Vice President interjects loudly, leaning back in his chair and throwing up his hands. "Are you kidding me? Everybody always wants more time. I will tell you what CANNOT happen. This report can't EVER see the light of day," Nixon declares firmly, ignoring the medical side of it. "This is supposed to be a done deal by '59," he says, calculating the political damage this could do to his upcoming Presidential campaign. "The American people will go bananas if we tell them now the vaccine isn't ready. We have been researching and developing Salk's vaccine for years, promising a cure. THERE IS NO MORE TIME! Christ, the word has been leaking out for months. The public is expecting a working polio vaccine next spring. We HAVE to deliver!"

"If it helps, Dr. Eddy and her staff are sworn to secrecy by non-disclosure agreements so they can't make this public, even if they want to," Dr. Sebrell assures him.

"What about leaks?" the Vice President asks, suspicious.

"The only WRITTEN report is the one that WAS spread all over your desk," Dr. Sebrell says, pointing. "I gave you the exact same document Dr. Eddy handed me yesterday. None other exists. The ONLY way this gets out is if the government publishes it."

The Vice President perks up, encouraged. "Okay. So we contain the report and proceed as planned," he orders.

“More R & D?” the NIH Director inquires, hoping against hope that he is NOT hearing Nixon correctly. He knows differently though. The rollout is already underway. He knows this because his fingerprints are all over it.

There is a press conference already scheduled for next spring at the University of Michigan. The press knows something BIG is brewing – political events are not planned this far in advance for SMALL announcements. The White House is quietly promoting the upcoming festivities in Ann Arbor as historic. The Vice President of the United States will preside over a ceremony honoring Jonas Salk at the conclusion of the press conference. A prominent medical historian is even trying to get Salk nominated for the Nobel Peace Prize. The media, alerted to the distinguished guest list through a series of leaks by its stable of reliable – and anonymous – sources, is doing its part, publishing headline stories that claim in above-the-fold, all-caps, bold-lettering, “SALK’S VACCINE WORKS!! More importantly, millions of doses of the vaccine have already been pre-ordered.

The medical and political communities are celebrating

as if the war is over and they won. In a way, they have – if true. Unfortunately, it is NOT true. A couple days ago, only Dr. Eddy and her tiny staff knew that. Then she brought Dr. Sebrell and his associates into the loop. Now the Vice President of the United States knows. Will anybody stop this madness?

"No goddammit," Nixon barks, frustrated. "I expect the NIH to license Salk's vaccine without further delay. That means YOU, Dr. Sebrell – YOU ARE the Director of the National Institutes of Health, aren't you?"

"But the vaccine doesn't prevent polio, it causes it," Dr. Sebrell protests. "We will have a public health crisis on our hands," he insists, very aware that it will be HIS and not the Vice President's signature on the license.

"That's YOUR god-damn problem," Nixon shrugs, standing to his feet. "Keep working on a fix, but in the meantime, get the doses ready. We begin the vaccination program next spring."

***

Washington D.C.

January 15, 1955

The folder is lying open on the Vice President's desk. *Sloppy,* thinks Beasley, surprised. *That is not like him.* It is the same yellow folder he noticed Nixon holding when he returned from his latest trip to California. As a trusted – and senior – staffer for Nixon, Jakub Berman has virtually unlimited access to the Vice President's office, which is why he does some of his best work AFTER hours. He takes a seat behind his boss's desk and begins examining the contents of the file.

The bulk of the file is a government contract with Cutter Laboratories, a giant pharmaceutical firm based out of Berkeley, California – Richard Nixon country. Everyone who has ever worked for him knows Cutter Labs well. *Nixon's biggest campaign contributor,* Beasley reminds himself. According to the terms, Cutter is the sole manufacturer of two-hundred million doses of Jonas Salk's IPV polio vaccine – at ten dollars per dose. Beasley quickly does the math in his head. "Two BILLION dollars," he blurts aloud. "Jesus...Cutter Labs is a monster," he realizes, shaking his head. Cutter estimates the first one-hundred million doses to be completed and ready for distribution by the end of THIS month – *that is only two more weeks,* he realizes. After that, the second hundred million doses will be "in the pipeline." Beasley leans back in Nixon's chair and closes his eyes, suddenly realizing the REAL purpose of the Vice President's weekly sojourns to the west coast.

Beasley finds a receipt for a money order stapled to a two-page memo tucked away in the middle of the file. Several items on the receipt immediately catch his attention. "July 15, 1954 – this is dated EXACTLY six months ago," he says. "Twenty-five THOUSAND dollars and signed by Richard Nixon," he adds, curious what a politician who constantly cries poor might be spending that kind of money on. *Better yet,* he wonders, *where did he even GET that kind of money?* Beasley remembers well the press having a field day with then-candidate Nixon's pitiful financial disclosure forms during the 1954 presidential campaign. Certainly, by now it is a well-known set of facts. The former Senator did not come from money. His wife has never worked. His family lives on a public servant's income and has zero investment income. He really IS poor! In fact, Richard Nixon is probably the poorest Vice President in American history.

The memo is even more intriguing. Written by Cutter vice-president Edward "Ted" A. Cutter, it clears up any questions about the money order in the first paragraph. According to Mr. Cutter, Richard Nixon invested twenty-five thousand dollars in Cutter Labs' stock on July 14, 1954. It occurs to Beasley that the Vice President submitted his financial disclosure forms to the Federal Election Commission in May 1954 – eight weeks BEFORE the transaction. He knows this because HE helped prepare the forms. "Welcome to the family!" Mr. Cutter writes, congratulating Nixon. "We thank you for your personal and professional support," he continues, adding, "With your help, the future of Cutter Laboratories looks very bright!"

Mr. Cutter is not finished. "After August 1, 1954, the lab will no longer produce blood plasma and penicillin. From then on, one-hundred percent of Cutter's production capabilities will be focused instead on the manufacture of the IPV polio vaccine." *Salk*, Beasley thinks. *Cutter AND Nixon are both going all-in on Jonas Salk,* he concludes silently, holding the government's two billion-dollar contract with Cutter Labs in one hand and the receipt from Nixon's twenty-five thousand-dollar purchase of Cutter stock in the other. "Son-of-a-bitch," he exclaims loudly. "No wonder the test results have been so hush-hush," he says, chuckling. "There's NO going back now..."

***

New Orleans, Louisiana

April 25, 1955

A little over two weeks ago, above-the-fold headlines across the country screamed in bold print, "POLIO VACCINE IS SAFE, EFFECTIVE, AND POTENT" and, "POLIO ROUTED!" Only one week later, the same newspapers' headlines told a much different story, announcing "CUTTER WILL WITHDRAW SALK VACCINE AMID NATIONAL OUTCRY."

This week, government doctors from the National Institutes of Health (NIH) – sent by the Surgeon General – are traveling to Cutter Laboratories to investigate its production methods; lawyers with dollar signs dancing in their eyes are filing a massive class-action lawsuit and Congress, with political points to make is preparing hearings – televised of course.

The "Cutter Incident" is quickly becoming the biggest rolling fiasco in medical history, at least in the United States. It has wrecked the reputation of Cutter Laboratories – Vice President Nixon's favorite pharmaceutical company – whose name is now synonymous with tragedy. What happened in two short weeks?

Thirteen days ago, the White House advance team held back nothing. Medical royalty, Jonas Salk and Cutter executives received the red carpet treatment in Ann Arbor, Michigan. All the bigwigs from the Food and Drug Administration (FDA), the Center for Disease Control (CDC), and the NIH were present, peacocking across a makeshift stage on the front steps of the University of Michigan's Rackham Auditorium, lending their gravitas to the occasion. The spectacle bore a close resemblance to a political campaign rally. American flags adorned the stage. Red, white, and blue bunting overlaid the auditorium's front entrance. Banners, streamers, and balloons hung from every sidewalk sign and light pole. Sound filled the springtime air as the Michigan Marching Band played an endless loop of patriotic themes, much to the delight of an enthusiastic crowd. Vice President Nixon made a convincingly sincere speech, comparing Dr. Salk's polio vaccine to Dr. Edward Jenner's smallpox vaccine and presenting the always-pretentious doctor with an honorary medal. The schedule itself was intentionally ironic. The event took place EXACTLY ten years after the death of the world's most famous polio victim – President Roosevelt.

It was official. Amid such pomp and circumstance, the White House sanctioned the release of Jonas Salk's IPV polio vaccine. As expected, there was a rush to get the vaccine. Parents waited in long lines to make sure their kids received the injections. Hundreds of thousands of people received the doses – administered in just two weeks. Everything went according to plan – until it didn't. What MOST people did not know was one-hundred-and-twenty thousand of those doses contained the live poliovirus. As Dr. Eddy predicted, the bottom fell out suddenly with an outbreak of polio unlike anything the American people had ever seen before.

The "lucky" kids who had been first in line to receive the miracle injections were now the unlucky ones filling up giant, hastily constructed warehouses populated by colonies of hospital beds and iron lungs.

Since then, thousands have died. Thousands more have been left permanently crippled. The numbers are positively staggering. Forty-thousand kids infected with polio in just TWO WEEKS! Naturally, the public outcry has been ferocious.

On this day, Dr. Alton Ochsner is determined to save the Salk vaccine. A prominent cancer research doctor from New Orleans, Dr. Ochsner has been somewhat of a medical sensation since 1927 when he burst on the scene as a thirty-one-year-old hotshot surgeon appointed to serve as chairman of the Tulane University Hospital Department of Surgery. A very public spat with Louisiana's legendary Governor – Huey "*Kingfish*" Long – eventually forced his departure from Tulane, after which he opened his own medical center in 1942. Today, The Ochsner Clinic is where the rich and famous (and politically connected) from Latin America come to receive their medical care. More importantly, Dr. Ochsner's research in New Orleans is pioneering the link between cigarette smoking and lung cancer. Word is he is on the verge of curing cancer.

There is no bigger defender of Salk's vaccine than Alton Ochsner. From the beginning of the Cutter Incident, he has stubbornly maintained that the Salk vaccine is safe. While most in the medical community are taking a wait-and-see approach, Dr. Ochsner is not. He is out front leading the charge, defending Cutter Laboratories and Jonas Salk.

On its face, the doctor's gung-ho support of the Salk vaccine is bewildering. Why would a prominent cancer researcher, with seemingly no connection to Cutter Labs or Jonas Salk, risk his reputation on a polio vaccine? Especially one that has demonstrably proven itself NOT to be safe?

Those people do not know him very well. Nicknamed the "Bull of the Bullpen," Ochsner is notorious for his use of confrontation and intimidation in his "classroom" – the clinic's amphitheater – where he teaches young medical students how to perform under stress. Undaunted by a hostile Governor earlier in his life, he is likewise unfazed by this little controversy.

The room hushes as Dr. Ochsner makes his entrance, displaying his trademark cocksure stride. Waiting for him on the stage are two young children accompanied by a nurse. In an effort to prove his point, Dr. Ochsner is staking their health on his judgment and Dr. Salk's vaccine. Supremely confident and self-assured, he invited the local media and gathered the entire clinic staff to witness the event. In typical Ochsner fashion, he intends for this to be an in-your-face rebuke.

The young boy goes first. He looks up at Dr. Ochsner with an aw-shucks, gap-toothed grin. The doctor ruffles his hair playfully as the nurse prepares the needle. Cameras flash during both injections and the whole assembly applauds as the children show off their wounds afterwards. Behind them, Dr. Ochsner is all smiles, his stagecraft a rousing success.

***

Berkeley, California

April 27, 1955

After the spectacle at The Ochsner Clinic, Ray Broussard, a frumpy, old-school New Orleans reporter from the *Times-Picayune* was suspicious of Dr. Ochsner's over-the-top interest in Salk's IPV polio vaccine. Having a little tread on his tires has honed Broussard's bullshit meter and it was registering off the charts while he watched the children interacting with the good doctor on that stage. Something about this whole affair just does not square with him so he does what any capable reporter would do – he begins digging. Experience has taught Broussard to start with the seven deadly sins and eliminate them one-at-a-time, methodically narrowing the list of possible motives. He assumes the first sin to be a given.

Hubristic pride, he thinks, rolling his eyes. *What doctor IS NOT an arrogant asshole?* Number-two on the list seizes his attention though. After a little research and close examination of Cutter Laboratories' 14-A proxy statement – made public at its annual shareholder meeting – he has his answer.

Aware this will be a major scoop, Broussard hurries to the newsroom to show it to his hard-to-please editor. "Good stuff," the boss growls, taking another huge bite of his apple. "Makes THIS even more sick and twisted." He thrusts a juice-stained news bulletin in his veteran reporter's chest. Broussard's face blanches as he scans the first few lines. "Oh my god," he whispers, barely audible, "this is just awful..."

"...Two headlines, two separate stories," his unsympathetic editor interrupts abruptly, all business. "We'll lead with the tragedy and follow up with the corruption." Broussard nods his head quietly, barely hearing the instructions. *What a disaster*, he thinks, lost in his own mind and frozen in place like a slab of granite. "Snap out of it!" the editor finally barks, slapping his hand on a nearby table. "These stories aren't going to write themselves!"

Hours later, extra copies of the *Times-Picayune* have

been printed and delivered to newsstands all across the city. New Orleans is soon to be the epicenter of a medical earthquake. The above-the-fold headline now screams "OCHSNER GRANDSON DEAD; GRANDDAUGHTER PARALYZED: SALK VACCINE ADMINISTERED BY NEW ORLEANS CANCER DOCTOR!"

It gets even better – or worse – depending on your perspective. Below the fold is another headline accompanying a second story, one that promises to sprout very long legs. It reads "OCHSNER IS CUTTER STAKE-HOLDER."

***

Chapter Four

***

Mole & Marine

New Orleans, Louisiana

July 27, 1955

"Flying planes is a goddamn man's job," the CAP Captain begins with a bang. "The Civilian Air Patrol is dedicated to teaching all you little bastards how to be cadets in the United States Air Force. All of you sons-of-bitches are volunteers. You do not HAVE to be here but since you are, I am assuming you want to learn how to fly or get intelligence training. That is where I come in. I will teach you – the boys anyway. You goddamn girls can go to hell, for all I care." *Wow*, thinks Lee. *That is quite an opening statement.*

The Captain continues speaking; the longer he speaks though, the more his voice seems to fade into the background. Lee is fascinated as he examines the strange-looking little man standing in front of the group.

Apparently, the Captain is wearing painted-on eyebrows. They look almost clown-like. Stranger still, the Captain's eyes literally bug out of his head. Together, the bulbous eyes and awestruck eyebrows create a weird kind of surprised look on his face, like someone who has just discovered what a rectal exam is.

The grotesque ill-fitting wig perched on his head sideways keeps moving as he talks. Every time he attempts to straighten it, the wig becomes even more lopsided. Lee subconsciously fixes his own hair as if trying to align the cockeyed disaster on the Captain's head.

His voice is high-pitched and frantic-sounding. Words are tumbling out of his mouth so fast they are all mixed up or butchered. He likes to swear a lot too, that is obvious. Clearly, it does not faze him that he is speaking to kids. It's "god-damn" this and "son-of-a-bitch" that. *I thought my mom's mafia boyfriends cussed a lot, but damn, this fellow beats them all,* Lee thinks, impressed. He continues staring at the Napoleonic caricature before him in amazement. The Captain's herky-jerky body movements back-and-forth, up-and-down, and here-and-there are dizzying.

The entire spectacle is mesmerizing.

"What's your name son?" the Captain asks Lee. No answer.

"Excuse me, over here," the Captain snaps his fingers. "What's your name?" He repeats louder. Still no answer.

This time, the Captain gets right in Lee's face and yells, "What's your goddamn name?"

With a sudden start, Lee comes out of his trance just in time to hear the Captain screaming in his face. He wipes the spit from his cheek and quietly answers, "Lee, sir."

The Captain yells back, "Lee what? You got a last name, boy?"

Lee nods and replies, "Oswald, sir."

"Os – what?" the Captain looks sideways at Lee.

"OsWALD, sir" Lee clarifies.

"What the hell kind of name is that? You a Jew?" the Captain frowns.

"No, uh, I don't think so. Actually, I don't know,

maybe." Lee is obviously flustered.

"Jesus Christ," the Captain shakes his head in disgust. "You either are or you aren't – which is it? These are NOT difficult god-damn questions!" Lee tries to answer but nothing comes out.

"Never mind," the Captain says abruptly. "Can you spell it?"

"Spell what?" Oswald asks, frustrated.

"Uh, I don't know...PONTCHARTRAIN!" is the sarcastic reply. "What the hell do you think? Spell your LAST NAME for me boy!" the Captain shouts loudly.

"Oh, O-S-W-A-L-D, SIR" Lee shouts at him. He does not know why he is shouting, but the Captain seems to inspire that kind of a response.

The Captain does not blink. In fact, Lee is sure he has not blinked once since beginning the conversation. "Where are you from, LEE OSWALD?" he asks.

Lee can tell that the Captain is a close-talker, invading his personal space. He gets so close Lee can feel his hot breath and almost taste the spit flying out of his mouth. Lee wipes his face again.

"My mom and I just moved from New York City, sir."

"You a Catholic?" the Captain asks, suspicious.

"No sir," Lee answers quickly, trying not to let the Captain interrupt him. For some reason, he feels rushed, as if he is under interrogation.

"That's too bad. How 'bout girls, you like girls Mr. LEE OSWALD?"

"Uh, well, uh...I guess so, sir," stammers Lee. He is sure the Captain is mocking his name.

"That's too bad too," answers the Captain with an exaggerated huff.

Suddenly, the Captain sticks out his hand, "David Ferrie, flight instructor with the Moisant Cadet Squadron," his voice softening a little. He even forces a crooked grin. His eyes still do not blink.

Lee offers his hand apprehensively.

"It's nice to meet you, young Lee Oswald. Welcome to the Civilian Air Patrol."

***

Washington D.C.

July 15, 1956

Sasha leaves the path, descending through the weeds to the culvert below. The grass is soaking wet from the morning dew. He inspects the secluded dead drop location, reaching underneath into the darkness, feeling for the familiar magnetic box. He always hates this part. Sasha lives in fear that one time, his hand will latch onto a snapping turtle or a water moccasin instead of the box. He shudders just thinking about it.

Sasha sighs with relief when his hand contacts the metal. He pulls the box out quickly, opening it and removing the envelope. After carefully securing the box back in its place, Sasha retraces his climb through the brush to the trail that stretches along the Potomac River.

He walks briskly, glancing over his shoulder periodically to check for witnesses. It is early in the morning – the trail is deserted. Satisfied that he is alone, he takes a seat on a nearby park bench and unseals the envelope.

The message reads, “URGENT…tonight. Place & time – usual.” There is no need for anything further – only one agent uses this dead drop. Such precautions are necessary when safeguarding the identity of a CIA mole.

*Something is going down in Asia...*Sasha thinks, looking at the envelope in his hand...*something big.* His no-nonsense double agent inside Langley is not one to cause alarm or deviate from the bi-weekly schedule. *He is out of the country on special assignment for six weeks...and now this. What in the hell happened in Japan?* Sasha wonders, standing to leave.

He does the math in his head while he walks. *Fourteen years,* he complains silently. *Son-of-a-bitch that is a long time. Could this finally be the big break KGB counter-intelligence has been waiting for...justifying its investment of more than a decade in an agent who has so far delivered the Soviets almost nothing?* He finds himself getting excited and walking faster.

His whole life, Michael Overstreet idolized his father. Why not? After World War I, his dad was a member of the "Black Chamber" which worked side-by-side with the Army Signal Intelligence Service and Navy cryptanalysts to crack Japanese encryption systems. Tokyo's codes deciphered, the attack on Pearl Harbor should not have been a surprise...but of course, it was. Michael often wondered what went wrong on December 7, 1941. Except for that one time his father sat him down and described what he did for a living, his father never discussed work. Michael never had the courage to ask him about it either. *Maybe after he retires*, he kept telling himself.

In 1942, three events happened, changing Michael's life forever. First, in order to prevent future intelligence debacles like Pearl Harbor, President Roosevelt created the Office of Strategic Services, the forerunner to the Central Intelligence Agency (CIA). The OSS fanned out across the northeast, combing the Ivy Leagues, looking for the best and brightest recruits.

Second, Michael graduated with honors from Princeton. The academic distinction and his degree in international relations from such a prestigious school naturally made him a high-priority target for the OSS recruiters. Besides, it made sense. If he made the grades, he was always going to follow his father's path anyway. Now he had the requisite education from a well-heeled institution. Both parties saw it as a perfect match.

The third event happened during his first six months

on the job. One evening he was warming up under the cherry blossoms on the Anacostia Riverwalk, stretching for his daily jog on the Mall, when a fellow runner approached and asked him if he would be his running partner for the day – a common request. Michael oftentimes joined with one or more on his longer runs. In fact, on weekend mornings, runners would form little pelotons and fan out all over the capital city like colonies of hard-working ants. Predictably, someone in the group would comment that "misery loves company" and the runners would laugh and venture forth. Like a monastery of Catholic friars practicing unnatural asceticism, miles of running in the heat of summer or cold of winter was their particular bed of nails.

On this day, Michael, who normally was the one setting the pace, had trouble keeping up with his new partner. He started fast – *too fast*, Michael thought at the time – and continued to pick up the pace throughout the ten-mile run. An hour later after they finished, the two men sat down together on a park bench to rest, though it did not appear to Michael his partner was even breathing hard. *Who in the hell is this guy?* Michael wondered to himself, exhausted. He checked and rechecked his watch, thinking he was misreading the time. He could not believe he had just run ten miles at a six-minute pace. *Jesus...*

A few minutes later, in the middle of a rather tedious conversation about old injuries, the man suddenly reached into his waistband and removed a plastic-covered envelope sealed tightly with packing tape. Before Michael could react, the package was in HIS hands and the tireless Spartan was off and running away into the night. Michael watched until he disappeared then he looked at the package he was holding. His first thought was to dispose of the item but he talked himself out of it. *Strange things happen in intelligence – this might have something to do with work,* he convinced himself, curious.

The cautious type, Michael resisted the urge to open the package until he was safely at home. When he did finally open it, he was instantly sorry that he did. In his work, evidence is gold. What fell from this package was pure gold – photographs, receipts, coded messages, and copies of handwritten reports – every document authenticated by a familiar signature – in a hand he knew all too well.

The report on a covert operation called "Invisible Hand" was of special interest to him. He examined the date again – October 1941 – only two months before the attack on Pearl Harbor. *Pure genius*, Michael thought, shaking his head as he read. *Legal too...Jesus.*

According to Invisible Hand, the NKVD spent most of 1940 and 1941 exploiting the United States intelligence community's byzantine rules and procedures, preventing the various spy agencies from talking to one another and simultaneously executing an elaborate disinformation campaign, thoroughly corrupting their communication pipeline. The Soviets had a man inside who understood how and where to put sand in the gears of the entire American foreign intelligence apparatus without detection – even the best intel is worthless if not shared and acted upon in a timely manner.

These stalling tactics worked long enough for Japan to launch its "surprise" attack. Neither the Japanese nor the Americans were aware the Soviets were secretly manipulating them, acting as the unseen force to make the attack on Pearl Harbor possible. Stalin knew that America would only join the war if Japan attacked it first. He and the NKVD arranged it with the help of their mole inside the Black Chamber – Michael's father. *Holy shit!* His father was a double agent. The proof was right in front of him. *Which means Pearl Harbor was not a failure after all...*

By that point in the evening, Michael had poured himself a very stiff drink. It was clear to him his running partner was really a Soviet NKVD agent. He was also certain their meeting was not by happenstance. It was obvious the Soviets were blackmailing him into following in his father's footsteps.

The package contained a date, a time, and a meet location. Michael had no choice. He HAD to meet with the NKVD. He would not allow his father to be the modern-day version of Benedict Arnold. Moreover, he would not go through life as the son of a traitor.

He was right. His father's career as a US intelligence agent was nearing retirement. The NKVD needed Michael to pick up where his father left off and it was more than willing to apply force on a vulnerable pressure point in order to make Michael an offer he couldn't refuse. It worked. For the last thirteen years, Michael Overstreet has been a Soviet mole – inside the OSS at the beginning, and now the CIA. The codename of Sasha's most prized asset is "Arrowhead." A rotation determines their meeting locations. Tonight, the random numbering system chooses Ford's Theater – just blocks from their first meeting at the National Mall, near the Washington Monument.

Even though it is raining lightly, Sasha chooses to walk the short distance from his bookstore to the theater. He arrives early to find Arrowhead already waiting. Silently, they walk a couple blocks, find an empty bus stop and park themselves beneath the canopy. Sasha waits for his agent to open the conversation. *He called this meeting,* he thinks. Arrowhead clears his throat finally. "The Agency has developed a reconnaissance plane that is undetectable," he begins.

"Undetectable?" Sasha asks, skeptical. "HOW undetectable?"

"You didn't let me finish," Arrowhead growls. "It's an ultra-high-altitude plane. When I say high, I am talking seventy-thousand feet high – way out of reach of the Soviets' worthless radar and their shitty fighter jets. As we speak, CIA pilots are in your air space flying missions all over the Soviet Union gathering photographic intelligence and you don't even know they're there."

"Seventy-thousand feet!" Sasha exclaims. "How in the hell? The altitude record is sixty-five thousand feet – and even the best radar only reaches forty-five thousand feet."

"Uh huh," Arrowhead grunts. "That's why it's damn-near invisible."

Sasha sits in stunned silence.

"The plane cost millions," Arrowhead continues, "which is why we only have a few of them. Brass wanted to wait and see if they were worth the money. They are convinced now – the last I heard, they just ordered ten more planes. Program is run right off your coast out of our base in Atsugi, Japan."

"Son-of-a-bitch. How long?" Sasha asks slowly.

"One month," Arrowhead replies. "Eisenhower was pissed when Premier Khrushchev rejected his "Open Skies" proposal so he basically said, "fuck the Soviets" and approved us for ten days of overflights in June. Since then, we have been busy degrading a ton of classified photographs. The images are the best we have ever seen. The Agency hit god-damn pay dirt this time."

"Atsugi...? Son-of-a-bitch, that's right under our nose!" Sasha exclaims.

"Doesn't say a lot for Soviet intelligence in that neck-of-the-woods," Arrowhead quips, ever the provocateur. Sasha shoots Arrowhead a withering glare, not amused. Arrowhead just shrugs and laughs.

"Is that it?" Sasha asks. Arrowhead nods.

Sasha stands to his feet, repeating his signature expletive, "son-of-a-bitch."

He sticks his hand out from underneath the shelter. "At least the rain stopped," he mumbles. Then he turns and disappears quickly into the night.

***

Fort Worth, Texas

October 24, 1956

"Are you sure you really want to do this?" Robert asks his brother sitting opposite him in the passenger seat of his aging mint-green 1945 Chevrolet Bel Air.

Lee nods his head. "I'm sure," he says firmly.

Robert tightens his grip on the steering wheel of the parked car. He turns his head and looks at his seventeen-year-old brother. "Take it from me, I know. You can't un-ring THIS bell."

Though Robert Jr. is five years older than Lee, the brothers have a unique bond, united through years of family dysfunction and parental neglect. They have shared the same experience. Because of their mother's transient lifestyle, Robert Jr. and Lee have become each other's best friend. Surprisingly, they both have the same father. Because Robert Sr. died before Lee was born, Marguerite – their "maw" – and a whole platoon of inconvenienced boyfriends that came after raised the boys. At age eighteen, Robert took the first exit ramp he could find, escaping maw and her no-count paramours by enlisting in the Marines. Following his brother's example, Lee does not even want to wait that long.

"Jesus, maw's going to absolutely come unglued when she finds out," Robert sighs.

Lee shrugs his shoulders. "Not my problem anymore," he says coldly. "I've been nothing but a burden and a disappointment to her my whole life anyway. I'm actually doing her a favor."

"What about me? Do you even care what I think?" Robert asks.

"Of course..." Lee says.

"...Well I think you should finish school first and THEN do whatever the hell you want," Robert interjects. "You won't need me to sign for you then. You'll be eighteen, you'll have your high-school diploma, and you'll be a man in the eyes of the state."

"I'm DONE with school," Lee states defiantly. "HIGH SCHOOL, anyway."

"Have you thought about what job you'll do in the Marines?" Robert asks. "After Parris Island, they'll make you choose something and you'll have to go through a training school. You'll just be trading one school for another."

Lee nods. "Yeah, but the difference is, I'll be getting paid to go to school and learn about something important – like radar operation."

"Radar!" Robert whistles, impressed. "That means a security clearance."

"I know," Lee replies. "It shouldn't be a problem if I volunteer for intelligence training."

“Intelligence training too?” Robert asks, surprised. “Who put that idea in your head?”

“Captain Ferrie,” Lee answers. “He was my Civil Air Patrol instructor when we were living in New Orleans. I joined the squadron out at the Moisant Airport last summer. At first, I really wanted to fly planes in the Air Force but the Captain told me I should be a spy in the CIA. He knows his stuff; he even started teaching me how to posture.”

“Posture?” Curious, Robert turns, props his knee up on the bench seat and faces his younger brother who is full of surprises this morning.

“Act a certain way to project an identity,” Lee repeats verbatim words he had heard the Captain say many times.

“Is that what you’ve been doing all this time – PRETENDING to be a communist?” a bewildered Robert asks.

Lee smiles and nods his head. “He taught me how to create an image by the clothes I wear, the books and magazines I read, the way I talk, who I hang out with – it’s like multiple personalities. It’s kind of fun actually.” Robert’s eyes widen. He cannot believe what he is hearing. *Little brother sounds so grown-up*, he thinks.

Lee continues, his words accelerating with excitement. "You'd be amazed how easy it is. People are superficial. They make snap judgments off first impressions. Captain Ferrie told me if I was good enough, I would even be able to fool my own family. He said that is the true test because family knows you best."

His brother has grown quiet. "God almighty Lee, I can't decide whether to be relieved or pissed. On one hand, I am relieved this is an act, but on the other hand, you are pretending to be a damn communist! OUR daddy fought for this country. Your uncle was in the service. Me, John – this is a military family!"

"Captain Ferrie told me there are different kinds of soldiers," Lee replies. "He said soldiers that can fool the enemy into thinking they are one of them are the future. Double agents don't use guns and bullets to kill enemy soldiers. He said they win wars by leveraging information to their advantage. Anyway," Lee continues, "he taught me how to practice my cover. That's what I've been doing."

"Cover, huh? Well, the joke is on you because all that

foolishness got you moved again," states Robert. "You DO know that maw moved to Ft. Worth to get you away from that Captain Ferrie and those other crazy nuts you were hanging out with in New Orleans, don't you? She told me that herself."

"She hates the Captain," Lee admits. "And the thing is he was only my instructor at Moisant for a few months. He left our squadron in the fall. I may have gone to ten or twelve meetings total. He is the first person who has ever believed I could be good at something – that I could do something important. I think mom resented him for that."

"Have you ever even fired a gun?" Robert asks, changing the subject.

Lee shakes his head. "No," he says sheepishly.

"Well, get ready. ALL United States Marines are trained snipers. I wasn't too bad myself. Scored two-twelve which designated me a sharpshooter," he brags. Lee nods, smiling. He has heard that story before. Many times.

"But enough of that," Robert stops himself. "I just wanted to make sure you know what you're doing. It sounds like you've given this a lot of thought."

"I want to belong to something important," Lee says. "I want to do something that matters, be someone who makes a difference."

"Is the officer expecting us?" Robert asks, pointed at the recruiting station.

"Yes," Lee replies. "Everything's BEEN ready. He just needs your signature."

"Okay little brother," Robert says, opening his car door. "Let's go get you enlisted in the United States Marine Corps."

***

Tokyo, Japan

November 16, 1956

It is a fourteen-hour flight from the Washington Airport in DC to Tokyo's Haneda International Airport. Coincidentally, there is also a fourteen-hour time difference between the two capital cities.

Like a time-traveler, Sasha loses twenty-eight hours flying east but will gain it all back on his return flight.

Such dramatic skips forward and backward in a three-day span wreak havoc on his body clock every time he makes this trip. In fact, just thinking about it gives him a headache. Today, Sasha is on the losing end of time as his plane circles, preparing to land at the fourth busiest airport in the world. He feels groggy. *I need a nap*, he thinks, looking at his watch. *Not enough time*, he realizes. He has an important appointment to keep.

His usual driver is waiting near the airport terminal's front entrance like always. If he leaves the car unattended, the hyper-vigilant airport security will have it towed. It happened a few years ago when a different driver waited inside the terminal to help Sasha carry his bags. He has to manage his bags by himself now. The driver waves, motioning him to the limo's open door.

It was twenty-one degrees when he boarded his plane in DC. Snow was coming at him from all angles, forced along by a stiff winter wind like an airborne avalanche. He had to squint to keep the giant flakes from blinding him. It was so cold his nose hairs froze. They did not completely thaw out until an hour into his flight. A nonstop runny nose has left pinkish-red track-marks under his nostrils that curve down and around his mouth like a cartoonish handlebar mustache. What a welcome relief it is to be in Tokyo, Japan on a balmy, fifty-four-degree, sunny day. He strips his sweater off and happily discards it along with his winter jacket in the trunk of the car.

During the short twenty-minute drive, Sasha sees the few remaining geisha houses clustered together in little "flower towns." He read recently that a declining interest in the traditional art of female entertainment is causing many geisha houses to close. Tourists keep the struggling Japanese custom alive now.

They pass the US Embassy in the expatriate ward of Akasaka in central Tokyo. The streets have emptied. On a weekday, Akasaka is extremely busy, like Los Angeles or Chicago. However, weekends are quiet. Today is the beginning of the weekend so they make good time.

The KGB field office closed for the day, per Sasha's order. *Just the two of us – good,* he says under his breath. He is meeting with this particular agent without any other people around. She is waiting for him when he enters the conference room.

Sasha slowly looks the young woman over, from head to toe and nods approvingly. *Where in Russia did they find THIS cupcake*, he wonders. Though she is sitting, Sasha can see that she is tall. Her shoulder-length brown hair frames her enormous brown eyes beautifully. Her high and wide-set cheekbones are set against a stunning backdrop of flawless alabaster skin. Then his eyes wander south. *Wow.* "You'll…certainly…do," he finally says haltingly. He clears his throat and tries again. "Looking at your file, I'm very impressed with what I read. But looking at you, I'm even more impressed with what I see."

Not offended, the woman smiles graciously, showing off her ruby-red, luscious lips and perfect teeth. "Thank you, sir. I hope to be of useful service to Mother Russia," she purrs, a thick accent practically dripping with sexuality. *I am glad she cannot read my mind*, Sasha is thinking.

Anya Kozlov – codenamed "Anna Kelly" – is a KGB "swallow" in the Delilah Unit – a special services unit comprised of the Soviet Union's most intoxicating vixens. She, like the other swallows in the unit, use all the equipment in their God-given feminine arsenal to neutralize intelligence targets. Anna Kelly is Delilah's most prolific agent. She ALWAYS gets her man.

"Uh huh,' grunts Sasha nervously. "Your mission," he pauses briefly, clearing his throat, "is to fraternize with an American serviceman on the base, maybe several – whatever it takes. "Spend the money we give you, frequent the nightclubs – oh hell, I shouldn't have to tell you how to do your job."

Anna smiles again and bends down, enough to give him a glimpse of her spectacular breasts. He is sure she is doing it intentionally and makes a conscious effort not to stare.

Sasha rallies. "We have reason to believe the Americans are flying spy planes from their base in Atsugi over Soviet territory. We have to stop it, and soon. This is the information we need," he says, handing her a folder.

"We need data about the plane's altitude and speed capabilities and we need flight schedules," Sasha explains. "This should help you determine who is worth pursuing. A pilot is preferable but a radar operator would work too. Whoever it is MUST have security clearances," he adds emphatically.

"Anna," Sasha lowers his voice, "this is a highly-classified program you will be compromising. These men will be on guard against women like you – they are on high alert. If you succeed, you will be a hero in your country. These bastards and their spy planes have made fools of us long enough." Then he makes a dumb mistake.

Sasha leans in close to Anna, catching a big whiff of her perfume. The scent is so mind-altering he temporarily forgets what he is going to say. He sits back in his chair, disoriented. He shakes it off, trying to clear his head. Suddenly he remembers. "Your best effort, Anna – nothing less, your country is counting on you!" *Jesus, did I just say that?* Sasha thinks, embarrassed.

Anna uncrosses her long, gorgeous legs, a skin-tight short black skirt with a tantalizingly high slit giving Sasha a view unlike anything he has ever seen before. She stands up, slowly unwinding her long slender frame. Then she leans over Sasha and places both of her hands on his chair's two armrests. Her face is so close to his he can feel her warm breath. The close-up confirms what he observed earlier. Her skin IS without a single blemish.

Sasha eases back further in his chair and tries to

speak. Softly, she puts her index finger on his lips. Then she leans in even closer and whispers in his ear seductively, "Relax. I do not need your pep talk. You WILL NOT be disappointed. I assure you." His stomach in knots, Sasha feels like convulsing.

She stands up straight, turns, and slowly exits the room, looking back at Sasha with eyes that scream trouble, leaving him frozen against the back of his chair. *I know why they told me to meet with her alone*, he thinks after a several long minutes. *Whew...*

***

Irvine, California

July 9, 1957

"Don't get too comfortable Sergeant," the commanding officer growls. "Looks like you won't be here long."

"Yes sir," the fidgety Sergeant responds, his eyes darting suspiciously with every movement and sound.

"Here" is the United States Marine Corps Air Station El Toro located near Irvine, California. The CO motions with a folder he is holding for the young Marine to take a seat.

“Another short-timer,” he fumes, disgusted.

Though it is still morning, the office is hotter than the air outside. That is saying something because the air outside is hotter than Hades. A small, hapless rotary fan on the CO’s desk tries its best to move the sticky, humid air around but it is failing miserably. The CO is wearing a bath towel around his neck as if he is at the beach – an old trick he uses to battle his perspiration. Judging by the sweat rings under the arms of his uniform shirt, he and the towel are BOTH losing the battle.

The CO opens the folder. “It says here you scored high enough to grade out with a sharpshooter designation,” he notes. “And you finished seventh out of a class of thirty at Keesler.” He pauses and reads the title of the Sergeant’s course. “Aircraft Control and Warning Operator. What in the hell is that?”

“Lots of things, sir” replies the Sergeant, trying hard to suppress a smile. “Mainly instruction in aircraft surveillance and the use of radar.”

“Lots of things, huh? Well, not many boys come here with the kinds of security clearances you have,” sniffs the CO. "You already had a top security clearance in Mississippi," he reads from a document, "and now you are approved for crypto secret clearance. Jesus Christ Marine, that's black-box shit right there!"

"Thank you...yes sir," replies the Sergeant, beaming.

"Must be why they're sending you to Atsugi," the CO observes dryly, not easily impressed. *Sure doesn't look like much,* he thinks to himself, examining the Sergeant's stature. He steals a quick glance at the file again. *So this is what 5'8", 135 pounds looks like? Jesus, what a puny little pecker!*

"Sir, Atsugi?" the Sergeant asks, interrupting the CO's critique.

"That's right," the CO says. "Atsugi is our main Strategic Air Command base in the Pacific. You ship out next month for the Marine Air Control Squadron 1 near Tokyo – which explains all the security clearances and your training in radar operation."

"Sir, THIS August?" inquires the Sergeant, surprised.

The CO nods. "Hey, look on the bright side soldier. It could be worse. You might get lucky and hook up with a national while you're there," he says, tossing the file on his desk.

“Sir, a national?” the Sergeant questions innocently.

“A Japanese woman, Marine!” the CO bellows loudly, laughing at the rube sitting in front of him. “They like American servicemen – they like VERY much! But hey, I forgot...where are you from again?” He grabs the file. “What, they don’t have Asian women in Texas soldier?”

The Sergeant grins awkwardly. “Sir,” he begins meekly, “are there any European women who like American servicemen in Japan?”

“You mean white? It’s a god-damn military base, soldier,” the CO says abruptly, finished with the conversation. “What the hell do YOU think?”

***

Chapter Five

***

Inconvenient Truth – Part II

Washington D.C.

December 1, 1957

"We might have a winner – finally," Caleb announces to Joshua over their disappointing cafeteria lunch. He plays with his fork, using it to toy with the piece of rubber chicken on his plate, unsure if he is desperate enough to eat it. "So far," he says, pushing the tray away, "Dr. Sabin's vaccine isn't killing anyone in the field test and it's not paralyzing anyone in the control group either." He reaches inside his coat, remembering the package in his pocket.

"Samples?" Joshua asks.

"Right," Caleb tells him, sliding the small plastic container across the table. "Tell him this is everything."

Joshua nods. "The Sabin vaccine..." he asks, returning to the original topic, "...is it working just because the doses are lighter?"

Caleb nods. "A lighter dose is definitely part of it," he agrees. "But it's also an oral application – two drops of polio vaccine on a sugar cube rather than an injection directly into the bloodstream."

"I see," replies Joshua, sipping his apple juice. "A lighter dose AND a weaker application." He fumbles briefly with his straw, thinking. "Whereas Salk's injections were too strong, Sabin's vaccine gives the body a chance to develop antibodies against polio."

"Exactly," Caleb agrees. "Salk's vaccine overloaded the immune system and gave people the very disease it was trying to prevent. Unfortunately for Salk, his vaccine came first in the trial-and-error world of science. His work produced the science that DID NOT work. Dr. Sabin is countering with a fix that DOES work."

Dr. Albert Sabin is not a Johnny-come-lately to polio research. His first examination of the virus happened in 1936. He and a colleague grew poliovirus in brain tissue from a human embryo at the Rockefeller

Institute for Medical Research in New York City while studying on a fellowship program.

After World War II, Dr. Sabin made the revolutionary discovery that poliovirus first attacks the intestinal tract before moving on to nerve tissue. This allowed Sabin to grow poliovirus in non-nerve tissue, much more practical than embryonic brain tissue.

From the time Salk and Sabin began their work on a polio vaccine, the two doctors were head-to-head competitors – Salk's killed-virus injections vs. Sabin's live-virus sugar cubes. However, Dr. Salk finished his first. Since the entire US population was already serving as a field test for Salk's vaccine, Sabin had to return to his native Russia to conduct a field test for his.

Then came the Cutter Incident. All at once, a fiasco for Salk became an opportunity for Sabin. The same medical and pharmaceutical big shots who earlier preferred Salk's vaccine have switched sides and are now rooting for Sabin's field test to succeed.

"It's not a done deal yet," cautions Caleb. "Remember Dr. Eddy?"

"You mean 'Bad News Bernice'?" Joshua replies with a

chuckle.

“It’s in her lap again – poor gal. I sure wouldn’t want her job,” says Caleb.

“They might do well to listen to her THIS time,” says Joshua.

“Whoever they get to license this vaccine might want to have a conversation with Dr. Sebrell first,” Caleb notes. “Salk’s vaccine wasn’t even off the market two days before they threw him under the bus...”

“...And backed over him several times,” Joshua interjects dryly.

“Speaking of that, I hear Sasha is pretty frustrated,” Caleb mentions. “Razor worked Wild Bill like a pro. Their relationship netted Sasha years of primo NIH intelligence. But there was no way to warn Wild Bill he was being set up without compromising Razor so Sasha had to sacrifice a valuable source.”

“An unfortunate outcome for all of us, no question,” agrees Joshua. “Who could predict Nixon’s madness would hurt the KGB?” Both doctors laugh as they rise to leave.

"You'll see to it Sasha gets those Sabin samples?" Caleb reminds Joshua.

"They'll be in his hands tonight, probably in Moscow by the end of the week," Joshua reassures him.

***

Atsugi, Japan

June 21, 1958

Sasha signs the courier's ledger and opens the secure envelope marked "**CONFIDENTIAL.**" The cipher-text ensures message secrecy and integrity while also authenticating the sender. Sasha keeps the only key hidden away in one of his bookstore light fixtures. In order to decipher the plaintext, he has to disassemble the light to access the key. The process is painstaking and time-consuming, which, of course is the point. An hour after the courier leaves, he is finally ready to start reading.

The heading on Anna's report reads, "Eyes Only. Intelligence Report #1 – Atsugi Operation."

"I've already made contact with several US Marines

based at Atsugi," the report begins. "One in particular is the most promising. Ideal candidate. Very young, quiet, reclusive, moody. Seems to be quite troubled too."

Anna continues.

> *I have met with him several times in Tokyo at the Queen Bee (a local nightspot frequented by US servicemen). To date, I have learned the following –*
>
> - *Subject arrived at Atsugi last September (1957).*
> - *Subject has multiple security clearances.*
> - *Subject speaks fluent Russian.*
> - *Subject is a radar operator for a secret high-altitude plane he refers to only as "racecar".*
> - *As radar operator, he supplies wind information up to 90,000 feet to racecar's pilot.*

Sasha examines the photo of the US Marine included in Anna's report. *Pretty nondescript*, he says to himself with a shrug.

> *From what he has told me, I believe "racecar" is*

a codename for the spy plane you described in our meeting. I am proceeding very slowly and carefully with the subject. Perhaps he is too good to be true. By that, I mean he shows signs of counter-intelligence training. Some observations I have made –

- *He claims to be a Marxist.*
- *He speaks fluent Russian. He did not finish high school and yet he has learned the Russian language well enough to converse with me flawlessly??*
- *He spends a lot of money on me and girls like me frequenting the priciest nightclub in Tokyo (The Queen Bee) three or four times a week.*
- *He complains constantly about the evils of capitalism.*
- *Information is easily (too easily, I suspect) extracted from him.*
- *He has a telltale nickname. His unit mates call him "Oswaldskovich" because he reads so much communist literature (such as Pravda). He is proud of this nickname.*
- *I observed him playing chess. He chose the red pieces and called them the*

"victorious Red Army".

The report is signed, *AK.*

Sasha re-reads Anna's report with great interest. After finishing, he transmits the following four-word message in response – "PROCEED WITH EXTREME CAUTION!"

***

New York City, New York

February 14, 1959

"Simians," the doctor begins her speech, "are essential in the production of Dr. Sabin's vaccine. The poliovirus used in the preparation of the vaccine is grown on monkey kidneys." The New York Cancer Society's featured speaker tonight is Dr. Bernice Eddy. Her assigned topic is "Cancer-Causing Viruses." She is prepared to speak about two viruses in particular.

"Like humans," Dr. Eddy continues, "simians are social animals. Like humans, their welfare depends on interaction. Without social interaction, psychotic behaviors such as self-biting, hair pulling, and rocking are common. For this reason, thousands of monkeys captured in the rain forests of two different continents – Africa and Asia – ship together in steel cages. Even after import, laboratories continue to house the primates together for social and practical reasons."

The crowd begins to stir uncomfortably. Some are wondering – *where is she going with this? Is Bernice protesting the use of simians in medical research?* Dr. Eddy ignores the clamor of anxious murmuring, mindful of the fact that she is the one risking her professional career to make this speech, which qualifies her to be a LOT more unsettled than anybody in the crowd listening.

"The problem is," she pivots, "simians from different continents have different viruses. What is so difficult to understand about Asian monkeys having viruses unique to Asia, or African monkeys having viruses that are exclusive to Africa? By caging them together however, the viruses have mutated and strange NEW viruses are appearing in these monkeys."

Dr. Eddy pauses for effect. She clears her throat and swallows hard. Then she boldly presses on. "It stands to reason then, using these monkey kidneys to manufacture Sabin's polio vaccine has resulted in a product contaminated by mutated 'monkey viruses'." The crowd gasps in unison. Alarmed Cancer Society stuffed shirts start looking at each other, whispering incredulously – "monkey viruses?" Some of them even pick up their programs and begin searching in vain for anything with the word "simian" in it.

Since its introduction in 1957, the Sabin vaccine is on a two-year win streak. Polio is no longer an epidemic. It poses no public health threat. Aside from the early bumps in the road thanks to Jonas Salk, Vice President Nixon's polio crusade is a rousing success. His master plan is working – just in time for the 1960 Presidential election. That is, unless Dr. Eddy ruins everything.

"The Sabin vaccine contains at least forty "monkey viruses" – two of which appear to be game-changers," she claims. "The first – Simian Virus #40 – is a cancer-causing virus. Research is showing it to be a catalyst for brain, bone, leukemia, and lung cancers. The second – Simian Immunodeficiency Virus – is a wildcard. We don't know WHAT it is yet."

The stunned room now goes silent. The gathering is allowing Dr. Eddy to hang herself – or perhaps it is listening. Probably a little of both.

"It gets worse," Dr. Eddy says. "How could it get worse?" she asks rhetorically. "First, SV-40 and SIV are absorbed directly into the bloodstream – notwithstanding Sabin's oral application. Second, both viruses transmit sexually. Meaning if a mother is a carrier of either virus, she can, and most likely will, pass it down to her children."

"This SHOULD scare us all to death," the doctor lectures, her tone serious. "As of tonight, one-hundred million Americans have already received the vaccine and are unknowingly carrying SV-40 and SIV. Tragically, because these viruses transmit sexually, many of these carriers have unwittingly infected their kids. How many MORE children are at risk? I submit there are not enough actuaries in the entire United States government capable of forecasting numbers that big. Again, it gets worse. OUR government," she pauses again, "is preparing to distribute one-hundred million MORE doses of this vaccine. That's two-hundred million contaminated doses total – two-hundred million PEOPLE," she emphasizes firmly. Even without looking up, Dr. Eddy can feel the daggers directed her way. She stands a little straighter.

"The REAL tragedy is our public health officials know

all of this," she declares. "They have my report. However, they also know that SV-40 and SIV both have 30-year incubation periods. They are gambling that the short-term gains will justify a long-term public health crisis. For the record, I requested permission to publish these findings publicly. I also recommended an immediate halt in the production of the contaminated polio vaccine."

She steadies her aim and readies her trigger-finger. Then she fires. "My government superiors instead censored my report and rejected my recommendation. Five years ago, I warned many of these same people about the dangers of the Salk vaccine. They covered up my report then and released the vaccine anyway. People ended up paralyzed or dead because of that terrible decision. Now, they are trying to cover up my report again." By now, Dr. Eddy is visibly angry. "But this time, I WILL NOT stand by and be silent. Consider yourself forewarned."

Finished, Dr. Eddy turns quickly and marches off the stage – not even bothering to wait and accept her National Institutes of Health "Woman of the Year" award. Flabbergasted attendees glare at her in stony silence, condemning the whistleblower with hostile eyes as she makes her way slowly through the disapproving gauntlet toward the front entrance. “Okay everybody,” the hapless emcee pleads after Dr. Eddy’s dramatic exit, “please give a nice hand to tonight’s featured speaker...”

***

Washington D.C.

March 5, 1959

Sasha re-reads the message, absorbing its meaning. The words are more than a little unnerving, especially considering who authored them. In the hierarchical labyrinth of Soviet intelligence, only two men outrank Sasha. Both are tough. Both are survivors. After all, both DID serve under Joseph Stalin and live to tell about it. A message from either one is rare. Something he is doing or has done is drawing attention in Moscow and he knows that is NEVER good.

The First Chief Directorate – codenamed “Father” – directs all foreign intelligence operations and espionage. Like a phantom, he stays out of public view, cloistered deep inside the “Lubyanka” – the

KGB's garrison-like headquarters in Moscow – adding to his mystique. In his five years of service, Sasha himself has only seen Father face-to-face one time. He keeps a very low profile, which is why this message is so alarming. Father does not use the radio transmitter often but when he does, he knows how to rattle Sasha's cage.

Father's real name is Aleksandr Panyushkin. When the NKVD reorganized as the KGB in 1954, Lavrentiy Beria appointed Panyushkin to be the head of the KGB's foreign intelligence division. Beria believed Panyushkin's decade of experience as Soviet Ambassador, first to the United States and later China, uniquely qualified him for the post. He was right. The USSR's only potential adversaries in the post-WW II world were the United States in the west and China in the east. Now five years later, it STILL only has two real threats – the United States in the west and China in the east. Just as Beria hoped, Panyushkin's past is helping shape the Soviet Union's future.

Sasha reads the message marked "**URGENT**" one more time.

Attn: Second Chief Directorate:

After careful study of the samples, Russian scientists' report the American "Sabin" polio vaccine to be contaminated with viruses – more than likely because of its use of monkey kidneys during development. Two of the viruses are game-changers. SV-40 causes many lethal cancers. SIV is not clear at this time but it seems to attack the immune system, which would be even more deadly than SV-40.

Moreover, Dr. Sabin's recent exploitation of Russian citizens as a control group for the field-testing of his vaccine concerns us greatly. Moscow views this ex post facto as an American preemptive strike against the Soviet population. Determining if this was experimental or intentional is of highest priority.

I will expect a full report from your office regarding the following:

- *The extent to which the American institutions responsible for the public health are aware of the dangerous side effects of the Sabin vaccine.*
- *The extent to which the American political institutions are aware.*

Finally, the part Sasha keeps reading repeatedly...

> *...The question in Moscow is, if we are learning this before you, WHAT IN HOLY HELL IS GOING ON WITH YOUR OPERATION? REPORT BACK, FORTHWITH.*

"What in holy hell..." Sasha echoes Father's words aloud, worried. *This is serious*, he thinks. *This is how wars get started and people like me end up in Siberian gulags.* He quickly makes contact with his two doctors for an urgent get-together later in the day. As usual, the meeting takes place at Sasha's bookstore.

"Does CDC know the Sabin vaccine is giving people cancer?" Sasha asks Joshua, putting him on the spot immediately.

"Cancer? No, I don't think..." Joshua stammers.

"...What about FDA?" Sasha interrupts, looking at Caleb. "Does FDA know about SV-40 and SIV?" Caleb shakes his head, taken aback by the aggressive tone.

Sasha is exasperated. "Somebody knows something! What about Razor and the boys at NIH? All they do is biomedical research. Can the Americans really be this goddamn stupid?"

“What are you talking about?” Caleb asks, bewildered.

“The Sabin vaccine – remember the samples we sent?” Sasha reminds them.

“Of course,” Joshua replies.

“The results are in,” Sasha tells them. “And they aren’t good. Our scientists say the vaccine is loaded with nasty viruses. Father mentioned cancer and something about the immune system. He wants to know why WE did not know this. In my world, that is code for ‘somebody is going to be hauling rocks in a Russian labor camp over this!’ You MUST find out if FDA, CDC, or NIH knows what we know.”

Inquisition complete, Sasha escorts them to the front door of the bookstore and practically shoves them both into the street. “Report back in two days!” he orders them.

The stunned doctors are standing on the sidewalk, paralyzed by the news they just heard. Neither one speaks for what seems like minutes, wheels spinning inside their heads.

Finally, Caleb breaks the silence. “They DO know. I suspected something was up when Razor told me they took Dr. Eddy's lab and equipment from her and demoted her. He said rumors are going around that she was fired for violating the non-disclosure agreement."

"Bullshit. Her team was in charge of testing the vaccine," Joshua says. "I bet Dr. Eddy found something they didn't want her to find..."

"...And then told the wrong person," Caleb concludes.

"The first one-hundred million doses already went out," Joshua continues. "But another one-hundred million doses are scheduled for distribution in the next year. That's why they have to shut her up."

"I wonder what Dr. Eddy found," Caleb ponders aloud. "Somewhere, there is a report with her name on it. I'd sure love to get my hands on it."

"Good luck with that," Joshua replies sarcastically. "There may have BEEN a report with her name on it but there isn't one now. No, if they did not publish it then, they never will. I guarantee you it's been buried in somebody's file thirteen," he says, nodding at a nearby trashcan.

"Can you imagine if this ever leaks?" Caleb asks,

incredulous. “The American government will be out of the vaccine business forever. First the Salk fiasco and now Sabin. Son-of-a-bitch!”

“NIH, CDC, FDA – they’re ALL in full cover-up mode now,” Joshua says. “That’s why we haven’t heard anything...”

“...Which kind of tells us what they plan to do with it, doesn’t it?” interjects Caleb.

***

Washington D.C.

March 5, 1959

Beasley arrives at Sasha’s bookstore a few hours later. By then, it is dark outside. The sign says “Closed, Please Call Again.” After signaling his arrival with a coded knock, the door swings open and he disappears inside. Sasha gets straight to the point.

“Sabin’s polio vaccine is tainted,” he begins. “It cures polio but it causes cancer. The question is, does Nixon know?”

"The simple answer?" Beasley asks rhetorically. "Of course he does. He knows everything. Polio is his second obsession. The REAL question is does Nixon care?"

"This IS an election year," Sasha notes.

"There's your answer," agrees Beasley. "Nixon's FIRST obsession is becoming President. He knew five years ago that Salk's vaccine was bad but he forced the NIH to certify it anyway to protect his Cutter investment. Now, he's forcing Sabin's vaccine on the American people to protect his electoral chances."

"So this has nothing at all to do with the Russian people," Sasha concludes, relieved. "It's just about Nixon becoming President..."

"...Russians?" Beasley interjects, startled.

Sasha waves him off. "Never mind," he says. "I'm just thinking out loud."

"I thought this might be tonight's topic," Beasley says cryptically, as if holding back something important.

"Oh?" Sasha asks, interested.

"The last week or so," Beasley begins, "Nixon's office

door has been like a turnstile – I've never seen so much activity."

"What kind of activity?" Sasha asks him.

"The curious kind," Beasley replies. "He's been meeting with FDA, CDC, and NIH white-coats, you know, the standard entourage of public health officials, nothing unusual about that. Now, intelligence is involved too. FBI, NSA, all of The Agency boys. I checked with our people at Justice and CIA – both say the same thing, 'national security'. But it's not WHAT they're saying; it's HOW they're saying it – like they always do when they're hiding something."

"What is the connection between public health and intelligence?" Sasha wonders.

Beasley shrugs. "I don't know yet, maybe it's nothing. Even though it looks like something big is going down on the medical front – something top secret…"

"…Something that involves all the highest levels of American intelligence," Sasha observes cynically, interrupting Beasley. The Bookstore quiets as both men try to imagine all of the possibilities. "Jesus, this Vice President is up to something very sinister," Sasha finally declares, frustrated.

“The election?” Beasley asks, suddenly unsure of his boss’s motives.

“I’m not sure…” Sasha replies haltingly, “…but I suspect it’s even BIGGER than the Presidency.”

***

Chapter Six

***

Fake Defector

El Toro, California

August 11, 1959

"What's on your mind, Private?" the commanding officer demands with a loud sigh, a stack of paperwork piled high in front of him. He taps his pencil impatiently.

"Sir, I need a discharge from the military. My mother hurt her head recently at work. She needs my care immediately."

"Well, I'm sorry about your mom..." the CO replies, motioning for Lee to take a seat, "...but you DO need to know how long and hard it is to receive a hardship discharge from the United States Marine Corps."

"Yes sir," Lee says, sitting down, eyes straight ahead.

The CO opens a desk drawer and pulls out a folder. “The application process is a bitch. First, the Marine Corps determines if the hardship is severe enough to qualify. Your mom or her work will have to provide an affidavit from a doctor.” He looks up at Lee. “Is she under a doctor’s care?”

“Yes sir…well, sort of,” Lee answers, unsure. “But she should be able to get a doctor’s report.”

“There’s more – trust me,” the CO grunts. “You will have to provide answers to a bunch of questions.”

“Sir…what kinds of questions?” Lee asks, leaning forward anxiously.

“Is the hardship temporary?” the CO reads from a sheet in the folder. “Will it get worse if the hardship isn’t granted? Have you and your mother made all reasonable efforts to improve the situation short of a discharge? Is a separation from the military the only solution or could a humanitarian reassignment closer to home solve the problem? Is there no one else that can provide the same help?”

“Sir, that sounds like a lot,” Lee observes. He shifts backward in his chair, not happy.

"Son, the United States Marine Corps is easy to get into and hard to get out of," the CO replies bluntly, unsympathetic. "And before a final decision is made Private, you will have to provide documentation and supporting statements."

"Sir, how long does all of this usually take?" Lee inquires, aggravated.

"Ten weeks if everything goes smooth," the CO barks. "Ten...maybe twelve weeks."

***

New Orleans, Louisiana

September 20, 1959

Anna watches Lee boarding the SS Marion Lykes, a freighter bound for Le Havre, France. Nine days ago, she was watching him leave the Marine Corps Air Station in El Toro, California, his hardship discharge papers in-hand. Next came a couple of days in Dallas and a week in New Orleans...*and now he is on his way to Europe...*she says to herself knowingly...*to start his REAL job...*

He bought his ticket three days ago. After a hefty gratuity from Anna, the sales representative at Travel Consultants, a New Orleans travel bureau, said he filled out a "Passenger Immigration Questionnaire" on which he listed his occupation as a "shipping export agent", claiming his two-month expedition to Europe would be strictly pleasure. He told the sales rep he chose the freighter instead of a luxury passenger liner because the rates are so cheap – he only paid $220.75 for his fare. Because it is a working ship, she informed him there would only be three other passengers aboard. "That's perfect," he replied. After leaving Travel Consultants, Anna followed him to the Liberty Hotel – a seedy joint with another cheap rate – where he registered and stayed until this morning. After watching him board, Anna hurriedly prepares her report – *nothing like waiting 'till the last minute,* she thinks, feeling the pressure to alert Sasha.

The next day, Sasha's courier is waiting at the bookstore for him with a secure envelope – this one from New Orleans – marked "**CONFIDENTIAL**". *Anna?* He guesses silently, uncertain. *What in the hell is she doing in New Orleans?* He holds the envelope, lost in thought while he watches the courier disappear.

It has been almost three years yet even the smallest reminder conjures an image of her curvy backside teasing – more like torturing – him from beneath her barely-there skirt as she exited their meeting in the KGB field office in Tokyo. *And her perfume – son-of-a-bitch!* He breathes deeply, sighs and blinks his eyes several times, trying to clear his head. *Get yourself together!* Sasha chastises himself silently.

The cipher begins ominously –

> *URGENT! This is a status update on the subject described in my Eyes Only report dated June 21, 1958. Since then, the subject has been granted a hardship discharge from the United States Marine Corps effective September 11, 1959. The subject's application was processed and approved in less than thirty days...*

Shit, Sasha thinks. *A rabbit hole...*

> *...A thirty-day timetable for a discharge of any kind (even medical) is unheard of in the military, especially the Marines. It prompted me to take a closer look...*

Good girl, Sasha thinks, also suspicious.

...Based on circumstances related to the subject's training, job description, security clearances, discharge and other events on the subject's timeline while serving at Atsugi and later El Toro, I am prepared to conclude he is a US intelligence agent (probably CIA). His job description allowed him unrestricted access to the spy plane and knowledge of classified information about the spy plane.

I have been able to confirm the following information –

- *Subject assigned to Marine Air Control Squadron 1 stationed at Atsugi Air Force Base from September 1957 to October 1958. After Atsugi, subject transferred back to the Marine Corps Air Station in El Toro, California.*
- *Subject had MULTIPLE Top Secret security clearances while at Atsugi and El Toro.*
- *Subject SELECTED to receive Russian language training while at Atsugi.*
- *Subject was a radar operator for the classified spy plane codenamed "racecar" while at Atsugi.*

- *Subject has had several unexplained absences from his unit while at Atsugi and El Toro.*
- *Subject court-martialed twice, demoted once, and imprisoned in the brig once while at Atsugi. Subject faced military discipline for illegal discharge of his weapon (twice) and fighting with a superior officer.*
- *Subject met several times with known US intelligence operative David Ferrie in New Orleans while on leave from Atsugi. Upon returning to base, subject lied about it on his leave report, claiming he was with his mother in Dallas.*
- *Subject claiming his mother severely injured at work – necessitating his hardship discharge. According to the injury report, a sixteen-ounce cardboard candy box fell on her head from shelf twelve-inches above her workstation.*
- *Subject applied for passports to Russia and Cuba one week before his discharge. He received both passports the day before discharge granted.*
- *Subject spent only two days in Dallas with his mother after discharge…*

"Jesus Christ!" Sasha exclaims to no one in particular. "Anna's right. He's being prepped for an operation." He turns the page. What he reads next changes everything.

> *PLEASE BE ADVISED: Intelligence asset (subject) is active. He left the Port of New Orleans very early this morning on the SS Marion Lykes, a freighter headed for France. I believe his ultimate destination is Russia. I also believe he is planning to defect! Be alert for a US intelligence agent posing as a defector!*

The report is signed, *AK*.

Sasha hurries to the radio transmitter to forward Anna's report to Father. Before he sends it, he hastily scribbles a postscript to Father at the bottom. "We won't need to steal the spy plane after all. The spy plane is coming to us."

***

Washington D.C.

October 12, 1959

"There CANNOT be any US footprints in Cuba," the President declares firmly, turning in his swivel chair. He gazes out the windows of the Oval Office, watching a groundkeeper on the south lawn trimming the bushes. "And I will NEVER approve an operation with ANY military fingerprints..."

"...I know. That's the beauty of this plan," the Vice President interjects, standing behind the President and his desk. "It's a CIVILIAN operation."

"And WHO exactly are you calling civilians?" Eisenhower questions him, unfazed by Nixon's interruption. He turns again, facing his Vice President, hands clasped.

"Well, as you know," Nixon begins, "Miami and New Orleans are chock-full of exiles who love Cuba and despise Fidel Castro. As long as he is in power, they cannot go home. Recruiting them will be easy. They are a motivated bunch. And the best part is these Cuban exiles will be joined by Cuban dissidents after the landing, making the operation entirely civilian AND Cuban..."

"...And how do we KNOW the exiles will be joined by Cuban dissidents after the landing?" the President asks, HIS turn to interrupt.

The Vice President squirms, glancing over his shoulder at a seated Jakub Berman who has been busily taking notes. “If I may Mr. President?” Berman asks, taking Nixon’s cue.

Eisenhower waves at him. “Go ahead, I’m listening.”

“Sir,” Berman says, holding up a manila folder. “Intelligence reports indicate a sizable dissident population searching for a partner to join them in launching a counter-revolution to overthrow Castro.”

“So what you’re saying is it’s a god-damn crapshoot,” Eisenhower shrugs, unimpressed. “Those CIA boys and their intelligence reports – have you both forgotten Guatemala so soon?”

Nixon shakes his head. “Different set of encyclopedias,” he argues. “Jacobo Arbenz was elected President of Guatemala by his own people, Castro wasn’t. We screwed that up by taking the wrong side. We’re on the right side THIS time.”

The President stands up and walks slowly across the office to the door facing east. He looks out over the Rose Garden, saying nothing. “No US troops?” he asks finally, skeptical. He remembers similar assurances less than a year before.

Vice President Nixon shakes his head again. “No sir. No US military – plausible deniability. It will be an Agency covert operation. The CIA will arm the exiles, train them, and support them.”

“What’s the contingency plan if the operation goes south?” Eisenhower questions him. He is in very familiar territory now, the old general in him kicking in.

“We’re counting on the element of surprise,” Nixon responds.

“Something ALWAYS goes wrong in these kinds of things,” the President says, admonishing the overeager Vice President with his professorial tone. Nixon nods, not appreciative of the lecture, especially in front of his aide, Berman.

“When?” Eisenhower asks after a brief pause.

“Next spring...” Nixon replies matter-of-factly, “...BEFORE the election.”

***

Washington D.C.

October 13, 1959

The two men arrive from opposite directions and meet at the west end of the National Mall. It is early morning, which means one thing in Washington DC – both men arrive with coffee cups in hand. They sit on the bottom steps of the Lincoln Memorial and look out over the water sipping their liquid narcotic. One removes a pastry from a small sack and begins munching on it. After a few minutes, they discard the remains of their breakfast and begin walking east along the reflecting pool.

The autumn air is unseasonably cold and crisp. Steamy clouds of hot breath shroud both men's faces as they walk. It is too early in the season for snow but a thick blanket of frost over the frozen ground looks like a carpet of fog.

A beleaguered jogger passes by, sounding like an angry woman in the advanced stages of labor. They watch him, laughing. After they bypass the usual herd of ducks squatting in the middle of the sidewalk, they are alone.

Caleb's source as NIH – Razor – accompanies him this morning. The two men don't have the kind of history Caleb and Joshua share but as long-time colleagues, they have gradually become friends – the kind of relationship that develops later in life when circumstances, like work, or a common purpose, brings people together.

Ken Rudolph is a career bureaucrat. His life is what happened while he was making other plans. His father's original plan for his son was what Ken called the "footstep plan" – four years of NYU followed by medical school at Georgetown University. After residency – a career in surgery just like dear old dad. As fate would have it, Ken took after his mother. Science turned out NOT to be his thing so he switched his major and graduated with a degree in public administration instead – much to the disappointment of his father, of course.

The next plan was to get a post-graduate degree in public policy and run for political office. His first few jobs at NIH were so energy and time-consuming though, he never could seem make it back to school. Putting aside the plans for a political career, Rudolph climbed the career ladder at NIH instead.

In thirty-three years of service, Rudolph has literally become "Mr. NIH." He has worked in supply, budgeting, human resources, purchasing, accounting, information technology, contracts, some middle-management positions, and most recently, as an administrative officer. Becoming a Soviet spy was NOT part of Rudolph's plan.

It all began innocently enough on a racquetball court. During an intense game of cutthroat, the NIH ringer impressed the new player from FDA. Dr. Cherry was the best racquetball player NOT named Ken Rudolph – and competitive as hell. The two soon became court regulars.

Rudolph noticed Dr. Cherry gently extracting NIH information from him at first. He never asked for classified information. Just stuff he already knew but needed confirmed. Rudolph suspected malfeasance but the racquetball was just too good to pass up.

Everything changed one day when Dr. Cherry offered Rudolph money for the same information he had been giving up for free. His daughter was in her first semester of a private college. His wife had just filed for divorce. Rudolph's finances were hemorrhaging. From then on, Rudolph was on Dr. Cherry's payroll. That is what HE thought anyway.

Then there was the day Dr. Cherry informed him he did not have a payroll but the KGB did and his name was on it. That was a memorable day. He tried thinking of ways to extricate himself but alas, by then it was too late. His two choices were clear: Continue passing information to Dr. Cherry – and become rich – or turn himself in and go to jail a disgraced traitor. That was the same day he learned his KGB codename. From then on, Rudolph still played racquetball with Dr. Cherry but it was "Razor" and "Caleb" who exchanged classified NIH information.

Rudolph eventually reconciled himself to the idea of trading medical secrets for money. As a doctor, he convinced himself improving people's lives through medicine was just as important in the Soviet Union as it was in the United States. As a humanitarian, his "work" did not involve weapons that threatened his country, thus – in his view – it was not treason.

Through the years, Razor's years of work experience at NIH and his relationship with Dr. Sebrell has yielded a treasure-trove of classified information for Caleb, who has then forwarded it on to Sasha. In return, the KGB has made Razor financially comfortable.

"I spoke with Wild Bill," Razor tells Caleb as they walk. "I thought when he resigned I would lose him as a source but it turns out, he's still in the game and unencumbered by the job. Best part is his circle of friends is intact – good for us."

"Does he suspect anything?" asks Caleb.

Razor shakes his head. "No way. We have been friends since we were eleven and sharing a paper route. Hell, we even swapped high school girlfriends a couple times," he says, laughing. "We've worked together professionally for the last thirty-plus years. I was his best man in his wedding and he was mine. He helped me through my divorce and I was with him when Linda died. To be honest, I think it unburdens him to have someone to talk to, especially since he lost his wife. He tells me stuff all the time he's not supposed to," Razor brags. "I didn't even have to ask for what I'm about to tell you."

They stop walking. For a moment, both men gaze at the water glistening in the bright morning sun. Even the birds cooperate. There is no sound, only silence.

"It's beautiful this time of day," remarks Razor.

"Uh huh," Caleb agrees, lost in his own thoughts.

"Okay, let's have it," Caleb says, suddenly out of his trance. "Is the United States government going to intentionally give the American population cancer?"

"It might be worse than that," replies Razor. "In fact, it IS worse. MUCH worse." He takes a big breath.

"The short answer is yes," he begins. "The program will continue without interruption. Orders have come down from the Vice President to carry on – this is AFTER we gave monkey viruses to one-hundred million Americans – which has to qualify as the biggest mistake in medical history."

"That IS one hell of a mistake," Caleb observes dryly.

"It's bad I know but that's really what it was – a mistake," Razor shrugs. "But now? Now it IS NOT a mistake because we know. Now it is intentional. Now we are going to give one-hundred million MORE contaminated doses to the American people – on purpose! That's premeditated murder – something none of us signed up for."

"What's the justification?" Caleb asks, unwrapping a piece of gum.

"Curing polio now is worth causing cancer later,"

Razor replies quickly. "The incubation period gives them a thirty-year head start to having a cure ready when the cancer epidemic hits."

Caleb starts to say something but Razor cuts him off. "Wait, there's more, straight from Wild Bill. It is classified, and after you hear it, you will know why. It's the latest research – scary stuff."

They stop at a park bench. Caleb wipes the morning dew off with a handkerchief and takes a seat. Razor remains standing. He props his leg up on one end of the bench and hunches over, resting both elbows on his knee.

"Everybody's heard of SV-40," Razor explains, "but there's another virus in the vaccine that's even more deadly according to Dr. Eddy's report that nobody saw. It comes from Africa..."

"...What is it?" Caleb interrupts his slow-talking friend.

"Simian Immunodeficiency Virus, or SIV," Razor answers.

"What does it do?" Caleb asks.

"It attacks the immune system and practically renders

it useless. The common cold could kill you if you get it. Like SV-40, it lies dormant in a person during a thirty-year incubation period before it manifests itself."

Caleb swivels on the park bench and stares at Razor in amazement.

"Think about this," Razor continues. "Thirty years of sexual encounters will spread the virus exponentially. Parents, kids, and sexual partners – the principle of multiplication will go into effect. America could wake up in the late 1980's with virtually its entire population infected with cancer or SIV – which I am sure they will have renamed by then – or worse, they could have both. We thought the polio epidemic was bad. If Wild Bill's information is correct, we will regret the day we cured polio. By then, the cure might kill us all."

"Holy shit," Caleb says quietly as he exhales.

"Holy shit is right," Razor agrees.

Razor joins his partner on the park bench. They both sit in silence for several minutes allowing the meaning of the words to sink in.

Finally, Caleb breaks the silence. "This is something

Stalin would have done."

"He DID," Razor replies morbidly. "Remember Ukraine?"

"Jesus Christ," Caleb mutters under his breath. He kicks at the dirt, disgusted.

Razor rises to leave and Caleb joins him. "It's warmed up," Razor says, removing his jacket. The two men nod and shake hands. Then they turn and walk away, again in the opposite directions – Nick, east toward Washington's monument and Razor, west toward the Lincoln Memorial. The irony is not lost on Caleb.

Two American leaders memorialized, he thinks as he walks. *One for creating a free country and the other for preserving it. I wonder what they must think now of the man who is killing it?*

***

Moscow, Russia

October 21, 1959

The loud knocking startles Lee. He has been waiting

for hours...*finally!* He thinks. Even though he knows better, he had started to think nobody would come. He jumps up to answer his Moscow hotel room door.

The short, balding man is NOT what he is expecting. His rumpled black suit is at least one size too small. *THIS does not look like a KGB agent,* Lee is thinking, examining him closely. The man offers his hand. "I am Abram Shaknazarov," he says with a nasally voice. "I have been ordered by the Soviet Interior Ministry's Office of Visas to interview you." He gestures at Lee with an official-looking briefcase in his other hand.

Office of Visas – sure, whatever, thinks Lee, amused. "Please, come in," he says, taken aback by the man's fluent English.

"Mr. Oswald, may I call you Lee?" the OVIR functionary asks routinely, helping himself to the only chair available in the austere accommodations. Recommended by the locals when he first arrived in Moscow, Lee is still surprised how Spartan the furnishings in the Berlin Hotel are. He chooses the only other seating option – the edge of the bed.

Lee nods. "Of course..."

"...Lee," he interrupts, "...what exactly do you want

here in Russia?"

"I want to become a Soviet citizen," Lee answers. "I want to live in the great Soviet Union."

"The USSR is only great in literature..." Mr. Shaknazarov declares with a sigh. "...you should return to the United States."

"I've planned this for two years," Lee says, distressed. "I want to be a Soviet..."

"...That's too bad," the OVIR agent interrupts again. "I fear you wasted your time."

"Please sir, I'll do anything," Lee begs.

"Mr. Oswald, your visa expires tonight. I will check again with my superiors and find out about an extension. You must remain here until I contact you." Mr. Shaknazarov rises to leave. "Someone will be in touch," he tells Lee, who is too stunned to move.

That was seven hours ago. Lee tries passing the time by writing in his diary. "I am shocked! My dreams! I only have $100 left. I have waited two years to be accepted. My fondest dreams are shattered because of a petty official!" Writing is not helping him. He is beside himself.

At six o'clock, there is another knocking on the door – this time more forceful and accompanied by loud voices. Lee opens the door hesitantly. Three large police officials stare at him. "Sir, you are ordered to report to the Soviet Interior Ministry's Office of Visas in two hours," the biggest of them barks, thrusting something into Lee's hand. "Your ticket. The train for Helsinki departs at eight o'clock. You MUST be on it."

"What about my visa – was it not extended?" Lee asks meekly, already knowing the answer.

"Your visa expires in two hours," the police officer answers firmly. Lee watches the three officers' march away. *I have failed because of bad planning,* he concludes silently. *I planned too much!* He closes the door and leans against the wall. *Damn!*

Suddenly, he remembers something that gives him a renewed sense of purpose. He scribbles a few words quickly on a scrap piece of paper, after which, he enters the bathroom and turns on the water – hot in the bathtub and cold in the sink – filling both. He dips his left wrist in the basin, soaking it in the freezing water, numbing it. Then he slashes at it violently and plunges his wrist into the scorching bath. Lee watches the water slowly turn pink, then red. *When the OVIR returns and finds me dead, it will be a great shock,* he thinks. "I have made a long journey to find death but I love life," he whispers – barely audible- reciting the words from his own hastily written suicide note. A few seconds later, he passes out.

***

Moscow, Russia

October 31, 1959

The Soviet Interior Ministry's Office of Visas DID return to the Berlin Hotel that night and find Lee but he was NOT dead. After a week in the psychiatric care unit, the Botkin Hospital released the troublesome foreigner into the care of the KGB, which registered him in the relatively plush Metropole Hotel until the Kremlin could decide what to do with him. After his attempted suicide – real or fake – one thing the Soviet government HAD already decided was to keep a closer eye on him this time.

"How is your arm?" one of the KGB agents assigned to

Lee taunted him upon his release from the hospital.

"Okay," Lee replies, defensive.

"Do you want to go to your homeland now?" the agent asked him, smiling mockingly. The rest of the agents laughed.

Lee shook his head stubbornly. "No. I want Soviet citizenship," he replied firmly, surprising the entourage of ill-mannered KGB officers.

"We will see about that," another agent taking notes told him. He looks over his glasses at Lee. "What papers do you have to show who and what you are?"

"These," Lee answered. He reached into his jacket pocket and pulled out his discharge papers from the United States Marine Corps. Then he handed them to the agent.

"Wait for our answer," the first agent ordered him. "And don't try anything stupid this time."

"How long?" he asked, ignoring the comment.

"Not soon," he replied, smirking. "Stay in your fancy room and eat well."

That was three days ago and Lee is feeling insulted. "I must have some sort of a showdown!" he writes in his diary. He exits the lobby of the Metropole and hails a cab. "American Embassy" he tells the driver.

Lee feels the stitches under the bandage on his left wrist. He pulls his sleeve down and enters the nine-floor monstrosity on Tchaikovsky Street. He looks at his watch. It is 12:30 in the afternoon.

"Richard Snyder," the Consul introduces himself pleasantly, shaking Lee's right hand and escorting him into his office.

"I intend to renounce my United States citizenship," Lee declares, coming right to the point.

"I see," the startled Consul responds. "Well, uh…I, uh…don't have the necessary papers on hand to accept your renunciation today. As you know, today is Saturday," he says, obviously stalling. "You'll have to return on Monday, during normal business hours."

Lee does not flinch, as if he already knows the embassy will not consummate his business on a weekend – especially this kind of business.

"If you don't mind, why are you doing this?" Snyder

inquires, pen in-hand, reaching for a legal pad.

"I was a radar operator in the Marine Corps," Lee begins. "Once I become a Soviet citizen, I am prepared to make known to Soviet officials all of the information concerning the Marine Corps I possess, including one program of special interest that was my specialty."

The Consul is startled. His writing stops suddenly and he looks up aghast. "What did you say?" he asks stupidly, his voice cracking. He clears his throat. "Pardon me, what did you say again?" he repeats.

"I intend to become a Soviet citizen, after which I intend to tell the Soviets everything I know about my time in the Marine Corps," Lee repeats, sounding rehearsed.

"That's...treason...son," Snyder stammers.

"Not if I've renounced my American citizenship and become a Soviet citizen it isn't," Lee replies, again sounding practiced.

"Well..." the Consul stalls again, "...as I said earlier, you'll have to come back on Monday."

"Great, I'll see you then." His mission accomplished, Lee jumps up to leave.

Stunned, a helpless Snyder watches Lee make a hasty exit from the embassy, leaving behind his passport on the desk. Snyder picks up the phone and begins dialing. “Get me Washington,” he tells the operator urgently. “Sir, this is Moscow. We might have a big problem...”

***

Moscow, Russia

November 1, 1959

“What do we know about the US Marine?” Father asks, offering Yuri a shot of vodka. With a wave, Yuri politely declines the alcohol and slips into the chair nearest Father’s desk, placing the heavy briefcase on his lap and opening it.

Yuri Annikova is the KGB’s Seventh Chief Directorate. His codename, “Kandinsky,” is a family surname from generations past, but he rarely uses it – counter-intelligence is not his specialty. Yuri’s area of expertise is the surveillance of Soviet nationals and foreigners. In other words, Yuri does most of his work from his office in Moscow. Nobody can sniff a rat, or an opportunity, like Yuri.

When World War II ended, thousands of German war criminals escaped international justice. Like a fog lifting across the entire continent, Nazi fugitives seemingly melted away without a trace. Rumors of Nazi sightings in far-away places such as Syria and Spain abounded. Some accused the International Red Cross of helping them run away to Canada. Others thought they had been smuggled out of Europe to South America by money-grubbing Vatican officials and the Jewish treasure-hounds Juan and Eva Peron, trading Argentine passports and visas for Nazi treasures stolen during the war. Soviet officials suspected Western intelligence services recruited them to help in the forthcoming Cold War struggle against the East. Whatever happened to them, they were gone.

In 1949, Stasi agents arrested a British spy. The NKVD sent Yuri to East Germany to participate in the interrogation. After just a few minutes with the subject, Yuri was sure he had found one of the missing Nazis. Furthermore, after a few days alone with him, Yuri was convinced he could turn the MI6 agent.

The Stasi was skeptical. NKVD higher-ups thought

flipping him was a fool's errand, giving Yuri a very short leash to prove them wrong. His instincts – honed by hundreds of interrogations of suspected spies – made Yuri confident this one would be worth the extra effort.

In the next several weeks, under psychological and emotional duress, the captured MI6 agent grudgingly confirmed what Yuri suspected – he WAS indeed a Nazi officer during the war.

That revelation did not surprise Yuri. What DID surprise him was what he learned next. According to the agent, there were several hundred former Nazis scattered over Eastern Europe gathering intelligence for the CIA and MI6. Alarmed, the NKVD suddenly did an about-face, green-lighting Yuri to carry on.

In a subsequent interview, Yuri demanded ten names and locations from the MI6 agent. After securing the list, the NKVD began scouring the Communist bloc, looking for a spy ring that had been operating under its nose for the last four years.

It only took the NKVD two days to verify the MI6 agent's list. Former Nazis working for British and United States intelligence were uncovered in

Czechoslovakia, Poland, Romania, Hungary, East Germany, and even Russia itself. Yuri's instincts were right after all. His next task was to flip the script.

First, in order to account for the MI6 agent being off the grid for six days, he knew he needed a trumped-up charge to convince the Crown its agent had not gone rogue. The Stasi filed two counts against him – charging him with failure to produce proper identification papers and attempting to escape East Berlin.

Second, he needed to make contact with the British government offering a trade. It was a common Stasi practice – granting politically connected or moneyed prisoners of the West a shot at "buying" their release if the offense was minor. Why risk an international incident? Besides, it was an easy revenue source for the cash-starved country.

The Stasi "allowed" the prisoner to contact the British Embassy with the extortion offer, after which, embassy officials pretended to contact "family members" to negotiate the transaction. Within twenty-four hours of the offer, embassy officials wired the ransom payment – quietly – and the NKVD's mole, "X" was on a plane headed east to the South London borough of Lambeth

– MI6 headquarters.

Upon his return to Century House, X endured an extensive debriefing, during which he "sold" interrogators the lie that he had simply been in the wrong place at the wrong time. X HAD to sell it, or Yuri promised to leak the transcript of his Stasi interrogation to his MI6 superiors. X was convincing. After an extensive observation period, MI6 reassigned its agent to Warsaw, Poland.

Since then, X has become an intelligence bonanza for the Soviets. Scores of former Nazis were outed in the five years after his arrest. In 1955, MI6 promoted X to counter-intelligence, giving him access to an even wider array of British and American agents.

Simply eliminating those spies would have been a short-term fix at the cost of a long-term opportunity. Instead, information is Yuri's weapon of choice. Many times, X has forwarded reports to Yuri that have enabled the KGB to frustrate CIA and MI6 covert operations. Since X has been in counter-intelligence, Yuri has used him to pass false information to foreign agents, compromising the integrity of American and British intelligence in Eastern Europe. In the world of espionage, the USSR is the kingfish of the decade. In the KGB's clandestine services, Yuri is the maharishi of counter-intelligence.

"His name is Oswald. Lee Harvey Oswald," Yuri reports, reading from the file. "Mr. Oswald first entered the USSR on October 15, 1959. Based on the intelligence report from field agent Anna Kelly, his request for asylum was initially denied." Father takes a sip of his vodka. "And while awaiting deportation, Mr. Oswald attempted suicide on October 21," Yuri adds.

"Jesus," Father says sarcastically, coughing on his drink. "Let me guess...he lives!"

Yuri nods and continues reading. "Doctors do not consider the attempt to be a serious one. In fact, our intelligence guide believes it was just a stalling tactic. Mr. Oswald did receive medical treatment for minor cut wounds to his wrist at our psychiatric facility in Moscow, October 21-28."

"How minor?" asks Father, demanding specifics.

"Five stitches," Yuri answers quickly.

"Beautiful," says Father, rolling his eyes. "We DID learn something THERE, no?"

Yuri continues, unaffected by Father's editorial outbursts. "During his stay in the hospital, Mr. Oswald was observed to be extremely cooperative during interrogations..."

"...Too cooperative perhaps?" Father interjects skeptically.

"Yes," agrees Yuri. "Discussions with Mr. Oswald yielded an intelligence windfall. Mr. Oswald served most recently at Atsugi Naval Air Base in Japan. His training is in radar – specifically for the spy plane he calls, 'Racecar'. The official name of the plane is 'U-2'."

"All of this information we already know from Anna," Father says impatiently, looking at his watch.

"I wasn't finished," Yuri responds, reaching into his briefcase for a second folder. "I think you will be pleased," he says, handing the folder marked "CLASSIFIED" across the desk.

Father opens the folder and takes a quick look. *His head is nodding up and down like a bobber on the end of a fishing line*, Yuri observes. A few moments later, Father looks up at Yuri. "Very good, very good," he states, obviously pleased. "Where is Mr. Oswald now?"

Yuri resumes reading from his report. "On October 28, he was released from Botkin Hospital and scheduled for deportation," answers Yuri.

"Deportation?" Father exclaims loudly. "Is this one of your tricks?"

Yuri ignores him. "THREE DAYS LATER," he looks up at Father, emphasizing his words, "Mr. Oswald entered the United States Embassy in Moscow claiming he wanted to renounce his American citizenship. Whether he followed through with it or not – nobody knows for sure. However, we HAVE learned that the US Marine Corps is changing Mr. Oswald's discharge status from honorable to dishonorable. Anna is also reporting that Atsugi Naval Air Base is in process of changing all of its radar codes."

"You STILL plan to deport him after these TWO episodes?" Father quizzes him with a relieved smile, knowing the answer now.

"Not a chance," Yuri declares. "We'll wait and see the next move. It's clear the Americans sent him here to give us what you hold in your hands," Yuri points at the classified folder. "At some point, they will want him back. If so, there is enormous opportunity in it for us.

Mr. Oswald will remain in Soviet custody until further notice."

***

Moscow, Russia

January 6, 1960

The secure phone line on Father's desk begins blinking. He answers. "Minsk it is," Yuri informs him.

"Are you sure?" asks Father, unsure of the pick. "It rains one-hundred and eighty days a year in Minsk. Even the summers are cold there. Mr. Oswald is from the Deep South. You didn't forget that Texas and Louisiana are hot and humid, did you?"

"You said to put him on ice," Yuri counters sarcastically. "Besides, we don't have a Deep South. Find me a city in Russia that's NOT cold and rainy."

"Good point," Father concedes, chuckling.

"Minsk IS the largest city in Belarus," Yuri explains. "To the extent that any American can blend in, he has a much better chance in a population of six-hundred thousand than six thousand."

"He could do MUCH worse than Minsk, no doubt," agrees Father, conceding the point.

Minsk is on the Svislach and Nyamiha twin-rivers – beautifully situated. On sunny days, of which there ARE a few, the picnic areas and walking trails next to the meandering waterways are full of pale-skinned Russians. Given the weather most of the year, Minsk is a city of optimists, with more outdoor parks and recreation areas than any other similarly sized city in the entire USSR.

Minsk is the economic capital of Belarus, one of the founding republics of the Soviet Union. The factory sector serves the needs not only of the city but also the nation, making it a critical cog in the industrial gear of the Soviet economic engine.

By Soviet standards, Minsk is also a cosmopolitan city. Home to the only subway system in Belarus, mass transit is remarkably swift and convenient. It has an international airport, a Soviet rarity, with flights to Europe and the Middle East. It also has a fashionable theater district, plush museums, movie cinemas, and at last count, thirty colleges and universities.

Moreover, if the mayor is telling the truth, there is a public library every six blocks. The weather in Minsk may not remind Mr. Oswald of Dallas or New Orleans but the culture might be able to come close.

"The large population will also allow us to observe him without being detected," Yuri continues.

"What about money and housing?" Father asks, looking at a checklist.

"I have arranged for a payment of five-thousand rubles from the MVD (Russian Secret Police) to be given to Mr. Oswald upon his arrival, along with a key to his new apartment," Yuri says. "The mayor will greet him and personally escort him to his new home."

"Have you made Mayor Zorin privy to his file?"

"Yes. Eyes and ears will be watching and listening to him all over town," Yuri assures Father.

"The apartment – has it been made suitable for our American guest?"

"Yes," Yuri responds. "It's already been wired for surveillance. It's also within walking distance of the Byelorussian Radio and Television Factory..."

"...I know this factory," Father interrupts. "My son worked there for a brief time before serving in the Russian Navy."

"Good," Yuri declares, relieved. "The factory director is a lifelong friend of mine. He has agreed to do this as a favor. Mr. Oswald will be working with metal. In addition to his factory wages, he is set to receive a monthly stipend from the Ministry of Internal Affairs Secret Police. Together, the sum will be more than the factory director receives. Obviously, Mr. Oswald will live quite comfortably."

"Amenities?" Father renews his inquiry.

"His apartment rises above the Svisloch River. It has two private balconies – each overlooking the river. Mr. Oswald has unlimited travel privileges, within Russia, of course. We also arranged with MVD for him to have a sixteen-gauge firearm for hunting purposes. He is a former US Marine. We thought he would be appreciative of this gesture."

"Very well," Father says, finally appeased. "Now that Mother Russia has satisfied him, we will wait to see if his information satisfies Mother Russia."

***

Chapter Seven

***

Faustian Bargain; Sabotage

Chicago, Illinois

January 10, 1960

"The meeting is on for tonight at five o'clock right here in my chambers," Judge Tuohy confirms, looking around nervously. "You tell Mooney and I'll let the Ambassador know," he orders. "One more thing, I want you here too."

"Right," notorious mob attorney Bob McDonnell replies, standing next to the judge's desk. "I'm sure you'd prefer we not come in the front..."

"...Please don't," Judge Tuohy says, interrupting. "For everybody's sake. Park around back. This door will be open," he says, walking McDonnell toward a back exit.

Three hours later, the judge and former US Ambassador Joe Kennedy are already waiting when

McDonnell returns, this time escorting Sam "Mooney" Giancana – infamous boss of the Chicago crime syndicate. After quick introductions, Tuohy and McDonnell both turn to leave the judge's chambers, their jobs complete. "Please turn out the lights and close the doors behind you when you are finished," the judge requests, looking at Kennedy, his long-time friend. The Ambassador nods, saying nothing.

"I'm sure glad I'm not privy to any of this," the relieved judge discloses, glancing behind him as they exit the Cook County Circuit Court Building together. A devout Catholic, Tuohy has spent a lifetime zealously guarding his reputation for being a man of unimpeachable character – a public servant whose integrity shines like a beacon in a city darkened by corruption. "I can't believe he asked me to arrange this," he complains, resentful of his friend's maneuvering that has put him in this position. "Joe Kennedy is taking advantage of our relationship. He knows I would never do it for anyone else..."

"...What's it about?" McDonnell interjects, unconcerned about any moral implications. As usual, Giancana's personal legal slave is in the dark.

"The Ambassador needs Mooney to help him get his

kid elected President," Judge Tuohy blurts, forgetting for a moment that discretion is the reason he is facilitating the meeting in the first place.

McDonnell whistles. "That'll cost him," he predicts, calculating his boss's considerable advantage in this bargaining session. "Which kid?"

"John," the judge replies. "Joe doesn't think Bobby is presidential timber. Ever since Joe Jr. died in the war, he's been obsessed with John's political career – kid is on the fast track."

"It makes sense," McDonnell observes. "Sam's organization controls eleven of Chicago's biggest labor unions. Win Chicago and you win Illinois," he adds.

"Win Illinois and you win the White House," Judge Tuohy concludes matter-of-factly.

***

Washington D.C.

March 17, 1960

There is a new envelope from Arrowhead in the

magnetic box. There is no actual message – the envelope IS the message. The random numbering system chooses tonight's location, a parking garage on Pennsylvania Avenue, two blocks from the White House – purely coincidental.

Arrowhead is already waiting when Sasha arrives. He looks impatiently at his watch. He cannot help himself. He lives by a creed his father taught him – *if you are early...you are on time, if you are on time...you are late.* He and his prized Movado Thin Classic wristwatch have been inseparable for years. It has become Sasha's running joke – "they will bury you with that stupid watch," – he often tells Arrowhead.

"Cuba is a go," Arrowhead blurts out. "Eisenhower has finally signed off."

"The plan?" Sasha asks quickly before Arrowhead can continue.

Arrowhead looks annoyed. "The PLAN has several parts," he says, pausing. "First, recruiting a paramilitary invasion force of Cuban exiles from Miami and New Orleans. Second, assembling the covert intelligence operation inside Cuba, using local dissidents. Third, constructing a way to communicate with the masses inside Cuba. And fourth, preparing a group outside Cuba to oppose the Castro government."

Sasha nods, scribbling furiously on a notepad. "What about the money?" he asks.

Arrowhead does not miss a beat this time. "Eisenhower is giving us $4.5 million to start. That is nothing. He's promising a lot more as we need it."

"Is there a target date?" Sasha asks.

"Not yet. Nixon is obviously pushing for it to happen before the 1960 election. But Eisenhower will only commit to a general time frame before the inauguration – election results be-damned," Arrowhead replies.

Sasha sniffs. "Yeah, right. Nixon usually gets what he wants. The invasion WILL happen before the election."

"Maybe, maybe not," says Arrowhead. "A lot has to happen first. The Cuban exiles are a bunch of crazy-ass roughnecks. They will need a lot of training. Weapons, logistics, and supplies – you name it. This is not just to bang-and-burn or cause mayhem. This is an invasion to overthrow a dictator and his government. We have to form an exile government and make it ready. Most importantly, all of this has to be covert, which complicates things. Castro has his eyes and ears all over Florida and Louisiana. If this were just a conventional military invasion of Cuba, it would be easy. The problem is we MUST be invisible. That's hard as hell."

"What about location?" Sasha asks, ignoring Arrowhead's lecture.

"Don't know," Arrowhead shakes his head. "I'll keep you posted on The Agency end here in DC. If you want operational intelligence, the name you need to know is Guy Bannister. He is ex-FBI, CIA, everything – and he is a militant anti-Castroite. Since the early 1950's, there's not been an anti-communist revolution in Central or South America that he's NOT been involved in..."

"...I've heard the name," Sasha interjects. "Where is he?"

Arrowhead clears his throat and pauses, composing himself after another interruption. "He's in New Orleans now, right in the middle of the Cuban-exile community. New Orleans is the HEART of it all. Whatever you need to know about Cuba you will learn in New Orleans. I would get an agent – check that – I would get a few agents and camp out down there – and quick. Those dumbasses will lead you to all the action, I promise."

Sasha is scribbling in his notebook again. He looks up. "That all?" he asks. Conversation finished, the two men leave quickly – neither looking back.

There are some nights when even Sasha, a devoted fifth-column Soviet saboteur, marvels at the sights in America's capital city. Tonight is one of those nights. He has always admired the District's linear design. *Somebody put a lot of thought into this*, he thinks, appreciating the scenery as he walks. From every direction, the four quadrants of the city seemingly stand at attention, facing the garden-lined grand avenue in the center.

The National Mall really springs to life after dark. It seems like the whole area is aglow. The marbled monuments, the tree-lined walkways, the Reflecting Pool, the Capital dome, the north lawn of the White House – all illuminated by natural or manufactured light. Even the sky is beaming with a twinkling array of stars and a full October blood moon.

Passing one landmark after another, Sasha goes over some mental notes he made to himself as Arrowhead was talking. *Polio vaccine, Cuban invasion – the VP seems to be driving the agenda right now. Eisenhower is deferring, probably setting the table for Nixon in '60. The Cuba thing is big. I have to message Father and let Moscow know. Arrowhead is right. The time has come to activate New Orleans.*

The longer he thinks about it, the more Arrowhead's cryptic portrayal of New Orleans intrigues him. *Whatever you need to know about Cuba you will learn in New Orleans.* Like a bad song, Arrowhead's words keep repeating in his mind.

I wonder if there's any connection between Guy Bannister and the strange Marine who made all those side trips to New Orleans, Sasha questions himself as he recalls Anna's earlier report.

Whom did she say Lee was visiting in the Crescent City? What was his name...Ferrie? David Ferrie. Yes, that's it. Didn't Arrowhead just say New Orleans is the HEART of it all? These thoughts stop Sasha in his tracks. *The heart of WHAT?*

***

Moscow, Russia

May 1, 1960

"This is a god-damned political provocation!" Russian Premier Nikita Khrushchev fumes. "On a Soviet national holiday...and only two weeks before our Summit in Paris! Son-of-a-bitch! What are you all waiting for? It's a coffin-with-wings – shoot that motherfucker down!"

Marshal S. S. Biryuzov, Commander-in-Chief of the Soviet Air Defense Forces, is the primary target of Khrushchev's profane tirade. The Premier still has not recovered from the disgrace of April 9 when the Americans utterly humiliated him and the Soviets with a U-2 reconnaissance plane. First, the U-2 flew several legs at sixty-nine thousand feet above the Semipalatinsk nuclear test site before jetting over surface-to-air missile (SAM) forces at Saryshaghan and the Tyuratam strategic missile testing range. The final touch was a "FUCK YOU" victory lap high above the city of Mary, after which it finally departed Soviet air space into Iran. The entire overflight nightmare lasted more than six hours.

"Shame!" the Premier thunders on, eyeballs bulging from his bald head. "The country is giving air defense everything it needs, and still you cannot shoot down this aircraft!"

Marshal Biryuzov is an intensely emotional man, a high-wire act with no safety net. Khrushchev knows this. Frustrated, Biryuzov finally spits out, "If I could become a missile, I myself would fly and down this damned intruder."

Clearly, the high-altitude flights are driving the Soviets nuts. Sixty-nine-thousand feet is a big problem. Stealth is another. The U-2 is on the Soviets and gone before they have a chance to react. The biggest issue however is radar. On the rare occasions the Soviets have managed to shoot at the intruders, homing devices in their missiles have gone haywire, causing the weapons to malfunction, veer off course and strike unintended targets. Everyone from the Premier on down is wondering...*what in the hell is wrong with Soviet radar?*

It is maddening to watch one U-2 after another raping the Soviet skies. Reality keeps undercutting Khrushchev's repeated statements about the high degree of Soviet air combat readiness. The American military is making the Russians all look like a bunch of boobs.

After the April 9 disaster, Soviet leadership appointed a commission to investigate the reasons Soviet air defense forces were failing. Predictably, the commission's findings were bureaucracy CYA. The report highlighted deficiencies in air combat training, command and control systems, Air Force personnel, weapons systems, and in the operation of advanced radio equipment. It also found information relating to the U-2 languishing in the communication pipeline – not passed on to the command element in a timely manner – and thus not available until the planes have come and gone.

More than anybody, Marshal Biryuzov understands all of these things are probably true but also knows three weeks is not enough time to fix all the problems. If there is ever a time to put the work of Soviet intelligence to the test, this is it.

New information has been flowing through the KGB pipeline recently about American radio frequencies and authentication codes for entering and exiting the Air Defense Identification Zone (ADIZ). Also included – instructions about counteracting the MPS 16 height-finder radar gear, and most importantly, the TPX-1, a genius instrument used by the US military to confuse enemy radar by transferring radar and radio signals AWAY from the potential target – such as a U-2 spy plane. Essentially, this equipment renders homing missiles virtually useless.

"Where are we getting all of this Intel?" Biryuzov keeps asking, thinking it is too good to be true. The only reply he keeps hearing is, "Moscow." The Marshal, hung out to dry by KGB intelligence before, would rather depend on military precision based on scientific laws. *If I wait for the scientists and generals, I will be toast*, he thinks. *Fuck it; we are going with the KGB this time...* He picks up the phone after his ear rimming from Premier Khrushchev. "Use the KGB intel," he orders with a growl, slamming the receiver down when he is finished.

The May Day parade is just about to begin. Everywhere, red flags are flapping in the wind. Tens of thousands of Soviet workers will march through Red Square in a celebration of Russian labor. Many of those same workers busily prepped thousands of posters – bathing powerful images of workers in glorious red and displaying the posters before members of the Soviet Politburo – the unelected leaders of the state. The esteemed Red Army stands at attention, waiting its turn to march in lockstep formation behind rows of trucks loaded with ICBMs, parading past an estimated crowd of two million citizens in a muscular show of Soviet might to the whole world. Everyone who matters attends this annual extravaganza. Party leaders, government officials, and the military generals are front-and-center, seated on stages as usual. Except one – Marshal Biryuzov – who is somewhere else, trying to spare the Soviet Union another U-2 humiliation.

The Soviets spotted the plane at sixty-two thousand feet above the Tajikistan SSR (Soviet Socialist Republic) in Central Asia. That was over an hour ago. Now the U-2 pilot, who is flying with a devil-may-care confidence, is entering the engagement zone of a SAM battalion near Sverdlovsk.

The unit's commander issues the order, "Destroy target." The first missile explodes behind the U-2, its fragments piercing the tail section and the wings. The battalion's radar screen starts to blink, indicating the target is either radar jamming or breaking up. They all wait to see, straining with their eyes, searching the sky. First, the smoke, then a parachute becomes visible, answering the question. The commander is shocked. It worked! A second missile makes a direct hit on the damaged plane. His men let out a whoop. Both plane and pilot are helplessly falling from the sky. Within minutes, the fuselage, engine, wings, and cockpit lie scattered on the ground over an area of several square kilometers – the pilot captured and whisked away to Moscow.

Investigators immediately begin rushing to the scene, combing the fields and groves, searching for aircraft parts and high-resolution cameras. They do better than that, finding cases of large, extra-wide rolls of exposed film.

Back in Moscow, Marshall Biryuzov receives the word. He grabs his jacket and rushes from his office toward the parade, which has just started. *Thank God for the KGB,* he mutters to himself, wiping the perspiration from his forehead with a handkerchief.

***

Moscow, Russia

May 5, 1960

In the late 1950's and early 1960's, one could hardly blame a U-2 pilot for being careless. The spy plane flew at a height of seventy-thousand feet, five-thousand feet higher than the world altitude record. Most radar only extended to forty-five-thousand feet. The U-2 spy plane was untouchable. Until May 1, 1960 when the Soviets all of the sudden proved that it was not.

U-2 pilot Francis Gary Powers was not careless, just unlucky. It happened fast. In fact, he was not able to take any evasive measures – the Soviets knocked his plane out of the sky with their first shot.

The U-2's disappearance in Soviet airspace is forcing the Eisenhower Administration to cover its tracks, hurriedly releasing a clumsy statement about a lost "weather plane". Very smart people make up the White House staff but the story the Administration chose to put out first about a "disoriented pilot" wandering across the wrong border as he "experienced difficulty with his oxygen equipment" sounded dumb.

Initially, the US was operating under the assumption that only its pilot was in Soviet hands. What the Americans DIDN'T know was Powers had NOT activated the plane's self-destruct mechanism before he bailed. Instead, the top-secret plane crashed to the ground wrecked and in pieces, but not destroyed. Minutes later, both pilot AND plane were in Soviet custody, handing an intelligence treasure trove to the United States' Cold War nemesis.

Now, the "U-2 Incident" is having far-reaching consequences. First, the intelligence-gathering advantage the US had achieved due to the air superiority of its U-2 plane is gone – a decade of dominance ended. The successful program is now useless.

And second, after the Soviets made details of the captured U-2 plane public – including images of highly-sensitive photographic equipment onboard – the US has been shamed into admitting that it has been flying covert intelligence missions over Soviet territory. This news is having an effect both on American credibility in the world and US-USSR relations.

"I realize I'm in the minority in this town but I'm not sure this is an event to celebrate," reveals an apprehensive Father. "We did next to nothing to extract the information from Mr. Oswald. He gave it up – too easily in my opinion."

"Don't tell anyone else that..." Yuri cautions.

"...WHY in the hell would the Americans sacrifice their U-2 plane?" Father says abruptly. "They were absolutely killing us with that damn thing." Yuri remains silent, thinking.

"Do you think Mr. Oswald might be a head-fake?" Father asks.

"I think he is the bait and the U-2 plane is the misdirection," Yuri replies. "They knew we would act on the information he gave us in order to verify it. Therein lies our dilemma. If we don't act on it, the U-2 flights continue and they keep right on reaping an intelligence windfall, but if we do...well, I guess that's what we're going to find out, aren't we?"

Father leans across his desk, glaring at Yuri. "We need to war-game this right now – play out the different scenarios. We CAN'T sit around waiting for the next shoe to drop."

Yuri nods, "Alright, you go first." Father sits back in his chair and runs his fingers through his hair, formulating his thoughts.

"The spy plane IS CIA, no? Atsugi IS home to the CIA's

operational base in the Far East, no? Mr. Oswald WAS stationed at Atsugi, no? He WAS a radar operator for the spy plane, no?"

"Yes, yes, yes, and yes," answers Yuri. "Look, there's no question we shot down the right plane. However, it is also true that the US Marine Corps granted him an expedited discharge. Why? According to Anna, that almost NEVER happens. Why did Mr. Oswald defect to Russia less than a month after his discharge? There is NO doubt our denial of his asylum request precipitated his fake suicide attempt. It worked too – he forced us to extend his stay. And like you said, he DID give up the altitude and radar information WAY too easily during interrogation."

"I'm trying to wrap my head around where all this leaves us," Father says.

"Six months ago, none of us had ever heard of Mr. Oswald," Yuri says. "And six months ago, we couldn't even find the U-2, much less shoot it down. Now because of him, America's prized U-2 spy plane is sitting in pieces in one of our hangars in Sverdlovsk. That CAN'T be a coincidence."

"A lot of smoke in that scenario," Father agrees. "Let's

assume Mr. Oswald is exactly what Anna suspected he was – an American intelligence agent sent to the Soviet Union on a mission to give up the spy plane. He arrives and discovers he is going to be returned immediately."

"If he is deported on schedule, his mission fails," explains Yuri. "The suicide attempt was a ruse to buy him seven extra days in a Moscow hospital alone with the KGB – time and opportunity. He played it like a pro, like a TRAINED intelligence asset."

"Goddammit. That brings us back to the original question," Father pivots. "Why would they do it?"

"It could be a Queen's Gambit," guesses Yuri, a chess aficionado.

"A what?" Father asks.

"The Americans used a worthless pawn to dangle an important piece in our face," Yuri answers. "And we just took their pawn AND their knight." Father betrays his ignorance with an empty stare.

You don't play chess, do you?" Yuri asks Father, smiling.

"Never learned how," Father acknowledges with a

shrug.

“A good chess player will bait and misdirect an opponent into making moves that advance HIS strategy,” Yuri explains. “It’s why it’s as important to know your opponent’s strategy as it is to know your own.”

“Are you saying the mission wasn’t really to give up the U-2?” Father asks, incredulous.

“They didn’t sacrifice two pieces for nothing,” Yuri replies. “Especially the U-2. It is too valuable. There’s a more important reason they gave it up – a bigger picture.”

Father stands up and walks over to his window that overlooks Red Square. He stares out across one-thousand feet of perfectly laid bricks at the fortified Kremlin, standing guard over Moscow like a motionless sentry. Deep in thought, he says nothing for several minutes. Taking Father’s cue, Yuri remains quiet. The office is thick with a heavy silence.

Finally, Father turns, faces Yuri and states nervously. “You’re right. They goddamn handed it to us on a silver platter. We might have lost this one Comrade,” he states, nodding at Yuri.

“The good news is...” Yuri begins.

“...Good news, my ass,” Father blurts, disgusted.

“The good news is...” Yuri repeats calmly, ignoring Father’s interruption, “...it’s NOT checkmate. We MIGHT still have a move.”

“This isn’t one of your damn chess games...” Father protests.

“...Ah, but it IS a game, is it not?” Yuri counters quickly.

“Okay, I’ll play along. What game are we playing now?” Father asks, clearly exasperated.

“Dumb,” Yuri replies. “The smart move now is to play dumb.”

***

Soviet Union

May 16, 1960

“The U-2 shit is already hitting the fan,” Father informs Yuri. “Khrushchev just walked out of the Paris summit and rescinded his invitation for President Eisenhower to visit Moscow."

Suddenly, like a lightning bolt out of the sky, a thought occurs to Yuri. "Mission accomplished," he blurts, like someone who has an epiphany and HAS to share it. "Six months ago," he begins, "the Americans deployed an agent to give up U-2 secrets. The mission succeeded. Then, two weeks before Paris, the Americans deployed the U-2, knowing we would shoot it down and all hell would break loose. Again, the mission succeeded..."

"...The Americans wanted the summit to be cancelled..." Father realizes, a sick feeling coming over him.

"...They sabotaged it," Yuri interjects, completing Fathers' thought.

"Son-of-a-bitch. Why kill a PEACE summit?" Father wonders.

"Maybe the Americans don't WANT peace?" Yuri guesses, shrugging with eyes wide.

The Four Powers Summit began yesterday in Paris. Though France and England are included, the whole world knows the United States and Soviet Union are the powers that really matter. The mood a month ago was one of optimism. Premier Khrushchev and President Eisenhower both held out hope the summit would result in an easing of tensions between their countries. There have even been hints of a limited nuclear-test-ban treaty – which would be the first major Cold War accord between the two superpowers. That was before Francis Gary Powers and his U-2 plane went down.

Premier Khrushchev is taking it personal – blasting Eisenhower for destroying whatever trust existed between the two governments. Years of hard work ruined by the events of one day. Khrushchev's outrage, though understandable, is disingenuous. The Soviets knew about the flights since 1956. They just could not do anything about them – now they can. They did not have PROOF of American espionage before – now they do.

The Premier went to Paris intent on demanding an apology from President Eisenhower but Eisenhower rebuffed him. In protest, Khrushchev and the entire Soviet delegation stormed out, boarded their plane, and flew back to Moscow. The summit is dead, as are the hopes of a détente between the Cold War superpowers.

“And why might the Americans NOT want peace?” Father asks rhetorically, talking more to himself than he is Yuri. “What if it’s just old-fashioned material greed?” he says finally.

Yuri thinks for a second. “Money, huh? THAT might just be it,” he agrees.

“This damn Cold War is a financial boondoggle for the Americans,” Father says. “It’s absolutely killing OUR economy but it’s making THEM rich…”

“…Which is why they would want it to continue,” Yuri interjects. “Anything that is a threat to the money spigot will be sabotaged or terminated…”

“…Or ANYONE,” Father chimes in ominously, his turn to interrupt.

“Any-ONE or any-THING…” Yuri repeats, nodding his head.

“Paris was a threat,” Father says finally. “Peace isn’t as profitable as war.”

“The question is now, what do we do with Mr. Oswald?” Father asks, changing the subject.

"We hope like hell he IS a spy," responds Yuri without hesitating. "If not, he will be stuck here forever. They will never allow him back, except to try him for treason. However, if he is intelligence, they will recall him soon to prep him for a future operation. That is precisely the moment WE will countermove," he adds, already plotting the strategy in his mind.

Father pauses, allowing Yuri's words to sink in. "Are you thinking what I'm thinking 'Ulysses'?"

"Trojan Horse," Yuri says, smiling.

***

Moscow, Russia

September 8, 1960

"It shouldn't even be close," Father predicts as he pulls a report from his briefcase.

"So it's Nixon..." Premier Khrushchev assumes.

"Yes, yes. Without question," replies Father. "Nixon is the prohibitive favorite. He is the sitting Vice President under a popular President. He has name-recognition and experience. He's from the largest state, and he has all the Republican Party big-money donors in his pocket."

"Plus..." Father peers through his glasses and begins reading from the report, "Nixon's role on the House Un-American Activities Committee (HUAC) solidified his anti-communist bona-fides with the American electorate."

Father looks over his bifocals at the Premier. "You remember Nixon outing Alger Hiss, right?"

"Of course," Khrushchev sneers with contempt. "He's been taking credit for that for twenty god-damn years."

Father tosses the report aside. "He's good at taking credit, no?"

"A born politician," the Premier agrees, admiringly.

He should know. Nobody plays the political game better than Nikita Khrushchev does. At the start of his career, Khrushchev served in the Red Army as a political commissar, indoctrinating the new recruits in Bolshevism. His political fortunes began rising soon after his first wife died of typhus. In an effort to prove his loyalty to Bolshevik principles, Khrushchev would not let her coffin enter the church, even though it was the only entrance to the cemetery. He made the pallbearers lift the casket up and over the back fence into the churchyard instead.

Like any good politician, Khrushchev used two relationships to aid his political rise.

In 1917, Khrushchev met Lazar Kaganovich, a rising star in the Communist Party. The pair hit it off immediately, becoming virtually inseparable. Promoted in 1925 to Communist Party boss in Ukraine, Kaganovich exploited the power of his new position to reward some of his own people – one of which was Khrushchev – to fill the plum party positions. Two years later, Kaganovich rewarded Khrushchev again – this time appointing him head of the Organizational Department of the Communist Party's Central Planning Committee in Ukraine. It was during his years in Kharkov that Khrushchev and Stalin launched the infamous famine that would eventually kill millions of Ukrainians.

In 1929, Khrushchev met Nadazhda Alliluyeva, a fellow student at Stalin's Industrial Academy – the school of choice for all young party risers. Though she was married, Nikita and Nadazhda became friendly.

She even told him how she spoke well of him to her husband. “What is his name and rank?” he asked Nadazhda, oblivious.

“Joseph Stalin,” she told a stunned Nikita with a wry smile. “You might have heard of him, no? He is the General Secretary of the Communist Party.”

Though Khrushchev did not graduate from the Stalin Industrial Academy, Stalin DID make sure Khrushchev’s career in the Party continued to blossom. By 1932, Khrushchev was second in command, behind Kaganovich, of the Moscow City Party Organization. Two years later, his dream came true. He became Party leader for the city and finally, a member of the Communist Party’s Central Committee.

In 1934, Stalin initiated the Great Purge. Moscow was host to thousands of show trials, all of which Khrushchev presided over. Thirty-five of the top thirty-eight Party officials in Moscow died, many of whom were friends of Nikita Khrushchev. As Party leader, he was required to approve the arrests and sign off on the executions.

In 1937, Stalin named Khrushchev head of the Communist Party in Ukraine. There, he purged any government officials and Red Army commanders who remained after years of purges by Stalin. Everyone arrested by Khrushchev received the death penalty. Stalin had found himself a loyal hatchet man – which made Khrushchev's "Secret Speech" on February 25, 1956 all the more remarkable.

In 1953, Stalin finally died and Khrushchev succeeded him as First Secretary of the Communist Party of the Soviet Union. What he inherited was a Stalin-fatigued Soviet Union. Three years later, Khrushchev did the unthinkable. In a speech to the Politburo, he denounced Stalin and his purges, ushering in the "Khrushchev Thaw." It was a stroke of political genius. He knew the trauma the Soviet people experienced during years of Stalin brutality. It also displayed Khrushchev's remarkable chutzpah.

Although he had once been one of his right-hand-men, Khrushchev began "de-Stalinizing" the Soviet Union. Slowly, he dismantled the cult of personality around Stalin. The entire country started breathing a cautious sigh of relief, hoping the reign of terror died with Joseph Stalin.

That is why the Premier appreciates a kindred soul when he sees one. Richard Nixon is Nikita Khrushchev in the looking glass.

"Well, he's getting credit now for something he shouldn't," Father says abruptly.

"A thief too?" Khrushchev asks with a sarcastic smirk.

"More like a liar," answers Father. "The American population thinks Nixon cured polio. What they do not know is that Nixon forced the Salk vaccine on them in 1955 to protect his financial investment in the company that manufactured it. People ended up paralyzed or dead because the doses were bad. Most of the victims were kids. Anyway, they had to cancel the program after just two weeks."

"How in the hell did he cover that up?"

"He's smart," Father replies. "It wasn't his signature on the vaccine license. He hung the whole debacle around the necks of the government medical boys who approved it. Of course, he was the one who pressured them to sign off on it to begin with."

"What about now?" the Premier asks. "Whatever they're using now seems to be working. It's not a front-page story anymore."

"In a manner of speaking, you're right. It does SEEM to be working," Father agrees. "But, the end of the story hasn't been written yet. And if Nixon has his way, the truth might NEVER get out," he adds.

"What IS the truth?" Khrushchev demands.

"The new vaccine is contaminated with monkey viruses," answers Father. "Two of the viruses are lethal. One causes cancer and the other destroys the immune system. Worse, both have a thirty-year incubation period and both transmit sexually. Since 1957, one-hundred million Americans have received this contaminated polio vaccine."

"Jesus Christ!" The Premier exclaims. "How do WE know this and the Americans don't?"

"Oh, they know." Father clarifies. "The first two years the doses were administered, they didn't know. However, one of their doctors reported the monkey viruses earlier this year. Instead of halting the program, they fired her and Nixon ordered another one-hundred million doses."

Premier Khrushchev is doing the calculations in his head. "Two hundred-million people, plus all their sexual partners, plus children – multiplied by thirty years. That's a big number," he claims, eyes widening. "They better find a cure for both or they'll have a god-damn public health crisis that will rival the Plague on their hands soon."

Father nods. "The clock is ticking."

"But in the meantime," Khrushchev realizes, "Nixon's campaign gets to run around taking credit for curing polio."

"How does Kennedy campaign against that?" Father asks rhetorically.

"He can't," Khrushchev states flatly. "But he's got bigger problems. Nixon couldn't have chosen a more flawed candidate to run against," he says, rolling his eyes contemptuously.

"American voters have never elected a Catholic to be President," Father agrees. "Kennedy's a far-left liberal and Americans tend to lean more conservative. Also, he's going to have trouble with southern voters..."

"...What's wrong with southern voters?" the Premier asks, interrupting Father.

"Nothing," replies Father, chuckling, "they just don't

tend to vote for northeastern liberals who try forcing civil rights laws down their throats."

"I can't believe anybody would vote for a Kennedy after what his daddy did, the Ambassador," Khrushchev reminds Father. "He sided with Hitler and the Nazis in the late thirties remember? FDR had to fire him."

"You're right. He might not want to put that in his campaign literature," Father says. Both men laugh.

"Relatability and experience will be issues too," says Father, concluding his report. "It's not just that Kennedy's from privilege, but again, it's his daddy and how he made the money in the first place – bootlegging illegal whiskey during Prohibition. Nixon grew up poor. He paid his own way through college, working and then serving in the Navy. Tough comparison for Kennedy. There is also the issue of experience. When he's compared side-by-side with Nixon, Kennedy looks very young and much too inexperienced to be President."

"So how in the hell is he winning?" the Premier asks, perplexed.

***

Washington D.C.

October 8, 1960

"Talk to me about John Kennedy," Sasha instructs Beasley as they stroll through Lafayette Park. "How is he doing it? Why is he winning this election?" The two men are alone in the park. They are virtually alone in the city too – Washington D.C. is a veritable ghost town.

Every year, the city begins emptying in the days before Christmas. By Christmas Eve, nobody is left. Senators, congressional representative, judges, staff, aides, lobbyists, news media – all off somewhere else causing trouble – taking with them the unrelenting commotion they create.

With the racketeers gone, the business of government also stops – some say mercifully – during the holiday season. The bureaucracy closes, sending one-hundred-thousand administrators of red tape to their idyllic homes and communities in Virginia and Maryland. Almost nobody who works in the District actually lives in the District.

The park is eerily quiet tonight though, the sounds of their footsteps and conversation muffled by the gently falling snow. A nearby church displays its seasonal wish in lights – "PEACE ON EARTH." For the moment, it IS peaceful, just like Christmas should be.

Beasley shrugs. "It's pretty simple. His daddy made a deal with organized crime. The Chicago outfit, Sam Giancana, and the labor unions will win it FOR him. When it is over, he will owe them all. His first act as President will be to appoint his brother Attorney General. He will order the Justice Department to back off and leave the crime families alone – the unions too since labor and organized crime are two heads of the same coin. Then the new President will overthrow Castro and Cosa Nostra will be back in business. The money the mafia's lost in Cuba since Castro...let's just say there hasn't been a leak like it since Noah built himself a boat." Sasha laughs.

"Kennedy's pretty smart too," Beasley admits. "The CIA spoon-fed him some garbage about a missile gap – how the Soviets have more nuclear warheads than we do – and he hasn't stopped talking about it since on the campaign trail..."

"...Nixon should just deny it..." interrupts Sasha.

"...He can't!" Beasley interjects quickly. "That's the point! He would have to reveal classified information to argue the point, and that is illegal! That is what I mean about him being smart. Kennedy is boxing Nixon in with a false narrative about national security. He's taking Nixon's strength and making it a weakness!"

"Hmm," Sasha grunts. "What am I missing here? I thought the mafia was helping Nixon invade Cuba," he says, confused. "Now you tell me it's helping Kennedy win the election – and HE will invade Cuba instead? Has organized crime switched teams in the middle of the game?"

"Yep," replies Beasley. "I guess Kennedy made them an offer they couldn't refuse. The 1950's have not been kind to the crime families. The Kefauver and McClellan hearings, the FBI raid at Apalachin – it is a long list. Kennedy promised relief, at home and in Cuba. The mob will have a hot line to the White House. It's a no-brainer."

"So is the Cuban invasion still on?" Sasha wonders.

"Yes, but the timing isn't the same," Beasley explains. "Nixon still wants it to happen before the election but the CIA and organized crime are now content to wait.

JFK is a game-changer. Giancana will own him after the election, and the CIA too ever since it hoodwinked him with that missile gap bullshit. Why would either want to help Nixon now? Why not stall until after the elections, when you have the President in your back pocket – then invade?"

Beasley pauses before adding, "And then of course, there IS the other thing..."

"...What other thing?" Sasha asks, impatient.

"Giancana's not stupid," Beasley begins. "After he decided to do business with Joe Kennedy, he took out an insurance policy. It was not hard. Rumors have swirled around JFK for years. Bottom line? Jack likes his women, especially the young and willing ones."

"Oh man, that's right in the mafia's wheelhouse," Sasha observes, chuckling.

"Absolutely," Beasley agrees. "Giancana's mistress, Judith something-or-other, is a high-priced call-girl, available for hire. She has previously been with Johnny Roselli and Frank Sinatra. Hell, the rumor is half the Chicago outfit passed her back and forth. Now she belongs to the Don. The Senator came to town on a campaign stop a few months ago and Giancana baited the hook. He ordered Sinatra to introduce his own mistress to Kennedy at a party."

"And…?" Sasha starts to ask.

"…And Kennedy took the bait, hook, line, AND sinker," replies Beasley, laughing. "He couldn't keep his eyes off her – or his hands. They left the party together and went upstairs to his hotel room. Nobody saw them again until late the next day. She's been his lover ever since."

Sasha is skeptical. "How do YOU know all this?"

"Opposition research," Beasley replies. "Nixon's entire campaign staff is talking about it non-stop," Beasley says. "They know everything. In fact, they know more, lots more – some unbelievable stuff. Kennedy must have the libido of ten sailors on shore leave. Nixon and his staff are frustrated though. He keeps telling them to leak stories but the press is not publishing them. The Nixon campaign thinks the fix is in, which of course it is."

"Hold on…so Giancana and Kennedy are SHARING a girlfriend?" Sasha asks incredulously.

"Yes," Beasley says, nodding. "Ordinarily, that'd be a

big problem for Kennedy," he laughs. "Mafia godfathers tend to be a little on the jealous side. But this was all Giancana's idea."

"Does Kennedy even know?" Sasha asks.

Again, Beasley nods. "Yep. Doesn't seem to give a shit. It is actually a handy set-up for both of them. They use her as their carrier pigeon. She carries a satchel full of cash and messages back-and-forth between Chicago and Hyannis Port so nobody sees them together. It's still careless as hell though. Imagine if the FBI or some nosy reporters ever find out that the future President of the United States is sharing a prostitute girlfriend with the most notorious gangster in the country..."

"...Those would be million-dollar photos," Sasha interrupts. "Jesus, if Kennedy wins the White House, the mob can blackmail him anytime it wants to. Giancana WILL own him..." Sasha says, shaking his head. "What a dumb-ass."

"WHEN he wins the White House," Beasley corrects Sasha.

"So it's over?" Sasha asks.

"It's over," Beasley declares.

***

Chapter Eight

***

Clusterfuck

Arlington, Virginia

January 31, 1961

Arrowhead, Sasha says to himself quietly as he retrieves another envelope from the magnetic box. This time, the numbered rotation sets the meeting at Arlington National Cemetery.

Sasha usually catches the express bus at the Mall for his trips out to Robert E. Lees' place but today, he decides to walk instead. Why not? It has been a mild winter so far. Today is almost too bright and sunny. The glare from the sun reflecting off the snow-covered landscape forces him to wear sunglasses. *Sunglasses in January...now that is a first*, he thinks. Although the temperature is only in the high thirties, it feels warmer without a northeastern wind biting his neck and face.

Sasha strolls onto the Arlington Memorial Bridge, beginning his journey. Each time he crosses the Potomac River, he pictures George Washington with his hapless Continental Army in boats, dodging the chunks of ice floating in the middle of a freezing Christmas Eve darkness. *I wonder how much of that is true*, he asks himself, chuckling. Somewhere near the middle of the bridge, he leaves DC behind and enters Virginia.

As he nears the meeting spot, he can see Arrowhead patrolling the front entrance to Arlington House, chomping unmercifully on a cigar, checking and rechecking his prized wristwatch. He keeps looking in Sasha's direction, finally spotting him. Then he peeks at his watch again. Sasha laughs.

The neoclassical Arlington House sits majestically at the region's highest point, overlooking the river and the Mall. No matter the season, the views from the columned mansion are gorgeous. From the city below, the aristocratic manor house resembles the temple of an ancient Grecian goddess peering down on her subjects.

The builder of Arlington House drew his inspiration from his adoptive father's estate stationed just thirteen miles downstream. Except for the Greek revival architecture, George Washington Parke Custis stayed remarkably true to Mt. Vernon's layout.

When construction was finished, his first inclination was to name the estate "Mt. Washington," in honor of the nation's most important Founding Father. Sasha often marvels at the irony of its most famous occupant – the Confederacy's most important general.

"The operation is STILL a go," begins Arrowhead, coming right to the point. "After the election, a lot of people didn't think the plan would survive without Nixon, but Kennedy surprised us all and authorized it to continue three days ago."

"How soon?" Sasha asks.

"Fourteen weeks, give-or-take," says Arrowhead. As usual, he speaks rapidly. "Target date will be April 15. American B-26 bombers painted to look like stolen Cuban planes will take off from Nicaragua and take out Castro's airfields. Two days later, the Cuban Brigade will land at the Bay of Pigs and invade Cuba with about fourteen-hundred men."

"What about support behind them?" Sasha inquires. "If the Brigade is in trouble, will Kennedy allow the US military to step in?"

"Supposed to but it gets a little fuzzy there," Arrowhead replies. "The new President has been waffling all over the place. Getting a commitment from him is like trying to hold water in your hands. Most of my colleagues at The Agency think he's chicken-shit. They are afraid he will bail out at the first sign of trouble. We could be wrong though. I'd prepare for it just in case."

"It sounds like Kennedy isn't very confident in Nixon's plan," Sasha observes.

"Nope, but he's stuck," Arrowhead replies. "What's he going to do? Tell the CIA no? If he does that, The Agency will leak his lie about the missile gap and make him look like a fool. Now HE IS the one in a box. He cannot deny what he said during the campaign and he cannot blame us for deceiving him or people would think he is a naïve rube who might believe anything. He also cannot reveal classified information – a felony. Besides, the operation has been in the works for a year. What CAN he do...start over? He has other debts to pay now. He does not have time to mess around. He's just crossing his fingers and hoping we pay off for him."

"Jesus, he must really trust you guys..." Sasha says, "...to place his political future in the CIA's hands..."

"...Hell no he doesn't!" Arrowhead exclaims, interrupting loudly. A little TOO loud. Sasha and Arrowhead both pause and look around.

"He doesn't trust us," he explains, resuming his normal voice. "We DID mislead him during the campaign – had him spinning like a top so he could become President. Now he IS the President. He gets our daily security briefings. He knows the truth."

"Which means he knows the CIA lied to him..." Sasha concludes.

"...Hell yes we lied, that's what we do, god-dammit," Arrowhead interjects. "He knows that we played him like a fiddle," he says with a wicked laugh. "Kennedy feels dumb for saying what he said during the campaign. That's not our fault – everybody has a right to be wrong. He won't make that mistake again though, you know – fool me once, shame on me..."

"...So if things go to hell at the Bay of Pigs," Sasha says, interrupting, "Kennedy won't follow the plan OR listen to the CIA."

"Probably not," Arrowhead agrees. "Kennedy only trusts one person – his little brother. The real opportunity in this is – Bobby has about as much military and intelligence experience as you and I do cross-dressing. If it comes down to them, those two will fuck it up all by themselves."

***

Moscow, Russia

February 13, 1961

"This is the same guy that was in my office less than two years ago trying to dissolve his American citizenship," Mr. Snyder announces, nodding at the just-opened letter lying on his desk. He rubs his forehead. The senior consular officer at the American Embassy in Moscow is bewildered.

"Maybe he just changed his mind," fellow consul John McVickar speculates, shrugging.

"No," Snyder disagrees, shaking his head. "Something's not right. This man is a former United States Marine. He stood right where you're standing and threatened to turn over information he claimed was of 'special interest' to Soviet intelligence."

"Classified information?" McVickar asks, alarmed.

"What else COULD it be? Snyder wonders. "He had several Top Secret security clearances while he was in the Marine Corps. I tried to tell him he would be committing treason but he denied it, saying something about it not being treason if he renounced his US citizenship first."

"Semantics," McVickar sniffs. "Read it to me again," he says, pointing at the letter.

Snyder sighs and picks up the letter.

> *Since I have not received a reply to my letter of December 1960, I am writing again asking that you consider my request for the return of my American passport...*

"...What letter?" McVickar interrupts Snyder. "I don't understand...is this his SECOND letter?"

"No," Snyder answers. "I don't know what he's talking about. Everything's in here." He holds up a file. "There is no letter dated December, 1960. In fact, this is the first time I've heard from him directly since he showed up in my office almost two years ago."

"Then the KGB intercepted his first letter," McVickar states matter-of-factly. "Why is he asking for the return of his passport – do we have it?"

"He left it on my desk when he walked out," Snyder replies. "We had agreed he would return the following Monday but he never came back. So yes, we have it right here," he says, holding up the passport. "At the time, I thought it was an accident but now I'm starting to think he left it on purpose."

"Like he's leaving a trail behind him – letters, meetings, passports..." McVickar agrees, his voice trailing off.

Snyder nods and resumes reading.

> *I desire to return to the United States – that is if we could come to some agreement concerning the dropping of any legal proceedings against me...*

"...Sorry, what legal proceedings?" McVickar asks, interrupting again.

"I assume he did what he said he was going to do. He must have turned over military secrets and now he's afraid he'll be charged with a crime," replies Snyder. "It's certainly not a crime to renounce your citizenship."

"Jesus, he's got SOME god-damn nerve," McVickar sputters angrily. He motions for Snyder to continue.

> *If so, then I would be free to ask the Russian authorities to allow me to leave. If I could show them my American passport, I am of the opinion they would give me an exit. At no time have they insisted I take Russian citizenship. I am living here with non-permanent type papers for a foreigner. I cannot leave Minsk without permission; therefore, I am writing rather than calling in person. I hope that in recalling the responsibility I have to America, you remember yours in doing everything you can to help me since I am still an American citizen.*

"This is fucking incredible," McVickar declares after Snyder finishes. "This asshole is lecturing YOU to do your job no matter what you might think and get HIM off the hook..."

"...Like he knows something about the legalities of citizenship," Snyder interjects, suspicious. "Clearly, this is no ordinary case," he adds.

"Did he sign the letter?" McVickar asks, maneuvering himself behind the desk and peering over Snyder's shoulder.

"Signed, 'Lee H. Oswald'," Snyder replies, pointing at the signature.

***

Moscow, Russia

March 13, 1961

"You MUST remind your niece again the importance of this mission," Father says sternly. "All of her training – hell, all of her life – has been pointing to this moment in time. The Soviet people are counting on her."

"Yes sir," replies the uncle, a ranking officer in the Russian Ministry of Internal Affairs, known as the Russian Secret Police, or more simply, the MVD.

Father stands and walks around to the front of his massive desk. He loosens his tie and removes his glasses, cleaning them with the sleeve of his jacket.

Then he props himself on the edge of his desk and addresses the MVD Colonel less formally.

“The American who gave us the U-2 is proving us right. Three months ago, he wrote a letter to the US Embassy – the same embassy where he tried to renounce his citizenship two years ago. Now all of the sudden he wants to return home to the United States. Surprise!” Father’s voice rises. “It gets better. We’ve just gotten word that the American, having completed his mission in enemy territory, is being recalled by the US State Department!” He leaps off the edge of the desk and starts pacing back and forth, gesturing with his arms. “The Americans think they have duped us. But they don’t know about your lovely niece, do they, Colonel Prusakova?”

“No sir,” the Colonel responds nervously.

“The Americans used defection as a ruse to sneak THEIR spy into OUR country. Well, the Soviets will use marriage as a pretext to sneak OUR spy into THEIR country – as THEIR spy’s wife!” Father declares, emphasizing the words loudly. “The time has come to activate Marina.”

“It’s brilliant, sir,” the Colonel gushes. “Sir, I CAN

speak for Marina. You choosing her for this critical assignment – she feels honored. We have discussed it many times. This is her destiny."

"Good. See to it immediately." Father orders, dismissing the Colonel with a wave of his hand.

Marina Prusakova's father died in WW II when she was a little girl. After that, she bounced from Archangel to Moldova to Leningrad with her nomadic stepdad – all before age twelve. Two years later, she moved to Minsk to live with her uncle, the MVD officer. Officially, Marina received her training for the next five years in pharmacology – earning her diploma in 1959. Unofficially, Marina has been receiving counter-intelligence training from the MVD while working the past two years in the pharmacy of a hospital in Minsk. She is now twenty-one and attractive – a loaded weapon in the hands of Soviet intelligence.

Like usual, Marina has dinner waiting for the Colonel when he returns home later that evening. He is unusually quiet at the table. Afterwards, he motions for his niece to join him on the patio for his after-dinner cigar. "Marina dear, we must talk." Marina grabs her coat and pulls it tight. It is still cold this time of year in Minsk, especially after the sun goes down.

“For two years now,” uncle Prusakova begins, “you have been receiving special training for an important mission for your country. You are aware how important this is, no?”

Marina nods and smiles playfully, shivering. “Yes, of course uncle. What a silly question!” Her teeth are chattering.

He puts his arm around her. “Sweetheart, the time has come. I was in Moscow today meeting with a very high-ranking man from the KGB. He gave me your assignment. Are you ready to do your part for Mother Russia, comrade?”

“I am,” answers Marina confidently, without hesitation.

“You must know the sacrifice Marina,” uncle Prusakova says. “You will leave this country, your home, me – maybe never to return. You will be the wife of a total stranger. You will most likely have children with that stranger. All the while, you will be gathering intelligence. Sometimes, your mission will involve passing information from me to him that will serve Soviet interests.”

"I understand perfectly," Marina claims. "Who is this man you speak of? Do I know him?"

"You don't know him yet," he answers her. "He is also an intelligence agent – just like you. Only, he works for America. He has completed his mission here and is preparing to return home. We think he needs a wife to go with him. The KGB will provide the time and opportunity for you to win him before he goes. You MUST be convincing."

"Uncle," she addresses him in a suddenly grown-up, more serious tone. Her gaze is steady and reassuring. "My father died serving his country. You have given your life to the cause. Now it is my turn. I have trained for this moment. It is my honor to follow in in our family's footsteps and serve my homeland."

"Good," he replies, kissing her on the forehead. "You will need a nice dress. There is a dance in your near future!"

***

Minsk, Russia

March 30, 1961

I cannot believe my luck, Lee is thinking, watching the most beautiful girl at the dance stealing furtive glances at him across the dance floor. He is accustomed to this kind of attention by now. Seemingly, all of Minsk is aware of the American in their midst – a novelty in Russia. *This one is different,* he thinks; s*he is too pretty to be desperate.*

He cannot keep from noticing her frame as she dances gracefully – slender, athletic-looking legs, slim-waist, perfectly proportioned bosom. Her soft-brown hair is long and flowing with waves and curls that take turns framing her innocent-looking face. Her green eyes sparkle and droop seductively. A shy smile. Ivory skin and a killer body, especially in that sinfully low-cut, black halter dress. *Gorgeous*, he mutters to himself, admiring her from a distance.

Lee's employer, the state-owned Minsk Gorizont (Horizon) Radio Factory is sponsoring a dance for its trade union workers. The event is one of relief – half for making last year's quota and half for having endured another very long Russian winter. Although he is not much of a dancer, Lee thoroughly enjoys mingling with the younger company these kinds of gatherings attract. The hors d'oeuvres and punch are ancillary enchantments – ones he enjoys very much.

The hostess smiles and hands her repeat customer another glass of punch. Lee noticed a funny taste in his mouth after his last cup. *Maybe another one will get rid of it,* he thinks, taking a big gulp.

"Excuse me," a charming voice behind him says. He feels a light tap on his shoulder.

Lee turns around and there she is, standing in front of him. He almost chokes on the swallow of punch still in his mouth. "Yes?" he sputters.

"You are American, no?" she asks sheepishly, a playful grin on her face.

"Lee," he answers, extending his hand awkwardly. "And yes, I am from the United States," he adds, suddenly remembering her question.

"Marina," she says sweetly as she offers her hand – the soft touch of her skin pressed against his hand in a gentle handshake sends tingles up his spine. "Your Russian is so excellent I thought you were native Russian with a Baltic accent when I first heard you speak. I couldn't help but overhear you talking to them," she tells him, pointing at the greeters near the front entrance.

Lee smiles nervously. “Thank you,” he says, swallowing hard. He wipes beads of sweat from his forehead. *What is wrong with me?* He wonders. *Why do I feel so faint?*

He hazily listens to her explaining details about her work and her family but he is having a hard time concentrating. His head hurts and he suddenly feels dizzy.

“What about YOUR family?” he hears her far-away voice asking him.

“Oh, it’s just me,” he answers, lying. “Both my parents are dead. My father died before I was born and my mother just recently passed.” he says quickly, blinking and wiping away more sweat.

“Are you okay?” she asks him. “You look flushed.”

“I don’t feel very good,” he replies, loosening his shirt collar. “I need to sit down.” Seated, Lee takes a deep breath before everything goes dark. “I…can’t…see,” he stammers, slumping over on his chair. The commotion around him continues for a few seconds until, complete silence.

***

Washington D.C.

April 21, 1961

Jesus, what a clusterfuck, Sasha thinks, amused by the debacle he is watching unfold live on the television screen in front of him. *I guess Arrowhead WAS right.*

Sasha is a professional. Rarely does he take pleasure in the enemy's misfortune. It is the nature of his business – win some, lose some. However, this is a train wreck of epic proportions – with the whole world watching. The talking heads are trying their best, but even they cannot spin this away. With some help from Sasha and Co., the Americans utterly botched the Cuban invasion. *This was TOO easy*, he tells himself, smiling.

If nothing else, the misadventure does confirm what Arrowhead had predicted. When the shit storm hit, the President and his brother got cold feet and cancelled the air support. Now, after the plan failed, they are both blaming the CIA for a bad plan.

Look who is on TV doing all the talking for the Administration, Sasha says to himself as the news coverage continues. *Bobby, accusing the military and intelligence brass of setting up his brother again. Arrowhead was right about that too. JFK will not trust ANYBODY but Bobby now.*

Of course, Arrowhead's intelligence had forewarned the Soviets, who in turn, gave a heads-up to Castro. The element of surprise then-Vice President Nixon was counting on DID happen, just not the way he planned it. The only ones surprised were the Americans. *Somewhere right now, Nixon is laughing his ass off,* Sasha thinks.

First, the planes, then a few diversionary attacks meant to throw off Castro, a naval landing at the Bay of Pigs, followed by an inland drop of the paratroopers – a good plan in theory. In real life however, excellent intelligence work and Murphy's Law ruined the plan. The diversionary attacks fooled no one.

The naval landing bogged down immediately because of ship engine failures, rough seas, and unforeseen coral reefs, all of which held up the landing long enough for the Cubans to counter with rocket fire. The ensuing scrum damaged some of the ships and disoriented the landing troops. Soldiers' weapons and equipment were lost in the surf – resulting in unarmed men staggering onto the beaches – right into the waiting arms of Castro's men.

The paratroopers dropped into the middle of a swamp, along with their weapons, supplies, and equipment. The orders had been to work their way back to the beaches, trapping Castro's men in a pincer movement between two invading forces. Instead, they were ALL sitting ducks.

The CIA knew right away that the operation was a disaster. Its fallback plan was to request military backup from the President. It had happened before. In the 1954 Guatemalan coup d' etat, The Agency's black-ops similar to the Bay of Pigs also got off to a shaky start. Eisenhower provided military support just in time and the covert operation ultimately succeeded.

That was Eisenhower though – no stranger to the fog of war, and certainly not scared to adjust mid-stride and go to plan b. "War is nothing but a series of contingency plans," he used to say. This is Kennedy. When the live bullets started flying, he pulled the chicken-switch.

In his address to the American people yesterday, Kennedy said there are "useful lessons" to be learned from this failure. Sasha was much more interested in something else he said. "Nor is it by any means the final episode in the eternal struggle of liberty against tyranny, anywhere on the face of the globe, including Cuba itself." *This is NOT over,* Sasha realized as he reviewed the transcript of the President's speech. *Castro and Cuba will be ongoing issues...*

Today, John Kennedy is the one taking live bullets. *The press is eating his lunch,* Sasha says to himself, now watching the split-screen images of former Vice President Richard Nixon leaving the White House after an emergency meeting yesterday next to Kennedy answering withering questions from the press today. The White House press corps shouts their questions rather than ask them.

"Mr. President, can you tell us anything about your talk with Vice President Nixon last night?"

"I brought – the Vice President came to the White House at my invitation – and I informed him, I brought him up to date on the events of the past few days," the President responds calmly.

"I call bull-shit on that," Sasha scoffs at the TV. "You want everyone to know that you inherited Nixon's plan."

The inquisition continues. "Mr. President, a published report claims you made the decisions to continue training Cuban refugees with arms provided by this Government and to release ships and fuel for the launching of the current operations in Cuba. Furthermore, this report says that you reached these decisions against the advice of your Secretary of State and his predecessor. Is this true?"

The President takes a deep breath. "There is an old saying – I don't know where it comes from." Kennedy allows for a pregnant pause in the room. "'Victory has a hundred fathers and defeat is an orphan'. The reality is I am the responsible officer of the government."

The President's statement floors Sasha. "Wow, a politician taking public responsibility?" he says, impressed. "Maybe I was wrong about him..."

Regardless, the United States is embarrassed in front of the whole world. The American people are humiliated. The President and his brother are indignant. Moreover, the CIA is in big trouble. *Not bad for a day's work*, Sasha congratulates himself silently, still smiling.

***

Washington D.C.

April 28, 1961

The dead drop is loaded. Sasha cannot wait to make the pick-up. Arrowhead's intelligence made all the difference in Cuba. Three days after the fiasco, Sasha listened to Kennedy give a speech to the American people. He heard the President offer his mea culpa at a press conference the following day. He wonders what the internal fallout will be. He will not have to wait long.

The rotation places this meeting at Mount Vernon – George and Martha's place. There will not be any walking this time – it is much too far. Sasha leaves the din of the District behind, driving fifteen miles south on the George Washington Memorial Parkway – a beautiful route along the Potomac River. Every road of any consequence in the DC area eventually bumps into the Potomac.

First glimpse of the handsome white estate emerging in the foreground against the backdrops of a flaming-red evening sun, the luscious canopy of green, and the grandiose waterway steals Sasha's breath away. Like usual, Arrowhead is already there, waiting impatiently, looking at his watch.

"This is WAR now," Arrowhead declares, startling Sasha with his opening broadside.

Arrowhead senses Sasha's alarm. "Not with the Soviets, with the CIA," he clarifies quickly. Sasha nods and exhales slowly, trying to pretend he already knows that.

Arrowhead continues, rapid-fire. "Kennedy is pissed. Bobby is pissed. Hell, Jackie is pissed too. Don't be confused by the President's statement at the press conference, 'I am the responsible officer of the government...' Fact is he and his brother blame us. They are out for scalps now."

"What about The Agency – how does it feel?" Sasha asks, interested in the intramural conflict.

"Like we got left out in the cold with our dicks in our hands," Arrowhead replies, with his usual coarseness. By now, Sasha is used to Arrowhead's bluster. He listens without batting an eye.

"Rumors are that our top three guys are going to be fired," Arrowhead says. "And, Kennedy's looking at ways to use executive orders to strip powers and money from The Agency…"

"…Hold it," Sasha interrupts, incredulous. "The President's going to FIRE Allen Dulles?"

Arrowhead nods his head. "God-damn right he is."

"Wow. Allen Dulles BUILT the CIA," Sasha remarks. "He is THE sacred cow of intelligence around the world. Are you sure about this? The US isn't quitting the intelligence business…" Sasha counters, skeptical.

"…Of course not," Arrowhead interjects. "The President is going to transfer intelligence and covert-ops to the military, over which he and his brother have direct control."

"Sounds personal," observes Sasha dryly.

"Damn right it's personal," Arrowhead agrees. "It didn't get a lot of attention in the media but Kennedy's scapegoating was in high gear yesterday at the American Association of Newspaper Editors' meeting. His staff circulated the room, leaking info to reporters and blaming the failed invasion on everybody but the

Administration. From the podium, the President even said 'How could I have been so stupid to trust the CIA and the Joint Chiefs of Staff?' But what he said next is what has Langley really up in arms." Arrowhead pauses for effect.

"Well...what the hell did he say?" Sasha asks, not at all interested in Arrowhead's theatrics now.

"He promised to 'splinter the CIA into a thousand pieces and scatter it into the winds'," Sasha announces suddenly.

Sasha shrugs. "He probably overstated, trying to make a point..."

"...Nope," Arrowhead interrupts, disagreeing. "It's just like I said, this is war now. The President of the United States has declared war on the CIA."

It is Sasha's turn to pause now, mulling the ramifications. "It's WAY too early in his first term for the President to be making these kinds of enemies," he says finally.

"Nobody's saying its smart," Arrowhead smirks, "but that ship has already sailed."

***

Washington D.C.

May 3, 1961

The CIA is a convoluted jungle of human intelligence gatherers, processers and analyzers, each grouped into departments, divisions, and operations. The covert nature of the job only adds to the confusion. Most times, the right-hand does not even KNOW the left-hand, much less, what it is doing or how well it is doing it.

In that kind of environment, it can be hard to rise through the ranks. A good agent is difficult to come by. Most operations directors try to hang on to the good ones rather than promote them. Michael Overstreet is a good spy. In nineteen years of service, he has only climbed three rungs of the CIA's career ladder.

He began as a Paramilitary Operations Officer with the Special Operations Group (SOG). His job was gathering and processing intelligence in Soviet-controlled Czechoslovakia. CIA agents do not commute to work if they are in counter-intelligence. They LIVE where they work. During his nine years in Prague, agent Overstreet knew if he was careless and was outed, the CIA would disavow all knowledge of his existence. For those nine years, he was the TIP of America's Cold War spear.

After Czechoslovakia, The Agency transferred Overstreet to the relative safety of Langley, Virginia. He worked in the Special Activities Division, overseeing all covert operations or "special activities" in hostile territory. For the last six years, he has been an intelligence analyst with the Directorate of Operations (DO). For that entire decade, he WAS America's Cold War spear.

Today is a big moment for him. The CIA is promoting him to Deputy Director of the Directorate of Operations. Promotions within The Agency are low-profile events – necessarily so. There will not be a public announcement. There will not be a notice in the local newspaper. There will not even be an intra-office news bulletin. The Agency will not be hosting a ceremony to congratulate him or anybody else. No cake. Nothing – just a quiet internal shifting around of office spaces and co-workers.

Aside from his changing job description and a modest pay bump, Overstreet will not experience any significant changes in his daily routine; nor will his co-workers or the public. That is the point. The CIA does not even publish the names of its Deputy Directors.

As big a day this is for the new Deputy Director, it is an even bigger day for the Soviet Union. Arrowhead is now the Directorate of Operations' number-two, overseeing the collection of ALL foreign intelligence from clandestine sources (human) and covert actions. The KGB has not EVER had had a mole this high up on the American Intelligence Community's food chain. From this day forward, the SOVIETS will be holding America's Cold War spear in THEIR hands.

***

Chapter Nine

***

Ulysses, Mongoose & Anadyr

Minsk, Russia

May 16, 1961

"This operation has succeeded beyond even MY expectations," a very satisfied Father remarks to Yuri, tossing the file onto his desk. "The girl, the dress, the dance, the illness..."

"...Poisoning him was a stroke of genius," Yuri interjects, complimenting his boss. "He was out-of-his mind sick. That can really mess with a man's mind – being so close to death."

"Especially one who's been drugged into a state of delirium," Father adds, grinning.

"The poor bastard was in a windowless hospital room for two weeks with no human contact except the beautiful Marina," Yuri declares, chuckling. "Christ, he didn't have a chance!"

"I wish I could have seen the look on his face when Marina came into his room the first time to give him his sponge bath, wearing nothing but her skimpy little nurse's outfit," Father says, laughing heartily. "He probably thought he died and went to heaven!"

"A one-man fantasy camp courtesy of the KGB – pure genius," Yuri repeats with a far-away look in his eyes.

"The American had been entertaining Russian girls in his fancy riverside apartment for weeks – two, sometimes three at a time," Father explains. "His exotic lifestyle and foreign status made him too tempting to resist evidently. Reports said he was living the life of a Hollywood playboy in Minsk. We had to isolate him with Marina to make the match. Her job at the hospital made it a natural occurrence," Father brags.

"Marina WAS the perfect choice for this operation," agrees Yuri.

"Just look at the results," crows Father. "Six weeks after their first meeting at the dance, the happy couple is now married! She sure did a number on that damn fool."

"Would that someone as sexy as her would do a

number on ME like that," Yuri says, suddenly envious of the American. "The last six weeks have been the BEST six weeks of his life, I'm sure. Sign me up. I'd GLADLY play the part of a damn fool..."

"...Wouldn't we all?" Father agrees. Both men laugh. Yuri taps his briefcase impatiently.

Father holds up a piece of paper. "Listen to this before you leave:

> *Since my last letter, I have gotten married. My wife is Russian, born in Leningrad. She has no parents living and is quite willing to leave the Soviet Union and live in the United States. I will not leave here without my wife. Arrangements need to include her, as she will be leaving at the same time I leave.*

Signed by Lee Oswald," Father finishes with a flourish. "The US Embassy just received this yesterday."

"Sounds like Operation Ulysses won't be domestic much longer," Yuri states confidently. "It's ready to go international..."

"...Not quite," Father interrupts, shaking his head. "But close. Very close. The wheels turn slow. My guess is that sometime this year, Mr. Oswald and his new bride – and our spy – will both be on a ship headed west. And if all goes to plan, with a new baby…"

"…Ah, yes. A family," Yuri interjects. "The oldest trick in the book."

"There's a very good reason it's the oldest," Father says, leaning forward in his chair.

"Because it works," Yuri acknowledges with a chuckle, standing to leave.

Father accompanies Yuri to the door. "Something on your mind?" he asks, sensing hesitation. Yuri's hand is fumbling with the doorknob. Finally, he stops and turns toward Father.

"We would NEVER recall a Soviet agent with an American spouse in-tow, much less a family," he says, baffled. "Can the Americans really be this dumb?"

"Not dumb – they want their agent back," Father replies. "Either they want him permanently silenced or they're not finished with him yet. Let's hope for the latter."

***

Washington D.C.

August 13, 1961

Kennedy has not been in office very long, but already, the Soviets know. "Fuck it, EVERYBODY knows," growls Petr Solomin. Codenamed "Pete Sandusky", the massive Russian is Sasha's babysitter inside the personal protective detail of Attorney General Robert Kennedy.

Sandusky is the walking-talking embodiment of a KGB agent – if such a stereotype exists. At six-feet, eight inches tall and "squared-up and built like a brick shithouse" – as Sasha describes him – his appearance is a physical absurdity. His frame resembles an Egyptian pyramid standing on its head with rock-hard muscles bulging in all the right places – Sasha laughingly claims that "Pete's muscles have muscles." His crew cut is so white it looks bleached – it is not. Instead of speaking in a normal tone, he thunders. Like a subterranean earthquake, his unfathomably-deep voice rumbles an octave or two below most humans. To hear Sandusky talk sends a shiver down a sane person's spine.

Before becoming a KGB agent, Sandusky was a "mechanic," or a hit man, for the Russian mafia. Not many occupations in the Soviet Union outshine KGB agent, but EVERYBODY knows there is NOBODY in this or any other world tougher than a hit man with the Russian mafia. His physical presence and his previous job make for some interesting "Sandusky stories" – so legendary they almost require their own literary category.

One of these stories had him surviving a wrestling match with a bear on a hunting expedition in the far north of Russia. Another time, two terrified bystanders witnessed Sandusky rip a gaping hole in a man's neck with his thumb and forefinger and hold him up in the air with one massive arm, watching the victim bleed out all over the ground. According to the traumatized gawkers, Sandusky calmly smoked a cigarette with his free hand during those horrifying minutes.

Without a doubt though, the most amazing story – whether it is true or not does not really matter – was the time he allegedly grabbed the landing gear of a helicopter with one gigantic hand and a steel railing attached to the top of a building with the other. This, as the helicopter tried to take off. According to witnesses, Sandusky flat REFUSED to let go. The story ends with the helicopter crashing and the merciless death of a rival gang member. Nobody doubts Big Pete's special skills. In fact, everybody with a working brain is terrified of him.

Sandusky's front is the one-man security service he operates out of a dilapidated DC storefront. During the '60 Presidential campaign, the Kennedy team brought him on board to provide extra security for the Kennedy brothers during a swing through rowdy South Florida. Good thing.

On one memorable day, a crazed anti-Castroite Cuban broke through the rope-line and charged the Presidential candidate with a serrated Bowie knife. JFK's own security guard tripped and fell over a speaker cord, rendering him helpless to stop the assailant. Sandusky saw the Cuban from a distance and watched as the bodyguard went down. Pete sprang into action, plowing through the crowd, knocking everyone in his way to the ground. Then he grabbed the Cuban by the back of his hair, spinning him around and hitting him ONE time in the face with an angry fist of iron. The blow was so hard and fast, witnesses heard the man's facial bones snap like twigs. His nose ended up on his forehead. One witness even found some of the Cubans' teeth IN her purse. The man later died of his injuries. Having made an impression, the Democrat nominee asked Sandusky to stay on with him through the remainder of his 1960 campaign.

Reportedly, Sandusky is also a big score with the ladies. Like a modern-day Samson, his libido is as legendary as his feats of strength. Sasha is convinced Sandusky's sexual prowess is the REAL reason he is so popular with the Kennedy family.

When the '60 campaign ended, President-elect Kennedy fell under the protection of the Secret Service – rendering Sandusky's services unnecessary. Pete so wowed JFK during the campaign he recommended him to Bobby. That is how a Soviet spy became part of the Kennedy inner-circle.

"Everybody knows JK doesn't have an independent thought," Sandusky continues, 'JK' being his nickname for the President. "That's not news. He's Bobby's little bitch. The AG is the power behind that throne," he adds, referring to the Attorney General.

Sasha replies, "True, but most importantly, whenever we've pushed them, in Cuba for example, they back down. Father is beginning to think it IS the Kennedy family DNA. Remember Joe and Hitler?"

"They're ALL pussies," agrees Sandusky, matter-of-factly.

"Moscow thinks we can advance our agenda in SEVERAL places while the Kennedy brothers are in the White House. Berlin is just the first step," Sasha explains.

"The military and intelligence boys are going ape-shit over Berlin," laughs Sandusky. "They told the Kennedys the Berlin Wall was our strategy to take all of Berlin, and eventually Germany. JK disagreed and said, 'Let them build the wall. It will protect West Berlin from an invasion and it's a public relations nightmare for the Soviets – building a wall to keep their people in'."

"He's got an answer for everything, doesn't he?" observes Sasha, disgusted. "The bottom line, we're going to keep pushing him until we find a line he WON'T cross. All he's done is bend over and take it..."

"...And like it!" Sandusky roars. Both men laugh at the crude joke.

"He IS feeling the heat on Cuba though," cautions Sandusky. "You know he still owes his mafia pals big-time for the election and you don't double-cross those boys. The Bay of Pigs mess has many folks wondering about his manhood. Now he's trying to overcompensate."

"Mongoose?" Sasha wonders, somewhat rhetorically.

"Yep. Here is the fuck in their cluster though. It is supposed to be a CIA operation but JK wants Bobby to run it from Justice instead. He doesn't even trust his own intelligence people! Bobby wouldn't know a black-ops if one bit him in the ass. Operation Mongoose is as covert as tranny-hookers in Vegas," Sandusky says, smirking contemptuously.

"So Robert's in charge?" asks Sasha, shaking his head and chuckling at Pete's colorful image. He remembers Arrowhead's prediction after the debacle in Cuba.

"Uh huh," grunts Sandusky. "In a manner of speaking anyway." Sasha opens the front door of the bookstore as Sandusky unwinds his massive frame, getting up to leave.

"Stay in touch," he orders. "We need to stay on top of Mongoose. Keep your head down and your ears open, big fella."

***

Moscow, Russia

March 5, 1962

"Ellen Rometsch, huh?" Premier Khrushchev whistles, holding up and examining the image from a file lying open on his desk. He lowers the picture, looking at his foreign intelligence operations chief seated directly in front of him.

"You said the finest piece of ass in the Stasi," Father reminds him. "She comes with the highest recommendations..."

"...I'll bet she does," Khrushchev interrupts, a far-away look in his eyes. "NOBODY in this world gives a better blowjob than that broad. I mean it. NOBODY. Even so, how do you plan to get an East German cupcake inside the President's pants?"

"We snuck her into a refugee camp three years ago," Father explains. "Both of her parents are Stasi officers so we had to create a non-official cover for her. She did the rest. She's a NOC inside the West German Diplomatic Corps now."

"Ellen Rometsch is a mole?" the Premier asks, surprised.

"That's right," Father nods. "Officially, her title is Third Secretary to the Foreign Minister – just a glorified hostess at Embassy functions. She feeds the West Germans information from clients at her other jobs and counter-intel that we give her. Bonn is scared of two things – the Berlin Wall and President Kennedy. The Wall because it exists and Kennedy because he has not done a thing to stop it. The West Germans are assigning Miss Rometsch to Washington to find out who their friends are. Her cover will be the Embassy but her REAL work – for them AND us – will be done as a hostess at The Quorum Club."

"I've heard of that place," Khrushchev says, smiling. "No one hires more European flesh than The Quorum – so I've heard anyway."

"And American politicians DO love European girls," Father agrees. "Anyway, she'll mingle with key politicos at state functions. With her killer looks, it will not be long before they appreciate her unique social skills if you know what I mean. After that, word-of-mouth will do the rest. Either he will hear about her from someone else or he will sniff her out himself. Kennedy is a damn bloodhound. Once he lays eyes on Miss Rometsch, it'll be over."

Khrushchev smiles a knowing smile. "She IS a honey trap if there ever was one. But still, do we think that son-of-a-bitch is really that stupid?"

"Not stupid, just incredibly reckless," replies Father. "Since the campaign in '60, he's been with mob women, Hollywood actresses, staffers – hell, he fucked BOTH of Jackie's secretaries in the White House swimming pool! THIS guy has a threesome EVERY Tuesday afternoon in FDR's old basement pool with Fiddle and Faddle..."

"...Fiddle and Faddle?" Khrushchev interjects. "What, are you joking?" he asks, unsure if Father is putting him on.

"That's what the Secret Service calls them," Father answers with a shrug.

"God-damn!" Khrushchev exclaims, suddenly envious of his American counterpart.

"Bobby's already had to get him out of a couple jams," Father adds. "One with Hoover and the other with reporters who were snooping around. Honestly though? Nothing can stop him. He is relentless, which is exactly why this will work. He cannot help himself. He's addicted to pussy."

"Aren't we all?" Premier Khrushchev replies with a smirk, dismissing Father with a wave.

***

Washington D.C.

March 21, 1962

The random numbering system chooses Washington National Cathedral for their meeting tonight. Arrowhead is waiting under the haunting Darth Vader-like stained-glass window when Sasha arrives. Like clockwork, he checks his watch. They talk as they walk.

"Congrats on the promotion," Sasha begins. "I don't have to tell you what a big deal this will turn out to be for all of us," he adds with sincerity.

“Thanks,” Arrowhead replies, for once appreciative.

“We have a chance now to rat-fuck the entire American intelligence community and sabotage its foreign policy. Jesus, you could even be Director someday,” Sasha realizes.

“Not likely,” Arrowhead replies with a huff. “The position is too political. And I do not consider myself a politician.”

“Good, because you’re not,” Sasha agrees, laughing. “What you ARE is a quick study. You are NOT the decider yet, but you ARE in the same room as him now. Just play the game.” Arrowhead groans his displeasure, never one to play ANYONE’S game.

“Never mind,” Sasha chuckles. “This is about Cuba again, no?” he asks, changing the subject.

Arrowhead nods. “The difference is, it’s their plan this time and Bobby’s running it. We are just pawns in the game. Bobby is sticking his neck out on this one. He gave a pep talk the other day and said, ‘deposing Castro is the top priority of the U.S. government – all else is secondary – no time, money, effort, or manpower will be spared’."

"Top priority, really? What's the plan THIS time?" Sasha asks sarcastically.

"Counterinsurgency," Arrowhead says, rolling his eyes. "The Kennedys love that word. Instead of one large-scale invasion, it will be small, pin-prick covert-ops – lots of them."

"Death by a thousand cuts," Sasha deadpans, sighing. "What kind of cuts exactly?" he asks.

"Bang-and-burn sabotage, crop-burnings, mining of harbors, propaganda, small-scale terrorist attacks, aid to guerillas, psych-warfare, and assassination attempts, just to name a few," says Arrowhead.

"Assassination attempts?" Sasha asks, taken aback by the last item on his list. "We call that burying the lead," he tells Arrowhead.

"Maybe," Arrowhead concedes. "Bobby wants the government to have plausible deniability," he explains. "The black-ops will be carried out by Agency-trained Cuban exiles. The mob will take care of Castro." Sasha laughs.

"What's so funny?" Arrowhead wants to know.

“I think it is god-damn hilarious the mafia has to do its own dirty work now,” he says, recalling the election-year deal the Kennedys made with Sam Giancana. “First the mob sides with Nixon to get rid of Castro, then switches and supports Kennedy because he promised to get rid of him, and now? Now they have to do it themselves! They probably think Kennedy isn’t up to the job, or maybe he’s just that much smarter than them.”

“It’s not Jack,” Arrowhead clarifies. “It’s…”

“…Bobby, I know,” Sasha interjects. “Bobby, Jack – what does it matter? They are the same. How is it working?” he asks.

“Johnny Roselli has been hired to carry out the hit,” Arrowhead explains. “And how might we know all this? Because WE hired him on Bobby’s instructions! WE are the ones who gave him the poison pills and ten-thousand-dollars cash!”

Sasha looks flabbergasted. “The US Government pretending not to notice the mob plotting the assassination of a foreign leader is ONE thing…” he maintains, “…but paying them to do it is just dumb as hell. Poison pills? Just plain dumb,” he repeats.

"It IS stupid, I know," Arrowhead agrees. "Roselli leads back to Giancana in Chicago. Whom did Joe Kennedy make a deal with in '60? That's right, Giancana and the Chicago family. The whole thing is incestuous."

"Why the mob...can't The Agency be invisible?" questions Sasha. "It's what you guys do!"

Arrowhead shakes his head. "That's not the point. There can never be any evidence that the American government conspired in a plot to assassinate a foreign head-of-state."

"What about cash and poison pills – that's NOT evidence?" Sasha asks the obvious question.

"Plausible deniability," Arrowhead replies, shrugging. "The cash was a payoff to an informant and if anybody starts asking, we've never heard of poison pills..."

"...It's STILL illegal as hell..." Sasha says, "...assassinating foreign leaders."

"Of course it is," Arrowhead admits. "Actually, it's tailor-made for MKUltra..."

"...The mind control program?" Sasha interjects.

"Yes," Arrowhead answers him. "It started under

Eisenhower as a way to get easy confessions but now we're having success using hypnosis to control human behavior."

"Programming," Sasha says, familiar with the experimental practice.

"Right," Arrowhead agrees. "We can now hard-wire an asset to do virtually anything we want. The best part is we can wipe assets' memory clean. Which means the CIA has the capability to program an asset to shoot Castro and confess to it afterwards, while having no recollection of the programming or who was behind it. The Agency walks away scot-free."

"So why not...?" Sasha begins asking.

"...Because Castro knows about it," Arrowhead admits sheepishly. "It would lead the god-damn Cubans right back to us."

"So the mob is cover," Sasha concludes. Arrowhead nods his head.

"Does Sam Giancana even have the people to get close to Castro?" Sasha asks, skeptical.

"Probably not," Arrowhead answers. "But Carlos Marcello does. Santos Trafficante CERTAINLY does.

When you link up with Roselli, he brings more than one family to the table. New Orleans is Marcello territory – overrun with crazy-ass Cuban exiles. Trafficante practically owns the whole state of Florida and where do you think the largest Cuban-exile population is in the United States?"

"Miami," replies Sasha, beginning to understand.

"And you know the best part?" Arrowhead asks. "They're motivated as hell – and expendable," he adds cynically.

"Where is Bobby's counterinsurgency operation based?" Sasha asks.

"At the JM/WAVE station in Miami. Everything's being run out of the CIA's Camp Swampy." Arrowhead replies.

"How much money is being budgeted?" Sasha inquires. He has learned the allocation of cold, hard cash determines the priority level of everything in Washington D.C.

"Are you kidding me?" Arrowhead exclaims, irritated. "I already told you what Bobby said. 'NO time, money, effort, or manpower will be spared'," he repeats. "Cash is flowing like a damn lava flow in South Florida – all of it government money. They're using gun stores, travel agencies, and boat shops as fronts to launder it all but I promise you, the cash is coming straight out of DC."

"This is for real then," Sasha concludes, finally convinced. "I guess Bay of Pigs wasn't enough. We're going to have to do MORE to defend Cuba from these assholes."

"That's for damn sure," agrees Arrowhead.

Sasha and Arrowhead have timed it perfectly. They are standing where they started, staring up at the Cathedral's sinister-looking stained-glass window again. Conversation over, the two men turn and walk away in opposite directions.

***

Gagra, Russia

April 6, 1962

The two highest-ranking Soviets – Premier Khrushchev and Defense Minister Rodio Malinovsky – are strolling the cliffs of Khrushchev's famous estate, stopping every few steps to gaze down at the Black Sea churning far below. Even with a morning fog, the view is stunning. "That's where the American rockets are pointed at us," Malinovsky says, eyes squinting southward across the water, pointing in the direction of Turkey. "They need only ten minutes to reach our cities, but our rockets need twenty-five minutes to reach America."

"Kennedy is no Eisenhower," Khrushchev states. "Why don't we install our rockets in Cuba and point them at the Americans? Then we will only need ten minutes too."

Malinovsky smiles and shakes his head. "We both know El Presidente won't agree to it."

"Then he must be convinced," replies Khrushchev. "The Americans already invaded Cuba once. Fidel has grown too full of himself after the Bay of Pigs. They will try again. What are allies for?"

"It would solve a lot of other problems too," Malinovsky agrees, adjusting his military-issued fur Ushanka ear hat.

As the Soviets are well aware, there IS a missile gap.

However, contrary to CIA propaganda and JFK's dire campaigning in 1960, it is the United States with the advantages, not the Soviets. The Americans are far ahead in long-range ICBM production, reliability, and accuracy. The US is also ahead in strategic bombers – the B-52 and the supersonic B-58 Hustlers being far superior to the TU-95 Bear. The US air defense against bombers is also superior, featuring computerized threat tracking, dew-line radar systems and pine tree line radar systems. The US has large numbers of interceptors, including the F-104 Starfighters with the most advanced digital radars. These have the speed to intercept Soviet bombers far away from US bases and US cities. The US has at least four Polaris nuclear submarines in operation – each equipped with Minuteman solid-fuel missiles that have one-thousand-mile range and digital guidance computers.

"The Americans' first strike capability keeps me up nights..." Khrushchev admits, "...twenty god-damn cities..."

"...And military bases," Malinovsky interjects, "all wiped out in one nuclear attack. Actually, the Americans have first-strike AND long-term advantages," he continues. "Our response would be limited because our missiles are one-time use. They could then attack our missile silos, bomber bases, and air defenses. By day three, we would be really hard-pressed to get more than one or two weapons to the US, while they would still have hundreds of B-52s capable of reaching anywhere in the Soviet Union – and thousands of weapons available."

"This is entirely unacceptable," Khrushchev mutters angrily. "Every dam and railroad would be demolished. And our water supply – I will not preside over the end of Russian history."

"It would be North Korea all over again," Malinovsky predicts. "Those American sons-of-bitches waited and blew up the dams at night, drowning everybody downstream. Twenty-five percent of North Korea's population was killed by US bombers."

"Cuba is a short boat ride from Miami," the Premier states. "If we put short and medium-range missiles on the island, we could penetrate deep inside US territory, counteracting their missiles in Turkey."

"And restore the balance of power," Malinovsky concludes. "The missiles would also provide us with a bargaining chip to be used against the west."

"American missiles in Turkey for Soviet missiles in

Cuba," Khrushchev wagers, squaring his jaw.

"Or, when the west leaves Berlin, Soviet missiles will leave Cuba," Malinovsky counters.

"We must arrange a meeting with Mr. Castro soon," Premier Khrushchev declares abruptly. "The Soviet Union is going to send America and the west a powerful message."

***

Havana, Cuba

May 6, 1962

"I will not be a Soviet puppet!" Cuban President Fidel Castro maintains, frustrated, chewing on his snuffed-out cigar. "Ask the Americans. They desired a puppet and ended up with a thorn in their side instead," he blusters.

"Of course," replies the leader of the Soviet delegation. "But the Americans will not stop until that thorn is removed," he warns. "You turned back the Bay of Pigs invasion because of Soviet intelligence, no? These missile sites will prevent future invasions."

Castro mulls the idea silently, somewhat chastened. Khrushchev's delegation – Soviet military and missile construction specialists – are in Havana under the guise of an agricultural junket to convince the Cuban leader it is in his best interest to approve the installation of nuclear missiles on his island. "Well, for the goal of strengthening the socialist camp, I agree," Castro reluctantly concedes after a few moments. "But I want the rockets brought in openly."

Khrushchev's representative shakes his head. "No, the Premier said we will do it like they did in Turkey. We will confront them with an established fact. The Americans are a pragmatic people. They will have to accept it just as we had to accept it in Turkey. THEN we'll be able to negotiate with America on a basis of parity."

"Fait accompli," mutters Castro, discerning the strategy. "Kennedy will avoid a confrontation."

"Moscow believes he will back down,' the spokesman replies, nodding. "For this to happen," he stresses, "Operation Anadyr will require elaborate measures to deceive and deny. In Russia, we call this 'maskirovka'. Transporting and deploying the missiles must be of the utmost secrecy. The troops assigned to the mission must be misdirected. We will tell them they are heading for a cold region. We will outfit them with ski boots, parkas, and other winter equipment. 'Anadyr' is a river that flows into the Bering Sea. It is also the capital of Chukotsky District and the name of a bomber base in the far eastern region. We picked this name to conceal the operation from both internal and external audiences."

"How many troops?" Castro asks. "And how will the Soviet government explain their presence in Cuba?"

"Forty-thousand," the delegate replies. "The specialists in missile construction will be in Cuba under the cover of machine operators, irrigation specialists, and agricultural experts."

"And how does the Premier plan to hide these missile sites from American U-2 pilots?"

The Soviet envoy smiles broadly. "The missile sites will be concealed and camouflaged by palm trees."

***

Moscow, Russia

May 10, 1962

Yuri knocks on Father's office door. He is in such a hurry he suddenly remembers he forgot to call ahead and make an appointment. *Shit,* he says to himself. *Too late now.*

"What is it?" he detects agitation in Father's voice.

"Sir, I'm sorry to disturb you but I thought you'd want to see this." Yuri cracks opens the door enough for Father to see the piece of paper he is holding in his hand.

"Come," says Father motioning Yuri inside. "Give me a minute. I am in the middle of something. Help yourself," he adds, pointing at the mahogany liquor cabinet in the corner. Yuri ignores the offer and settles into a chair instead, pretending to read the paper again.

A few minutes later, Father finishes his writing, takes off his glasses with a sigh and looks up at Yuri. "Alright, what is it?" He asks, clearly annoyed at the distraction.

"The American has been granted permission to return to the United States – along with Marina and their newborn child," Yuri announces.

“Good. Very good,” Father says, his countenance improving a bit.

“That’s not even the BEST part,” Yuri declares, unfolding the paper.

“What ELSE does it say?” Father asks, leaning forward with his elbows on his desk.

Yuri scans the document quickly, looking for the key paragraph. “Here it is,” he points. “It says that ‘OSWALD WENT TO RUSSIA WITH STATE DEPARTMENT APPROVAL’…”

“…Let me see that!” Father cuts him off, reaching for the document.

“That’s their reason for allowing him to return,” Yuri continues. “They put it in writing – he was SENT here, just like we thought!”

“Anna called it first,” Father says, leaning back in his chair. “What bureaucratic ass-hat thought it would be a good idea to write this,” he wonders aloud, examining the form once again. Father spins in his chair and looks out the window. “Yuri, it’s a god-damn wilderness of mirrors out there. Things are NEVER what they seem. The CIA did not want Eisenhower and

Khrushchev to meet. They needed an incident to subvert the peace process." Father pauses as he walks through the timeline in his mind. "So they sent their trained asset to Russia as a fake defector in order to hand over classified information about the U-2. We used it to shoot down the plane. Both sides got what they wanted. We have their plane and they have their incident..."

"...And Khrushchev's walkout at the Four Powers Summit," Yuri adds quickly.

"Right, exactly," Father agrees. "Mission accomplished."

"And now it's time for their agent to come home," Yuri concludes.

Father pauses again, this time cleaning his glasses. "What they don't know is that we were wise to their little scheme all along, thanks to Anna. And like YOU said," Father says, recognizing Yuri with a nod, "playing dumb HAS indeed been the smart move."

"Not deporting him cost us the Summit..." Yuri calculates. "...but gave us the plane and a chance to trigger Ulysses."

"Come into my parlor said the spider to the fly..." Father quotes, smiling. Yuri laughs.

"Marina will help guide us through that wilderness of mirrors," Father says, pouring himself and Yuri a drink. "She is the riddle they can't solve – unless we fuck it up. Her training and access will present Mother Russia with unlimited opportunities." He is smiling now, his mood considerably bolstered by good news and a stiff drink.

"You know," speculates Yuri, "if the Americans want him back this badly, they must be planning to use him again, probably for something important. They are not going through all this just to retire his ass. In their reports, his mission was an unqualified success."

"He's a modern-day Trojan horse. Remember how that turned out?" Father asks rhetorically as he rises from his chair.

Yuri takes Father's cue and stands up to leave, saying ruefully, "I hate that the Americans think they fooled the Soviet Union though."

Father laughs and pats him on the shoulder as they approach the door. "Yuri, Yuri," he repeats, "let the Americans think whatever the hell they want. In fact, let them take a victory lap if they want. WE know who won this exchange."

***

Chapter Ten

***

Medical Manhattan Project

Moscow, Russia

June 1, 1962

"Your cash, Mr. Oswald," Mr. Snyder says, paperwork completed for the repatriation loan. He pushes an envelope across the desk, reading from a receipt. "Four-hundred, thirty-five dollars and seventy-one cents. These funds are furnished to you by the State Department to cover all travel expenses related to you and your family's journey to the United States, including tickets for the train leaving Russia, ship fare, hotel accommodations, and food."

"What happens when we get to New York?" Lee asks, thinking ahead.

"We've made contact with your brother in Ft. Worth," Mr. Snyder replies. "Mr. Raikin will help you from there..."

"...Mr. Raikin?" Lee interjects with a sideways glance.

"Permit me to acquaint you with your itinerary," Mr. Snyder says quickly. "First, you will travel by train from Moscow to Amsterdam. West German and Dutch customs officials are expecting you – you should not have any problems at their borders. When you arrive in Amsterdam, a Spas Raikin from the Traveler's Aid Society will be waiting for you. He will assist you, beginning with your trip across the Atlantic on the *S.S. Maasdam."*

"How long will our layover in Amsterdam be?" Lee asks, expecting it not to be short.

"Three days at most," Mr. Snyder answers. "American intelligence officials will be arriving the same time to debrief you. You cannot board the ship without this debriefing – you must know this. The schedule allows for two days, maybe three – depending on your level of cooperation."

"I understand," Lee says, nodding. "How long will Mr. Raikin be escorting us?"

"He will stay with you until you leave New York for Texas," Mr. Snyder replies. "He has already arranged temporary living quarters for you and your family in

New York City and as I started to say earlier, been in touch with your brother Robert regarding your flight to Fort Worth."

"Will this money cover that too?" Lee asks, motioning at the envelope still lying on the desk.

"Probably not," replies Snyder. "The United States State Department is committed to securing for you a hassle-free reentry into the country. After that, you are on your own. I believe Robert HAS offered to pay for your flight to Fort Worth if I'm not mistaken."

Lee is quiet. "What time does our train leave today?"

"The embassy will send a car to pick you and your family up at noon," Snyder replies, standing to his feet behind his desk. "I would advise you to be ready; your train pulls out at one o'clock sharp."

Lee gathers up the paperwork and puts the cash envelope in his pocket. He stands awkwardly, extending his hand.

"Mr. Oswald," Snyder states in his most official tone, rebuffing Lee's courtesy. "Don't take this wrong. Unofficially, I hope I never see or hear from you again. Officially, I wish you good luck back in America."

***

Washington D.C.

June 6, 1962

“Nixon and the heads of NIH, FDA, and CDC are terrified of a cancer epidemic,” reports Beasley. “They’ve been in cover-up mode since 1955. While he was VP, Nixon could control the research apparatus in DC. But after he lost in ’60, everything had to be moved to a secure location, away from prying eyes.”

“And where might that be?” Sasha inquires, curious.

“New Orleans,” replies Beasley. “Carlos Marcello is a big Nixon supporter. In fact, he gave him a half-million-dollars cash during the ’60 campaign. He was one of the crime bosses helping Nixon in ’59 with the Cuban operation. And now he’s helping him with medical research.”

“New Orleans! For crying out loud, are you kidding me?” exclaims Sasha, calculating in his mind the rapidly growing number of nefarious actors and activities intersecting in the Crescent City.

Beasley is startled, "I'm NOT making this up..."

Sasha waves him off, interjecting, "...What's the goal NOW, to cure cancer before an outbreak begins?" he guesses impatiently.

"Well, that's PART of it, yes," responds Beasley. "Nixon's hoping the research in New Orleans WILL lead to a cure for cancer. If that happens obviously, he will be credited with curing polio AND cancer," he says.

"What politician WOULDN'T want that?" Sasha asks with a quizzical look on his face.

"There's another part – the sinister part," Beasley says, clearing his throat. "It's not just WHAT, it's WHO."

Sasha looks exasperated. "Christ almighty, land the airplane already!" he exclaims, frustrated.

"When you hear the words cancer research..." Beasley begins, feeling rushed now, "...you think of prominent doctors, lab technicians, and medical research teams, right?"

"The American Cancer Society, the Cancer Research Institute..." Sasha adds, nodding.

"...Exactly," Beasley interjects. "Legitimate research by

licensed medical professionals. So why is the CIA involved in cancer research in New Orleans? What medical prowess does an intelligence agency bring to the table? The cast of characters involved in this project makes me question what in god's name is really going on down there."

"Cast of characters?" Sasha asks.

"Mafia, covert Agency types, local extremists with big money, oil tycoons from Texas, and the doctors," Beasley lists. "The doctor in charge is a flaming right-wing extremist. He co-founded the Information Council of the Americas (INCA) to fight the spread of Communism in Latin and South America. He absolutely hates Castro. Last year, he narrated an INCA film called, 'Hitler in Havana'."

"I've heard of INCA," Sasha claims. "Another John Birch Society – a bunch of radicals."

"The question is – are these misfits only working on a cure for cancer?" Beasley shakes his head, "Hell, no. HELL NO!"

"Maybe you're right," replies Sasha. "Cancer research might very well be a front for something else they don't want anybody to know about. But what's it got to do with us?"

"I believe it's connected to the CIA's TWEP program," Beasley blurts. "I can't prove it, but I have been hearing the word 'bio-weapon'."

"Termination-With-Extreme-Prejudice," Sasha mumbles, pieces beginning to fall into place. "A bio-weapon, huh? It could be this is less about a cure FOR cancer than it is a weapon FROM cancer."

"Why else would The Agency be involved in cancer research?" Beasley wonders.

It is a valid question but Sasha is no longer listening. His mind is racing, thinking about Nixon's final year as Vice President. In 1959, Beasley reported Nixon's office occupied by medical and intelligence officials. He remembers wondering then about connections between researchers and spooks. He might finally have his answer. *I need to talk to Arrowhead*, he thinks.

Sasha quickly dismisses Beasley and closes up the bookstore. He hurries on foot to the nearest Washington Metro bus stop. While he is waiting for his bus, he locates a pay phone nearby and dials the number. Only Arrowhead will understand the coded message.

The bus deposits Sasha at a crosstown Greyhound bus terminal. He buys another ticket and takes a seat in the waiting area. Fifteen minutes later, Sasha is on a bus heading thirty miles east to Annapolis, Maryland.

Upon arriving in Annapolis, Sasha hails a cab, directing the driver to the theater district. Arrowhead is already in front of the Colonial Players Theater, standing next to the display, reading a poster. Sasha is surprised. *How in the hell,* he mutters to himself as he pays the cab driver cash.

Silently, Sasha and Arrowhead begin walking. It is the beginning of the summer tourism season in the home of the United States Naval Academy. The sidewalks are crowded with slow-walking sightseers, some carrying brochures, all sporting cameras. Sasha and Arrowhead know the quiet spots of the historic town. After a few hectic minutes swimming against the current of mostly-Asian tourists, they are strolling by themselves in a peaceful neighborhood.

"What's going on in New Orleans?" Sasha gets right to the point.

Arrowhead sighs. "It's a long story," he says, pausing,

anticipating a follow-up question. Sasha remains quiet.

"What do you know about the polio vaccine?" Arrowhead begins.

Sasha plays dumb. "Polio vaccine? What's that got to do...?"

Arrowhead cuts him off. "...The vaccine the government used to inoculate two-hundred million Americans has serious problems."

"What kind of problems?" Sasha asks, still playing dumb.

"It's loaded with monkey viruses," Arrowhead says bluntly.

"Monkey viruses!" exclaims Sasha, skepticism in his voice.

"Yes," replies Arrowhead. "Two of the viruses happen to be lethal. One is cancer and the other has something to do with the immune system – nobody seems to know much about it. What we DO know is that everybody who received the vaccine now has these viruses in their blood. Anyway, since 1959, the same bigwigs who promised the vaccine was safe and forced sugar cubes down people's throat have been working around-the-clock to find a cure for cancer..."

"...Who are these bigwigs?" Sasha interrupts.

"Is former Vice President Richard Nixon big enough?" Arrowhead asks. "He and the directors of the medical establishment – like NIH, CDC, and FDA – are all in this together. Of course, Nixon has more to lose since he still wants to be President one day."

Sasha points at a street sign. "Turn here," he tells Arrowhead.

"During one experiment," Arrowhead continues, "radiation was used to kill the cancer cells. The exact opposite happened instead. The radiation treatment actually made the cancer cells MORE aggressive. What they accidentally created was something they now call a 'galloping cancer'."

"Sounds like they just swung and missed," Sasha replies.

"Maybe, for medical purposes," Arrowhead agrees. "But for OUR purposes, it is the biggest breakthrough in bio-weapon research in a generation!"

"Jesus," says Sasha. "So researching a cure for cancer IS just a mirage. The CIA is turning cancer into a bio-weapon it can use to kill people."

"Exactly," agrees Arrowhead. "A medical Manhattan Project if you will. We know how to create the galloping cancer cells but now the question is – can we convert these cells into a weapon? If so, how aggressive can we make it? Can we use it to assassinate somebody? Can we use it as a means of population control? Can we control the timetable? Can it be introduced other ways, besides injections?"

"It fits the TWEP profile perfectly," Sasha says. "If the bio-weapon is perfected and a delivery system, like food, is developed, the CIA could make people die of natural causes."

"Theoretically yes," Arrowhead agrees. "But the timetable is tricky. The beauty of a bullet is in its immediacy. Cancer can take years to kill someone. That wouldn't do us any good," he chuckles.

"Those issues will be ironed out in New Orleans..." Sasha predicts.

"...Bet your ass they will," Arrowhead interrupts, nodding his head. "A cancer bio-weapon will revolutionize the science of assassinating people. No traces, death by natural cause – plausible deniability."

"A spy agency's wet-dream," replies Sasha.

***

Washington D.C.

August 18, 1962

Even though it's Saturday, Sasha is still careful. The subject and location of today's encounter has him feeling a little more paranoid than usual.

The Americans and West Germans can never know that Ellen Rometsch is waiting in the East German Embassy for Sasha – the KGB's Second Chief Directorate in charge of Soviet counter-intelligence in America. *What a fucking disaster that would be*, Sasha thinks.

Miss Rometsch's codename for this operation – "Lace" – is an ironic choice. If the Stasi NOC succeeds in her mission, Lace will be sharing President Kennedy with the First Lady. Sasha figured she might as well share Jackie's Secret Service handle, too.

After parking his rental car in the underground garage, he enters the basement of the East German Embassy through a tunnel that links Reservoir Road Garage with government and non-government offices nearby. A grim-faced security officer is standing guard, waiting for Sasha as he approaches the end of the tunnel.

Together, they enter the elevator, ascending to the third-floor lobby. The guard escorts Sasha deep inside the bowels of the massive building, navigating him through the jungle of half-rent cubicles warehousing a small army of diplomatic aides. The aristocratic offices with glass walls, posh mahogany doors and views of the city belong to the diplomats.

Neither one speaks as they walk. Except for the clicking of heels on marble tiles and the muted sounds of heavy, wood-paneled doors opening and closing, it is eerily quiet.

The guard stops and points at a corner office. Sasha cannot be sure but he thinks he detects a slight smirk on his face. Satisfied, the guard turns and shuffles away, looking behind him once. Sasha waits until the uniform disappears through a set of double doors. He listens for the door to click shut and the sounds of footsteps to end. Finally, he breathes deeply, reaching for the door handle.

He remembers the warning. "If you do not prepare yourself, you'll hyperventilate the first time you lay eyes on her and get a whiff of her perfume," Father told him. "She is fucking intoxicating."

He opens the door and there she is, seated elegantly, smiling seductively, and looking amazing. Her hair is pinned up, perfectly coifed, exactly like the picture Sasha saw earlier in the file. Her tantalizing bedroom eyes with the playfully mischievous sparkle, her bronzed and perfect skin, the ivory-white smile, and the aroma – w*hat is that wonderful fragrance?*

He stands in the doorway, staring. Her tanned legs are long and athletic, attractively crossed and stunningly exposed by a strategically placed slit in her provocative skirt. Her silk blouse is under considerable duress – NOT designed to do what Miss Rometsch is expecting of hers without the support of a bra...*and that damn scent!*

Sasha recalls reading in her file what the Premier told Father, "the best blowjob," He steals a quick and nervous glance at her luscious red lips and imagines.

Jesus, he thinks.

As if on cue, she stands to her feet and begins approaching him. Sasha's heart is racing. He can feel himself sweating. He is sure she sees every drop of perspiration on his forehead. He hopes his eyes do not betray the panic he is experiencing in his mind.

He finally open his mouth to introduce himself, his voice cracking awkwardly like a pubescent boy. Suddenly, he feels lightheaded and in desperate need of a chair. *I need some air* Sasha recalls thinking. That is when the lights went out...

The next thing he knows, Lace is standing over him wiping his forehead with her handkerchief. He sees her lips moving. Like a far-away echo, he hears her soothing voice but he is not able to make out the words. Then something else catches his attention...

Her celestial breasts swing divinely in front of his face, the silk blouse accentuating her not-so-hidden treasures, teasing him. *Where in the hell is the smell of incense coming from?*

Sasha cannot remember how he ended up on the floor. *Where is my briefcase?* He struggles to his feet, panicking. "It's okay," Lace says calmly, pointing at his briefcase on the table. He feels his head, searching for bumps or bruises. Nothing. “You must have blacked out,” Lace tells him. “I caught you before you could hit your head on the corner of that desk.” Sasha tries shaking the cobwebs from his brain.

After a few minutes, Sasha is himself again. Embarrassed, but capable of carrying on. He sits down and pours himself a glass of water from a pitcher on the office table, drinking it down in big gulps. He cannot help noticing how unaffected Lace seems by the entire episode, almost as if it has happened before. *Jesus, who IS this woman?* He wonders.

Clearly, Lace is no amateur. Sasha remembers her file. He is aware of the many times she’d used her considerable assets to reduce even the most hardened Cold War spies to a series of puddles. *President Kennedy does not have a chance,* he thinks, pretending to busy himself. He opens the briefcase and begins reviewing his notes one more time. Lace sits quietly, waiting.

Finally, Sasha summons what remains of his dignity and begins the debriefing. “Item one is contact with the subject – has it been established yet?” He finds himself hoping it has not.

"Yes," she purrs softly. "MANY times since our introduction at the party." *Many times*, Sasha thinks, disappointed. *Of course. What man could resist this tasty treat? Shit.*

"Anything to report?" Sasha asks, trying desperately to resist his lust-filled thoughts.

Lace reaches for her purse and pulls out a small spiral notebook. "The President is a very sick man," she begins. "He is being treated for Addison's disease and hypothyroidism. Symptoms include fatigue, dizziness, muscle weakness, weight loss, difficulty standing up, sweating and nausea – and changes in mood and personality," she reads, pausing to look up at Sasha. "I've personally witnessed bouts of severe depression, which is another common symptom."

"This is very good," responds Sasha, somewhat taken aback by Lace's meticulousness. "Any medications?"

"A ton," Lace answers. "His dinner tray looks like a pharmaceutical buffet. This is a list," Lace pulls a small document from her notebook. "Do you want me to try to read them all to you?"

"Go ahead," says Sasha, nodding. *Anything to extend this little visit*, he thinks.

Slowly, Lace sounds out the names of the President's prescriptions. "Twice daily, he takes the following: hydrocortisone and prednisone, methyltestosterone, liothyronine, fludrocortisone, diphenoxylate hydrochloride, and atropine sulfate."

"What the hell?" Sasha asks incredulously. "Let me see," he says, reaching across the table.

"He even told me what some of the meds are for," Lace adds. "The Liothyronine is a synthetic thyroid hormone. It regulates his metabolism. Diphenoxylate treats chronic diarrhea, and the testosterone is supposed to help him gain weight. Believe me, he's a bag-of-bones."

"Christ, he sure doesn't LOOK sick," Sasha says, perplexed.

"Trust me, he doesn't ACT sick either," Lace agrees. "He's a tiger when he's had his meds..."

"...Okay, okay, I get it," Sasha interrupts, gesturing with his hand for her to stop. "God damn, I was actually starting to feel sorry for the man." Then he changes the subject. "In your contacts with the President, has he made any mention of Cuba?"

"Oh yes," she chuckles. It's ALL Cuba ALL the time it seems," Lace replies. "The President calls Cuba his 'never-ending Caribbean quagmire'."

"Because of the Bay of Pigs?" inquires Sasha, playing dumb.

"More than that. My sense is he feels obligated to PRETEND that he wants regime change in Havana, but if truth be known, he'd prefer to make nice with Castro," she says. "He's honest about it. More than once, he's admitted he owes favors to some powerful people who want Castro overthrown but he is tired of tiny little Cuba dominating America's foreign policy. He complains all the time that Cuba is the tail wagging the dog."

"That's interesting," Sasha says, surprised. "So his Cuba fixation isn't as real as it appears?"

"Not even close. He certainly won't ever go to war over Cuba," she says confidently.

"What about a COVERT war?" Sasha asks. "Anything about a counterinsurgency?"

Lace nods her head. "Yes. Bobby talks a lot about sabotage, crop-burnings, propaganda, you know –

small stuff. They call it Operation Mongoose," she adds.

"How about assassinating Castro?"

"Not in so many words," she replies. "But I HAVE heard him say the people he's in debt to want Castro out. Overthrowing Castro means killing Castro, no?"

"Probably," Sasha agrees. "Have either of them said anything about money and weapons flowing into the Cuban exile communities in Miami and New Orleans? Or training camps?" Sasha asks, hoping to corroborate Arrowhead's information.

"Yes, they both have," Lace nods. "He and Bobby want to shut all that down."

"SHUT IT DOWN?" Sasha questions her, unprepared for THAT answer. "Are you sure?"

Lace nods her head. "Yes sir," she says firmly. "The Administration doesn't trust the intelligence community. It has been using organized crime figures to do the dirty work instead. Bobby is scared to death the CIA will expose White House links to the mafia in retaliation. He might be right; the CIA hates Bobby AND Jack."

Sasha listens closely. Though he is baffled, he does not show it. "This has been helpful," he tells her after a brief pause. "I'll be in touch." Then he packs up his notes, careful to avoid looking at her, excuses himself and begins retracing his steps quickly.

As he walks, questions begin flooding his mind. Sasha is juxtaposing Arrowhead's reports with what Lace just told him. He wonders how to reconcile the contrasting intelligence. Because he does his best thinking aloud, he begins conversing with himself.

Which spy is right? Is Operation Mongoose for real...or is it just a half-hearted front designed by the Kennedy brothers to keep the anti-Castroites and Sam Giancana at bay? Are Bobby and Jack willing to expend any amount of time, money, effort, and manpower to overthrow Castro...or are they secretly trying to shut it all down? Does either Kennedy even give a shit about Cuba and Castro?

Sasha knows he has to choose wisely. The truth could prevent a war – or provoke one. Though Arrowhead has never been wrong before, his instincts tell him the Kennedy brothers are toying with the CIA, and since Arrowhead is Agency...*I am going with Lace,* Sasha decides, reaching for his car keys.

Chapter Eleven

***

Cosmic Chicken

Washington D.C.

October 25, 1962

"They have photos," Sandusky thunders, slamming the bookstore door shut behind him.

Sasha is sitting in his favorite armchair, almost hidden behind a tall counter stacked high with books. Most people might not even see him but Sandusky towers over the workspace, taking in everything. He leans over, resting his enormous frame on the counter.

"Of what exactly?" asks Sasha quietly, closing the report he was working on and looking up at Sandusky over his bifocals.

"Of our god-damn ballistic missile sites in Cuba!" roars Sandusky.

On October 14, an American U-2 pilot raced over

Cuban territory, taking almost one-thousand pictures and capturing images of an ICBM construction site in western Cuba. The CIA examined the images and identified the objects as medium and intermediate-range ballistic missiles. Only ninety miles from America, the offensive warheads could reach Portland, Oregon and Portland, Maine – the two farthest corners of the continental United States. Two days later, the CIA briefed the President.

The following week, he and his advisers searched for a way to communicate to the Soviets that the United States will not permit Soviet offensive missiles in the western hemisphere. The USSR, unaware that the Americans had photographic evidence, repeatedly lied, claiming there were no weapons of that kind in Cuba.

The President had a big decision to make. The military and intelligence communities wanted to invade Cuba and overthrow Castro, a Bay of Pigs do-over. The State Department recommended diplomatic pressure to force the Soviets to REMOVE the missiles. The Air Force favored limited air strikes against the bases to DESTROY the missiles. Meanwhile, Bobby argued for a blockade of Cuba by the US Navy to STOP the missiles from coming to the island. On October 22, eight days after the U-2 first captured the images, President Kennedy addressed the nation. He had made his decision.

Hardly a surprise, Jack went with Bobby's idea. He called it a "quarantine", a semantical trick so as not to offend the Soviets with the more-aggressive word "blockade". Critics panned the idea, saying a quarantine could not do anything about the missile sites nor would it destroy or remove the existing warheads but so far, Kennedy is holding fast. Yesterday, he received this letter of protest from Soviet Premier Nikita Khrushchev.

> *His Excellency,*
> *Mr. John F. Kennedy,*
> *President of the United States of America*
>
> *Mr. President, what if we were to present to you such an ultimatum as you have presented to us by your actions – how would you react? I think you would be outraged at such a move on our part. This we would understand.*
>
> *Having presented these conditions to us, Mr. President, you have thrown down the gauntlet. By what right have you done this? Our ties with the Republic of Cuba, as well as our relations*

with other nations, regardless of their political system, concern only the two countries between which these relations exist. If it were a matter of quarantine, only states agreeing between themselves may establish it, not some third party. Quarantines exist, for example, on agricultural goods and products. However, in this case, we are not talking about quarantines, but rather about much more serious matters, and you yourself understand this.

You Mr. President are not declaring a quarantine, but rather issuing an ultimatum, and you are threatening that if we do not obey your orders, you will then use force. Think about what you are saying! And you want to persuade me to agree to this!

What does it mean to agree to these demands? It would mean for us to conduct our relations with other countries not by reason, but by yielding to tyranny. You are not appealing to reason; you want to intimidate us.

No, Mr. President, I cannot agree to this, and I think that deep inside, you will admit that I am right. I am convinced that if you were in my place you would do the same.

This Organization of American States has no authority or grounds whatsoever to pass resolutions like those of which you speak. Therefore, we do not accept these resolutions. International law exists; generally accepted standards of conduct exist. We firmly adhere to the principles of international law and strictly observe the standards regulating navigation on the open sea, in international waters. We observe these standards and enjoy the rights recognized by all nations.

You want to force us to renounce the rights enjoyed by every sovereign state; you are attempting to legislate questions of international law; you are violating the generally accepted standards of this law. All this is due not only to hatred for the Cuban people and their government, but also for reasons having to do with the election campaign in the USA. What morals, what laws can justify such an approach by the American government to international affairs? Such morals and laws are not present, because the actions of the USA in relation to Cuba are outright piracy. This, if you will, is the madness of a degenerating imperialism. Unfortunately, people of all nations, and not least the American people themselves, could suffer heavily from madness such as this, since with the appearance of modern types of weapons, the USA has completely lost its former inaccessibility.

Therefore, Mr. President, if you weigh the present situation with a cool head without giving way to passion, you will understand that the Soviet Union cannot afford not to decline the despotic demands of the USA. When you lay conditions such as these before us, try to put yourself in our situation and consider how the USA would react to such conditions. I have no doubt that if anyone attempted to dictate similar conditions to you – the USA, you would reject such an attempt. We likewise say no.

The Soviet government considers the violation of the freedom of navigation in international waters and air space to constitute an act of aggression propelling humankind into the abyss of a world nuclear-missile war. Therefore, the Soviet government cannot instruct captains of Soviet ships bound for Cuba to observe orders of American naval forces blockading this island. Our instructions to Soviet sailors are to observe strictly the generally accepted standards of navigation in international waters and not retreat one-step from them. If the American side violates these rights, it must be aware of the responsibility it will bear for this act.

To be sure, we will not remain mere observers of pirate actions by American ships in the open sea. We will then be forced on our part to take those measures we deem necessary and sufficient to defend our rights. To this end, we have all that is necessary.

Respectfully,
N. Khrushchev

Clearly, the Soviet Premier is willing to play a dangerous game of cosmic chicken. What he does not know is the US President has something else up his sleeve. Today, the world will know what it is. The United States is requesting an emergency meeting of the UN Security Council to argue its case. International pressure has been mounting on the Americans over the last eleven days to provide evidence of a Soviet military buildup on Cuba.

Meanwhile, confident the Americans DO NOT have evidence, the Soviets are continuing to deny the presence of offensive weapons in Cuba. It appears to be a standoff. Except the Americans have one last card to play. A card the Soviets do not see coming.

Sasha stands slowly and removes his glasses. "Are you sure?" he asks, alarmed.

Sandusky straightens, crossing his massive arms. "Fuck yeah, I'm sure. There were easels set up in the White House Situation Room with about twenty black-and-whites. EXCOMM was looking at them."

"EXCOMM?" Sasha is unfamiliar with the term.

"It's JK and Bobby's dream-team," Sandusky replies. "The National Security Council plus four or five other dudes. It's called Executive Committee of the National Security Council, or EXCOMM for short."

"Can the photos be explained, in ANY reasonable way?" asks Sasha, aware of the impact the photographs would have if they appear publicly.

"You mean, 'these aren't missiles you see,' or 'those aren't Soviet soldiers building the missile silos' – cover shit like that?" Sandusky asks sarcastically, smirking.

"Something like that," Sasha nods, hopeful.

"NO FUCKING WAY." Sandusky has a way of slamming the door on Sasha's hopes. "The idiot that thought palm trees would be enough camouflage should be strung up," he declares. "The images show twelve ICBM sites protected by a perimeter of surface-to-air sites. I also counted forty ICBM launchers. That's enough pay-load to wipe half of the US right off the map..."

"...Perhaps they are DEFENSIVE warheads to protect Cuba from another US invasion," Sasha interjects, searching for a plausible explanation.

Sandusky laughs. "They'll call bull shit on that one," he says bluntly. "Bobby's been talking a lot about an inside source in Soviet Military Intelligence (GRU) that must be protected. His reports were the reason they ordered the U-2 pilot to take the photos to begin with. They ALREADY knew."

"Mother-of-god," Sasha says, aghast. "Photos AND a mole – sweet Jesus."

"This mole reported forty-thousand Soviet troops and a caravan of trucks carrying long, canvas-covered, cylindrical objects being transported through villages in western Cuba," Sandusky tells him. "These are the same objects in the photos. He also said the trucks had trouble making the narrow turns through towns. EXCOMM discussed it. They all agreed that defensive missiles are shorter and easy to maneuver. There's just no believable way to explain it all away."

"Gromyko will look like a fool if the photos do come out," Sasha realizes, recalling the Foreign Minister's repeated public denials that the Soviets were introducing offensive weapons in Cuba.

"WHEN the photos come out," Sandusky clarifies.

"Damn it!" exclaims Sasha, his face suddenly pale. "This information might be too late! The Security Council is meeting as we speak. How am I supposed to get word to Zorin?" He looks frantically at his watch. He gets up and hurries to his office.

Inside, Sasha fumbles with the old television on his desk. "Too fucking late," he says calmly. "Too fucking late," he repeats, shaking his head as the images come to life on the screen.

"What's he saying?" Sandusky asks, straining to hear the antique. The old set does not want to produce a clear picture. Finally, a distorted image of Valerian

Zorin, the Soviet Ambassador to the United Nations, begins coming to life. Sitting beside him is Anatoly Dobrynin, the Soviet Ambassador to the United States. Zorin is speaking in front of the UN Security Council.

"Anatoly has Zorin denying everything," Sasha replies. "He is telling the whole world there aren't any Soviet offensive missiles in Cuba."

"The company line," Sandusky says quietly. "Son-of-a-bitch, those cocksuckers set him up."

Sasha shakes his head, disagreeing. "No, they set us ALL up. Those photos – if they have them like you say, the whole god-damn world is about to see them."

***

Washington D.C.

October 26, 1962

They meet outside Smithsonian's Museum of Natural History on Constitution Avenue. As usual, Sasha arrives to find Arrowhead waiting for him, sitting on the front steps smoking a cigar. He checks his watch twice, looking annoyed as Sasha approaches.

After a quick greeting, they begin walking the loop around the US Capitol. The Chesapeake Bay region is always drop-dead gorgeous but late in the fall, it is a perfect Garden of Eden. With its number-one industry – the government – in full swing at this time of year, it usually packs with people. Students, tourists, politicians, lobbyists, and bureaucrats – all scurrying hither and thither. Not today. Not since the Missile Crisis began.

There is a pall over the capital city. A quiet soberness in the passing faces, reflecting a collective inner angst about the future of humanity. A potential nuclear holocaust hangs in the air.

Ever since the President announced the quarantine of Cuba, the whole world has been on edge, teetering on the brink with each televised confrontation in the Caribbean between the US Navy and Soviet freighters trying to reach Havana. This slow-motion dance with Armageddon is stressing everybody out.

After walking several blocks, Sasha breaks the silence. “So who is Kennedy listening to now?”

“Not us – thank God,” replies Arrowhead. “The Pentagon and CIA are still pushing for a full-scale invasion. Bomb the missile sites first and follow up with boots-on-the-ground. According to our people, this crisis is a gift from God. A second opportunity to do what we should have done the first time at Bay of Pigs. I DON'T think the President appreciates that sentiment very much," he adds, chuckling.

"A gift from God, huh? Jesus," Sasha says, shaking his head. "Are there any other alternatives EXCOMM is considering that won't get us all vaporized?"

"Yes," Arrowhead declares. "The State Department believes the quarantine IS working. It's kind of buying time for both sides, allowing for cooler heads to prevail," he explains.

"Which side does Bobby favor?" Sasha inquires, confident that Bobby is really the only one in the room that matters.

"He agrees with State," Arrowhead answers. "He also wants to set up a diplomatic backchannel and negotiate directly with Khrushchev. As you know, it is a matter of time before the President agrees with him. They're BOTH scared to death of a military confrontation."

"This negotiation you speak of – might there be the

possibility of a trade?" Sasha asks, hoping to sow the seeds of a deal.

"Hell yes there is," replies Arrowhead quickly. "Everything is on the table if it will prevent a war. Privately, I think the Kennedy's will give almost anything away to avoid conflict AND piss off the generals. But publicly, they need a win after the Bay of Pigs," Arrowhead says.

"What's the atmosphere inside the room?" asks Sasha.

"Pure, unadulterated hate," Arrowhead responds. "After Bay of Pigs, the CIA doesn't have ANY confidence in Jack or Bobby, and the White House certainly doesn't trust us. And the Pentagon, holy shit, military brass is furious with Kennedy for cutting so many of its bases and for backing down to the Soviets in Berlin."

"The bottom line is," he continues, "both the military and intelligence communities believe the President is soft on Communism. Both Kennedys think military and intelligence are hell-bent on nuclear war. It's toxic."

"Good," replies Sasha. "They're divided. We can exploit that."

***

Moscow, Russia

October 26, 1962

"Read it back to me," Premier Khrushchev orders his administrative assistant, removing his glasses and handing him the letter. He lights a cigar and leans back in his chair, listening to his own words.

"Dear Mr. President," the secretary begins solemnly.

> *Our purpose has been and is to help Cuba, and no one can challenge the humanity of our motives aimed at allowing Cuba to live peacefully and develop as its people desire. You want to relieve your country from danger and this is understandable. However, Cuba also wants this. All countries want to relieve your country from danger. But how can we, the Soviet Union and our government, assess your action, which, in effect, mean that you have surrounded the Soviet Union with military bases, surrounded our allies with military bases, set up military bases literally around our country, and stationed*

your rocket weapons at them? This is no secret. High-placed American officials demonstratively declare this. You station your rockets in Britain and in Italy – pointing them at us. You also station your rockets in Turkey.

You are worried over Cuba. You say that that it worries your because it lies at a distance of ninety miles across the sea from the shores of the United States. However, Turkey lies next to us. Our sentinels are pacing up and down and watching each other. Do you believe that you have the right to demand security for your country and the removal of such weapons that you qualify as offensive, while not recognizing this same right for us?

You have stationed devastating rocket weapons, which you call offensive, in Turkey literally right next to us. How does recognition of your equal military possibilities tally with such unequal relations between our great states? This does not tally at all.

Respectfully,
Nikita Khrushchev,
Premier, USSR

The assistant, finished reading looks up. "Do you require any changes, sir?"

"Nyet!" the Premier barks. "What I have written, I have written."

***

Moscow, Russia

October 27, 1962

"Never let a good crisis go to waste," Father advises Khrushchev.

"Words easily spoken," the Premier sighs, unimpressed. "If this crisis gets any more out of hand, we'll all be finished."

"Sir," Father begins, slightly chastened. "What have we observed in this President so far?" Khrushchev shrugs, less interested in psychoanalysis than he is a solution to his problem.

"He backs down," Father declares. "If we learned anything from Bay of Pigs, Kennedy will cut-and-run at the first sign of trouble. He let us build a wall in

Berlin for Christ's sake! I think he will do anything NOT to fight. He just doesn't have the heart for it."

"But his advisers aren't quite so dovish," the Premier argues.

"It's true," Father agrees. "His military and intelligence brass ARE advising another invasion to make up for their first failure, I imagine. However, the President is not listening to them. Since Bay of Pigs, he does not trust them. In fact, he will do the exact OPPOSITE what they tell him. Fighting goes against Kennedy family instincts. Their instincts are always to back down."

Khrushchev chuckles. "So the Kennedy's are too weak to stand up to US but too strong to give in to THEM?"

"I didn't say it makes any sense," Father says, acknowledging the dichotomy.

"Lace is reporting that Kennedy is shutting down Operation Mongoose," Father tells him. "Sir, he won't even fight a COVERT war. What are the odds he will fight an OVERT one? Lace also said we are dealing with a sick man, doped up on god-knows-what. He is not in his right mind. This is a strategic opportunity for us if we press him. He is too weak to push back.

He does not have the will OR the energy for a fight."

"I agree with you up to a point," The Premier responds. "Any negotiation must BEGIN with our missiles for theirs in Turkey – an even swap. That would be a victory for BOTH sides, no? I could press for more then, maybe a promise from the Americans never to invade Cuba again – victory for US, no?" Khrushchev pauses, measuring his words. "But if I press TOO hard and fail – is that not a victory for the devil? We'll ALL be in hell then."

Now it is Father's turn to sigh, relieved that Khrushchev appreciates the opportunity before him. "Bay of Pigs almost ruined the Kennedy Presidency before it started," he says. "Kennedy NEEDS a victory. You can give him that and still win." Khrushchev nods, thinking.

"If we agree to remove our missiles, dismantle the sites, and broadcast the images around the world, he gets his victory – publicly," Premier Khrushchev proposes. "In exchange, we expect a guarantee that they will remove their missiles from Turkey. Moreover, the Americans promise no more invasions of Cuba. We get our victories...privately."

"A two-for-one," Father calculates, smiling. "Would we not gladly take that deal every time?"

Premier Khrushchev jumps to his feet and walks briskly toward the exit. He stops at the door, turns his head, and looks back at Father. "Goddammit!" he exclaims. "What are you waiting for? Start the back channel! Make the offer!"

***

Washington D.C.

October 28, 1962

Thanks to Soviet intelligence, the crisis is over.

Opposing reports from two of his best agents forced Sasha to choose between them. He chose wisely. His reports convinced Father the Soviets would win a confrontation with the Americans. Father's counsel to Premier Khrushchev proved decisive in the end. The system worked.

When pushed to the brink in Cuba – again – the Kennedy brothers folded – again – like cheap suits. The American President got his much-needed PUBLIC victory. More importantly, the Soviet Premier achieved a two-for-one deal for the USSR, which reveled in its victories PRIVATELY.

"JK and Bobby are on top of the fucking world," laughs Sandusky, entering the office in Sasha's bookstore, eclipsing the open doorway with his huge frame.

"It's the way America works," Sasha explains, cleaning his glasses. "While we are trying to win a war, Kennedy and his brother are worrying about winning the next press conference."

"Americans like to brag about freedom of the press," Sandusky complains. "But the US media is no different than ours. It regurgitates the government cover story without questioning it. There is no expectation of Pravda. It has no amendment protecting it. Everybody knows it is under the control of the Party. On the other hand, the American press DOES have constitutional protection. It is one thing to be the government's bitch when you have to be. It is another when you don't. The Americans waste their freedom. They don't deserve their precious first amendment."

"You've been watching American TV, no?" Sasha asks, detecting his frustration.

Sandusky nods. "Watching, reading, listening – it's the same damn story over and over." He clears his throat, imitating Walter Cronkite. "'President Kennedy stared down the barrel of a loaded gun, backed Premier Khrushchev into a corner, and caused the panicked Soviet leader to blink!' Ha! That is what the foolish Americans think!"

Sasha chuckles. "Let the Americans celebrate – they don't know what they don't know. This is only Kennedy's second year in office. Look at what we have accomplished in two years! We have backed him down in Cuba twice and Berlin once. With a little bit of luck, he will win re-election in '64 and we will make America OUR bitch for the next six years. Maybe we should start calling him 'Premier Kennedy' because he is the best friend we've got!"

"Jesus, we better hope he survives," Sandusky warns ominously. "He's made enemies, LETHAL enemies, and LOTS of them in two short years. Wait until the anti-Castroite Cuban exiles down in South Florida and Louisiana find out he promised never to invade Cuba again. Son-of-a-bitch, he'd better stay out of Miami and New Orleans. Those people are god-damn fanatics."

"Don't forget the mafia," Sasha adds. "It got him elected on a promise he'd re-open Cuba for business."

"Those wops don't like being double-crossed," Sandusky agrees.

"Not just once, TWICE!" Sasha says, amazed. "The deal was Kennedy would eliminate Castro AND stop government harassment of all the crime families. That is why they named Bobby the Attorney General. It was HIS job! Instead, he can't prosecute them fast enough..."

"...I heard he had Carlos Marcello deported to Guatemala in '61," Sandusky interjects, "almost right after the election was over. Customs agents swooped in and picked him up, put him on a plane and flew him out of the damn country. He had no clothes, no money, no warning."

"He might be able to stab some people in the back and get away with it," Sasha replies. "But NOT the Sicilians. If they didn't invent the vendetta, they sure perfected it."

"You can put the Pentagon and CIA on the list of Kennedy-haters too," Sandusky adds. "Damn, watch your back, Jack!"

***

Chapter Twelve

***

New Orleans Intrigue

Washington D.C.

April 25, 1963

"The file," Sasha says, handing a folder thick with documents to the new guy. "You will need to catch up with the rest of the team today in New Orleans. Your plane ticket," he adds, giving him a sealed envelope. "The meet time and location is enclosed."

Sasha points at the folder. "Anna and Yuri's reports are included along with Father's analysis. Marina is reporting the subject left Ft. Worth for New Orleans yesterday afternoon. According to his cover story, he is looking for work. We know he's not LOOKING for work – he IS working." Sasha pauses, watching the most recent addition to his team.

"The subject being assigned to New Orleans is not a coincidence," he continues. "We've been watching New Orleans become a rats' nest of US intelligence black-ops recently. Something is brewing down there – that's why Moscow sent you here," he adds.

The "new guy" is KGB agent Anatoly Kournikova – codenamed "Andy Katz".

Surveillance is Andy's specialty. According to Father, he is the best. In fact, the KGB only assigns him its most important cases. In over twenty years of tracking, he has never once blown his cover.

A quick look and Sasha understands why. He has no distinguishing physical characteristics. He has a face seemingly without features. His height and weight are average. His hair color is brown, medium length – not too short, not too long. Though he is presently clean-shaven, he could easily carry off facial hair. His clothes are dull and nondescript. Even his voice is unremarkable. Andy is a person that is easy to forget, or more importantly, hard to remember.

New Orleans is rapidly becoming the nerve center of American intelligence activity. Operation Mongoose, the Medical Manhattan Project, Carlos Marcello and his crime family, and now Mr. Oswald. "We need an asset in New Orleans whose only job is to follow him," Sasha indicated to Father in an earlier message marked "URGENT." Andy Katz is Father's choice for the job.

Andy takes the file and asks, “The team?”

Sasha clears his throat. “We’ve pulled assets from all over. Marcos and Felix have been in the Cuban exile communities of South Florida infiltrating the anti-Castroite movement. The contact they made in Miami is now in New Orleans working with Operation Mongoose, so they are following the action north.”

“We embedded Big Russ in Giancana’s Chicago outfit to learn the White House connections to the mob,” continues Sasha. “Instead, we discovered a bunch of pissed-off gangsters plotting to kill the President. When the plot moved south to New Orleans, Big Russ followed it. Now he finds himself neck-deep in a ring of cancer research doctors.”

“How is organized crime in Chicago involved with medical doctors in New Orleans?” Andy asks, perplexed. “And what does a plot to kill the President have to do with cancer research?”

“Good questions, both,” Sasha responds. “That’s what WE’RE going to find out.”

“Any others?” Andy inquires.

"Billy is already there," Sasha says. "He's our inside-guy in the Marcello crime family. Marina is still in Ft. Worth playing her domestic role but she will be with us in New Orleans by the end of summer. Steven is working the field office by himself right now. You will not see him; he will be too busy helping me with research. All of these operatives," Sasha acknowledges, "might seem like overkill but we're talking about the CIA, organized crime, a cancer research team, and a whole bunch of loose ends we think are acting under the umbrella of a single covert action operating out of New Orleans."

"Single covert action," Andy repeats thoughtfully. "And if I understand correctly, we're hoping Mr. Oswald is the single common denominator," he says, detecting Sasha's game plan.

"Exactly," Sasha confirms, escorting his new recruit to the front door of the bookstore. "That's where you come in. Instead of us chasing our tails, you will follow him. We're pretty confident Mr. Oswald will solve the New Orleans riddle FOR us."

***

New Orleans

April 26, 1963

One-by-one, the team is assembling inside the oversized and poorly lit conference room in the rear of the Crescent City Travel Agency – a front for Sasha's New Orleans headquarters. There is a rectangular table in the middle of the space, surrounded by brown metal office chairs. A map of the continental United States hangs on one wall. Next to the doorway, a pushcart with dirty coffee cups and an unopened container of decaffeinated coffee sits abandoned.

Though the morning rush-hour traffic finished several hours ago, Canal Street is still hustling. In many ways, it is New Orleans' societal Line of Demarcation.

North of Canal lie the hoity-toity neighborhoods of both Garden Districts and the distinguished University District. South of Canal resides the decrepit Lower Ninth Ward and the filthy, touristy French Quarter. The streets, too, are segregated – street signs indicating "uptown" names in the north and "downtown" designations in the south. The Crescent City Travel Agency is downtown in the Central Business District, very much the low-rent part of town. After the last arrival, Sasha begins handing out assignments.

“Marcos and Felix are assigned to the Cubans,” Sasha begins, looking up from his notes at the assemblage in front of him. “Big Russ will stay with the doctors. Billy is working Marcello and the mob. Steven will help me with subject research and Andy will be with Mr. Oswald.” He removes his glasses, wiping them with his shirtsleeve. “Andy, you will need to coordinate with Marina throughout. You can do that through me. We will probably have to reassign once we know all of the key players and their roles,” he explains. “Be flexible. It looks like we are all going in different directions at the beginning. But we believe this operation will land us in the same place.” There are nods all around. His “troops” say nothing. They have their marching orders.

“Here’s what we know,” Sasha says, standing up and walking over to the US map. “Operation Mongoose has moved north. The epicenter of all covert-ops in Cuba is New Orleans instead of Miami now. It is the NEW ground zero.” Using his left hand, he places his thumb on Miami and his ring finger on New Orleans, pointing out the most notorious hotbeds of anti-Castro activities. “There’s more,” Sasha turns, looking at his agents. “Reportedly, New Orleans is also the home of a top-secret medical research project run by the CIA.

Sources are telling me that the goal is to weaponize cancer by converting cancerous cells into a bio-weapon. I shouldn't have to tell you the advantage this would give the Americans in covert operations." He pauses. "They call this their 'MEDICAL Manhattan Project.' It's THAT big."

"Might Operation Mongoose and Medical Manhattan be two heads of the same coin?" Big Russ blurts out suddenly, suspicious. "I mean, if the CIA is running two covert operations in the same city at the same time..."

"...They MIGHT indeed," Sasha interjects, agreeing with Big Russ.

***

New Orleans, Louisiana

May 21, 1963

"They must have more than one lab," Big Russ thunders, slamming the heavy wooden door of the travel agency loudly behind him.

Russell Pratt – codenamed "Russ (or, Big Russ) Prater" – was born in Ireland. After the Great War, his family migrated to America, settling in the Central Ward of Newark, New Jersey. The Pratts were lucky. The International Longshoreman's Association (ILA) hired Russell's father to be a worker on the container shipping docks of Port Newark. From then on, he had one of his feet planted firmly in organized labor and the other in organized crime.

After high school, Russell joined his father on the docks, hiring on as a dockworker and taking to the life enthusiastically. Because of his prodigious size, it seemed he was destined to become a union enforcer, mafia wise guy, or both. Then in 1949, his life took a curious left turn.

In an effort to infiltrate the ILA with pro-communist agents, the KGB managed to recruit young Russell. It was not that big of a leap for him. His union upbringing had instilled principles such as solidarity and collectivism in him from a young age. Socialism was right in his wheelhouse. Besides, the money was just too good to pass up.

Because of Big Russ's experience – his savviness in negotiating the shadowy realm of organized crime – the Soviets were understandably delighted to have found themselves a cunning twofer. Since that time, Big

Russ has proved to be one of the KGB's most reliable sets of eyes and ears in Big Labor AND organized crime.

In Chicago, he uncovered a mafia plot to kill President Kennedy. When Giancana's family joined forces with Carlos Marcello's, Sasha ordered him south to the Gulf Coast. He was not there a week before uncovering another layer of the conspiracy, one that involves medical doctors and cancer research.

Now his assignment is Dr. Mary Sherman and Big Russ is clearly frustrated. In the world of labor thugs and made-men, he has become accustomed to simple, one-dimensional subjects. He is used to uncomplicated plots. This is obviously a completely different set of encyclopedias.

Dr. Sherman is clearly NOT the conspirator behind Medical Manhattan. More like the intermediary in a highly compartmentalized operation – the doctor is the BRAIN the conspiracy needs for it to work. Somebody is using her. Sasha jumps up and motions for Big Russ to follow him to the back.

"Now. Why do you say that?" Sasha asks quietly, closing the conference room door carefully behind him.

"Because I see two Cubans delivering samples to Dr. Sherman's apartment," Big Russ blusters. "She takes the samples to work with her and roasts the material at the lab. When she finishes, she repacks it and returns home. The same two Cubans reappear, make the pick-up and leave MORE samples. They NEVER leave Dr. Sherman's place empty-handed," Big Russ says, shaking his head. "That stuff is going SOMEWHERE!"

"Hold it. What do you mean, 'she roasts it'?" asks Sasha, a puzzled look on his face.

"She zaps the samples with a high-powered linear particle accelerator," Big Russ replies.

"Back up a second," Sasha tells him, "What did you say? A linear WHAT...?"

"...A linear particle accelerator," Big Russ bellows, interrupting Sasha. "It's like a laser. A high-powered radiation beam they use to aim at a target, in this case Dr. Sherman's samples."

Sasha says nothing, remembering a conversation with Arrowhead a year ago about the CIA using radiation to create galloping cancer cells.

"Hospitals use accelerators for x-rays and radiation

treatments all the time," Big Russ says, not paying attention to Sasha's far-away stare. "But this is no ordinary accelerator. There are only a few this size in the whole world. Hell, it is bigger than a goddamn silo. My sources inside Entergy Louisiana says it requires five million volts of electricity."

"Seems like that would attract attention..." observes Sasha.

"...Oh, they don't want anyone to know about it," Big Russ interjects. "It's hidden away behind security gates and armed guards at the Infectious Disease Laboratory on the grounds of the US Public Health Service Hospital."

"So they don't want anyone to know it's there or what it's being used for," Sasha concludes before asking, "What in god's name is she's roasting?"

"I don't know...YET," replies Big Russ, shrugging.

"But the samples originate somewhere else and NOT with Dr. Sherman?" Sasha asks, making mental notes about the chronological pattern.

"Right. The material comes to her from the other labs," Big Russ confirms. "Then she returns it to the other labs after she's poisoned it with radiation."

"We've GOT to find those other labs," Sasha declares, a sense of urgency in his voice.

"Just follow the Cubans," Big Russ barks.

***

New Orleans

May 23, 1963

"The photos of 531 Lafayette Street, The Newman Building," Marcos explains, as Felix, his long-time partner and friend, hands Sasha a large envelope. "That address IS Mongoose," he adds, pointing at the location indicated on the front of the envelope.

"Walk two blocks in any direction from that building and you'll be at the FBI, CIA, and Office of Naval Intelligence (ONI)," declares Felix. "531 Lafayette Street is in the middle of the entire US intelligence community."

Carlos Huerta – codenamed "Marcos Rodriguez" – and Fernando Garcia – codenamed "Felix Lopez" – are by-products of Castro's 26th of July Movement. When the Cuban Revolution began in 1953, Huerta and Garcia were two of Castro's most trusted right hands.

In 1959, once the rebels had ousted US-backed Cuban dictator Fulgencio Batista, thousands of Cuban refugees fled to America. These “first wave” immigrants were aristocratic, former elites of Cuban society. Proprietors of sugar plantations and mills, executives of top firms, merchants, cattlemen, business professionals, foreign company reps, and crime bosses were forced to flee Cuba when Castro began overturning the old social order and nationalizing American industries. It was evident Castro's declaration “Cuba is for Cubans!” did NOT include them.

Calling themselves “those who wait,” the aristocratic refugees hoped their exile would be brief. Their faith was in the United States helping them overthrow Fidel Castro. That faith crashed when Bay of Pigs happened.

After the disastrous invasion, the exodus from Cuba nearly doubled. “Second wave” exiles were different though. Radicalized by the Bay of Pigs debacle, they were not waiting around for others to help them anymore. Calling themselves “those who escape,” they came to America with only one purpose – to build their OWN army and overthrow Castro's government themselves. Back in Cuba, Castro called these counterrevolutionaries “gusanos,” or worms.

Not all of them were worms. Castro sent some of them as pseudo-refugees to infiltrate the ever-growing anti-Castroite population in South Florida. Huerta and Garcia were among the posers sent to pretend to be Cuban exiles while acting as informants for the Cuban dictator.

When Cuba and the USSR became blood brothers in 1961, Castro's Intelligence Directorate and the KGB joined forces to safeguard the island. Ever since, "Marcos" and "Felix" have worked for Sasha as his eyes and ears in the Cuban exile communities of Miami and New Orleans.

Sasha opens the envelope and lays out the black-and-white photographs on the conference-room table.

"Okay, so we've established 531 Lafayette as the perfect location for Mongoose headquarters. How do we know that it IS Mongoose headquarters?" Sasha quizzes them.

"Because the Cubans led us right to it," Felix responds, chuckling. "The Newman Building might look like a shithole," he says, pointing at the pictures, "but it's a busy little shithole. The people coming and going out of that place all day and night – shady characters, all of them. It CAN NOT just be a coincidence."

"It IS Mongoose's New Orleans command center," Marcos agrees, nodding his head.

"Who's running the show?" asks Sasha, moving on.

"Former FBI agent, Guy Bannister," replies Marcos. "Big-time connected guy – Agency, mob, and the Cubans. Bannister ran weapons for Bay of Pigs and is supplying Mongoose now. He is also in charge of the Cuban Revolutionary Council and the Crusade to Free Cuba Committee, both anti-Castro organizations. He gets his money from a local socialite named Clay Shaw. Shaw does not come around very much but when he does, Bannister rolls out the red carpet for him."

"Good," Sasha says. "The Cubans served their purpose. Now we know Bannister IS Mongoose. If we stay with him, HE WILL lead us through the whole operation. Those shady characters – do you have any information on them yet?" Sasha inquires.

"Just a few names so far," Marcos replies. "We're compiling a list. David Ferrie appears to be one of Bannister's main lieutenants. Brass balls, that one. He doesn't try to hide the weapons – parks the truck on the damn curb and starts carrying the crates inside."

"What about Oswald?" Sasha asks, impatient.

"I was just coming to that," Felix informs him. "If you see Ferrie, you see Oswald and visa-versa. He comes and goes with Ferrie all day long. It appears that he works FOR Ferrie."

"And they ALL work for the CIA..." Marcos adds.

"...Of course they do," Sasha responds quickly, chuckling. Finished with their report, Felix and Marcos lean back in their chairs, waiting for Sasha to dismiss them.

"Let's see if I have this right," Sasha says, reading his notes. "Mr. Oswald receives a discharge from the Marines and defects to the USSR. While he's there, he gives us classified U-2 material, TRIES to renounce his American citizenship and marries a Russian woman. Now he works side-by-side with Anti-Communist agitators Guy Bannister and David Ferrie?"

"It looks that way..." Felix tells him. Marcos nods.

"...Jesus," Sasha says, interrupting. "The CIA is putting that poor fool together like a dummy corporation."

***

New Orleans

May 25, 1963

Andy boards Magazine Street bus eleven on the thirty-nine hundred block, taking his seat near the back. One stop later, the pretty young lady boards. Andy guesses her age to be eighteen or nineteen. She takes her usual window seat near the front, leaving enough room for him. At the forty-nine hundred block, Mr. Oswald hops aboard and sits next to her.

At first, they were discreet, choosing seats across from one another and conversing lightly. The two friends were just sharing a ride together on their way to work. It was all very casual.

After a few weeks, things heated up. Sitting together, they started acting more suggestively – talking, laughing, and flirting openly with each other. Lately, Andy has even noticed her holding his hand and Oswald adding a good-morning kiss to his repertoire.

This morning, they cannot keep their hands off each other. The bus takes them downtown to the job they also share at the Reily Coffee Company. Andy watches them get off the bus separately and mix with the other workers as they enter the building – separately. Andy knows subterfuge when he sees it.

As entertaining as the bus rides are, Andy knows it is what is happening DURING and AFTER the workday – those are the keys to unlocking the secret that is Oswald. It began on his first surveillance, almost four weeks ago...

An hour after they enter Reily Coffee to begin their shifts, Andy observes a man walking briskly away from Reily toward Lafayette Square. He is not sure why – perhaps boredom – but something makes him take a second look. Even though he can only see the back of the man, he looks a lot like Oswald. Intrigued, Andy decides to follow him. He looks back at Reily, hoping he is not making a mistake by abandoning his post.

Andy has to speed up to keep contact with the fast-moving target. He sees the man turn ahead onto Camp Street and enter a building. Andy continues walking past the building. He notes the address – 544 Camp Street. Centered above the entryway is the engraving "The Newman Building".

Once inside, the man begins taping flyers to the front

windows. Andy positions himself in a bus stop shelter across the street, pretending not to watch the activity. The sun's glare on the glass is making it impossible for him to see the man's face clearly, frustrating him.

A half-hour later, the man exits the building and staples a couple flyers to the corner telephone pole. When he is finished, he turns to re-enter the building. For the first time, Andy can now see the man's face and make a positive identification. It IS Oswald!

Satisfied with his work, Oswald again disappears inside The Newman Building. Andy would very much like to see what the flyer says but he cannot get too close and risk blowing his cover. So the reconnaissance continues from a safe distance instead.

An hour passes without any activity at the Camp Street address. In the meantime, Andy notices the side entrance on the Lafayette Street side of the building. He cannot HELP noticing the traffic. People are coming and going nonstop. To pass time, he watches the parade of peculiar people.

Mostly Cubans, he thinks. *I wonder what...* Andy stops himself mid-sentence as the door swings open and three men exit the building onto the sidewalk. One of them is Oswald. The other two he does not recognize. One is much older than Oswald and his partner. It seems the older one is their ringleader. He carries himself with an air of authority, like someone used to giving orders, not receiving them.

The other figure is a small, strange looking man. He gestures wildly as he talks. *Is that David Ferrie?* Andy wonders.

The three men stroll back to the corner and turn onto Camp Street. They begin pointing at the flyers hanging in the windows of the 544 Camp Street address, laughing. They are close enough that Andy can hear the little one saying something about "those dumb-ass cocksuckers." Then, the boisterous little mob turns and walks away together, still cursing and laughing.

Andy waits until he is sure they are gone before crossing the street to examine the flyers. They read, "FAIR PLAY FOR CUBA COMMITTEE." The pro-Castro recruiting posters list a "Lee Oswald" as the contact person. Andy notes the "544 CAMP STREET" address stamped at the bottom. He eases around the corner and checks out the listing on the 531 Lafayette Street entrance. It says, "GUY BANNISTER – PRIVATE INVESTIGATOR."

So the older one WAS Bannister, Andy says to himself, assembling the puzzle pieces in his mind. *Two entrances, one building*, he thinks, suspicious. *Must be an inside hallway that connects the two*, he guesses. *If Bannister's building IS Mongoose headquarters in New Orleans – the operation to get rid of Castro – why is Oswald leafletting pro-Castro literature from it as well?*

Ever mindful of blowing his cover, Andy continues walking past the Newman Building, retracing his steps back to his original post outside Reily Coffee.

His mind races with unanswered questions. *Oswald's entrance to The Newman Building is pro-Castro; Bannister's is anti-Castro. That is like having the CIA and the KGB share the same office space. If they are on different sides, why are they walking down the street together like best of friends? ARE they on different sides? If not, which one is pretending?*

Before resuming his surveillance, Andy cases the perimeter of the Reily Coffee Co. building and finds a partially hidden back entry that leads to an alley. He guesses this to be how Oswald had escaped unobserved from the building earlier in the day.

Sure enough, in the weeks to follow, Oswald slips out of Reily nearly every day, exiting through the back door and sneaking down the alley. The Newman Building is only a three-block walk to Lafayette Street and around the corner to Camp Street. Interestingly, Andy notices that Oswald always enters The Newman Building in the front – Camp St. – and exits on the side – Lafayette St. On each of these little day trips, Oswald lets himself in through the hidden door before his shift ends at Reily, just in time to clock out for the day.

The obvious questions in Andy's mind are – *how is Oswald able to leave work every day without any consequence? Does his supervisor know of his walkabouts? What kind of job is this?*

In the afternoons after work, Oswald and the young lady follow a much different pattern. Four days a week, they board the Magazine Street bus eleven again and backtrack. However, passing their usual stops they continue to the sixty-four hundred block where Audubon Park is located. The next few hours are spent doing what young lovers do, publicly anyway.

They hold hands and go for long walks, always speaking in fluent Russian, or they just sit in the grass and read to each other. Judging by the time they spend doing it, Andy guesses reading to be their favorite pastime. Sometimes, they join the children in a local tradition by rolling down Monkey Hill and ending up in each other's arms at the bottom.

When the frivolity ends, the same bus takes them back to their same morning stops. Oswald is the first to get off, followed by the young lady nine blocks later. For those four days, the starry-eyed twosome lives the dream – not realizing someone is always nearby, watching and listening to them.

The other three days, however, they follow a much different itinerary.

Instead of leaving work together, they depart separately, taking different buses. The first time this happened, Andy stayed with Oswald, who boarded first. The bus took them out of the city, heading east toward the suburbs. Oswald got off on Louisiana Avenue and began walking.

Andy waited two more stops, getting off just in time to see Oswald disappear behind an olive-green, Mediterranean-style house. Andy noted the address, 3330 Louisiana Avenue.

A few minutes later, Andy was startled to see Oswald's young lover making her way toward the same house.

Though it had a front entrance, she too made her way around back to the rear entry. Andy thought to himself as he walked, *Is this a love nest...if so, why all the countermeasures?*

The next day, the young lovers were back at Audubon Park. This pattern has continued, one day at the park, the next day in the suburbs. In the meantime, Andy has been doing some research.

He has learned that a Mr. William Reily owns the Reily Coffee Company. Coincidentally, Mr. Reily is a known financial backer of Guy Bannister's Crusade to Free Cuba Committee AND the Cuban Revolutionary Council. The groups and Bannister are notoriously anti-Castro. Evidently, so is Reily. More intriguing – Andy has also learned that Oswald's supervisor at Reily Coffee is ex-FBI agent Bill Monaghan.

He dug and found out that the house on 3330 Louisiana Avenue is actually an apartment leased to David Ferrie, Guy Bannister's right-hand man. After seeing his picture, Andy is positive Ferrie is the man he saw on the sidewalk in front of The Newman Building with Oswald and Bannister.

Oswald has definitely mixed up with an anti-Castro crowd, thinks Andy. *Most likely Mongoose, but what about the pro-Castro poster with his name on it? What about the girl? How does she fit in? Is she just an innocent girlfriend?* He knows he has to find out what is going on inside that damn apartment.

Andy plans today's stakeout around the pattern he has observed. This time, he uses a car to follow the bus. Before Oswald's stop, Andy finds a place to park about a block away and settles in. Within minutes, he is watching the same routine unfold.

First, Oswald gets off the bus and disappears around the back of the house. Then his girl arrives and does likewise. Andy waits, unsure of what to do next.

While he's thinking about his next move, the strange-looking little man Andy saw several weeks before outside The Newman Building makes a sidewalk appearance of his own, creating quite a spectacle.

He is a dwarfishly small fellow with cartoon-like facial features. He does not walk as much as he darts, speeding up and slowing down, weaving in-and-out. He keeps looking around him, as if he is worried about someone following him – or watching him. He is plainly a nervous wreck.

Andy was right – *it IS the notorious David Ferrie*, Andy

says to himself, laughing. Suddenly, Ferrie zigzags his way around to the backside of his house and enters through the backdoor. *He is even uglier in person,* Andy thinks. *I did not think that was possible.*

Just then, Oswald reappears on the back steps carrying a small package. His head jerks when he hears a sharp whistle. Andy does not look but he knows the signal came from the sidewalk by his car. At that moment, two poorly dressed Cuban men carrying large, covered containers pass by, walking briskly in Oswald's direction. Andy watches Oswald nod in their direction and sit on the steps, waiting for the two Cubans.

When they arrive, the two Cubans place their containers on the ground near the back steps and Oswald hands them his package. After the quick exchange, they turn and leave, heading back in the same direction they came. As they near Andy again, he suddenly becomes interested in the newspaper. After they pass, he takes a quick peek over the paper at Ferrie's apartment. It is too late – both containers and Oswald are gone.

Andy lowers his newspaper and uses his mirrors to watch the Cubans crossing the street behind him. He is surprised when he sees them enter the house almost directly across from where he parked. Andy makes a note of the address – 3225 Louisiana Avenue.

Driving away, Andy is wondering – *what is going on inside those two houses – one block apart – on the same street? What was in Oswald's package? What were the Cubans carrying?*

An hour later, he is in the Crescent City Travel Agency's conference room making a full report to Sasha. After the scribbling stops, Sasha examines his notes again, putting pieces together.

"Reily Coffee is obviously a cover job. His time card provides him an alibi while he's attending to his real job," he concludes. "The pro-Castro leaflets are cover too. The CIA is prepping Oswald – for what I do not know yet. It is profiling him now as a Communist for a future mission. My guess is there will be a public spectacle soon to draw attention to that fact."

"Public spectacle?" Andy asks, "...something contrived perhaps?"

"Something that will attract a lot of attention..." Sasha replies, "...and will create a media event or generate a police report. Clearly, they're sheep-dipping him."

Andy wonders aloud, "For what?"

Sasha shrugs his shoulders. "I don't know…yet."

"The good news is you may have just found the other labs," Sasha reasons aloud. "Big Russ said to follow two Cubans…" He pauses in mid-sentence. "…I sure want to know what's in those containers," he says, finally finishing his thought.

"And Oswald's package," Andy adds.

"Yes." Sasha agrees. "Absolutely."

"I wonder how this all connects to the cancer bio-weapon project?" he asks. "We know the two Cubans definitely link the two labs, Oswald, and Ferrie to Dr. Sherman. We know the doctor is working the bio-weapon, which means somehow, Oswald and Ferrie are too. What the hell?"

"And don't forget Oswald's girlfriend," Andy reminds him.

***

New Orleans

June 6, 1963

The 500 Club is hopping tonight. Nude dancers are trying their best, putting everything out there on stage, recruiting customers in the lobby, flirting with the patrons at the bar, and servicing the high-paying clientele waiting in the back. The bartenders are busy, as usual. The customers, mostly men and rowdy, are here thirsting after wine and women. Everybody is in a festive mood and the cash is flowing like lava. It is always this way when "Big Daddy" is in the house.

He is hard to miss, arriving with his colorful entourage of bodyguards, women, and some of the lucky associates he has chosen to honor with his presence for the night. He sits at his favorite table – closest to the stage – the best seats in the house. Big Daddy loves his ladies.

Everybody at the 500 Club kicks it into a higher gear when Big Daddy arrives. The dancers shake it harder, the servers are friendlier, and the bartenders work faster. Why not? It is HIS club.

Big Daddy is Carlos Marcello, nicknamed the "Big Daddy of the Big Easy." Estimates are his criminal empire is worth hundreds of millions of dollars – nobody really knows for sure. Big Daddy runs all the gambling rackets in Louisiana and skims profits from the legitimate gaming casinos in Las Vegas, the far-away high-stakes mecca of odds making. He is not a man to trifle with.

High-powered and big-moneyed interests from Washington D.C. to Los Angeles offer Big Daddy and his outfit millions of dollars to provide the "muscle" needed to consummate their lucrative business deals. Naturally, no deal is complete without the obligatory kickback to Big Daddy.

Billy Kyle is some of that Big Daddy muscle. Billy's quirky habit of repeating everything he says has earned him a Marcello-family nickname, "Two-Times." Like most wise guys, he started with a crew, distinguishing himself for his fighting skills and, more importantly, a willingness to use those skills. It did not take him long to climb the ranks.

Opportunities for advancement happen all the time in his line of work. People die, go to prison, disappear – the possibilities are endless. Each time opportunity knocked on his door, Two-Times took advantage. He is now Big Daddy's main bodyguard. Marcello does not go anywhere unless Two Times is by his side. Unbeknownst to Big Daddy, Two-Times is NOT Billy Kyle. His real name is Boris Konnikov. "Billy Kyle" is his KGB codename.

In 1959, the Soviets learned about the special relationship between the Kennedy family and the mafia, particularly Sam Giancana and the Chicago crime family. Immediately, the KGB infiltrated the three major syndicates to gain an advantage with America's new President. Soviet agents fanned out in three regions – Chicago, New Orleans, and Florida – and penetrated Sam Giancana's, Carlos Marcello's, and Santos Trafficante's families.

What they found was a triangular treaty of money and blood that started in Washington DC and included Big Labor and organized crime. Each of these interests had a common goal – to kill Fidel Castro, overthrow his government, and reopen Cuba for business. No one could be sure but the best estimates were that Castro was costing American businesses and organized crime interests one-hundred million dollars every year he stayed in power. At a minimum.

What had started as a Soviet attempt to outmaneuver President Kennedy became a Soviet plan to protect its interests in Cuba. It was working too. The KGB had already thwarted the American invasion at Bay of Pigs. It had provided the intelligence Premier Khrushchev needed to bluff the US President during the Cuban Missile Crisis. The pipeline of information flowing from the three crime families is now helping the USSR win the Cold War. Billy Kyle is the KGB's agent inside the New Orleans outfit.

Seated with Big Daddy at the head table tonight is Jacob "Sparky" Rubenstein. Most people call him Jack Ruby. Owner of the Carousel Club in Dallas, he is in New Orleans on business. The 500 Club has something he wants – a dancer who can earn. From the moment he walked in, he has kept his eyes on the remarkable Jada, known around town as "the heavenly body." One look and he knew instantly how she earned THAT nickname.

For now, though, Jada belongs to Big Daddy. Everybody has a price though. After watching Jada dance, Ruby has decided he will find out what Big Daddy's price is and meet it. He has done business with Marcello many times before. He knows she will NOT come cheap. It is ALWAYS a seller's market when Big Daddy is doing the selling.

Seated at a nearby table is an assortment of other, less-distinguished guests. Like practically everybody in New Orleans, three are on Big Daddy's payroll. David

Ferrie is the "family" pilot. Guy Bannister helps Marcello with legal matters, and Lee Oswald is a long-time runner for the family – introduced to the racket by his mother while she was dating one Marcello soldier after another through the years.

Two-Times does not recognize the girl sitting with Oswald tonight. Dark-haired and pretty, Two-Times thinks to himself, *who is the piece of ass and why is she with that douchebag? Who is the piece of ass and why is she with that douchebag?*

The evening slowly turns to morning and the crowd begins to thin. As is the custom, Big Daddy starts holding court with his guests. Those who remain in the 500 Club gather around, listening in. By then, the liquor and ladies have loosened enough lips. If there is something to learn, Billy knows from experience, this is the time to pay close attention. Especially THIS time. Tonight's topic is President Kennedy and his brother, Bobby.

The latest rumor is that the President is back-channeling secret communications to Castro in an effort to normalize relations between the US and Cuba. Leaked by the CIA to the anti-Castroites in Miami and New Orleans in its ongoing war with the White House, the rumor has Cuban exiles and refugees everywhere in a state of panic. Even worse, the CIA is also reporting that Kennedy is scuttling Operation Mongoose as a show of good faith toward Castro.

David Ferrie is furious. Pacing back and forth, he is on one of his epic, wild-eyed rants, screaming. “He fucked us in ’61, he fucked us again in ’62, and now Bobby is shutting down all the training camps! He took our C-4, took 10,000 fucking rounds of ammo, took 3,000 rounds of gunpowder, and took all our fucking weapons, goddamn it – he’s fucking us again in ’63! If the bastard is re-elected in ’64, he’ll make peace with that commie-bastard in Havana and fuck us all over again!”

Big Daddy raises his glass and shouts angrily, “Livarsi na petra di la scarpa!” amid loud jeers and curses. Two-Times has heard Marcello issue the old Sicilian curse before. The English translation is, “Take the stone from my shoe!” Only a few people know the history behind Marcello’s curse. Two-Times is one of them.

In 1959, during its investigation of racketeering, the US Senate called Marcello to testify in front of the McClellan Committee. Two members of the committee were Senator John Kennedy from Massachusetts and his little brother Robert, chief counsel of the body.

During his testimony, Marcello repeatedly pleaded the Fifth, refusing to give answers that could incriminate him or his associates. Bobby in particular was not amused. Mockingly, in a singsong rebuke, he accused Big Daddy of hiding behind the amendment "like a little schoolgirl." The godfather was not used to being insulted privately, much less on national TV.

Marcello had one problem. He was not a US citizen. Worried about deportation if Kennedy won the election, Big Daddy became a Nixon supporter in 1960, contributing a cool five-hundred thousand dollars to his campaign. Alas, Nixon did not win. In the spring of '61, Bobby got his revenge.

Marcello was a regular at the offices of Immigration and Naturalization Services in New Orleans. The law required aliens to report four times a year. This time, acting on Bobby's orders, officers handcuffed and blindfolded Big Daddy and drove him to the Moisant International Airport.

The plane flew Marcello twelve-hundred miles to Guatemala City and unceremoniously dumped him like a stray dog in the middle of the night. One of the richest, most powerful men in the world was a vagabond. Courtesy of Bobby Kennedy, Big Daddy had no luggage, no money, and just a few shredded remains of his trademark Sicilian pride.

Marcello might still be wandering the streets of Guatemala City if family pilot David Ferrie had not smuggled him back into the US aboard his Stinson Voyager single-engine plane.

Marcello is from the old school, when vendettas reached back centuries. He had not forgotten. He will NEVER forget.

He looks at David Ferrie promising, “Don’t worry about that little Bobby son-of-a-bitch. He’s going to be taken care of.”

“His brother is the fucking President!” Ferrie protests angrily, waving his arms wildly. “The little cocksucker is protected!”

Marcello nods calmly. “You’re right. There IS a better way. A dog will continue to bite you if you cut off its tail. But if you cut off the dog’s head, it will cease to cause trouble.”

Marcello’s words get Ferrie excited. He jumps up again and begins pacing back and forth, out of his mind with rage. "I want him killed," he suddenly screams. "In the fucking White House! Stab him in his fucking heart! Somebody's gotta get rid of this fucker...!"

Two-Times interrupts, skeptical. "David – how you gonna get the President of the USA? How you gonna get the President of the USA?"

"It won't be long, mark my words," Ferrie predicts. "That fucker will get what's coming to him!" He pauses as if expecting someone to interrupt him again, but no one dares.

"It can be blamed on Castro – hell the whole country will want to invade Cuba then," Ferrie says. "If it's planned right, it's no problem – a motorcade with an open-top car. Hell, even Eisenhower rode around in an open-top limousine. Three different locations. An office building with a high-powered rifle, triangulation of crossfire, that's the key, that's the key. A diversionary shot gets the Secret Service looking the other way. Then the kill shot. In all the commotion of the crowd, the job gets done!"

"Sounds like a good plan, sounds like a good plan," Two-Times agrees, twice, as usual.

"It is," Ferrie declares. "There's only one catch, but it's

important one." Everybody leans in close to hear.

Ferrie lowers his voice, almost whispering, "The crucial thing is – one man has to be sacrificed."

***

Chapter Thirteen

***

Crisis of Conscience

New Orleans, Louisiana

August 13, 1963

"She's being used like a two-bit whore," announces Steven, entering the conference room with a thick file under his arm. He places the bundle on the table with a thud.

"CIA?" Sasha asks, reaching for his glasses.

"The very same," Steven nods, taking a seat across from Sasha.

"Go on," Sasha says, motioning Steven to continue while he is examining the report.

"Ever since the missile crisis last year," Steven begins, "developing a cure for cancer has taken a backseat to national security. What began as a project to cure cancer is now a scheme to make cancer into an untraceable bio-weapon, to be used in black-ops, specifically executive actions."

"Oswald's mistress is an assassin?" Sasha asks incredulously, looking closely at the file photo of a cute, brown-eyed debutante.

"Not literally and definitely not by choice," Steven replies, shaking his head. "No. She is just young and extremely naïve – no match for the people exploiting her."

"But why her anyway?" quizzes Sasha.

"Several reasons, for starters, she's god-damn brilliant," answers Steven.

KGB agent Sergei Lipov – codenamed "Steven Lindbergh" – is finished with his assignment, finally. Sasha was starting to get antsy. How long does it take to research a subject as uncomplicated – seemingly anyway – as Oswald's New Orleans' goomah?

This is Sergei's first assignment in the field. Barely twenty years-old, he will not be reconnoitering or infiltrating – the fun stuff – any time soon. The recent graduate of the Higher School of the KGB in Moscow is stuck researching instead. He is not happy about it.

"What do the Americans call it?" Steven asks rhetorically. "A prodigy – yes – it turns out Oswald's pretty little girlfriend is a child prodigy."

"Tell me about her," Sasha says, leaning back in his chair.

"Her name is Judyth Vary. She just turned twenty years old. Even though she's young, her age is not indicative of her achievements – already," Steven begins, opening one of the folders lying on the table.

"The short-story version is, her grandmother died of breast cancer when young Judyth was only fourteen years old. They were very close – grandmother and granddaughter. Judyth took it hard. Ever since, she has dedicated her life to cancer research. She converted an old equipment shed under the bleachers of her high school's football stadium into a make-shift lab and began using mice in her experiments..."

"...Wait, she was researching a cure for cancer when she was fourteen?" Sasha interrupts.

"That's right, and evidently, she was pretty good," Steven answers, nodding. "Good enough the Bradenton Herald published several stories about their town's teenage savant. She was winning award after award at different science fairs in Florida by then. In one interview, Judyth was up-front about her ambition – finding a cure for cancer. She claimed it would be her life's work – for her grandma."

"All of this on her own?" Sasha wonders aloud, skeptical.

"Actually no," Steven replies. "She was influenced by some fairly interesting people. Dr. Canute Michaelson was an Agency radiobiologist during WW II. After he retired, he took an assignment teaching at Judyth's high school. In fact, he was her biology teacher. Dr. Canute arranged for his old CIA contacts back at Oak Ridge to send him equipment for Judyth and her homemade lab."

"A CIA doctor..." Sasha mumbles, shaking his head, a look of sarcasm on his face. "What are the odds?"

"Retired Army Colonel Phillip Doyle was her science teacher," Steven continues, still reading the same file. "He and Dr. Michaelson mentored Judyth. She was their prize student throughout her high-school years."

"Sounds like she was well worth their efforts," observes Sasha.

Steven nods. "They had a lot to work with," he

comments. "Florida records indicate Judyth Vary has the highest IQ of her age classification in the entire state. Sure enough, in less than one year, she was inducing lung cancer in mice. This was faster than all the high-tech labs and their high-dollar researchers," he adds.

"Wow," Sasha says, impressed. "So why in the hell is she involved in Medical Manhattan? She doesn't realize nobody's trying to CURE cancer in that outfit?"

"You're getting ahead," cautions Steven. "It's not that simple."

"Sorry. Proceed," Sasha replies with a wave.

"There's a political side to young Judyth," Steven tells him. "In high school, she was best friends with a boy named Tony Lopez-Fresquet. Tony's father used to be Castro's finance minister until 1960 when he was forced to flee Cuba with his family..."

"...Let me guess," Sasha interrupts Steven. "Tony turned Judyth into a right-wing extremist."

"Well, judging by her comments in several of the newspaper stories I read, she's definitely anti-Castro," acknowledges Steven.

"Is that how she got noticed by the Central Intelligence Agency?" Sasha asks.

"Not really," answers Steven. "No, it was her success with the mice that attracted the attention of Dr. Alton Ochsner, President of the American Cancer Society. He has been trying to prove a link between smoking and lung cancer for years. Anyway, he was so impressed by Judyth's work that he got her an invite to work at the most important cancer research center in the United States – the Roswell Park Institute in Buffalo, New York."

"How old was she?" Sasha asks, jotting notes in the margins of Steven's report.

"Seventeen," replies Steven.

"Jesus!" Sasha exclaims. "A god-damn kid!"

"Two years later," Steven adds, ignoring Sasha, "Dr. Ochsner recruited Judyth to New Orleans to work at HIS hospital, the Ochsner Clinic, and help HIM cure cancer – her dream come true." Steven pauses, as if expecting another outburst from Sasha.

"Go on," Sasha demands impatiently.

"In 1957, the US government discovered a cancer-causing virus in the polio vaccine. The CIA set up in the neighborhood of one-hundred-and-fifty covert research facilities across the country to develop a vaccine for cancer before the epidemic hits. The Ochsner Clinic is one of the facilities. Dr. Ochsner recruited Judyth to join the team, or so she thought. He promised a scholarship to Tulane Medical School in the fall if she'd intern for him this summer."

"So she's going to Tulane in the fall?" Sasha asks, curious. This is the first he has heard a time frame for the Medical Manhattan project.

"That's the plan," Steven replies.

"This is important," Sasha declares. "They plan to be finished with this by then – or at least her part of it, whatever THAT is. Continue," he instructs Steven.

"It was a classic bait-and-switch," Steven continues, taking a deep breath. "The doctor recruited her with the promise she'd be working on a cure for cancer. But once she was here, he assigned her to the bio-weapon project instead."

"Son-of-a-bitch," Sasha mumbles. "Poor girl."

"What's she going to do?" Steven asks, shrugging his shoulders. "Quit – and lose her scholarship in the fall?

Not likely. Besides, it is no secret the bio-weapon is to kill Castro. Given her prior relationship with Tony, she probably rationalizes her role – hell, she may even consider herself a patriot…" A sudden realization causes Sasha to stop Steven in mid-sentence.

"…The CIA doesn't need her because she's brilliant," he interjects. "The CIA is using her because she doesn't exist. She has no credentials yet – which means nobody can ever connect her work to them. She's damn-near untraceable."

"I guess that's true," Steven agrees, nodding his head.

"So what EXACTLY is her role in Medical Manhattan?" Sasha asks, leaning forward in his chair.

"She is doing the same things she did six years ago in her homemade lab in Bradenton, Florida," answers Steven. "First, she injects the mice with cancer cells. After a period of observation, she cuts out the biggest tumors – the most aggressive ones – and grinds them up in a kitchen blender. Then she sends the macerated tumors to a separate lab for radiation treatment. When the now-radiated material comes back to her from the other lab, she injects a NEW batch of mice with it – and the new tumors grow bigger and faster. Then the process is repeated…" Sasha motions Steven to stop again. He is nodding his head and writing furiously.

After a lengthy pause, he begins thinking aloud. “So that’s what the two Cubans are carrying to her lab – mice. The first lab must be where they keep them – the ‘mouse house’. The second lab is the injection lab – where they grow the tumors, cut them out and blend them together. Then the third lab is where Dr. Mary Sherman roasts the tumors with the radiation...”

Steven wants to say something but Sasha shakes his head and holds up his index finger. He is not finished talking to himself. “The package Oswald traded with the Cubans was the material ready to go to Dr. Mary’s lab to be radiated. It all makes sense now.”

Steven is confused. He keeps looking at his report, wondering what he missed.

“Don’t worry about me,” Sasha reassures Steven. “I’m thinking out loud. These are large pieces of the puzzle – IMPORTANT pieces.”

Steven shrugs, relieved. He rises to leave, finished with his report.

“I DO question Oswald’s role in Medical Manhattan though,” Sasha says, rubbing his chin. “He’s no scientist..."

"...He's her handler maybe?" Steven suggests, halting his exit for a moment. "It's HIS job to make sure SHE does HER job."

"Makes sense," Sasha agrees, impressed with the young agents' work, forgetting for a moment how long it took him. "Oswald WAS assigned to New Orleans a couple days before she arrived. The jobs at Reily Coffee are obviously covers for both of them. Their real work is what's going on in those labs."

"I'm guessing Oswald and Judyth becoming lovers wasn't part of the plan," Steven notes wryly.

"He knows better," Sasha responds coldly. "At least he SHOULD."

Steven stops in his tracks, adding, "Actually, they BOTH should know better. Supposedly, Judyth is married to some mystery man who works offshore on an oil rig."

"Christ almighty," Sasha laughs a cruel laugh. "I was almost starting to feel sorry for her – there is one thing for sure – this WON'T end well."

"It can't," agrees Steven with a chuckle.

The door closes behind Steven, leaving Sasha alone, lost in his thoughts.

Since labs one and two are in houses leased to David Ferrie, we have to assume he is involved in Medical Manhattan too, he thinks. *If Ferrie and Vary inject the mice and grind the tumors, what is Oswald doing? He MUST be helping the Cubans move the mice and material from Ferrie's labs to Dr. Mary's lab...*

Ferrie, Vary, and Mary, Sasha thinks, smirking. *Sounds like partners in a law firm.*

***

New Orleans, Louisiana

August 20, 1963

The room is eerily quiet. Inside the lab, all work has stopped. Anxious faces are loitering about aimlessly, checking the door periodically, waiting for their leader. A nervous research intern in an unblemished white coat is biting her fingernails, staring blankly out a window.

Without warning, the door bursts opens and into the room strides Dr. Alton Ochsner. Entering behind the legendary and obnoxious "Bull of the Bullpen" is the buttoned-up gentle-genius, Dr. Mary Sherman. Her staff is as comforted to see her, as it is alarmed to see him. This must be important.

"The operation is a go," Dr. Sherman informs the assembly after a brief greeting. Like always, she talks in a measured tone – almost solemn. "The product is operational and the subject is undergoing preparations. Testing begins next week."

In a field dominated by Machiavellian alpha-males, Dr. Mary Sherman is a striking abnormality. Naturally, gender is a big part of that, distinguishing her in the testosterone-fueled industry of medical research. She is also an idealist, not common in her world of cutthroats. However, her rise to prominence in the medical community did not happen because she is a woman with pure motives. There are many nurses in this world with pure motives. Dr. Sherman did it the old-fashioned way. She earned it.

At sixteen, Mary studied abroad for two years in France. She then taught French while finishing work on a master's degree at the University of Illinois. Afterward, she began her graduate studies at the University of Chicago, during which she was a member of Phi Beta Kappa – billed as the nation's oldest and most prestigious academic honor society. Dr. Sherman's expertise in cancer research developed during her post-graduate work, also at the University of Chicago, one of the premier research institutions in North America.

Her research into state-of-the-art applications of radiation for the treatment of bone cancers is groundbreaking stuff – documented by the numerous published articles in scientific journals to her credit. An intellectual powerhouse, Dr. Sherman's credentials are impeccable. Unfortunately, like young Judyth Vary, she is also naïve.

After noticing her cancer work at the University of Chicago, Dr. Ochsner recruited Dr. Sherman to help him find a cure for cancer. Enticed with promises of a partnership in the Ochsner Clinic, her own cancer lab, and an Associate Professorship at Tulane Medical School, she relinquished her practice in Chicago and came to New Orleans, intent on making medical history.

Now she finds herself creating a super cancer. Rather than using radiation to CURE cancer, she is employing the linear particle accelerator to CAUSE galloping cancer cells. Instead of working with other researchers and doctors who are intent on making the world a better place, she is neck-deep in a squalid underworld of anti-Castroite Cubans, organized crime henchmen, and US intelligence operatives.

Dr. Sherman came to New Orleans to make history, just not THIS kind of history. It does occur to her that she has Dr. Ochsner to thank for all of this. It should not be difficult. He has become virtually omnipresent lately, always lurking nearby, peering creepily over her shoulder. The lab stays silent after Dr. Sherman's announcement.

"Where?" Big Russ finally asks.

"Jackson," Dr. Sherman replies. "At the East Louisiana State Mental Hospital, away from people with prying eyes." She glances nervously at Dr. Ochsner. "The volunteer is coming from Angola Prison."

"Who volunteers for something like this?" Big Russ asks the question on everybody's mind.

"A death row inmate," she responds sheepishly.

Loud gasps are followed by someone in the crowd exclaiming, "Good god!"

Someone else speaks up, "Twenty-eight days?"

She nods her head. "Yes, twenty-eight days is always the goal. So far, we have hit all the rungs of the testing ladder except one. It is now time to conduct the human test. I don't have to remind you that a lot of work here and elsewhere is at stake in next week's test," she adds, crossing her fingers.

They all knew this day was coming but now it is here. The realization is sinking in, weighing the group down. What did they think this day would bring – a celebration? It is one thing to sacrifice mice and monkeys – but humans?

The room is awkwardly still. There are wide eyes all around, but no one makes a move or says a word. Finally, Dr. Ochsner clears his throat. "Be proud of what you've done," he declares. "New Orleans is the Los Alamos of the Cold War."

People look at one another. Though no one has the courage to say it, it is clear each one is thinking the same thing. *Los Alamos? Really?*

"World War II had its heroes," he continues, increasing his volume. "Project Manhattan gave us Albert Einstein, General Groves, Enrico Fermi, and Robert

Oppenheimer. The Cold War is giving us heroes too – you. YOU are Medical Manhattan," he says, pointing at each of them. He pauses for effect. "YOUR work will change history, just as theirs did."

Dr. Alton Ochsner is an intimidating figure. Certainly not beloved like Dr. Sherman, most people fear him – for good reason.

Eight years ago, in a foolhardy stunt to convince the frightened populace that Salk's vaccine was safe, he inoculated his own grandchildren in front of hundreds of witnesses. His Hail Mary effort to save the vaccine was a disaster. The injections were lethal. One of his grandchildren died and the other was crippled.

Many times in the past year, Dr. Sherman wanted to flee New Orleans and get as far away from Medical Manhattan as possible. What prevents her is the realization, *if he can do that to his own blood, what can he do to me?*

The former President of the American Cancer Society lives by the creed – fear is the absence of discipline. In his view, permissiveness creates an insecure and unhappy person, and eventually, a fearful society. His goal is to drive out fear with harsh discipline.

As Head of Surgery at Tulane Medical School, Dr. Ochsner is notorious for his incendiary tactics. In an amphitheater he calls the "bullpen," Dr. Ochsner screams questions at assembled medical students, berating them over their answers.

He claims the humiliating drama is a necessary tool to teach them how to think under pressure. "MEDICINE IS STRESSFUL!" he yells at the terrified students. It is how he acquired the nickname, "the Bull of the Bullpen." He does not just strong-arm his students though.

In the early 1930's, an era when Governor Huey Long – the "Kingfish" – was dominating Louisiana politics, Dr. Ochsner demonstrated an uncommon fearlessness by refusing to hire one of Long's friends and put him on staff at Charity Hospital. The Governor was red-faced furious. He retaliated by having Dr. Ochsner fired and access to his patients denied.

In 1942, Dr. Ochsner responded with a middle-finger salute to the Governor's political machine by opening his own hospital called the Ochsner Clinic. The multi-disciplinary hospital is now the largest health-care provider on the Gulf Coast. Back in those days in Louisiana, NOBODY defied Huey Long and prospered.

Nobody except Dr. Alton Ochsner.

Meeting finished, Dr. Ochsner carefully begins guiding Dr. Sherman by her shoulder toward the exit. Somberly, the group watches her leave, dispersing afterwards.

After the coast clears, Big Russ leaves the US Public Health Service Hospital and takes the bus to downtown. He switches buses several times along the way just in case someone tries to follow him. Finally, he gets off and walks the remaining three blocks to the Crescent City Travel Agency.

“We’ve reached the final rung of the testing ladder,” Big Russ announces.

“Testing ladder?” Sasha asks, opening his notebook.

“The testing originated with mice,” Big Russ begins. “That went pretty quickly. Next were the monkeys – Marmosets, Rhesus, and finally African Greens. We just finished. The results are in. The last rung of the ladder is the human test. It’s already been scheduled for next week.”

“What’s the objective?” Sasha inquires.

“From injection to death – twenty-eight days,” answers

Big Russ.

Sasha whistles. "That's pretty ambitious," he states, impressed. "Who is the unlucky bastard?"

"Some poor fool on death row," Big Russ answers morbidly. "Inmates will do most ANYTHING to get out of their cells. This cat supposedly VOLUNTEERED for this. I guess if you are on death row – what the hell, right?"

"Volunteered my ass," Sasha replies, rolling his eyes.

"Yeah," Big Russ agrees. "I'd be willing to bet he fits Castro's height, weight, and ethnic profile exactly."

Sasha thinks for a second. Then he says, "Assuming the tests work, they still have to figure a way to inject Castro without him knowing it. I mean, after all the assassination attempts, he is extremely careful and almost paranoid and who can blame him? Anyway, body doubles and guards surround him. He knows the Americans are gunning for him. It's not going to be as simple as hand-picking three death-row inmates and strapping them down, that's for sure."

Big Russ nods his head. "Trust me, they know that. They are working on a couple different kinds of delivery systems. One is food. If they can inject the food with the cells, it will accomplish the same. I also heard The Agency is developing a cancer gun that uses a tranquilizer dart to deliver the cells."

"Who's doing the test next week?" Sasha asks, moving on.

"Clay Shaw is driving, Oswald is handling the material, and David Ferrie is doing the injections," Big Russ reports.

"The girl?" Sasha wonders.

Big Russ shakes his head. "Not at first," he says. "The injections are the easy part. She will be in the on-deck circle, waiting to conduct the follow-up blood work. They do not dare send Sherman or Ochsner – credentials attract attention – Judyth is invisible. Her data will determine if the bio-weapon is operational."

"And if it is?" Sasha asks, almost afraid of the answer.

"Bodies everywhere," Big Russ predicts. "The Agency won't take any chances. ANYBODY with knowledge of this project will be eliminated."

"Anybody except THE TARGET of course," Sasha declares, chuckling. "Castro escapes again!" Both men laugh.

***

Jackson, Louisiana

August 31, 1963

"I was starting to think he'd NEVER leave," Lee says, sitting on the couch looking at his watch. "We're a little behind schedule."

"I'm sorry," Judyth replies, closing the door behind her. "Robert is not in a hurry to get back to the oil rig today." She sighs and plops down next to him, resting her head on his shoulder.

The run-down shotgun house has two apartments, one in front and one in back, with an inside door connecting them. Judyth Vary "Baker" and her husband live behind Suzi Hanover, a close friend of Lee's. To keep their romance hidden from Marina and Robert, the Hanover place has become a convenient safe house where Lee and "Juduffki" – Lee's term of affection for Judyth – rendezvous after her hard-working husband leaves for another long week in the Gulf. Like a turnstile, the lover enters the front as the hubby exits the back.

Today, the clandestine lovers are on their way to the Jackson State Mental Hospital to see the project "volunteer" – injected with the bio-weapon serum two days ago. Judyth will be conducting blood tests to see if the "cancer soup" is doing its job. Lee will be doing the driving and carrying the materials.

The old Kaizer-Frazer four-door sits a block away, loaned to Lee for today's trip. It's a lot beat up and has no air conditioning, a problem in southern Louisiana. The owner also warned him the engine has a tendency to overheat. Other than that, the car is a peach.

"We have to make a stop," Lee informs her as she slides over in the bench seat next to him. He tries to steal a kiss while he is driving, swerving and making her giggle. "There are two letters in there," he says, pointing. She opens the glovebox and pulls out the envelopes. One reads "New York Communist Party" and the other – "Washington-Baltimore Socialist-Workers Party." Judyth looks bewildered.

"Subterfuge," Lee tells her, slowing down and pulling into a gas station on the outskirts of town. He parks in front of a mailbox.

"Is this the pick-up?" she asks, handing over the letters.

Lee nods, opening his door. "I'll just be a minute." After depositing his mail, he enters the gas station, returning a few minutes later with two Dr. Peppers and a small red cooler.

Two hours later, they arrive at the hospital's main gate. Lee recognizes the orderly from before. "He's with us," he whispers to Judyth. The orderly leads them around to a back entrance of the main building where they take a service elevator upstairs.

Lee had explained the next part to Judyth during the two-hour drive. No one, including her, would actually see the project volunteer. Her job would be to check the blood work data – slides and blood counts prepared for her in advance – and determine if cancer cells are present. If not, she would have to prepare a second round of injections, using the contents of the thermos in the cooler. Meanwhile, Lee would be in the hospital's personnel office, inquiring about a job. "To provide an alibi for me being here," he told her.

It has not taken Judyth long to find cancer cells in the blood samples. *After only two days*, she thinks, knowing this is an excellent sign the bio-weapon had worked and relieved that the thermos will stay closed after all.

She motions for the orderly to come over. "Why are there so many blood samples? These all cannot possibly be from one patient," she says, pointing at the slides lying on the counter, suspicious.

The orderly just shrugs, saying nothing.

"I want to see the prisoner," she demands, packing the thermos and the blood samples in the cooler for transport.

"No one is permitted..." the orderly protests.

"...I don't care what the rules are," she interrupts, voice raised. "I HAVE to see the prisoner!"

The orderly thinks for a moment. Reluctantly, he turns and gestures for her to follow him. He points at a door. "You can see him from there, but you can't go in," he tells her.

Inside a dark, Medieval-looking room, the "volunteer" lies in a bed, restrained with belts and straps. Judyth is watching him, pretending to be pleased with his status as he thrashes around, convulsing with fever and pain. After a few moments observing – more like forcing herself to stare into the horrifying torture chamber – Judyth turns to leave. Later in the car, she bursts into tears describing the patient to Lee.

"That's not the same guy I saw getting injected two days ago," Lee says matter-of-factly when Judyth characterizes the man that she saw as Cuban, about Fidel Castro's age and build.

"That means they injected more than one inmate," Judyth realizes, fuming. "I wondered why there were so many blood samples – way too many for just one patient."

***

New Orleans, Louisiana

September 14, 1963

To: Ochsner Clinic
ATTN: Dr. Alton Ochsner
From: Judyth Vary
Date: September 5, 1963
Re: Cancer research project (Dr. Mary Sherman's team)

Dear Sir,

As I know you are responsible for this project, I am addressing this letter to you. It has long been my dream to find a cure for cancer. When I accepted your invitation to join this project, I believed I would be working with a team of researchers on a vaccine for cancer. Instead, good science has turned bad.

Our team has spent the entire summer working on making cancer more lethal. In short, we have been creating a weapon, not a cure. Furthermore, we just crossed serious moral and ethical boundaries by testing these galloping cancer cells on unsuspecting human subjects.

It is with the utmost respect and humility that I must in good conscience object. It is abhorrent to treat human beings like lab rats. We must get back to saving lives, not destroying them.

Respectfully,

Judyth Vary

Sasha reads it again, for the third time. "Where did you get this?" he asks incredulously.

"You don't want to know," Steven chuckles. "It's dated September 5. It took me a week just to get my hands on it."

"She's toast," Sasha declares. "She knows too much

and it appears she's willing to talk about it. This is the CIA she's dealing with. Now that she's expendable, she's toast," he repeats.

"You said it, 'now that she's expendable'," Steven reports. "When he received this letter, he called her in and fired her from the team immediately. Then he took away her scholarship to Tulane and promised her she would never practice medicine again. Oh, and the next day, Reily Coffee fired both of them – Judyth AND Oswald. She's on her way back to Florida now with her tail between her legs."

"Jesus," Sasha exclaims. "In over her head, that poor girl. Lost love, lost jobs, lost scholarship, lost career – welcome to the real world, Judyth," Sasha says, shaking his head. "She's lucky to be alive though," he adds. "Damn lucky."

"I think it was destined to end this way, letter or no letter," Steven tells Sasha. "Her time was coming to an end here in New Orleans – him too. In the last three weeks, they spent five nights in Marcello hotels around town. Dinners at the 500 Club, honeymoon suites and room service – all comped by Big Daddy."

"Out with a bang," Sasha says with an ornery smile.

***

Chapter Fourteen

***

TWEP's New Target

New Orleans, Louisiana

September 20, 1963

Lee walks briskly past Audubon Park, as if trying to escape a summer's worth of enchanted memories with Judyth, made even more painful now by her recent banishment. A few minutes later, Oswald boards the St. Charles Avenue streetcar, hitching a ride downtown toward the warehouse district, arriving at the State of Louisiana Unemployment Office.

Andy is surveilling from a safe distance, watching Oswald practically sprint into the building. He enters the lobby a minute later, observing the long line already formed. Andy chuckles under his breath. Visibly aggravated, Oswald is loitering at the back of the line, alternately looking up at a clock on the wall and then down at his wristwatch, as if comparing the times. Some poor fool at the counter is having difficulty with the instructions. Oswald watches the confusion unfolding in front of him impatiently, sighing repeatedly as the transaction drags on. He looks around him at the other patrons, his eyes darting back-and-forth. Clearly, he is anxious – his head is on a swivel. In fact, several times, Andy ducks out of view to avoid detection.

An hour later, Oswald finally has his unemployment check in his hand and begins hoofing it again. Andy struggles to keep up. He catches a city bus to Loyola Avenue, getting off at the Greyhound Bus Terminal. After waiting in another line, Oswald buys a ticket and leaves on foot again. Andy waits until he is out of sight before approaching the clerk.

“May I help you?” an insincere clerk asks nonchalantly.

“I need some information,” Andy responds quietly, flashing a twenty-dollar bill.

The clerk, who cannot be older than seventeen-years old – just a kid – is suddenly alert. “What kind of information?” he asks, eyeing the money.

“Your last customer. Where is he going and what time is he leaving?” Andy inquires.

The clerk looks around, wary. He is the only employee behind the counter. "He bought a ticket for Mexico City with a stop in Houston."

"What time does it leave?" Andy quizzes him.

"Tonight at 7:30," the clerk answers quickly, looking around again.

"I need a ticket on that same bus," Andy says. "How much?"

"$15.75," the clerk figures, reading a rate chart in front of him.

Andy slides two twenty-dollar bills across the counter. "Thanks. Keep the change. One more thing," he leans over and whispers to the clerk. "This never happened, got it?" The clerk takes the cash and shrugs, disinterested again. Andy turns, hurrying back to the Crescent City Travel Agency to talk to Sasha.

"Oswald's on the move – probably been reassigned. He's leaving tonight for Houston and then on to Mexico City," he reports, taking a seat opposite Sasha.

"Mexico City, huh?" Sasha replies with a knowing nod.

"Actually the Cuban Embassy," Andy clarifies. "He applied for a travel visa to Cuba. Then he's due in

Dallas in early October," he adds.

"Dallas – what the hell? Slow down," Sasha orders Andy.

"I met with Marina," Andy begins, taking a deep breath. "She's in New Orleans right now, but not for long. Lee told her his work here in New Orleans is finished. Reily Coffee fired him AND the girl on the same day – end of cover jobs." He pauses. "You were right, by the way," he adds. Sasha raises his eyebrows, looking sideways at him. "They made Oswald into a walking-talking flapdoodle this summer."

"Oh?" Sasha asks.

"It started when Oswald came to New Orleans in April and started his chapter of the Fair Play for Cuba Committee," he begins. "So, he's PRO-Castro, right?" Sasha nods but says nothing.

Andy continues. "He passes an extensive background check and gets a job at the Reily Coffee Company, which is owned by a Crusade to Free Cuba Committee money-man. Meanwhile, he consorts with Guy Bannister and David Ferrie – both known Mongoose and Agency operatives. So now he's ANTI-Castro, no?" Sasha smiles and starts to say something.

"Wait, it gets better," Andy interrupts him, holding up his hand.

"He travels to Mobile, Alabama with his uncle and gives an anti-Soviet speech at a prominent Jesuit Seminary," Andy recounts, getting himself worked up. "As soon as he gets back to New Orleans, he visits Carlos Bringuier – The Agency's anti-Castro plant in the Cuban Revolutionary Council – volunteering his services. So now, he is DEFINITELY ANTI-Castro! Except a few days afterward, Bringuier bumps into him on a street corner – leafletting PRO-Castro literature!"

Sasha is belly laughing by now. He cannot resist this "I told you so" moment. "I told you..."

"...ANYWAY, Bringuier is pissed off," Andy continues, cutting Sasha off before he can finish his gloating. "So he confronts Oswald and they get into a fist fight right there on the sidewalk. Both men end up arrested. You may have heard about it – it was all over the news. After his release, Lee appears on several local radio and TV programs. During these programs, he claims to be a Marxist-Leninist! Son-of-a-bitch!"

"I saw one of those interviews," Sasha acknowledges.

"The arresting officer reported that the incident with Bringuier looked staged," Andy notes. "Like it was straight out of a playbook to attract attention..."

"...It's just smoke-and-mirrors," Sasha agrees, interrupting Andy. "Whether Oswald is anti-Castro or pro-Castro is irrelevant for our purposes because we know it's all a charade. It will make an interesting cover story in the future but right now, I'm more interested in why he's being reassigned to Dallas."

"What about Cuba?" Andy asks.

"Oh, I think we all know why he's going to Cuba," Sasha declares. "The bullet is now in the chamber. The bio-weapon must be ready to activate."

Sasha's comment reminds Andy of something. "Does Jackson, Louisiana mean anything to you?" he asks.

"Why?" Sasha inquires, always fishing for corroborating information.

"Oswald's been in Jackson twice in the past three weeks at the East Louisiana State Mental Hospital," Andy responds. "It didn't appear to be a big secret. They detoured first in Clinton, Louisiana and made a huge ruckus at the courthouse. They made sure everybody saw them, almost like they were creating an alibi."

"They?" Sasha asks, reaching for his notebook.

"Clay Shaw, David Ferrie, and Oswald," Andy answers him.

"What happened AFTER Clinton?" questions Sasha.

"They continued on to Jackson and joined a bus from Angola Prison," Andy recalls. "When they arrived at the hospital, both vehicles were waived through by security and escorted to the back of the campus. I saw three inmates walk from the prison bus to an isolated, run-down building. Oswald and Ferrie joined them – Oswald carrying several thermoses and Ferrie carrying a medical bag. An hour later, both exited the building with a prison guard – minus the inmates."

"How did YOU observe this?" Sasha asks him.

"I got lucky," admits Andy. "There is an old utility drive that runs along the perimeter of the campus so I just followed it until I spotted the two vehicles. Then I parked and used my field glasses."

Sasha nods, motioning for him to continue.

"Two weeks later, Oswald made a second trip to Jackson, but this time only Judyth was with him. Like before, they entered the same building and came out an hour later by themselves."

"Did Marina tell you WHEN Lee's going to Cuba?" Sasha asks, returning to the original topic.

"Yes. This week," Andy replies. "She said he is going to Mexico City first to get the passports."

"How long will he be there?" Sasha wonders.

Andy shrugs. "She doesn't know how long he'll be gone but didn't think it would be very long because he told her he'd meet her in Dallas in October. He said he already has a job in Dallas waiting for him."

"Oswald's the mule," a confident Sasha declares.

Andy looks startled. "What do you mean?"

"What you witnessed in Jackson was the human test," Sasha explains, finally getting around to answering Andy's question. "A successful test means the subjects died in twenty-eight days or less. Oswald going to Cuba suggests to me that the test worked and the bio-weapon is operational. It's Oswald's job to get it to his contact in Havana. We'll be ready for him though."

Poor sap, Andy thinks.

"What Dallas is about, I DON'T know," Sasha admits. "Maybe it's connected, maybe not. I've got to speak with Arrowhead," he concludes.

"What are my instructions? Andy asks. "Do you want me to...?"

"...Stay with Oswald!" Sasha interjects. "My gut instinct tells me too much has been invested in him to go to waste. He has been sheep-dipped for something big. I just don't know what it is yet!"

Something does not add up, Andy is thinking. He lets several moments go by before speaking. "I don't think sheep-dipping him as a Communist does any good if the target is Castro," Andy says finally, shrugging. "I mean, why would a Communist want to kill Castro anyway? Why would they set up a Communist to be Castro's assassin? It doesn't pass the smell test."

Suddenly, like a fog being lifted, Sasha remembers the after-hours conversation at Marcello's 500 Club – reported by Billy "Two-Times" four months earlier. *If Lee Oswald IS the patsy, the target cannot be Castro*, he thinks. *Andy is right. It is too obvious. Trying to go to Cuba will leave a paper trail a mile long. But what if KENNEDY is the target instead...what if Oswald is the sacrificial lamb – like Ferrie said? It would not be that hard to release a cover story implicating Oswald as a pro-Castro Communist. He DID defect to the Soviet Union…he IS trying to go to Cuba…*

“On the other hand,” Andy resumes, interrupting Sasha’s thought-filled trance. “What if that PRO-Castro Communist who just got back from Cuba took out the American President? Who would be…?”

“…Blamed?” Sasha interrupts loudly, “The American people would blame Castro! They would DEMAND an immediate invasion of Cuba and the overthrow of Castro in the process…”

“…Two birds with one stone,” Andy interjects.

“Oswald’s trip to Cuba is just a red herring,” Sasha reasons.

Andy shakes his head. “He’s is in way over his head. I almost feel sorry for him.”

“I will activate Mexico City and Havana if and when Oswald makes it that far,” Sasha says. “But intelligence agents don’t just pick up and go to other countries on their own. Somebody SENDS them. This is another breadcrumb. He will come back to Dallas when he has finished laying his trail. Dallas IS the key.”

"So you DON'T want me to go to Cuba with him?" Andy clarifies.

"No," Sasha says, shaking his head. "We'll have a thousand eyes on him in Cuba. No use wasting you too. Stay with him to the border. When he gets back, FOLLOW HIM TO DALLAS."

Andy nods, standing up to leave, checking his watch. *Oswald's bus leaves in one hour*, he thinks.

"In the meantime," Sasha adds, escorting Andy to the door. "I'll find out when the President is coming to Dallas."

***

Washington D.C.

September 22, 1963

Sasha exits the plane, stepping out of the luxurious first-class cabin into a cold, drizzling rain. *Never thought I would miss New Orleans*, he thinks, hurrying to the waiting cab. "Georgetown!" he shouts at the driver as the car splashes away from the curb.

Traffic is light this evening. The ride into the nation's

capital from Potomac Airfield in Friendly, Maryland is normally about forty minutes, but this cabbie is an overachiever. Sasha is hanging on, several times his life flashing before him. He breathes a quick sigh of relief as the campus comes into view. Thirty minutes after landing at the Airfield, Sasha enters the Georgetown University Law Library.

Approaching the biography section, he notices Arrowhead sitting alone, fiddling with his watch impatiently as if he has been waiting there for hours. *Some things never change*, Sasha thinks, laughing to himself.

Together, they leave the library and begin walking across campus, neither one speaking. They make a right onto Massachusetts Avenue, in the direction of the Supreme Court Building. The two men make another right when they reach Union Station, entering Lower Senate Park.

The rain has stopped but Sasha manages to step in an ankle-deep puddle camouflaged by fallen leaves. He now has a drenched sock inside a squishy shoe to aggravate him. He curses under his breath. “Is the President going to win re-election?” he asks, frustrated.

"Nope," answers Arrowhead curtly. "He's not even going to make it to '64."

"Jesus, I was right," Sasha says. "Castro's not the target after all."

"He WAS," Arrowhead replies. "But that was then. Now the President's enemies view him as the bigger threat than Castro. So they took the infrastructure of a plan intended to kill Castro and aimed it at Kennedy instead."

"These enemies of his – they must be the heavy hitters we've discussed," Sasha guesses.

Arrowhead nods his head. "Well, double-crossing the crime families certainly wasn't smart," he says sarcastically. "Joe Kennedy promised them a friend in the White House and the re-opening of Cuba if they helped his boy win in '60. Instead, Bobby's been on a crusade against the bosses and..."

"...And Jack's been busy fucking up in Cuba," Sasha concludes, jumping the gun on Arrowhead.

Arrowhead frowns, briefly losing his train of thought. "As you know, The Agency and Kennedy have been at each other's throats since Bay of Pigs," he begins again. "He fired our top three guys and put all covert-ops under his know-nothing brother Bobby, that cocksucker. Military and intelligence are BOTH pissed at him for letting the Soviets build that god-damn wall through Berlin and giving away the family jewels in the Missile Crisis."

"Hang on a second." Sasha cannot stand it any longer. He stops walking and props his soaked foot on a park bench, removing his shoe. Then he takes off his sock and begins ringing it out. "Sorry," he says. "It's driving me crazy. Keep going. I'm listening."

Arrowhead shrugs and watches Sasha in amusement before resuming his monologue. "He's talking about pulling out of Vietnam and ending the Cold War in a second term. Last year, he closed seventy military bases. Intel and the brass do not trust him. They think he is weak. They think he has to go. The Cubans – they are furious with him too. It was their families and friends who were butchered when Jack cancelled the air support at Bay of Pigs."

"Promising Khrushchev he'll never invade Cuba again probably didn't help," Sasha adds, tying his shoe.

"It only confirms to the Cubans that he can't be trusted to get rid of Castro," Arrowhead agrees. "And Bobby shutting down the training bases in Miami and

New Orleans is the last straw."

Sasha stands, drying his hands with a handkerchief. "That's a little better," he says with relief as he takes a couple steps, testing his footwear.

"And then there's Lyndon Johnson," Arrowhead says to Sasha as they resume walking. "LBJ won't EVER be President if Kennedy survives. Jack and Bobby cannot stand him. They've been searching for a way to dump him from the ticket since '60."

"That shouldn't be hard," Sasha notes wryly. "He's been corrupted and bribed so many times by so many people..."

"...Bobby's got the goods on him now," Arrowhead interjects, agreeing with Sasha. "But he's waiting for the right time to indict, probably early in '64. After that, Kennedy will replace him with a placeholder, preferably someone lacking any ambition to run for President in '68."

"What's so important about '68?" inquires Sasha.

"Jack's setting it up for Bobby to run," Arrowhead responds.

"A Kennedy dynasty," Sasha observes, impressed.

“Does Johnson know...?”

“...Johnson knows EVERYTHING that happens in Washington,” Arrowhead replies, interrupting Sasha again. “And what the Kennedy brothers DON’T know is that Johnson and his money men are searching for their OWN opportunity to erase Jack.”

Sasha laughs. “Jesus, those two sons-of-bitches deserve each other. Money men?” he asks.

“Texas oil barons,” Arrowhead replies. “Like most politicians from Texas, LBJ is literally bought-and-paid-for by big oil. Kennedy is trying to lower the oil depletion allowance and repatriate oil profits. If Congress agrees and passes the bill, it will cost the industry billions. Clearly, both sides benefit if Kennedy is taken out,” he says matter-of-factly. “So they made a deal.”

“When?” asks Sasha.

“Soon, probably in the fall,” replies Arrowhead.

“Where?” inquires Sasha.

“I’ve heard several places, Chicago, Miami, Dallas – if you ask me, Dallas makes the most sense because it’s in Texas. Even though he’s in DC right now, LBJ still runs the state. He has a million friends in Texas to help with the advance planning. Hell, the mayor of Dallas is Cabell's brother – one of The Agency's directors that Kennedy fired after Bay of Pigs. Talk about someone with motive. He can control the local investigation afterwards, and of course, the new President can control the FBI and Justice Department from DC."

"Somebody might put all this together," protest Sasha.

"No chance," Arrowhead shakes his head.

"How can you be so sure?" Sasha presses.

"Because there is a sacrificial lamb already being led to the slaughter," Arrowhead tells Sasha. "Hell, we're the masters at diversion. You just move a few pieces around, compile a believable cover story with links to Communism and Castro and release it when everyone is hysterical. The media will convict the poor bastard FOR us. All we have to do is eliminate him before a trial."

"The whole damn country will be seeing red," Sasha figures. "What if Congress investigates?" he asks.

"That's simple," shrugs Arrowhead. "Johnson will get out in front of it by appointing a blue-ribbon panel to conduct the probe. Then he will play puppet-master, stacking it with stooges he can control. They will wink and nod their way through a bullshit investigation, starting with the government conclusion and working backwards. Any evidence that does not fit the cover story will be conveniently lost or destroyed. Believe me – the dumb schmuck doesn't have a chance." Sasha listens, slowly processing Arrowhead's prediction.

"Dumb SCHMUCKS," corrects Sasha finally, emphasizing the plural form. Arrowhead looks confused, glancing sideways at Sasha.

"The American people – shows you what their leaders think of them," Sasha explains.

***

Washington D.C.

September 23, 1963

The next day, Sasha retraces his steps to the East German Embassy for his rendezvous with the seductress. This time, he prepares himself better for what awaits him.

He realizes now he should have paid more attention to

Father's warning about what he called "the Lace effect." Sasha knows he embarrassed himself. Not today. He has a simple strategy. Do not inhale!

Sasha is convinced her sweet fragrance acted as a gateway drug on him the last time. Once his keen sense of smell activated, it triggered a chain reaction that rendered him, a damn KGB Director, limp as a dishrag. Not this time.

Before entering the small office, Sasha removes a small vial of peppermint oil from his pocket, applying drops to both shirt collars and his tongue. Then he takes a deep breath. The aroma from the natural healing oil is so potent it steals his breath away. The taste jolts him like a dose of courage. Sasha is hoping the oil will overpower Lace's flavorful perfume, but just in case it does not, he carries a backup – lemongrass – in his other pocket. Finally, Sasha thinks he is ready and slowly opens the door.

Again, Lace is waiting for him and again, she looks amazing and yet again, Sasha stares. This time however, he catches himself before it is too late. He takes a deep breath and swallows hard. *Yes! Peppermint!* He thinks to himself. *It IS working.*

All the while, Lace is either graciously unaware of

Sasha's attention or she is accustomed to it. Whichever it is, nothing ever seems to faze her.

He comes right to the point. "I need to know the President's itinerary," he announces, clearing his throat.

"Today?" She asks. "Minute-by-minute?"

"No, no," Sasha responds, shaking his head. "Is he taking any trips soon? Campaign stops, anything like that?"

"These days it's nothing BUT campaign trips," she replies. "He's going to Chicago on a swing through the Midwest in a couple weeks. He was supposed to go on to Miami afterwards but they cancelled that part of the trip. I do not know why. Then he's going to Texas on a six-city…"

"…Texas? Are you sure?" Sasha interrupts her. "Is Dallas one of the six cities?" Lace laughs. *Damn, what a beautiful laugh*, Sasha thinks.

"I SHOULD know about his trip to Texas," she acknowledges. "I'm meeting him at the family compound in Palm Springs the weekend after he returns. And yes, Dallas is one of his stops."

"Any specifics?" Sasha asks.

"Two months from now, in late November," Lace answers. "November 21-24 to be exact. The last two days are pleasure. He is going to Johnson City for a weekend of fun at LBJ's ranch. But not the kind of fun you're thinking," she clarifies, chuckling. "The Texas trip is strictly business because Jackie's going to be with him. The First Lady will NOT be in Florida the weekend after though. That's where I come in."

"So Dallas is definitely on the list?" Sasha double-checks.

Lace nods her head. "Yes. The city is planning a parade or something for them, rolling out the red carpet. He knows people really want to see the Camelot Queen, not him. I can tell you, he is dreading it. Jack – that is what he wants me to call him – told me Dallas is full of right-wing wackos. He calls it the 'land of the crazies.' I am sure that's why they're taking the wife – to soften the edge..."

"...That's not the only reason," Sasha interjects.

"Oh?" Lace replies.

"It's campaign season," Sasha says matter-of-factly. "It's time to pretend girls like you don't exist."

***

Moscow, Russia

September 25, 1963

The door opens, signaling Father to rise. Premier Khrushchev rushes in, followed by a secretary and a few nondescript aides, all with the same pale faces. He shakes Father's hand hurriedly and dismisses his nervous entourage.

There are no pleasantries – the Premier is not one for small talk. "You requested a meeting, no?" Khrushchev asks loudly.

Father nods his head solemnly. "Yes sir. There's a developing situation in America that requires your immediate attention."

"Proceed," orders the Premier, unwrapping a cigar.

"As you know," Father begins, "the Americans have been trying to assassinate Castro for years – since Eisenhower at least. We have learned that the apparatus they built to kill him is now aimed at Kennedy instead. We've also learned that they intend to wave the red flag and make Soviets and

Communism guilty of the crime in the eyes of the world."

Khrushchev stops chewing on his cigar and pulls it from his mouth. "Shit," he says in his raspy voice. "Are we sure about this?"

"One-hundred percent," Father assures him.

"Inside or outside job?" inquires Khrushchev.

"Inside," answers Father.

"That means it's a policy decision, not a personal one – the worst scenario for us," Khrushchev says matter-of-factly. "Our free ride might be over."

"Should we leak this to our American contacts?" Father asks, preferring a proactive approach. "It might safeguard Soviet interests..."

"...Absolutely not!" Khrushchev thunders, interrupting Father. "We MUST protect intelligence assets at ALL costs. Not a word from us," he orders Father.

"Understood, sir," nods Father.

"We must also be prepared for all contingencies," Khrushchev adds. "How do the conspirators plan to make it the fault of Mother Russia?"

"Mother Russia's proxy, Cuba," Father answers him. "You remember Oswald, no?" Father asks.

The Premier is not sure. "Refresh me," he tells Father.

"He's the agent the CIA sent here in '59 to give us the U-2," Father explains.

Khrushchev suddenly remembers. "Ah yes, the fake-defector who tried to kill himself, no?"

"Yes," Father replies. "He has been on American radio and TV claiming to be a Marxist-Leninist. He is on his way to Cuba right now to deliver what he thinks is a bio-weapon to kill Castro. It is a phony mission. He is actually carrying a placebo in a thermos bottle. We think he's being set up as the fall guy."

"How long will he be in Cuba?" the Premier wonders.

"Not long. His orders are to return to America in October," Father replies.

"When is the hit?" Khrushchev asks.

"We're checking on the President's schedule," Father answers. "We think it's soon..."

"...I see," the Premier interrupts. "If the assassination happens right after Oswald's trip to Cuba, the

American people will demand an invasion of Cuba," Khrushchev calculates. "They will think Castro put him up to it."

"They will be MADE to think that, yes," Father agrees.

"Somebody better tell Fidel," Khrushchev advises. "You said it's an inside job. HOW inside?" he inquires.

"Military, intelligence, the Vice President..." Father answers.

"...Son-of-a-bitch, the holy, fucking trinity," Khrushchev interrupts Father again.

"Anti-Castro Cubans and mafia too," Father finishes.

The Premier shakes his head. "Jesus, let me guess, the military is pissed about Berlin and Cuba. The Agency never got over the Bay of Pigs and Johnson's in a hurry to be President, no?"

Father hands Khrushchev a file. "It's all in there," he points. "Basically, two-thirds of your "holy trinity" think he's too soft on Communism. Johnson is a different issue. The President wants to dump him from the ticket. He and his brother are cooking up a legal case against him. The Vice President WILL be indicted before the '64 campaign," Father predicts.

"So it's the President or him," Khrushchev states.

"Yes," Father replies.

"Lyndon will do anything the military wants," Khrushchev speculates. "And the CIA will be back in business. Both have been pushing for an escalation in Vietnam. They'll get it now."

Father nods his head in agreement. "Back in '60, after the Americans sabotaged your summit with Eisenhower, I thought they wanted the Cold War to continue for ideological purposes. I know better now. They want it to continue for financial reasons."

"Of course. It's big money for their military-industrial complex," the Premier agrees.

"BIG money," Father repeats. "But Kennedy is pursuing peace..."

"...Which means he's a threat to all that money – god-damned capitalists," huffs Khrushchev.

***

Washington D.C.

October 22, 1963

"Fucking Clark Mollenhoff!" Sasha exclaims. "What in the hell is *The Des Moines Register*?" He slams his fist on his desk in frustration. Backwater USA has just exposed one of his most useful and productive agents.

The gist of the story is simple. President Kennedy compromised the White House and national security by his repeated dalliances with an East German spy, a Stasi agent posing as a West German diplomat and Quorum Club hostess. According to Mollenhoff, the bewitching Ellen Rometsch or Lace – whichever – is not who she pretends to be.

The Quorum Club is wildly popular among the most senior members of the US government. Its "hostesses" are legendary for being the most beautiful in the entire District. For a very high price, they are the most willing too. Until Mollenhoff started nosing around, they prided themselves for being the most discreet.

It started with one. Probably an inexperienced cupcake with stars in her eyes. Once she spilled the beans about the Quorum Club and its prestigious clientele, a reporter with the experience of Mollenhoff was able to construct a scandalous story about Senators and prostitutes. Then the story became MORE interesting.

In a routine background check of one of the Quorum

hostesses, he discovered Lace's Embassy job, piquing his curiosity. *A West German diplomat doubling as a hostess at The Quorum Club?* From there, he learned Lace's real name. A conversation with a reliable anonymous source led him to Miss Rometsch's East German roots, causing him to suspect Stasi involvement. Another source at the NSA unwound the elaborate cover story the Stasi had woven, uncovering the real identities of Ellen Rometsch and her parents. That was enough for a smashing good story. Then he found out she had only one client. Mollenhoff obsessed over the identity of that one client – *he must be important*! Then he found out who it was, which is when the story took a turn for the scary.

The client turned out to be the President of the United States. A daring and careless President. Mollenhoff was amazed he was able to find out so easily. "It's as if he WANTS people to know," he told his editor.

Sasha knows what this story means. The Center – KGB headquarters in Moscow – terminates operations and operatives that risk exposure. Above everything, a spy MUST remain anonymous. Unless this story is miraculously contained, "Ellen Rometsch" is soon to be a household name. Though it certainly means the end of Lace's spying, he is hoping it is not the end of

Ellen Rometsch. *Now THAT would be a tragedy*, he thinks sadly.

He is also very aware how this White House deals with JFK mistresses who are outed. *Marilyn Monroe*, he thinks ominously – *exactly one year ago.*

According to the medical examiner, the Hollywood starlet died of an accidental drug overdose. Sasha's sources dug deep, discovering that the autopsy revealed no traces in her stomach to indicate she had taken drugs orally nor were there any needle marks on her body.

Sasha knows what few others do. Bobby Kennedy – his brother's keeper – gave the order. His people slipped Miss Monroe a "Mickey Finn" to knock her out and then drugged her with an enema bag loaded with Nembutal. End of Marilyn. End of problem.

Sasha also knows eliminating an over-sexed floozy and an East German Stasi agent are not the same. *That is a completely different ballgame*, he thinks hopefully.

The President's re-election campaign is in full swing. Politicians survive bimbo eruptions if they come clean. In fact, in some cases, squeaky-clean candidates who need relatability points even BENEFIT from them. The

American people are a forgiving lot, but this is not that.

Best case, President Kennedy has made himself AND the Executive Branch susceptible to blackmail. Worst case, he has compromised American national security. If they ever find out, the American people will NOT forgive that degree of recklessness, especially in the thick of the Cold War. They must scrub clean all traces of Ellen Rometsch.

A few hours later, the Stasi recalls Lace. Actually, the Americans did not give the Communist Bloc much of a choice. Within hours of the story breaking, the US State Department quietly informed Moscow and the East German government of Ellen Rometsch's "persona non grata" status. They also said she was "being deported for improper behavior befitting a diplomat while in Washington D.C."

Deported beats dead, Sasha says to himself upon learning her fate.

***

Dallas, Texas

October 29, 1963

The receiver clicks and the signal light engages. Andy sighs while he picks up the headphones. Oswald is on the phone again. With unlimited access to Big Daddy's numbers-racket phone service, Oswald is testing Andy's surveillance skills – and his endurance.

"Juduffki!" Lee calls out wistfully.

"Scarlet Pimpernel – my love!" Judyth coos in return.

I hate my life, a nauseated Andy groans silently.

After a dreamy summer of clandestine intimacy in New Orleans, Lee and Judyth make their love now by phone, blissfully unaware that a Soviet agent is on the line with them, listening to their every word.

The ciphered call wheel with dates, times, and locations of pay phones is supposed to ensure a private conversation. That was before Andy broke in and stole the call wheel from Oswald's apartment while he was at work, made a copy, and returned the original.

Once Soviet cryptanalysis experts deciphered the pilfered call wheel, Andy bugged every phone Oswald planned to use in advance.

"Where are you?" Judyth asks sweetly.

"Dallas," replies Lee.

"Dallas? What happened in Cuba?" Judyth inquires. "Did you make the drop?"

Lee clears his throat huskily. "No. I never made it. My contact no-showed in Mexico City. I went to the Cuban Embassy instead and tried to get a passport but they denied my application. The Agency told me that a hurricane in the Caribbean prevented the drop, but I don't believe it. Bad weather is not the reason they chose to call off this operation. No, there's been a change in plans."

"Change in plans – what about Castro? What about the bio-weapon?" Judyth asks, exasperated.

Lee sighs. "Do you honestly think they could have gotten a legitimate cancer researcher like Dr. Sherman to agree to create galloping cancer cells without using Castro as a bogeyman? How about you – would YOU have agreed to do it? Castro was a straw man. They needed the science more than they wanted Castro," he tells her. "Besides," Lee continues, "they've figured out a way to kill TWO birds with one stone – AND get rid of the stone."

Judyth pauses on the other end. "Who are the two

birds?"

"After Mexico City," Lee explains, "I was ordered to Dallas for a debriefing. My handler reassigned me to work in a book depository in the downtown area. Since then, I have learned there is a plot to kill the President when he visits next month. They tell me I am part of an abort team that is trying to stop it."

Lee hears a gasp. "The bio-weapon...?" Judyth tries to ask.

"No, it's not like that," Lee assures her. "The original plot was to take him out in Chicago a few weeks ago. I found out and tipped off the FBI. They asked for my name and I just said, 'Lee'. Do you remember the night at the 500 Club when David Ferrie was going on half-cocked about killing the President?" Lee asks.

"Yes, unfortunately." Judyth recalls.

"Well, that wasn't just crazy talk," Lee informs her.

"If that IS the case, why were you sent to Mexico City to deliver the cancer cells?" Judyth asks, confused.

"To set me up," Lee says matter-of-factly. "Think about it. I defected to the Soviet Union and I lived there for three years. While I was there, I tried to renounce my

US citizenship, which is a matter of public record. Then I married a Russian woman. After my recall to the states, I publicly masqueraded as a pro-Castro Communist all summer long before trying to go to Cuba in the fall. None of this I did on my own, of course. We both know I was just following orders – Agency orders. It won't matter though because no one will know. I will look like a flaming left-wing radical by the time they're finished with me."

Judyth is too stunned to respond. There is only silence as she processes Lee's words.

He takes a deep breath and continues. "Today, the Dallas newspaper published the President's motorcade route. It will turn and pass within feet of the front steps of my building. If the shots come from the building where I work, everybody inside will instantly become a suspect. With my history, it will not take long for me to become THE person of interest. Next, the people I work for will release the prepared cover story about my background to Dallas authorities and the media. If it's a long-range shot with a high-powered rifle like Ferrie said, my sharpshooting days in the Marines will be icing on the cake, especially since I was ordered to buy a rifle as soon as I got to Dallas."

Judyth gasps. “You not going to shoot anybody…”

“…Of course not,” Lee interjects quickly. “I doubt the rifle I bought could hit anything I aimed at anyway. It’s a cheap piece of crap. However, that is not the point. It is the fact that I own a rifle. They will plant evidence, linking the shots from MY building to MY rifle. No doubt, my prints will be on the weapon, making me the shooter. I DID use my alias when I ordered it but that will only take the FBI about five extra minutes to trace.”

Judyth is crying on the other end.

“Within hours, I will be a convicted in the eyes of the free world as a Castro-loving Communist, a defector, a traitor, and an assassin. The American people will be hysterical. They will demand a pound of flesh. An invasion of the Soviet Union is out of the question, but not Cuba. The CIA has been looking for an excuse to invade Cuba and kill Castro but two things have prevented it – Kennedy and a promise he made to the Soviets. Now Kennedy will be gone – the US President assassinated by a pro-Castro Communist – someone who just tried to go to Cuba. They will have a blank check to do whatever the hell they want. I am a means to an end.”

"The second bird," Judyth gasped, crying bitterly.

"No," Lee says, exasperated. "Castro is the second bird. I'm the stone..."

"...Why don't you just leave, run away – something?" she pleads in between sobs, interrupting him.

"Where can I go to hide?" Lee asks. "The government would hunt me down – to the ends of the earth. I know too much. I went to Russia for a reason. If that reason gets out, it will blow the lid off The Agency. Medical Manhattan, do you honestly think they will allow the public to find out it knowingly infected two-hundred million Americans with a cancer-causing monkey virus? Then, instead of working on developing a vaccine, it weaponized cancer and created a bio-weapon instead? God almighty! That would be the mother of all scandals."

"So what CAN you do?" Judyth asks softly.

"All I can do is stay and abort the mission," he answers firmly. "If I alert the right people, I might be able to save him again like I did in Chicago. If I alert the wrong people, well, he is a dead man. Right now, I do not know whom to trust. But one thing I do know, if I stay, it will be one less bullet fired at the

President."

"When will I see you again?" Judyth whimpers, changing the subject wearily.

Lee is silent. Finally, he says softly, "You won't. My sweet Juduffki, there is no scenario that ends well for me. If I succeed in Dallas, I become the OBSTACLE to their plans. But if I don't, I become the PATSY."

"Your trial, you could tell the truth!" Judyth exclaims, hopeful.

"You still don't get it, do you? There WON'T be a trial," Lee says with a sigh, resigned to his fate. "There CAN'T be a trial."

***

Chapter Fifteen

***

Crime of the Century

Dallas, Texas

November 22, 1963

"There are no faint hearts in Fort Worth," the President begins, lifting his hand to shield his face from the falling rain. "I appreciate your being here this morning. Mrs. Kennedy is still organizing herself. It takes longer, but, of course, she looks better than we do when she does it," he adds, sporting his trademark aw-shucks grin.

It is a friendly crowd. They have come to hear the President brag about Fort Worth being "second to none" in the space and defense industries. The sea of smiling faces presses against the makeshift platform outside the Texas Hotel, eager to hear more, longing to see Jackie.

They will have to wait – for the First Lady anyway. A few minutes later, President Kennedy retreats inside the hotel for a breakfast hosted by the Fort Worth Chamber of Commerce, speaking on military preparedness. "We are still the keystone in the arch of freedom...and we will still do our duty, with the people of Texas leading the way."

Unfortunately, the crowd outside earns only a passing glance at the First Lady as the motorcade speeds away after the President's speech, on its way to Carswell Air Force Base. The Fort Worth folks will have to wait a few hours to watch the main event on television – live from Dallas.

Air Force One departs Fort Worth, leaving behind rain and an overcast sky – landing thirteen minutes later at Love Field in Dallas. The rain had stopped about ten o'clock, a brilliant sun and a light breeze drying up the puddles on the ground. "It's almost seventy-degrees," one Secret Service agent observes, scowling. "I guess the Vice President will get his way – it's warm enough to remove the bubble-top after all. Dammit."

Dallas is not Fort Worth and the President's protective detail knows it. Everyone on the security team has seen the file. A well-known stronghold of the far right, the conservative city is hostile to liberal politics and especially, liberal politicians. Though Kennedy won the state narrowly in 1960, he lost the Dallas area big-time, even WITH native son Lyndon Baines Johnson on the ticket.

Three weeks ago, Kennedy's Ambassador to the United Nations – Adlai Stevenson – was spit on and nearly manhandled by raucous Dallas protesters in front of his hotel. Less than one week later, a prominent Dallas businessman made a speech during which he called JFK a "liability to the free world."

Dallas's Mayor is Earl Cabbell, brother of former CIA Deputy Director General Charles Cabbell. Charles is "former" Deputy Director now because the President fired him a year ago after the failed Bay of Pigs invasion. Earl has made no secret of his displeasure over that decision.

Dallas is also home to General Edwin Walker. Accused of distributing literature from the right-wing John Birch Society to his troops, Walker was relieved of his command of the 24th Infantry Division in Germany by the Kennedy Administration in 1961. The General blamed Kennedy for firing him, saying, "It will be my purpose now, as a civilian, to attempt to do what I have found no longer possible to do in uniform." In the two years since, the military hero has been true to his threat, stirring up all kinds of trouble for the Administration.

He organized protests against the enrollment of James Meredith – a black man – at the University of Mississippi in 1961. One year later, he incited a riot on the Ole' Miss campus while protesting Kennedy's use of federal troops to enroll Meredith. Two students died and rioters shot six federal marshals.

The government arrested General Walker on federal charges of sedition and insurrection against the United States, charged levied by the Attorney General himself – President Kennedy's brother. Walker made bail, returning to Dallas a hero to the right-wing conservatives resisting federal abuse of power and greeted at the airport by two-hundred cheering supporters.

He is now a national symbol, traveling the country giving speeches, railing against Communism, desegregation, and civil rights, denouncing the liberal establishment generally and the Kennedy Administration specifically.

Yesterday, someone plastered "WANTED FOR TREASON" posters with the President's picture front and center all over the city of Dallas. Storefront windows, utility poles and bulletin boards are becoming message boards for the far right's beef with JFK. Though it has no proof yet, the Secret Service suspects General Walker paid for the printing of the posters.

This morning, hours before his visit, the Dallas Morning News ran a full-page ad welcoming the President to Dallas. However, upon closer inspection, the ad asks leading questions like "Why have you ordered your brother – the Attorney General – to go soft on Communists, fellow-travelers and ultra-leftists...while you allow him to persecute loyal Americans who criticize you, your Administration and your leadership?" There are eleven more questions similar in tone and content. The ad concludes, stating, "Mr. Kennedy, we DEMAND answers to these questions and we want them NOW." At the bottom of the page, the local chapter of the John Birch Society – of which General Walker is a prominent member – claims sole responsibility for the ad.

These are just a few reasons the Secret Service is in such a foul mood over the President's foray into Dallas, Texas. Without question, it is enemy territory.

The motorcade procession begins slowly, crossing the

airfield's tarmac like floats in a parade. In front, the grand marshal of this VIP procession is Dallas Police Chief Jesse Curry in an unmarked white Ford accompanied by his friend, Dallas County Sheriff Bill Decker. Two stone-faced Secret Service agents are sitting on opposite sides in the backseat, staring out of their windows, taking turns talking into their wrist microphones.

Next, the Presidential limousine – a 1961 Lincoln Continental – with its top removed exposing the occupants and its three rows of seats. Secret Service agents Bill Greer and Roy Kellerman are in the front seat, with Greer doing the driving. In the second row of seats, waving his ever-present ten-gallon hat at the crowds, Texas Governor John Connally and his wife Nellie are all smiles. Of course, the back seat of the stately limousine is for JFK and his lovely wife Jacqueline – glamor and grace personified, dressed elegantly in a candy pink suit.

Behind the President is the follow-up car, a convertible nicknamed "Halfback" carrying a driver, two Presidential aides and seven more grouchy – and cramped – Secret Service agents.

The Vice Presidential limousine, also a convertible, is

car number-four in the line-up. In addition to Vice President Lyndon Johnson and his wife Lady Bird, the distinguished Texas Senator Ralph Yarborough is a guest passenger today.

Trailing the Vice President, three more cars – two of which are carrying various media members reporting on the President's trip to Texas – and the third and final car, packed full with local law enforcement.

Like bees buzzing around their queen, nineteen of Dallas's finest on two-wheel Harley-Davidson motorcycles escort the motorcade, encircling it in blue uniforms, completing the picture-perfect scene. Three of them serve as the advance team, cutting off crossing traffic at upcoming intersections. Like a Grecian phalanx, five bikes are out in front of the motorcade, leading in the inverted "V" formation, lights blinking and sirens blaring. Four stay in close ranks to each other, within arm's reach of the President, six space out, attending to the VIP's and their vehicles behind the Presidential limousine, and one lonely rider is trailing the procession, bringing up the rear.

Chosen in advance, the peculiar route for the President's motorcade started at Love Field in northwest Dallas. The seven-car parade began the forty-five minute loop at 11:40 am, traveling south toward Dealey Plaza in the downtown area, after which the motorcade will double back, taking the Stemmons Freeway to the Business and Trade Mart in northwest Dallas – only about ten minutes in real time from Love Field.

The spectacle moves in slow motion – coming to a halt twice so the President can shake hands. "God-damn wide-open windows everywhere," the agent on the left in car number-one states tersely, looking up at the high-rise buildings on his side. "I want to know what birdbrain came up with THIS idea."

Near the center of Dallas, it enters Dealey Plaza, slowing to make a ninety-degree, right-hand turn from Main Street onto Houston Street. Now directly ahead of the motorcade is the Texas School Book Depository building. About fifty feet before the Depository, the motorcade slows down again, coming almost to a complete stop to make the hairpin one-hundred and twenty-degree, left-hand turn onto Elm Street. The grassy knoll is on the right – people everywhere – calling out "Mr. President!" and holding their children up to see the leader of the free world pass by. The President and First Lady are smiling and waving, enjoying the intimacy of the close quarters.

"If we can just make it to the Triple Underpass, we're home free," the agent on the right of car number-one says, looking ahead, pointing. The Triple Underpass is now in plain view, less than one-hundred yards in front of the motorcade, and then on to the safety of the freeway.

"We're going WAY too slow," the first agent remarks. "I don't like it. I don't like it one bit."

Seconds later, all hell breaks loose.

***

Dallas, Texas

November 24, 1963

It happened just as Oswald predicted. Exactly. The President – shot dead in Dealey Plaza, just a few feet from the entrance of the Schoolbook Depository. Witnesses swore they heard shots and saw rifle smoke coming from the grassy knoll in FRONT of the President's car. Senator Yarborough, a former lieutenant colonel in the US Army during WW II, confirmed he smelled gunpowder as his car passed the grassy knoll.

Yet, the Dallas Police made the Depository building – BEHIND the Presidential limousine – their focal point, sealing the building within minutes of the shooting and demanding a roster of employees. With the help of Depository Superintendent Roy Truly, a roll call ensued, coming up one name short. The police radio sprang to life, the all-points bulletin identifying a "Lee Harvey Oswald" as an early "person of interest" in what was already being described as the "crime of the century".

Co-workers were inconclusive in their statements to police – most did not even know the recent-hire, much less, what he was doing during the motorcade. Carolyn Arnold, however, was a little more definitive. "I saw him sitting in one of the booth seats on the right-hand side of the break room," she said. "He was alone as usual and appeared to be having his lunch. I did not speak to him but I recognized him clearly."

Her statement rang true. Oswald spent a lot of time alone in the break room, mostly talking on the pay phone. During one reconnaissance of Oswald at his new job, Andy observed Lee on the same phone in the same second-floor break room three different times on the same shift. With some help from a Southwestern Telephone Company technician, a suspicious Andy planted a bugging device in the phone. After the shooting, Lee made a phone call. Andy was one block away listening in his car when Oswald's handler instructed Lee to "go to the regular meet location and wait for further instructions."

A few minutes later, Lee exited the building through the front doors, passed by the assembling police, slipped through the hysterical crowd, and made his way across town on foot with Andy in tow. It was then, once their man was out of the building, the Dallas Police closed all the exits and entrances to the Depository.

Meanwhile, though all of President Kennedy's Secret Service detail were at Parkland Hospital and accounted for, imposters flashing Secret Service badges were busy securing the scene of the crime. They rounded up witnesses, bullying or ignoring the ones whose accounts differed from the rapidly emerging official version that all the shots came from the Book Depository. The police disregarded Miss Arnold's statement almost immediately because Oswald could not have been eating in the second-floor break room at the same time he was shooting at the President from a sixth-floor window. Next, with Oswald on the loose, the Dallas Police set up the second patsy of the day – one of their own.

Forty-five minutes after the assassination, Officer J.D. Tippit stopped a man walking through the quiet Oak Cliff neighborhood, roughly two miles from the Depository building. Tippit radioed his dispatcher and reported a man matching Oswald's description. Tippit tried to question the man but never got the chance. The suspect shot him three times at point blank range. Before fleeing the scene, he leaned over and delivered a coup de grace shot for good measure.

Witnesses disagreed when confronted with Oswald's photo. Some shook their heads, saying the shooter was not Oswald. Others claimed it was actually TWO shooters, both fleeing the scene on foot in opposite directions. None of them identified the shooter as Lee Oswald. Nevertheless, the Dallas Police released a second all-points bulletin, this one with Oswald's image. The whole city of Dallas was now searching for Lee Harvey Oswald, alleged assassin AND cop-killer.

Coincidentally, authorities knew exactly where to find him, sitting by himself in the Texas Theater, waiting. Clearly, he was not there in the darkened theater during the middle of the afternoon to see the feature – *War is Hell.* Though he had thirteen dollars and eighty-seven cents in his pocket, Oswald had not even bothered to purchase an eighty-six cent ticket.

More than thirty Dallas Police officers stormed the theater, creating quite a ruckus. While they were inside arresting Oswald, their bosses were busy outside releasing the prepared-in-advance cover story – casting the necessary first impression – as their army of underlings escorted the guilty man out of the theater, through the assembled onlookers, to a waiting patrol car.

The .38 revolver found on Oswald at the time of his arrest matched the spent cartridges found lying in the street next to Officer Tippit – seeming to neatly tie up the evidence linking Oswald to the Tippit murder in a big bow. With one problem – .38 revolvers DO NOT eject their spent cartridges. No matter! Next, it was the media's turn to play along. Soon, the whole world was learning the Oswald story. Just as he had predicted, it painted a very guilty picture.

Yesterday, the state of Texas formally charged Lee Oswald with the murders of President Kennedy and Officer J.D. Tippit. Normally, the state provides a defendant with an attorney. Not Oswald. Instead, attempting to exhaust a confession out of him, the

Dallas Police spent the whole day moving him from one interrogation room to another, each time parading him before the assembled media horde and their cameras – flashbulbs and film producing the requisite guilty image needed to accompany the cover story.

“Did you shoot the President?” a bloody-eyed correspondent shouted accusingly during one of the transfers.

“No sir,” Oswald replied calmly. “I have not been charged with that. Nobody has said that to me yet. The first thing I heard about it was when the newspaper reporters in the hall asked me that question – I did not do it. I did not do it – I did not shoot anyone.”

“Do you even know the charges against you?” another writer asked breathlessly.

“Nobody has told me anything except that I am accused of murdering a policeman. I do not know anything more than that. I do request someone to come forward and give me legal assistance.” Then this kicker from Oswald. “I am just a patsy!”

Today, the police are transferring him yet again, this time from downtown police headquarters to the county jail. Like times before, a gaggle of reporters waits for him, frantic to witness the accused assassin escorted from the city jail's basement exit to a waiting vehicle. Included in the frenzy is mobbed-up nightclub owner and known Oswald associate Jack Rubenstein or, as Oswald knows him – Jack "Ruby" – waiting with the rest of them, pretending to be a gawker.

Jack Ruby is a well-known figure in Dallas, especially with Big D's finest. Since he relocated from Chicago in 1947 and opened the Carousel Club, he has cultivated a partnership with Dallas Police. He saves the best booze and the finest women for "his boys" in the DPD. Coincidentally, or not, one of his boys was Officer J.D. Tippit, a regular at the Carousel Club.

With Ruby's extensive underworld connections, the DPD found a use for him too, recruiting Ruby to be one of its most reliable informants. Ruby tips police about low-level vice and narcotics operations in the city – mostly giving up his competition. Ruby's payoffs to corrupt police officers provide him what HE needs – protection. His tips give them what THEY need – an impressive string of busts that bring notoriety and most importantly, promotions.

Everybody inn Dallas knows that Ruby is the liaison between Sam Giancana's Chicago outfit and Carlos

Marcello's New Orleans' empire – both of which operate in Dallas. Organized crime controls the prostitution rings and gambling rackets in Dallas. Due to Ruby's good work, it can also lay claim to the Dallas Police Department. That is why his presence in the police garage is not surprising.

Finally, the moment everyone is waiting for. As Oswald steps from the elevator, he recognizes someone in the crowd. The man steps out of the mass of people toward him. "Ruby..." Oswald says, his eyes locking onto the familiar face.

"...Oswald!" Ruby shouts, interrupting Oswald. Suddenly, his right arm raises, revealing the .38 revolver in his hand. A single shot rings outs. Oswald slumps to the ground, wounded eyes screaming their betrayal.

Confusion reigns as the assembled police officers wrestle the assailant's gun from his grasp and throw him violently to the ground facedown next to a bleeding Oswald. For a brief moment, the two men are side-by-side. One lies dying and the other lies handcuffed.

The Dallas Police quickly confirm Oswald's identification of the man as Jack Ruby. They hold him in an interrogation room, waiting for final word about Oswald's condition.

A Dallas Police detective assigned to the room is observing Ruby, noting his agitated state. The heart monitor they wired him to indicates a racing heart rate. Pacing frantically, smoking the detective's cigarettes one after another – his hands shaking – and soaking through a bath towel with his own sweat, Ruby is NOT the picture of a confident man. Every time the holding room door opens, the skittish Ruby practically jumps out of his skin. He does not say very much but when he does, it is clear he is a nervous wreck. Naturally, the detective assumes Ruby is concerned about Oswald's condition. After all, Texas IS a death penalty state.

Word finally arrives from Parkland Hospital, the same hospital where the President died only two days before. It is official now. Oswald too is dead.

Knowing his one and only bullet found its mark, Ruby's heart rate slows to normal and he stops sweating. A strange calm comes over him and he takes a seat. A stunned detective offers him a cigarette. Ruby declines, claiming he does not smoke. He begins joking with the other officers in the room, most of whom he knows personally. Obviously, Ruby is relieved that Oswald is dead.

Though his life is now in jeopardy with the legal system, Oswald's death squares him with the ones that matter most – the Giancana and Marcello crime families. He fears them more than anything the state of Texas can do to him. His debts to Sam "Momo" Giancana and Carlos "Big Daddy" Marcello now paid in full, Ruby smiles, satisfied. There can never be a trial of Lee Harvey Oswald for the murder of the President. He has made sure of that.

One of the reasons Andy is good at his job is the research he does on his subjects. By the time he completes his assignments, he has read every file, looked at every photo, heard every story, examined every record, followed every lead, studied every trait and learned every habit of his subjects. Like the successful actor who gets into character, Andy usually knows his marks better than they know themselves. In Oswald's case, he recognizes exploitation when he sees it – the reason his final report to Sasha includes these words of remembrance for a man Americans would rather forget.

Born into a life of aimless wandering, abject

poverty, and after-thought neglect, Oswald was a lost soul until David Ferrie took him under his wing. Ferrie steered Lee into a life of military intelligence. After the CIA recruited him, he served his country, following orders and trusting those who gave them.

He was, like most orphans or unwanted children, in constant search of a family he never had. He found a father figure in David Ferrie. His family became the CIA, and his life was covert-ops. Altogether, they gave his life meaning. For the first time in his life, he was somebody important doing something that mattered.

To him, The Agency was everything. To The Agency, he was nothing – something it could use and dispose of later, like garbage. Such is the tragic end of a true American patriot.

***

Washington D.C.

November 25, 1963

She kneels down, meeting the little boy's eyes with her

own. “Today is your birthday son. You are three years old. We have to do something for daddy first. Is that okay with you?”

The boy nods, aware something bad has happened to his daddy.

The young mother smiles through her tears, hugging her little man. “I love you,” she whispers.

Heartfelt messages keep flooding into the White House, too many for a grieving widow to read right now. The First Lady’s staff is collecting them. “There will come a time and place,” they are told. Except for one – from the Soviet Premier. They gave it to Jackie immediately.

> *It was with deep personal grief that I learned about the tragic death of your husband, President of the U.S. John F. Kennedy. All people who knew him greatly respected him, and I shall always keep the memory of my meetings with him. Accept my most sincere condolences and expressions of wholehearted sympathy with your grievous bereavement. –Nikita Khrushchev*

Khrushchev was not the only one grieving. Yesterday, in near-freezing temperatures, more than three-hundred thousand people gathered, watching somberly as the horse-drawn caisson carried Kennedy's flag-draped coffin down the White House drive, past the soldiers and flags, on its journey to the United States Capitol Rotunda to lie in state. A single horse – no rider – with a pair of boots reversed in the stirrups followed the caisson. The only sounds were the muffled drums and the clacking of horses' hooves.

Over the next eighteen hours, over two-hundred and fifty-thousand people paid their respects, waiting their turn, some standing for ten hours in lines ten-persons wide and forty blocks long.

Today, one-million people are lining the route of the funeral procession, from the Capitol back to the White House, then to St. Matthew's Cathedral, ending at Arlington National Cemetery. Millions more will follow the proceedings on television. Representatives from ninety different countries are present.

Unlike the silent procession yesterday, the funeral procession today will include other military units – some foreign. Kennedy's widow requested the Marine Band lead the funeral procession. She also requested pipers from the Scottish Black Watch to march from the White House to St. Matthew's and cadets from the Irish Defense Force to perform silent drill at the gravesite. The pipers and cadets are from Ireland, in Washington today paying tribute to Kennedy's Irish ancestry.

The procession began at 10:50 am, the caisson leaving the Capitol on its way back to the White House where all the military units except the Marine Company turned right off of Pennsylvania Avenue onto Seventeenth Street. A platoon of the Marine Company entered the northeast gate of the White House, leading the cortege into the North Portico.

Now, the procession is resuming on foot to St. Matthew's Cathedral, led by Jackie and the late President's brothers, Robert and Edward (Ted) Kennedy, walking the same route the President and First Lady often used when going to Mass at the cathedral. Behind them, John, Jr., turning three years old today, and big sister Caroline, nearly six, are riding in a limousine. The rest of the family is waiting for them at the cathedral.

New President Lyndon B. Johnson, his wife Lady Bird, and their two daughters Luci and Lynda are also marching in the procession. The Secret Service tried to talk him out of it, considering the potential risk in the wake of Kennedy's assassination. "Like hell I won't," he said, abruptly ending the discussion.

When the service ends, the Kennedy family takes its place outside the cathedral. Thousands of people hush respectfully. Photographers crammed into the tight space jockey for position. The moment they have all been waiting for is here – the caisson, carrying the late President's body, on its way to Arlington.

All eyes are on Mrs. Kennedy as the horses draw near. She leans over, whispering something in her son's ear again. John, Jr. looks up, his right hand letting go of his mother's grasp. He raises it to his forehead, open-hand, and palm down. His left arm stays at his side, pointing at the ground. As the caisson passes, the young boy stiffens, saluting the President – his daddy – one last time.

***

Moscow, Russia

December 1, 1963

Premier Khrushchev leans back in his chair and throws Father's report on his desk. "It's obvious who's calling the shots in America now," he barks, clearly agitated.

“You predicted it,” Father says, taking his seat.

“I was hoping I was wrong,” Khrushchev admits. He wheels around in his chair and looks out the window for a minute, lost in his own thoughts.

“President Kennedy was his own ambassador of détente,” remarks Father, ending the silence. “He gave, we took, and it cost him. It proves one thing, as long as there are profits to be made, the Americans will not be ready for peace.”

Disgusted, the Premier turns his chair back toward his desk and picks up the report again. Then he begins reading aloud. “The new President is reversing America’s foreign policy in Vietnam as set forth on October 11, 1963 by Kennedy’s National Security Action Memo 263. JFK’s order, a partial withdrawal of military advisors, was to be followed by a complete withdrawal of all American military personnel in Vietnam after the 1964 election.”

Khrushchev pauses briefly before continuing. “But November 26, 1963, President Johnson issued National Security Action Memo 273, authorizing an ESCALATION of covert actions in Southeast Asia.”

He stops reading and looks up at Father, exclaiming, "Son-of-a-bitch! Four fucking days! Kennedy's body is still warm! How do they get away with this shit?"

"He's got stones, I'll give him that," Father agrees. "A lot of us were dead wrong. We thought the Americans' immediate target would be Cuba, certainly not Vietnam," he says, mystified by the new American strategy.

"I disagree. I'm not so sure we were totally wrong," Khrushchev says, shaking his head. "It could just be payback with a sleight-of-hand trick, no?" Father remains silent, waiting for the Premier to continue. He has learned to let Khrushchev do his thinking aloud with minimal interference.

"We've been in Cuba, poking around in their hemisphere ever since Bay of Pigs," Khrushchev explains. "Now, they're going to meddle in Vietnam and create a mess in ours. Meanwhile, as the world is focusing on Southeast Asia, Castro will be dying quietly of cancer."

"Interesting theory," Father says with admiration.

The Premier is rolling. "Kennedy's enemies got exactly what they wanted. Vietnam is in play now, before it wasn't," he calculates. "In fact, it's become a god-damn blue-chip stock. War in Vietnam translates into billions for their military-industrial complex, a restoration of power for the CIA, and almost-certain victory for Johnson in '64. The only thing they need now is an excuse to go to war. This memo will give them..."

"...Ah, yes, the covert-ops playbook," Father interrupts. "There will be an incident, followed by a cover story that blames a Communist bogeyman, which in this case will be the Viet Cong," he predicts cynically.

"Indeed, just like Dallas," the Premier agrees. "If you can lie about murdering your President and get away with it, imagine how easy it will be to lie about the god-damned Viet Cong."

"Assuming its true, there could be a silver lining in this for us," Father says, already plotting the next move on the geopolitical chessboard.

Khrushchev looks at Father hopefully, "Yes?"

"It's a paradox," Father begins. "The Americans are willing to trade Cuba, which is ninety miles off their coast, for Vietnam, which is nine-thousand miles away. Cuba is IN their hemisphere, Vietnam is NOT. It makes no sense, but it does give us a strategy. Think of the logistics…"

"…Dammit! You are right! We'll bleed them!" the Premier interrupts loudly. "American taxpayers will choke on their precious social contract. They do not know it yet but they have given power to a corrupt government, which is going to take their money and men to fight a war halfway around the world. All they'll get in return will be their boys in flag-covered coffins."

Father nods his head in agreement. "If we do this just right, the war will drag on – more money, more men. Public opinion will begin to turn against the politicians. Hell, American containment might end up American capitulation instead! It could not have turned out better for us if we had planned it ourselves – east vs. west in Southeast Asia. If it was east vs. west in Cuba, they could have bled us."

Khrushchev laughs. "And to think, we thought all Americans were bastards. Turns out they are. But some of them are DUMB bastards!"

***

Chapter Sixteen

***

Cover-Up – Tying Off Loose Ends

Washington D.C.

February 12, 1964

The bookstore is dark. The red-lettered "Closed, Please Call Again," sign is hanging in the front window, dusty and crooked. *Has the sign ever said open?* Caleb wonders, chuckling to himself. Three months of northeastern snow accumulation covers the sidewalk. Large ice swords hang from the awning above the entry, aiming perilously at the few scattered passers-by. By the looks of things, Sasha's bookstore has not been open in years.

Caleb ignores the sign and knocks three quick raps. The door opens quickly and he steps inside. Sasha nods at him, glancing at his watch. He motions toward the back, escorting Caleb without a word to a room where Joshua is already waiting. Sasha takes a seat facing the door. Both doctors seat themselves at a table across from him.

"It's been awhile," Sasha begins, opening the file in front of him. "Where are we with the polio vaccine? Last time we met, the government knew that the Sabin vaccine was contaminated by monkey viruses." Sasha looks at the report. "I believe you said SV-40 and SIV. Is that correct?"

Caleb speaks first. "That's correct. Dr. Eddy made her report in 1959. By then, the government had already mass-inoculated one-hundred million Americans during 1957-1959. Afterward, the government decided to proceed with the vaccines anyway – in spite of her findings. Since then, the remaining one-hundred million doses have been administered."

"So you're telling me that two-hundred million Americans have SV-40 and SIV in their bloodstream..." Sasha says, doing the calculations in his head.

"...No," Joshua interrupts quickly, shaking his head. "Both viruses are sexually-transmitted. Who KNOWS what the actual number is after eight years of exponential multiplication?"

Sasha is confused. "Doesn't that mean EVERYBODY at some point will be diagnosed with cancer or the immunodeficiency virus, or both?"

"No, not necessarily," Joshua clarifies. "But two-hundred million-plus are carriers."

"When will we know the extent...," Sasha begins asking.

"...We should start seeing a spike in soft-tissue cancers in the early eighties," Joshua interrupts again. "The immunodeficiency virus is the wildcard. We simply do not know how it will manifest. However, we do know that the incubation periods are identical. In other words, we could have a double-whammy of first-time cancer diagnoses and catastrophic immune system failures at about the same time."

Sasha looks at Caleb. "What about you? You are being awful quiet. The government went ahead with the vaccinations in hopes of finding a cure for cancer in the meantime – is there progress to report on that front?"

Caleb shakes his head. "No. In fact, the goal has changed again. We are no longer trying to find a cure. Instead, the government and pharmaceutical companies are researching a whole menu of treatment options to be available when the epidemic hits. It seems there is more money in treating cancer than in curing it. The same is true for the immunodeficiency symptoms."

Sasha lets the words sink in. "Holy shit," he mutters. "Imagine the pile of money the Americans will shell out for treatment if just HALF of those vaccinated are diagnosed with cancer."

"A license to print money," Caleb agrees.

"Nixon started all this in '55 because he wanted to be President in '60," Sasha remembers. "It's too late for him to declare this cycle, but I would bet everything I own in this world that he'll be a Presidential candidate in '68 – with financial backing from the medical community and the big pharmaceutical companies of course."

"I don't know," Caleb shrugs, looking at Joshua. "Maybe."

Sasha ignores them, continuing his monologue. "Just mark my words, Nixon WILL be President soon. When it happens, FDA will suddenly approve cancer treatments the pharmaceuticals are quietly working on right now. When the cancer diagnoses begin happening and the people start panicking, the drugs will be ready and waiting, at a very high cost. Big-Pharma will make a killing…"

"…They'll make a killing together," Caleb interjects. "The drug companies need the government to approve their drugs and the politicians will need the pharmaceutical industry's money to get elected."

"The cruel irony," Sasha says, shaking his head. "Nixon cured Americans of polio but gave them cancer instead…"

"…And god-only-knows what else," Joshua says, finishing Sasha's thought.

***

Gettysburg, Pennsylvania

March 5, 1964

His day begins with a forty-minute drive to DC Metro Station in Shady Grove, Maryland. After parking in the rental car lot, he buys a day pass and boards a train to National Military Park in Gettysburg, Pennsylvania.

An hour later, he steps off the train at Westwood One-Metro Station. After a quick bathroom break, he sets out on foot, walking south toward the infamous Cemetery Ridge. Arrowhead chose this particular location, not Sasha. The view is spectacular though, and the privacy is impossible to beat.

Arrowhead had been specific – the south end of the Ridge near Little Round Top. Sure enough, Sasha sees him from a distance, a solitary figure planted on a wall of stones, smoking a cigarette. Aside from the sitting and the cigarette smoke, he looks like a sentry, manning a lonely post.

"What's the topic today?" Arrowhead asks without looking up or saying hello. Out of habit, he checks his watch.

"The Warren Commission," replies Sasha, taking a seat on the man-made barrier.

Arrowhead curses and snuffs out his cigarette. There is a long pause. "A dog-and-pony show," he says finally.

"Take me through it anyway," Sasha insists. "And don't leave anything out."

Arrowhead sighs. "The perps are in charge now," he begins. "Eliminating Oswald did foreclose on a trial, but it also opened the door to doubt. It does not take a genius to figure out someone shut him up – permanently. They were expecting the cover story to harden by now but it is not happening. Americans are unsure. Hell, just look at the polls. Half think Oswald had some kind of help – he could not possibly have acted alone. A growing number of people are beginning to suspect the government was involved. And if you ask most people in Texas, they believe LBJ pulled the god-damned trigger himself."

"So the Commission's main job is to sway public opinion," Sasha says, "NOT find the truth."

"Exactly," Arrowhead replies. "The conspiracy will only hold up if the American people believe the lone-nut, blame-Castro, cockamamie cover story. The conspirators DO have a trump card though. His name is Lyndon Baines Johnson. He's their ace-in-the-hole."

"What about the Commission?" Sasha asks. "It seems rushed after the assassination. And the members – almost like he had a list prepared in advance."

Arrowhead smirks. "You think?"

Sasha kicks at a nearby fence plank. "I don't often divulge inside information," he says. "But this is important. Military and intelligence officials are moving this new President around like a pawn in their chess game. There has already been a 180-degree change in America's foreign policy in Southeast Asia. The war hawks around Johnson seem hell-bent on keeping all of us on the brink of Armageddon."

"That's exactly what they want," Arrowhead states bluntly. "Kennedy was getting in the way so they killed him. Now Johnson's their little hand-puppet."

Sasha clears his throat. "The Soviet government is not the American people. We know the plot. We know the players. What we do not know yet is the get-away plan. Inside information on the Warren Commission would give us tremendous leverage opportunities. These conspirators will do anything to keep the truth from getting out. They THINK President Johnson holds the trump card. But if they know that we know what they don't want us to know, WE will be holding all the cards."

Arrowhead does not need convincing. "When and who explains what and why," he says gruffly.

Sasha stares at Arrowhead, waiting for details. "And?"

"The speed with which this commission was put together reflects the need to tie up loose ends, and quickly. It is the same reason a cover story was prepared in advance, to start the ball rolling in Oswald's direction before any other suspects or theories could fill the vacuum. As you know, timing is everything in covert-ops. The members themselves are telling. During the World Wars, Warren and Cooper were Army, Boggs and Ford were Navy, and McCloy was Assistant Secretary of War. Dulles was Director of the CIA for eight years, and Russell was Chairman of the Senate Armed Services Committee and a committee member of the Subcommittee on CIA Oversight. Anything jump out at you about that list?" Arrowhead asks Sasha, eyebrows raised.

"All seven members have military or intelligence backgrounds," Sasha answers.

"Damn straight," Arrowhead says. "You think that's an accident?" he asks rhetorically.

"Then you have Johnson's executive order," Arrowhead continues. "'To investigate all aspects of the assassination and produce an official report that will forever satisfy the American people'. You know, typical politician-speak."

"Hot air…" Sasha agrees.

"...People MIGHT have believed it too if Katzenbach hadn't gone out and stepped in a gigantic pile of shit," Arrowhead says, interrupting Sasha.

"Why in the hell did he write that memo to begin with?" Sasha wonders, incredulous. "He HAD to know it would get out eventually!"

Arrowhead laughs. "I don't know, dumbass, I guess. When the Assistant Attorney General – the number-two law enforcement officer of the United States – writes that 'the public must be satisfied Oswald was the assassin and he did not have confederates who are still at large, and that evidence was such that he would have been convicted at trial', people start believing the investigation is fixed – they can't help it. Dumbass or not, his words ring more true than anything the President is saying."

"Johnson stacked the god-damn commission," concludes Sasha.

"Of course he did," replies Arrowhead with a shrug. "What choice did he have? He cannot take a chance on a real investigation. He knows he'd get caught in his own dragnet."

Sasha rubs his chin. "Fox guarding the henhouse. By

choosing military and intelligence cronies, he's protecting them AND him at the same time."

"Like it or not, they're bedfellows now," Arrowhead agrees. "The kind that REALLY means, 'til death do us part'."

"This commission is going to begin with a conclusion and work backwards, Oswald acted alone," Sasha predicts.

"Obviously. But there's an even bigger picture," Arrowhead adds.

"Oh?" Sasha queries.

"New Orleans!" Arrowhead replies emphatically. "Imagine if Oswald had lived and there was a legitimate trial. How long would it take for his summer of '63 to come under scrutiny? Oswald's time in the Crescent City would lead investigators to a top-secret CIA cancer research lab, the Medical Manhattan Project, a cancer bio-weapon, and an assassination factory – with Oswald right in the middle of all that government hanky-panky..."

"...Jesus. The mother of all scandals," Sasha interjects.

"Oh, it gets better," declares Arrowhead. "The assumption that cancer research was covert to protect the bio-weapon is only partly true. The government is actually much more terrified that the American people will find out it mistakenly injected one-hundred million people with the contaminated polio vaccine. Talk about a scandal."

"It was a mistake. Governments survive scandals like that all the time," counters Sasha.

"Jesus, this isn't just a scandal!" Arrowhead exclaims. "The first one-hundred million injections might have been a mistake but KNOWINGLY injecting one-hundred million MORE people with the monkey viruses – both of which are lethal? Christ, that's god-damn genocide! Assassinating the President is bad enough, but mass murder?"

"You're right," Sasha admits. "No government would survive that. The American people's faith in government institutions would crumble overnight. The whole system would come apart at the seams."

"Sooner or later," Arrowhead says, "Somebody would testify the reason the government was working on a cancer vaccine was to head off a cancer epidemic it knew was coming. How did it know? Because Dr. Eddy

– the government's own researcher – gave them a written report predicting it. Why was the cancer vaccine necessary? Because they covered up her report and authorized one-hundred million more injections anyway, hoping to find a cure before the incubation period expired. At that point, the trial would be less about Oswald and more about the government playing Russian roulette with two-hundred-million Americans, injecting them with SV-40 and SIV. Son-of-a-bitch, talk about explosive shit."

"I thought the reason they didn't want a trial was to protect the JFK conspirators. They HAD to kill Oswald..." Sasha says before Arrowhead cuts him off.

"...They had to kill Oswald to protect SEVERAL conspiracies," Arrowhead declares. "Any of which even a half-ass public defender could expose in a trial. Can you imagine the fall-out if the American people found out the REAL reason Oswald went to Russia? Holy Christ!"

"It's amazing how all these CIA covert-ops point back to the same twenty-four year-old flunky," Sasha observes, shaking his head.

"Maybe he wasn't the flunky they made him out to be," suggests Arrowhead.

"Maybe not," agrees Sasha. "Regardless, without a suspect – there can be no trial. No trial – no witnesses. No witnesses – no depositions. No depositions – no testimony. No testimony – no problems. They put that poor boy together like a cheap suit. He did not have a chance then and he certainly does not have a chance going forward. The Commission will pin everything on a dead man."

"Anything could happen at a trial," Arrowhead states. "But an investigation with hand-picked members who understand the stakes and know their marching orders? It's a no-brainer. One they can't control, the other they can."

Sasha stands up, brushing residue from the stone wall off his pants. He looks up at Arrowhead. "The Warren Commission will produce a report and the media will masturbate all over it. Then, the textbooks will do the rest. Generations of Americans will be taught the official version, that Lee Harvey Oswald – a crazed, lone nut – acted alone and killed Kennedy." He stops, pausing for effect. "What a crock of shit."

"And what's worse," Arrowhead adds, "When they get away with it – and they will – they'll do it again."

***

Washington D.C.

June 14, 1964

Sasha carefully opens the envelope postmarked New Orleans. There is no return address but he knows who sent it. *Andy*, thinks Sasha. Since Oswald's death in Dallas, Andy's new assignment is to "follow the bodies" of his summer of '63 accomplices in New Orleans.

A singular newspaper clipping falls from the thin envelope onto Sasha's desk, names underlined and dates circled in red. "William Guy Bannister, born March 7, 1901 in Monroe, Louisiana died June 6, 1964 of coronary thrombosis at his home in New Orleans," reads the obituary. The date listed is June 7, last Sunday's edition of the New Orleans Times Picayune. The caption under the file photo provides more details.

> *'Guy' Bannister was an investigator with the Federal Bureau of Investigation from 1934-1954. He also served with the New Orleans Police as Assistant Superintendent from 1955-1957. After retiring from public service, he established Guy Bannister Associates, a private detective agency*

> *in downtown New Orleans.*

Andy highlighted the next paragraph in yellow. Next to it – scribbled in the left margin – are the words: “Suspected publisher of the Louisiana Intelligence Digest.”

> *Mr. Bannister belonged to several New Orleans-based anti-communist organizations including the Minutemen, the John Birch Society, and the State of Louisiana Committee on Un-American Activities. He also supported anti-Castro groups such as Friends of a Democratic Cuba, the Anti-Communist League of the Caribbean, the Cuban Democratic Revolutionary Front, and the Crusade to Free Cuba Committee.*

The article ends with a quote from the New Orleans States-Item.

> *Guy Bannister participated in every anti-Communist South and Central American revolution that came along, operating as the key liaison for all U.S. government-sponsored anti-Communist activities in Latin America.*

Squeezed in at the bottom of the obituary is Andy’s handwritten memo. “Did you notice the bio left out his involvement with Lee Oswald and the Fair Play for Cuba Committee, only listing anti-Castro credentials? Very interesting. Also, officially ruled death by natural causes. Timing is sure convenient. Heart attack scrubs WC testimony and his scheduled deposition with New Orleans District Attorney Jim Garrison in the Clay Shaw matter. Watching to see if any other Oswald associates die convenient deaths. Stay tuned.

There is no signature at the bottom, just the singular letter "A."

***

Washington D.C.

July 28, 1964

Six weeks after Andy's first envelope arrived from New Orleans, a second one arrives. There is no obituary from the newspaper this time, just a typed paragraph with an image of a horribly burned woman stapled to it. The face and body are beyond recognition but the victim's brown hair is surprisingly undamaged and unmistakably feminine.

Sasha studies the picture carefully, noticing that the

entire right side of the body appears to be missing from the waist to the shoulders. The right arm is gone and the right side of the torso is gaping wide open, exposing all of the internal organs. It is a gruesome sight. Finally, he puts the picture down and reads Andy's letter.

> *Police discovered Dr. Mary Sherman's badly burned body in her New Orleans apartment a week ago on July 21, 1964. Police say intruders killed Dr. Sherman during the burglary-gone-bad – trying to erase the crime scene by burning her apartment.*

Sasha cannot help himself. He looks at the photo again. *Something is not right*, he tells himself.

> *I sent you one of the autopsy photos. You will notice the catastrophic injuries to Dr. Sherman's right side. The severed right arm is completely gone. Vaporized.*

Sasha picks up the photo and examines it more closely. Not only is her right arm gone, so too is most of her right shoulder. *And that cavity in the right side of her torso – mother of God,* Sasha is thinking. He takes a deep breath and continues reading.

> *According to the medical examiner, the apartment fire caused those injuries after her death. A source of mine in the medical field said even cremation fire does not burn through bone like that. He confirmed the burns but attributed them to electrocution, not fire. He said it would take five million volts of electric current to do that kind of damage.*

That would explain the cauterization, Sasha thinks again, agreeing with Andy's source.

> *The only piece of equipment in the entire city of New Orleans that requires five million volts of electricity is the linear particle accelerator. The only person trained to use it was Dr. Sherman. I believe somebody used the accelerator to kill her. They then moved the body and tried to cover up the crime with the burglary/apartment fire. By the way, Dr. Sherman died on July 21. She was supposed to give her testimony to the WC on July 22.*

Again, there is no signature, just an "A" at the bottom. "Jesus!" Sasha exclaims. "Big Russ was right – bodies everywhere!"

***

Washington D.C.

September 28, 1964

Sasha's eyes, glued to the TV, watch Walter Cronkite summarizing the big news of the day. *I do not know how he keeps a straight face*, Sasha wonders to himself, shaking his head. The Warren Commission has finally issued its much-anticipated report.

Sasha already has his copy. A heads-up from Arrowhead alerted him the Government Printing Office (GPO) would be making 235,000 copies available to the public when it opened for business this morning. Thanks to the tip, he was one of the first customers waiting in what turned out to be a very long line for the bookstore to open.

The news day began with a ceremonial White House unveiling of the 889-page Warren Report. The White House photographed the seven-member Commission in the Oval Office presenting the President with his copy – all smiles and backslaps.

The day is continuing with Commission-member Gerald Ford seemingly omnipresent. After his live interview on CBS with Cronkite, Ford follows it with an appearance in the NBC studios with David Brinkley. *Poor bastard*, Sasha thinks, watching the Warren Report apologist launch into yet another hyperbolic defense of the panel's conclusions.

The report begins and ends with the premise that Lee Harvey Oswald, acting alone, fired three shots from the sixth floor window of the Texas School Book Depository, killing the President. In his get-away, Oswald shot and killed Dallas Police Officer J.D. Tippit. The report disavows the notion of a conspiracy, absolving everyone but Oswald for the "Crime of the Century," as Cronkite first – and now everybody – is calling it.

"I want to talk to you about the 'Oswald rifle'," the host begins. "As you know, the Mannlicher-Carcanos is a bolt-action rifle, requiring almost three seconds between shots. According to the Commission's own findings, the shooting lasted a little over eight seconds. So how could a lone gunman fire THREE times in less than nine seconds with the final shot being the most accurate, on a moving target no less?"

"That's easy," Representative Ford replies quickly, eager to explain the ballistics evidence. "The Oswald rifle doesn't require a full three seconds between shots. It actually only takes two-and-a-half seconds per shot. That equals seven-and-a-half seconds for three shots, which means Oswald had an extra second for the final shot."

"I call bullshit on that," Sasha sneers at the TV. "Why don't you talk about the home movie that shows the shooting really only lasted five-and-a-half seconds?" Arrowhead was right. He had predicted the Commission would "dick with the time" to make its case for a lone gunman.

"Did all three shots find their targets?" the interviewer asks Ford, obviously having not read the full report yet.

"No," Ford responds patiently. "There were two hits and one miss..."

"...And one of the hits nearly took the President's head off," the reporter interjects. "That only leaves one bullet..."

"...The Single Bullet Theory," Ford says, his turn to interrupt. "The trajectory of the bullets and the alignment of the victims inside the limousine allowed the remaining bullet to pass through the President AND hit the Governor, causing seven wounds between them," Ford tells him, clearing his throat.

Curious, Sasha opens his copy of the Warren Report to chapter three entitled, "The Shots from the Texas School Book Depository" and begins reading. In short, the Single Bullet Theory posits that the remaining bullet, zigged and zagged in midair, went up when the trajectory was down, did somersaults, and generally defied all the laws of physics. After which, it emerged in pristine condition on a Parkland Hospital gurney, presumably having worked its way out of Governor Connally's injured thigh. *A goddamn magic bullet,* Sasha says aloud, chuckling.

He looks back at the screen. Gerald Ford is STILL talking, STILL filibustering the truth. *I wonder how many DC chits this fool is collecting doing the Commission's dirty work*, he thinks. *Payday someday.*

***

Washington D.C.

January 7, 1967

Sasha opens the envelope postmarked New Orleans. Inside is another newspaper obituary. He recognizes the photo immediately. *Jack Ruby,* he thinks, sighing. He finds the date in the upper right-hand corner of the newspaper clipping. “Three days ago,” he says, not surprised.

> *Jacob Rubenstein (Jack Ruby) died Tuesday, January 3, 1967 at Parkland Hospital in Dallas. Ruby suffered from lung cancer. He shot and killed Kennedy assassin Lee Harvey Oswald on November 24, 1963. The Texas Court of Appeals had recently overturned his death sentence, granting him a new trial.*

New trial – lung cancer, Sasha observes silently, connecting the dots. He begins reading Andy’s attached note.

> *My source inside Marcello’s organization tells me Ruby begged the Warren Commission for a transfer to a secure location in Washington D.C. in exchange for his testimony in ’64. He was scared for his life. The members declined, saying they were not in the business of protecting witnesses. He told them his food was poisoned and he would die of cancer. The WC members thought he was crazy. My source also said Ruby was promising to talk at his retrial.*

Sasha cannot help remembering four years ago at the 500 Club, the night Ruby, Lee Oswald and Guy Bannister listened to David Ferrie rant and rave about killing President Kennedy. *Son-of-a-bitch,* he realizes suddenly, *four of those five people are now dead!*

Andy's note concludes with a paragraph prefaced by the word "IMPORTANT" in capital letters.

> *The Appeals Court granted Ruby a new trial on October 6, 1966. According to his medical records, Parkland Hospital diagnosed him with cancer on December 6, 1966. He died on January 3, 1967 – exactly twenty-eight days after his lung cancer diagnosis.*

Like always, Andy signed the letter at the bottom with an "A".

***

New Orleans, Louisiana

February 23, 1967

Sasha hears a knock. His courier holds an envelope up to the bookstore window so he can see. *Jesus!* Sasha exclaims. *Another one?* Inside the envelope is a hastily written letter from Andy.

> *Police discovered David Ferrie's body yesterday in his apartment. Preliminary reports indicate brain aneurism. My source inside the New Orleans District Attorney's Office reports an empty bottle of Proloid found lying next to Ferrie's body. You might check to see what an overdose of Proloid will do to someone diagnosed with severe hypertension, as Ferrie was. There were also TWO suicide notes with DIFFERENT handwriting found in his apartment.*

Sasha pauses briefly, scribbling on his note pad, "Proloid OD, hypertension – murder, suicide, or natural causes?" Andy's note continues.

> *David Ferrie was Jim Garrison's star witness in the upcoming Clay Shaw trial. The New Orleans States-Item broke the story last week about him testifying. The next day, Ferrie phoned Garrison's lead investigator Lou Ivan hysterical, yelling that the story made him a dead man. His exact words were – 'Do you know what this story does to me? I'm a dead man! From here on, believe me, I'm a dead man'!*

Andy ends his letter with another shocking timeline.

> *The story ran on February 17. Ferrie called the DA's office on February 18, forecasting his death. He died on February 22.*

As usual, the brief letter is signed "A" at the bottom. *Kennedy, Oswald, Bannister, Ruby – and now Ferrie too*, thinks Sasha, again thinking back on the ill-fated confab at the 500 Club. *AND Dr. Sherman too*, he reminds himself. *Bodies everywhere...*

***

Copper Canyon, Mexico

September 23, 1967

It IS her. Andy steals another glance at the young woman. She has put on a little weight and her face has aged considerably in the four years since he last saw her but it is definitely her.

Andy orders his lunch and takes a seat opposite her booth, watching for his opportunity. It has taken him enough time and effort to locate her. He can afford to wait a few more minutes.

The woman sips her coffee, half-absorbed by a book. Every couple of minutes, Andy observes her looking up from her reading and glancing around. She sits with her back to the wall, facing the door.

After a few moments, Andy takes a deep breath and makes his move. “Juduffki,” he murmurs softly, easing himself abruptly into the seat across from her. As he intended, the suddenness of the encounter catches her off guard.

The woman’s head jerks up, startled. Her book falls closed on the table. “Do I know you?” she asks with genuine alarm in her eyes.

“New Orleans, the summer of ’63. You were in love with someone I knew,” Andy says, ignoring the question. “I believe he was your ‘Scarlet Pimpernel’.”

She stiffens. Immediately, tears well up in her eyes. She begins scanning El Catrinas, searching frantically for clues that might identify her surprise mystery guest. She is clearly flustered.

“Judyth Vary, no?” Andy presses, leaning over the table toward her. A long pause. Then she wipes her eyes with a napkin.

“Judyth Vary BAKER,” she clarifies reluctantly, raising her hand and revealing her wedding band. “Who are YOU?” she asks, hesitant.

"It's not important," answers Andy, shaking his head. "Lee asked me to check on you and make sure you are safe," he lies. "Medical Manhattan is leaving behind a trail of dead bodies..."

"...Medical Manhattan?" she interrupts him, a quizzical look on her face.

"The cancer bio-weapon project you...," he says, catching himself.

Judyth drops her head. "I had NO idea," she replies softly. "I thought we were CURING cancer, not CAUSING it. Those poor prisoners..." her voice trails off.

"I know. That's why they killed Lee," Andy tells her. "And Dr. Sherman, and David Ferrie, and Jack Ruby," he adds.

Judyth looks shocked. "They're all dead?" Andy nods.

"How?" she asks.

"Dr. Sherman was electrocuted," he tells her. "David Ferrie's death was ruled a suicide but it was actually a murder-by-overdose and – Jack Ruby died of cancer."

"Cancer?" she questions, suspicious.

Andy nods again. “EXACTLY twenty-eight days after he was first diagnosed.”

“Dear god, the bio-weapon,” Judyth gasps. Her hands are trembling.

“You’re the only one left,” he says matter-of-factly.

“Dr. Ochsner too?” she asks hopefully.

“Sorry,” Andy clarifies, shaking his head. “I forgot about him. Unfortunately, he’s still going strong.”

Judyth sighs, a far-away look in her eyes. “I was in Gainesville, Florida when Lee was shot. I watched it all happen on live TV. I still can’t believe it was Sparky who killed him,” she says, remembering Ruby by his nickname. “Lee and I spent several evenings with him at the 500 Club. He even came by the lab a couple times.”

Andy is not interested in Judyth’s trip down memory lane. “This is a good place to hide,” he observes, looking around. “I had a hell of a time tracking you down.”

“We’re in the middle of the Sierra Madres Orientale Mountains in north-eastern Mexico,” she says, glancing out the window. “We don’t even have TV or

English-speaking newspapers. I am about as off the grid as I can get. That's why I didn't know about Dr. Sherman and the others."

"Does your husband know anything?" Andy asks.

Judyth shakes her head. "David Ferrie called me the day after Lee was shot. He told me as long as I stayed in Florida, Santos Trafficante would be keeping a close eye on me. If I wanted to live, he said I would have to lay low and stop trying to cure cancer. He said 'stuff like that gets your name in the papers'."

"How'd you pick THIS place?" Andy wonders.

"Robert is a Mormon," she says. "Copper Canyon has one of the largest Mormon communities in North America. After what happened in New Orleans, I converted. We came here to practice our faith and raise a family. Robert wants a lot of kids," she adds, shrugging.

"A perfect place to hide," Andy says again, looking around. He stands up, preparing to leave.

Judyth allows for a bittersweet smile. "It's funny," she adds, dabbing her eyes with a tissue. I've never seen you before and I don't know who you are but talking with you reminds me of him."

Andy leans over, speaking in a low voice. “Keep safe Miss Baker. I hope I never see you again.” Then he disappears.

***

Washington D.C.

June 8, 1968

“When they get away with it – and they will – they'll do it again.” Arrowhead's cynical prediction in the aftermath of President Kennedy's death still rings in Sasha's ears. Especially today.

They caught this one in London, he mutters silently, staring at the live footage on his TV screen. Like millions of others this morning, the stately funeral of another assassinated Kennedy – this time Senator Robert Kennedy – preoccupied him until this breaking news. The scene quickly shifts from New York City to London.

“The flight from London's Heathrow Airport to Brussels was already running behind schedule,” the reporter begins. “According to Heathrow security officials, the suspect was attempting to board after the scheduled time of departure. His two Canadian passports caught the attention of an alert immigration officer – a Mr. Ken Human – who asked to see both. Suspicious, he called Scotland Yard detectives. Within an hour, the man was taken into custody."

The image of the untidy would-be passenger being perp-walked through the airport terminal in handcuffs flashes before him, broadcasting a very guilty-looking image all over the world. Sasha shakes his head. *Another lone-nut, I'm sure*, he thinks.

"The suspect's passports identified him as 'George Sneyd', with 'Sneyd' misspelled as 'Sneya'," the reporter continues. "The passports are fake. His true identity is 'James Earl Ray', the FBI's primary suspect in the April 4, 1968 shooting death of Dr. Martin Luther King, Jr. in Memphis, Tennessee."

"James EARL Ray," Sasha chuckles. "Jesus, a southern, redneck hillbilly..."

"When Mr. Ray was searched, a loaded Japanese-made Liberty Chief Revolver with black gaffer tape on the handle was found in his back pocket," the breathless announcer says. "Tomorrow, Mr. Ray will be charged in the Magistrate's Court with carrying a false passport and possessing the unregistered firearm. And as early as next week, he will be extradited to the United States to stand trial in Memphis."

Interestingly, in the two months since he was killed at the Lorraine Motel, the King family has become more and more critical of the investigation. Just yesterday, the family issued a press release claiming it believes a conspiracy involving the United States government assassinated the prominent civil rights leader. "This is more than coincidental," the spokesperson for the family said, standing in front of a bevy of microphones and cameras. "First the President, then the civil rights champion of his time, and finally the next President, all taken out in their prime by lone gunmen? We don't think so."

Nevertheless, the government maintains that James Earl Ray, aka Mr. Sneyd, acted alone in the shooting death of Mr. King. According to FBI allegations, Ray aimed a high-powered Remington rifle at King from a Bessie Brewer's Boarding House window across the street from the Lorraine Motel while King was standing on the balcony of his second-floor room. His motive? He is a racist – a crazed lone-nut.

The sons-of-bitches are getting away with it again,

Sasha thinks, turning off the TV.

***

Los Angeles, California

April 17, 1969

"The defendant will rise," orders the judge.

"On the charge of murder in the first degree, how do you find?" the judge asks the jury foreman.

"Guilty as charged," he replies.

The defendant does not flinch. After all, he HAS confessed to the crime. He has even pleaded guilty. When the judge asked him about sentencing, he answered, "I will ask to be executed," which, in California means the gas chamber. Throughout the entire legal process, he has been unusually cooperative. This four-month trial sure was not his idea.

The judge refused to accept his confession. He also denied his guilty plea. When his defense attorneys entered a motion to withdraw from the case, the determined judge denied it too.

There is no question on June 5, 1968, the defendant shot and killed a man in cold blood. After all, it took four grown men to subdue and disarm him in the scrum afterwards.

The mystery is the defendant himself. From the beginning, he has been TOO willing to confess, TOO willing to plead guilty, and TOO willing to die. He claims to have no memory of the attack, almost as if programmed to carry out the shooting and take responsibility afterwards. Then, his memory was wiped of the programming AND the crime.

Sasha is convinced the defendant is part of the CIA's mind control program Arrowhead told him about in 1962. Back then, it was experimental. *MKUltra is operational now*, he realizes, reading the newspaper accounts of the bizarre trial.

Sasha begins digging through his old notes, searching for a conversation he remembers having with Arrowhead, though it was years ago. Finally, his search pays off. The relevant notes come from a conversation dated March 21, 1962.

> *MKUltra started under Eisenhower as a way to get easy confessions but now the CIA is having success using hypnosis to hard-wire (control*

> *human behavior) its assets. The Agency can program an asset to carry out an operation and confess to it afterwards, while having no recollection of the programming or the forces behind it. The Agency walks away scot-free.*

"The Agency walks away scot-free," Sasha says, rereading his notes. It reminds him of another more recent Arrowhead quote. *When they get away with it – and they will – they will do it again.*

Sirhan Sirhan is guilty of assassinating the man who most likely would have been the next President of the United States. Senator Robert Kennedy had won the California primary. The Ambassador Hotel in Los Angeles was alive with celebrating Kennedy supporters. After delivering his victory speech, the Senator ducked out the back of the ballroom, entering the back kitchen. Before exiting, a Palestinian immigrant stepped from the shadows, shooting Kennedy four times. He died twenty-six hours later.

Another assassination. Another lone-nut. This one a crazed Arab angry with the Senator's pro-Israel positions. This one a brazen crime at close range in front of eyewitnesses. This one a remorseless machine with no memory of his crime afterwards yet willing to give police a taped confession.

Just as they drew it up, Sasha thinks.

***

Washington D.C.

December 23, 1971

“WHITE HOUSE DECLARES WAR ON CANCER,” screams the Washington Post headline. Sasha is smiling as he reads the front-page story. It feels good to be right. It feels even better to have a NOC like Beasley working for him in the White House.

On November 5, 1968, Richard Nixon finally won his life-long bid to become President. The one responsible for the Cutter Incident and subsequent release of two-hundred million doses of SV-40 and SIV-contaminated Sabin polio vaccines is now President. Like Johnson after the JFK assassination, HE is now in the catbird seat. It is HIS turn to cover up.

The story says the National Cancer Act’s goal is to “eliminate cancer by 2015.” According to the President, the cancer campaign allocates hundreds of millions of dollars for the fight, “making possible new research and diagnostics, superior early-detection measures, and additional preventative measures. After all, wars DO cost money."

The last sentence in the article catches Sasha's attention. He reads it several times. *I knew it*, he thinks, reading Nixon's words aloud.

> *The Food and Drug Administration is ready to approve a whole menu of advanced therapies and radical treatments.*

***

Chapter Seventeen

***

Corrupt Bargain

Moscow, Russia

February 22, 1972

"This American President swings for the fences," Father opines, opening a file in front of him.

"Motherfucker's got brass balls," Brezhnev growls, unhappy as usual.

General-Secretary Leonid Brezhnev knows a little something about brass balls. In October 1964, a vacationing Premier Khrushchev received a phone call from Brezhnev demanding him return to Moscow for a special meeting of the Presidium of the Supreme Soviet. When he did, all hell broke loose.

Unbeknownst to Khrushchev, Brezhnev had conspired to have the Premier fired from all his party leadership posts. Worse, Brezhnev became Khrushchev's successor. Worse yet, Brezhnev had Khrushchev classified a "non-person" by the state until his death seven years later. Leonid Brezhnev plays for keeps.

"Castro, polio, cancer – now he's in China. Talk is he's going to pull out of Vietnam, too," Father says.

"Can you imagine the shit storm if Kennedy had tried to go to China?" snarls Brezhnev. "Son-of-a-bitch got his head blown off because he DIDN'T want to go into Vietnam. Nixon? He nailed Hiss – the alleged Soviet spy. The American people think he's god-damn bona-fide."

"There's an element of shrewdness to what he's doing," Father admits.

"God dammit, I know that," Brezhnev huffs. "He's trying to divide the Communist bloc. China's wet dream has always been to leverage us against the Americans. Nixon is there now getting a sloppy, diplomatic blowjob from those slant-eyed chinks. If we lose China, we lose almost a billion people and most of East Asia. If the Americans pull out of Southeast Asia..."

"...Then WE'LL win Vietnam!" Father interjects.

"Hell no we won't!" Brezhnev shouts, stomping his foot. "THEY win by losing. Vietnam is a gold mine for us. Economically and morally, the Americans are bankrupting themselves defending a corrupt regime halfway around the world. Strategically, they cannot win because they are not just fighting the Viet Cong. Most of the Ho Chi Minh Trail is in Cambodia. The Chinese will not let the Viet Cong lose, and we will not let the Chinese lose. Politically, for once, we look like the good guys, defending Vietnamese villages against Uncle Sam's napalm. Hell, Vietnam is a gigantic pile of shit for the Americans. Nixon is no dummy. He knows he can cut his losses. Kennedy could not – they literally crucified him for being weak against communism. Johnson did not – he was a wholly owned subsidiary of the military and intelligence. But Nixon? He's our worst fear come to pass."

Chastened, Father thinks for a second before adding, "You're right. Big picture, who really gives a flying fig about Vietnam anyway? Do we? Not really. Do they? I don't think so."

"We DO for what benefits it brings us," Brezhnev corrects him. "Whether Vietnam is unified as a Communist country or stays divided matters very little, strategically. However, the war is helpful to our overall cause. And that's precisely why Nixon will pull out."

"What do we do about China?" Father asks, bailing out on the Vietnam discussion. "We need a strategy." Brezhnev, for once says nothing, brooding over Father's question. "We could cut our own deal," Father proposes meekly after a few moments.

The General-Secretary looks at Father. "Jesus, with the Americans?" he asks, incredulous.

Father nods. "Why not? Nixon is walking a tightrope without a net – reaching out to China and pulling out of Vietnam. I believe he is communicating to us. He wants a partner. It would be his legacy – and yours too. A Brezhnev-Nixon Axis, a thawing of the Cold War, a détente!" Again, Brezhnev silently mulls over Father's words. This time, Father does not interject.

"The hard-liners in both governments will not allow it," Brezhnev says finally, shaking his head. "Eisenhower and Khrushchev tried in 1960 – remember the Paris Summit? The Americans used a fake defector and their U-2 spy plane to sabotage it."

"I DO remember," Father replies. "But a lot has changed in twelve years. Eisenhower was on his way out in 1960 and Kennedy was on his way in. US intelligence did not think Kennedy was tough enough to stand up to Khrushchev. Hell, we didn't either. Both of us were right. But Nixon? He has built an entire political career on the reputation of being strong against Communism. You said it yourself – the motherfucker's got brass balls."

"I AM surprised the American military and intelligence communities aren't publicly or privately challenging Nixon being in China right now," Brezhnev acknowledges. "That says a lot."

"They didn't trust Kennedy," Father explains. "They DO trust Nixon."

"That doesn't solve the problem with our own hard-liners though," Brezhnev argues.

"This endless military build-up is bankrupting us and everyone in the Politburo knows it," Father declares, closing the file. "If we miss opportunities like this, the American economy will beat us, not their military."

The General-Secretary knows Father is right. *This IS an opportunity*, he agrees silently. A phone on his desk starts blinking, interrupting his train of thought. Brezhnev curses, pressing a button. "Not now!" Then he turns toward Father. "Alright," he says gruffly. "Two things. First, we must find a new leverage instrument to use against Nixon. A vulnerability – political or personal. If his past is any guide, it won't be too hard."

Father nods. "And the second thing?"

"You're right. We must invite him to Moscow. FORTHWITH." Brezhnev says emphatically.

***

Washington D.C.

June 17, 1972

"Where did you get this car?" the outfit's locksmith, Virgilio Gonzales, asks from the back seat, unimpressed.

The group's leader, James McCord is sitting up front in the passenger seat. An important man – the security coordinator for both the Republican National Committee and the Committee to Re-Elect the president (CREEP) – also formerly with the FBI and CIA. He turns around, glaring at the snarky Virgilio. "What's wrong with it?"

"It looks like a hearse," Virgilio replies, laughing. "I sure hope it's not a premonition of tonight's operation." Four of the five men in the car join in nervous laughter.

“Everybody shut up,” McCord growls. “We have two missions tonight and not much time.” The car goes silent, tension building. Thirty minutes later, they park the car at the Watergate Hotel. Each man is carrying a briefcase, doing his best to look elegant. The group registers as business clients of the Ameritus Corporation in Miami before heading upstairs for the briefing.

Howard Hunt – codenamed “Eduardo” – is doing the talking. An advocate for the anti-Castroite Cubans to the Kennedy White House during the Bay of Pigs operation, Eduardo is a name they all know and appreciate, especially after he laid the blame at the politicians’ feet for plopping the Cuban Brigade in the lap of Fidel Castro like a Christmas present. Eduardo is different from other Company men, appearing more like a politician than a freedom fighter. His tan does not seem to match the complexion of a man who has been in the sun, and his motions – the way he looks at people and smiles – suggest even more insincerity. Everything about him seems fraudulent. Officially, Eduardo was retired by the CIA in 1971 and transferred to Mullen and Company – a front for The Agency where “retired” agents still work “off-the-grid”.

Ordinarily, he gives his orders through McCord. Tonight though, the group will hear from the famous Eduardo in person.

“Your first mission tonight will be another black-bag job – you will photograph all the documents at Democrat headquarters we missed the last time,” he begins. “The earlier operation netted us fourteen-hundred photos, mostly contributor lists. This time, I am giving you forty rolls of film, each with thirty-six exposures. That is fifteen-hundred photographs. Just make sure you wear your gloves! Afterwards, you’ll head over to McGovern headquarters to repair the broken phone tap.”

“I don’t like the second part,” Eugenio Martinez, a Cuban exile with CIA connections speaks up. “It feels too rushed.”

“You are an operative,” Eduardo replies coldly. “Your mission is to do what you are told, not ask questions.” Eugenio looks at his old friend and former boss, Bernard Barker, and shrugs. Barker is also ex-CIA, introduced to anti-Castroite Cubans like Eugenio during the Bay of Pigs operation.

The open briefcase on the table is for the five “operatives” to unload their identification. When they finish, Eduardo hands each two-hundred dollars in cash and tells them to use it as bribe money should police or security catch them. Like always, Frank Sturgis – another Barker associate from Miami and a Bay of Pigs alumnus – receives his fake identification just in case.

The five men exit the Watergate Hotel after Eduardo dismisses them, registering at the Howard Johnson's Motor Lodge across the street. There, in adjoining rooms, they take turns surveilling the Watergate Office Complex, waiting for the building to go dark.

McCord leaves first. Because he knows the officer behind the security desk, his job is to walk in the front door of the Watergate building and let him know that a group will be working on the eighth floor tonight in the Federal Reserve Offices. The officer will require McCord to sign in, after which he will take the elevator to the eighth floor. From there, he will work his way back down by the stairs, taping open all the door latches from the eighth floor to the basement. When he gets to the bottom floor, he will leave through the exit door in the parking garage. Then it is back to the Howard Johnson's to wait with the others.

Two hours go by after McCord returns and the

Watergate Office Complex is finally asleep. “It’s go time,” McCord tells his team. Virgilio’s lock-picking skills win him the privilege of leading the entourage with Sturgis close behind, serving as his lookout.

A few minutes later, the radio cackles. “Boss, we’ve got a problem.” It is Sturgis.

“What is it?” McCord hisses.

“The duct tape is missing. And there’s a sack of mail sitting in front of the door on the bottom floor.”

“Shit,” McCord curses.

“Should we abort?” Sturgis asks.

“Hold on,” McCord orders. “I’ll check.”

A minute later, Sturgis and Virgilio have their answer. “Eduardo says go ahead. Watch Virgilio’s back while he works the locks and re-tape the doors for Eugenio and Barker – they are on their way. I’ll remove it when I get there like usual.”

Twenty minutes go by and all five are inside the Democratic National Committee headquarters on the sixth floor. “Did you remove the tape?” Eugenio asks McCord.

"Dammit, I forgot," answers McCord, shaking his head. "I'll go back and do it in a minute. Turn your walkie-talkie off," he instructs Barker. "Too much static."

Barker starts opening file cabinets, pulling out handfuls of folders and laying the documents out on a conference-room table for Eugenio to photograph. "What's that noise?" he asks suddenly, looking over at the door. McCord turns out the light and holds his hand up, signaling absolute silence.

Beneath the door, shadows of people darting back and forth in the lighted hallway are visible. The men can hear muffled voices and footsteps outside, and then – the jiggling of door handles. "The tape. They found the tape," Barker whispers quietly. McCord peeks through the peephole in the door, squinting mightily. "It's nothing," he lies, reassuring his team in a hushed voice. "Just a routine check."

Now someone is at the door in front of them, playing with the knob. Like wooden Indians, the five intruders stand frozen, holding their breath. Then a familiar sound. "Keys!" McCord hisses. "They have keys!" All five men start searching for cover – diving under desks, scurrying behind doors, and wherever else they can hide.

All at once, the door swings open, flashlights piercing the darkness. “Come out with your hands up!” A voice rings out. Nobody budges. “Come out with your hands up or we will shoot!” the voice repeats. Then, the lights come on.

There is no way out. Security wins this round.

Barker turns his radio on, calmly asking the cops in plainclothes who they are and where they are from. No answer. Seeing their badges, he says, “So, it’s the metropolitan police who caught us,” before one of them can snatch the radio and shut it off. That is how Eduardo, camping out in a hotel room at the Watergate, finds out the mission has failed.

“Don’t give your names,” McCord orders his men as the police are handcuffing them roughly. “Nothing. I know people. Don’t worry. Someone will come and everything will be all right. This thing will be solved.” As the police lead them to the waiting cars, each one takes note of a lone figure watching from a window in the hotel overlooking the office complex. *Eduardo,* they all think. *He will take care of this for us.*

***

Washington D.C.

July 17, 1972

The bookstore is dark save for a single light bulb, swinging precariously by a wire from Sasha's cracked office ceiling, in rhythm with air moved by an oscillating fan in the doorway. Sasha is sitting behind his desk, cleaning his glasses with the bottom of his shirt. Compared to the surroundings and his present company, the other man standing in front of him looks like a million bucks.

A runner, Sasha determines quickly, observing the lithe muscles and tan skin of his new cut-out. A crew haircut makes him look even thinner. He is sporting an *Adidas* navy blue tracksuit with the three trademark white bars lining both sleeves and pant legs. His brand-new running shoes are sparkling white. It is a clean, linear look for the notoriously self-absorbed six-foot, two-inch specimen.

"It's a good problem for us to have," Sasha declares, sizing up his sleeper agent Aaron Feldman, ironically codenamed "Bob Kennedy". "One is a top aide for the President inside the White House and the other is the Deputy Director of Operations at Langley."

"Cover?" Kennedy asks, a look of condescension seemingly always on his face. Sasha was afraid of this. For years, he has heard the stories about Feldman, most of them including the description "arrogant asshole". For years, Sasha laughed at the Feldman stories. Cloistered inside The Center in far-away Moscow, he seemed harmless then. It is not so funny now. For Sasha's plans to succeed, Sasha knows he and Kennedy will HAVE to work together. More importantly, Beasley and Arrowhead will HAVE to trust him, a conversation he has already had with both of them. Nobody HAS to like him, which is a good thing. *I have to give them a heads-up,* he thinks.

Sasha shakes his head, handing Kennedy two thick file folders. "Nothing official. They are naked. NOC's – both of them..."

"...I know what the hell a NOC is," Kennedy says quickly, cutting off Sasha. He is looking at a file photo from Beasley's folder, examining it closely. "This one," he shows Sasha. "How long?"

"Don't fucking patronize me," Sasha replies angrily. "Read the files yourself. It is all in there. You probably already know everything about our operations anyway..."

"...You're right. I DO know the WHAT of everything," Kennedy interjects. "I've had a whole god-damn year to memorize files and get up to speed. These do me NO good now," he says, waving the folders in front of Sasha. "I want to know WHO I'm dealing with."

Sasha takes a deep breath, calming himself. "Fine," he responds finally, conceding. *For the sake of the operation*, he tells himself. "Beasley has been with us ever since we liberated him from a Nazi concentration camp in 1945. He was recruited and trained by the NKVD and sent here as a Jewish refugee. Senator Nixon hired him in 1947 as an interpreter for his office during HUAC and the Alger Hiss hearings."

"Twenty-five years," Kennedy does the math, impressed. "He should be embedded by now."

"He is," Sasha says. "Arrowhead's been with us even longer – since 1942 when The Agency first hired him. He was not a willing recruit like Beasley though. We had to make him an offer he could not refuse. You will probably like him. He can be a prick."

"That's fifty-five years combined..." Kennedy notes, ignoring Sasha's inference. "...And we STILL haven't won the Cold War," he says sarcastically, laughing at his own joke.

"It IS beginning to pay off," Sasha defends himself and his agents. "The Center obviously agrees or YOU wouldn't even be here."

Aaron Feldman came to America one year ago during a period when the Soviet Union expelled citizens whose only crime was being an ethnic Jew. His expulsion was cover for the KGB's true purpose – to sneak its spy into America. The policy should have affected thousands of Jews – perhaps tens-of-thousands – but it did not. As it turned out, the policy only targeted a few hundred – enough for Father's spy to blend in, infiltrating the refugee ship headed to the United States. Once ensconced safely in Washington D.C., the Soviet Union reversed itself and stopped expelling its ethnic Jews.

Father sent Feldman after a decade spent training the next-generation of Soviet spies at the Lubyanka Building – "The Center" – in Moscow. The rumor in Washington is Father got sick of dealing with Feldman and his antics so he got rid of him. His skill is acting as an intermediary, or cut-out, between agents, buffering them from direct contact with one another, facilitating the exchange of information – mostly verbal – and thereby safeguarding the agents and most importantly, their network. He is very good at his job.

Just ask him.

Feldman has relatives in New York City who own a modest tax filing company. It was Father's idea that he take KGB start-up cash and invest it in a new branch office in the nation's capital, expanding the family business AND establishing his cover. For the past twelve months, he has been filing people's taxes – mostly low income – under the "Feldman Bros. & Associates" name out of a rented, mice-infested office in a dilapidated DC strip mall. The District's many running paths redeem his personal purgatory – somewhat. He is in the best shape of his life.

The election of Beasley's boss to the White House means a Soviet mole is now working inside the West Wing. The ascension of Arrowhead to the Deputy Director's position at the CIA means a KGB double agent is presently collecting all foreign intelligence and directing covert actions on behalf of the United States government. Heady stuff – much too risky for more face-to-face meetings with the KGB's Second Chief Directorate. Father's words, "Dumb loses more than smart wins," have never left Sasha. Dumb would be blowing his own cover or burning one of his agents. If they want to stay clean, the smart move now is to work with this jackass Kennedy.

"You have three days before your first meeting with Beasley," Sasha informs Kennedy. "Let's meet back here afterwards to go over your report."

"I'll set my own schedule from now on," Kennedy says bluntly, heading for the door.

Sasha sits back in his chair, listening for the bookstore's front door to close behind Kennedy. "Jesus, what a cocksucker," he mumbles under his breath. "He god-damn better be worth it."

***

Washington D.C.

July 20, 1972

Beasley is watching him from a distance, running – not jogging – on a path coming toward him on the other side of the reflecting pool. *That is his third lap,* he thinks, wondering if this rendezvous is ever going to happen. This time, the runner stays straight rather than turn, heading straight for Beasley. He shakes his head, a little spooked. *He knew where I was all along.*

"What's the topic?" Beasley inquires as the new cut-out approaches, slowing to a jog. Kennedy motions for

Beasley to join him, ignoring the question for the moment. Together, the two men begin walking, neither one breaking the silence. *Son-of-a-bitch is not even breathing hard*, Beasley notices.

It is an idyllic summer day in the nation's capital. The bright sun and warm breeze has lured the DC "sidewalk mafia" out into the open air. The Mall is teeming with an assemblage of optimistic joggers and walkers. Starry-eyed lovers stroll along, hand-in-hand. Bureaucratic suits hurry past, sipping coffee, newspapers under their arms, briefcases in-hand.

Sounds of life ring out all around them. A cacophony of birds singing, dogs barking, and children laughing makes for a festive atmosphere. There were three kites darting about like fireflies until one snagged itself in a tree. Now a rescue operation has commenced. Kennedy points at an unoccupied park bench.

"Ratfucking," he finally answers, taking a seat next to Sasha's White House mole.

Beasley shifts in his seat, a look of surprise on his face. "The Watergate burglary, no?" Kennedy nods, saying nothing. "You get right to the point. The only people I've heard use the word work for Nixon's re-election team," Beasley says.

Kennedy stares straight ahead, uninterested in Beasley's commentary. "Would it help if I asked about the bugging of Democratic National Committee headquarters instead?"

Beasley clears his throat, looking away irritated. "Ratfucking applies the tactics of international black-ops to the domestic political process," he says finally. "The Agency's been fixing elections overseas since the early '50s. Nixon has never gotten past Kennedy stealing the election from him in '60. It was like a perfect storm. Nixon needed the election rigged and ex-Agency shop-hands needed an election to rig. The Committee to Re-Elect the President is now a staging ground for campaign covert-ops."

"ALL political campaigns use intelligence assets for opposition research," Kennedy argues.

"Right," Beasley counters. "But CREEP takes it to a whole different level."

"Impress me with facts, not opinions," Kennedy says bluntly.

"Political espionage mostly," Beasley answers. "But ratfucking has changed. Originally, it meant infiltration of the Democrat Party to sabotage it from within. As one successful operation begat another, the scope and sequence expanded to include burglaries, money-laundering, electoral fraud, dirty tricks, slush funds, electronic surveillance and wire-tapping – all of it illegal as hell, of course. That is not all. Everybody knows that Nixon has an enemies list. Jack Anderson would probably call it a hit list. You remember..."

"...Of course. He's the columnist who is always criticizing Nixon and the White House," Kennedy interjects, familiar with the controversial newspaper writer.

Beasley nods. "Well, according to my sources, Nixon's Plumbers tried to kill him, but failed."

Kennedy turns and looks at Beasley. "Plumbers?"

Beasley shrugs. "That's what Nixon calls them. Do you remember a series the *New York Times* published in '71 called the Pentagon Papers?"

Kennedy nods impatiently, not comfortable with being on the receiving end of the questions. "The bombing in Cambodia."

"Nixon was pissed," Beasley says. "After assuring the American people for months that he was drawing down US military involvement in Vietnam, somebody inside his Administration leaked information to the contrary. It turns out he was not just fighting the Viet Cong; he was bombing the country next door – Cambodia. Instead of pulling out, Nixon was escalating. The stories made him look like a liar. After that, President Nixon ordered CREEP to recruit spooks to plug his leaky White House – permanently."

"Plumbers," Kennedy chuckles. "Cute."

"Seems they were so good at it, Nixon and CREEP grew the mission to include the '72 election," Beasley adds. "NOT cute."

"Ratfucking," Kennedy guesses.

"Right," Beasley nods. "But don't let amusing words like 'plumbers' or 'ratfucking' mislead you. These people are heavy-hitters, serious people – mostly CIA and anti-Castro Cuban-exiles. They have infiltrated, sabotaged, and overthrown governments their whole careers. They have also plotted and carried out assassinations. Fixing an election is nothing. Hell, murder is nothing to these characters. LBJ called them 'Murder, Inc.' Experienced hands, all of them."

Kennedy is thinking aloud. "I wonder if these are the same ones that..."

"...The very same," interjects Beasley, anticipating what Kennedy is thinking. "Richard Nixon has been in bed with these characters since 1959. Bay of Pigs, Operation Mongoose, Medical Manhattan, Dallas, Jack, Martin Luther King, and Bobby – all black-ops, American-style."

Kennedy bristles, not happy with the interruption. "It makes sense. Who better to organize an intelligence operation than The Agency vets that wrote the book on covert warfare? They are retired, which means they can work on deep background and be anonymous. No traces."

"That's EXACTLY the point," Beasley agrees. "Nixon didn't hire them to infiltrate and sabotage the Democrat Party. That shit is easy. CREEP did not contract with them to rig the election. That has been going on for centuries. Like you said, they were recruited to be invisible."

"Oops," says Kennedy, rolling his eyes.

"Oops is right," Beasley smirks. "These geniuses fucked up – caught red-handed in DNC headquarters with sequenced hundred-dollar bills – brand new paper! Two of them had address books in their jackets with White House contacts and phone numbers!"

"Linking the burglary to the Administration," Kennedy concludes.

Beasley nods in agreement. "Two of them were ex-FBI, three were known CIA, and all of them had extensive covert-ops experience dating back to the Bay of Pigs. Within one hour of their arrest, all five burglars had high-priced DC attorneys representing them. So much for being invisible!"

Kennedy rubs his chin. "No wonder Nixon's press secretary keeps referring to it as some 'third-rate burglary'. It is the Administration's strategy to undercut a very big story. The Watergate break-in is just one of MANY covert operations."

"The tip of a very large iceberg," Beasley agrees. "The White House is trying to contain it. Nixon KNOWS where it could lead."

"I get the big picture," Kennedy tells him. "Are there any specific examples of ratfucking during this election season other than the Watergate break-in?"

"The Canuck letter didn't write itself," Beasley begins. "CREEP and Nixon were afraid of Edmund Muskie. They knew he would be a stronger candidate for President than George McGovern would. The Plumbers forged a letter using stolen Muskie campaign stationary and smeared the presumed Democrat nominee. By the time they were finished with him, Muskie was literally crying on national TV. Poof! End of candidacy, end of political career."

"Tom Eagleton, too?" asks Kennedy, pretty sure he knows the answer.

"He didn't engineer his OWN political demise," Beasley responds, chuckling. "His psychiatric file was leaked by the Plumbers to the press to publicly humiliate him and render him a radioactive candidate. It worked. On the other hand, do you ever wonder why they leave McGovern alone? He is goddamn untouchable. Why? Because he is the clusterfuck they want to run against. Hell, his own party even knows it. The poor son-of-a-bitch can't give away the VP slot!"

"A lot of dots there, if someone ever starts connecting them," muses Kennedy.

"Trust me, they've got every angle covered," Beasley disagrees, shaking his head. "It's 1963 and 1964 all over again. Nixon is to Watergate now what LBJ was to the JFK assassination then. The Justice Department is to CREEP what the Warren Commission was to the CIA. You don't think CREEP appointed John Mitchell to be its Director because he wins elections, do you?"

"Convenient," Kennedy admits, standing up and stretching his legs. "The Attorney General is doubling as the Director of CREEP. It's a Wild West racket – Mitchell is the crooked Sheriff and the Plumbers are his gang of bandits."

Beasley eyes Kennedy as he prepares to resume his run. "And the Americans think OUR system is corrupt."

***

Washington D.C.

June 1, 1973

"CIA DIRECTOR TO STEP DOWN," blares the Washington Post headline. The story documents the lengthy intelligence resume of James Schlesinger, including his stormy tenure as Director. His idea to commission reports – referred to as the "Family Jewels" – uncovering years of illegal activities by The Agency and his subsequent efforts to reform Langley have made him a pariah in the district. In fact, according to Arrowhead, The Agency had to install a security camera in front of his official portrait at CIA headquarters to discourage vandalism.

Sasha reads the article with heightened interest. Just one year before, Mr. Helms retired from the Directorship, creating an opportunity for Arrowhead. However, Nixon chose Schlesinger instead. *I bet he did not think to tell the White House of his plan to retire in six months*, Sasha thinks, remembering the thorough vetting process Arrowhead endured. He chuckles, thinking about an Administration scrambled by the news of yet another bruising confirmation process.

This time, it is Kennedy meeting Arrowhead at the Pennsylvania Avenue parking garage. Sasha has carefully explained the rotation, detailing the various locations in the file he gave Kennedy. Coincidentally, the rotation had just gone full-circle after their last meeting, returning them to stop number-one. "What are your chances this time?" Kennedy asks, getting right to the point.

"Did you run here in the dark?" Arrowhead asks, avoiding his question.

"What difference does it make?" Kennedy shrugs. "Are they going to give you an interview or not?"

"Administration have officials already contacted me," replies Arrowhead testily. "I don't know why. The reason they didn't choose me last time hasn't changed in six months."

"You've already been vetted," Kennedy contends. "Nixon might want a quick replacement this time."

"He wants a politician – a tool he can use," Arrowhead argues.

"Could be, or maybe after the Schlesinger disaster, he wants a company man. Somebody who won't play crusader and try to blow up The Agency," Kennedy counters.

"You mean a 'yes man'," Arrowhead says. "Not interested."

Kennedy curses under his breath, shaking his head. "No wise-guy, I'm talking about somebody who has climbed through the ranks."

Arrowhead mulls over Kennedy's theory. He had not thought of that. *It just does not seem real. A Soviet mole inside the CIA is one thing – but the Director?*

"So tell me what's going on inside the White House," Kennedy redirects, bringing both of them back into the present.

"Agnew's in deep shit," Arrowhead reports candidly. "Hell, the entire Administration is in deep shit," Kennedy does not flinch. Sasha was right. Arrowhead speaks his language.

"Less than one year removed from winning sixty-percent of the vote..." Kennedy's voice trails off as he states the obvious.

"Don't forget how he got that sixty percent," Arrowhead reminds him.

"He would have gotten away with it," Kennedy declares. "No one but the Washington Post has even touched the story until now. Talk about snatching defeat from the jaws of victory..."

"...Fuck the media," Arrowhead interrupts quickly. "It's full of idiots. Useful? Yes, but idiots just the same. For over a year, the Administration had the rest of the media convinced the Post was on a lonely witch-hunt."

"Tell me about Agnew," Kennedy says, returning to the original subject.

"The District Attorney in Baltimore has the goods on him," Arrowhead declares. "Apparently, before he became Nixon's VP, Governor Agnew ran Maryland like the Cosa Nostra. Tax fraud, extortion, conspiracy, and bribery – to the tune of at least one-hundred grand – he is dead man walking. Seems the only thing he didn't do was murder..."

"...He and Nixon make quite the pair," Kennedy interjects. "I should say, MADE quite the pair," Kennedy corrects himself.

"Word is a deal is on the table," Arrowhead states. "In exchange for his resignation, the state will reduce the charges. He'll serve no jail time provided he makes full restitution."

"So they're going to brush him back with the high heat and strike him out with a meatball out over the plate," Kennedy predicts.

"If you remember, it was Agnew who helped carry Nixon across the finish line last November," Arrowhead recalls, brushing off Kennedy's pitching analogy.

"Yes, but now the election's over," Kennedy argues. "He's outlived his usefulness. Nixon needs his NEW errand boy, someone who will help him contain Watergate. Any names on the short list?"

"One," Arrowhead answers. "Only one."

Kennedy pauses, waiting for the name. “Who?”

“Gerald Ford. The new Vice President will be Congressman Gerald Ford,” replies Arrowhead.

“That flaky Warren Commission guy?” Kennedy asks incredulously.

“Bingo,” Arrowhead replies. “He was the Bureau’s inside man on the Commission. He single-handedly protected the entire intelligence community and the cover story. His first task was steering inquiries away from Oswald’s CIA background and away from evidence of a broader conspiracy. His second job was reporting any Commission member who suspected CIA or FBI involvement in Dallas.”

“He had a third job,” Kennedy adds. “Don’t forget his media marathon on the day the Warren Report was published. Ford was the explainer-in-chief for the Commission. It was his face and voice on TV predicting the Report would ‘stand like a Gibraltar of factual literature through all the ages to come’.”

Arrowhead shakes his head, sighing. “If he makes dumb statements like that about a dumpster-fire document like the Warren Report, he’ll say anything. Nixon is gambling he’ll do it again.”

"Actually, it's pretty smart if you think about it," Kennedy concedes. "The Senate hearings start in May. Nixon will have thrown everyone beneath him under the bus by then. There will not be a soul left on Capitol Hill to fight for him. Who better to go to bat for him with key Senators than the most popular Congressman in DC? Christ, he has thirty years of favors he can call in."

"He's Nixon's firewall if Watergate gets out of hand," Arrowhead declares. "On the front end, he'll try to steer the investigation and finesse the hearings. On the back end, if it comes to it, he'll have to tie off a potential trial by pardoning Nixon – IF it comes to it."

"IF Watergate gets out of hand?" Kennedy asks, his voice oozing sarcasm.

"You know what I mean. Clearly, it's become a god-damn rolling disaster," Arrowhead clarifies. "They were hoping the story wouldn't have legs. But that was before the Post found a $25,000 check to CREEP in the checking account of one of the Watergate burglars."

"Some 'bureaucratic snafu'," Kennedy says, mocking the explanation the White House used for the cancelled check. "Jesus, you can't make this stuff up."

"One check exposed the entire CREEP slush fund," Arrowhead continues, ignoring him. "Then McCord and Liddy were convicted and the two White House Aids – Haldeman and Ehrlichman – had to resign. And just when they thought the worst was over, John Dean happened."

"But it was just a third-rate burglary, no?" Kennedy sneers, parroting another ridiculous White House narrative.

Arrowhead pauses, shaking his head. "The amazing thing is Nixon still won re-election in a god-damn landslide. The Teflon man!"

"I think he's finally used up all of his nine lives," Kennedy predicts. "Watergate is about to land on ALL of the front pages like a gigantic matzah ball."

"It's already starting," Arrowhead agrees. "It's not just Woodward and Bernstein stirring up the shit storm now. Radio, TV, and print media in markets across the whole country are requesting interviews. The two Post reporters have something none of the Johnny-come-lately's have – a White House source on deep background. Deep Throat's been driving everybody in the West Wing bat-shit crazy for months."

“Wait until the hearings start, when witnesses are testifying on live TV,” Kennedy declares. “I’ll bet Nixon’s White House Counsel – the John Dean fellow – sings like a Russian canary. Moscow’s known for years that Nixon has been neck-deep in crookedness going back to the mid-fifties. Now the American people are going to find out. They will lose their minds. This will be big.”

“He’s nervous, that’s for sure,” Arrowhead agrees. “Choosing Ford proves it. Normally, a President picks a VP who will balance the electoral map but Nixon has already won re-election. He could not give two shits about the electoral map. This is politics of a different kind.”

“The C-Y-A kind,” Kennedy states bluntly. Arrowhead nods.

“As for Ford, he must be thinking ‘power is where power goes’,” Arrowhead claims. “I can’t remember who said that...”

“LBJ said it when Kennedy offered him the VP slot,” the other Kennedy recalls. “He already had his eyes on the prize.”

“That’s right. Ford’s going to get his shot at the brass

ring too," Arrowhead predicts. "Even if President Nixon survives, Ford is set up to run for President in '76. If Nixon does not survive, he is President and can run in '76 as the incumbent. In exchange, Ford has to prevent an impeachment trial. Worst case, if he cannot and Nixon has to resign to prevent a trial, Ford will grant him a full and unconditional pardon. One thing is certain though; there absolutely cannot be a trial of any kind. I assure you, Nixon is a scab nobody in DC wants picked."

Kennedy nods. "Any of this sound familiar?"

"Oswald," Arrowhead responds, taking a deep breath. "I realize everything's hyper-political in this town but there is an element of trust at work here, too. Nixon and Ford have known each other since 1942 when they both served in the Navy."

"That's more than thirty years..." Kennedy observes.

"...A LOT of history there," Arrowhead declares, interrupting Kennedy. "Nixon and Ford became war buddies while they were stationed together in the Pacific. They resigned their commissions within months of each other in 1946. Nixon went into politics that same year and Ford followed two years later. Nixon has been the political climber, translating the

Alger Hiss hearings into a California Senate seat in 1950 and the VP slot in 1952. On the other hand, Ford has always been more of a grinder, proving to be a loyal supporter of Nixon throughout. This is his payback."

"Birds of a feather..." Kennedy mumbles, barely audible.

"Sort of," Arrowhead agrees. "The bottom line is Nixon trusts him. Ford knows how to play the game in DC. When it is time, he will know what to do and how to do it. Like you said, he's already done it before with Warren Report."

Kennedy is quiet for a moment. "It will be interesting whom Ford appoints to be the Secretary of State. If he keeps Kissinger, American foreign policy will not change much. If not, who in the hell knows? Either way, The Center is going to be very busy researching the Congressman from Michigan. Things sure are happening fast these days."

"Hell, we'll ALL be scrambling if Ford becomes President," Arrowhead states. "That would mean another VP vacancy. A complete turnover of the Executive Branch – without one single vote cast!"

"Lincoln is rolling over in his grave right now," Kennedy cracks, amused. "A government of the people, by the people, for the people doesn't mean what it used to, does it?"

***

Washington D.C.

July 20, 1973

Sasha does not have to wait to hear the news from Arrowhead. Again, the papers tell the story. "MICHAEL OVERSTREET TAPPED BY PRESIDENT FOR CIA DIRECTORSHIP." Senators from both sides of the aisle agree that expedited confirmation hearings are appropriate in this case. "Everybody knows Mr. Overstreet and the quality of his work," comments one prominent Democrat, adding, "Washington could use more public servants like Michael Overstreet."

Another Senator – this one a Republican – releases a prepared statement through his office. "Mr. Overstreet is an expert in foreign intelligence. He has been a reliable and trustworthy member of the clandestine services for thirty-one years. His experience is unimpeachable. I believe he is uniquely qualified to lead the Central Intelligence Agency and, most importantly, unite factions that presently divide Langley. The President has made an excellent choice." *He is a damn good Soviet spy too*, Sasha says to himself, chuckling.

He turns his copy of the Washington Post over, looking for bad news for the President. The Senate Watergate hearings have been above the fold, front-page news since June. Today's news about Overstreet has temporarily offered the Nixon White House some welcome relief.

So far, Kennedy's prediction has proven to be spot-on. The hearings have been a public relations calamity for the President, though not a legal one – yet. White House Counselor John Dean testified in June that he and Nixon discussed the Watergate cover-up at least thirty-five times. His testimony IS damaging – no doubt – but many dismiss it as the politics of grievance from a disgruntled – and discredited – ex-employee. Subpoenaed White House memos detailing plans for break-ins, burglaries, and wiretapping are incriminating. Displayed in open court, they prove a conspiracy at a high-level, but not the highest. Until last Friday, it seemed like Nixon's firewall was holding strong.

Friday the thirteenth was the day Alexander Butterfield dropped a bomb on the Oval Office. Mr. Butterfield, a little-known and lightly regarded White House appointment secretary, testified to the Watergate Committee and a world television audience that shortly after his inauguration in 1968, President Nixon ordered a taping system installed in the Executive Office Building.

When pressed on the subject, Butterfield maintained that the taping system had only one purpose – to record all conversations and phone calls in the West Wing.

The members were stunned. Notoriously paranoid, the President had sought to protect himself by spying on others. The obvious question on everybody's mind now is – *do these Oval Office tapes contain evidence that the President's men CANNOT discredit or discount? The President's own words? The smoking gun?*

***

Washington D.C.

November 18, 1973

“The President has requested air time from the networks for a prime-time address to the nation tonight,” a soaking-wet Beasley reports, easing into the booth facing the bar. Kennedy arrived before the rainstorm, choosing a table nearest the television. Beasley reaches for a handful of napkins from the holder in front of him and begins drying his hands. Kennedy ignores him, staring at the picture on the screen instead.

“I already know that,” Kennedy grumbles finally, turning toward Beasley. “Your job is to know WHAT he’s going to say.”

“I don’t have a damn clue,” Beasley replies, sighing. “Nobody in the office does.”

“Probably another Checkers speech,” Kennedy figures, disappointed, mixing the ice around in his water glass with a straw.

“It worked before,” Beasley shrugs, wiping his face. The pile of used paper towels grows taller on his placemat.

This will not be the first time Nixon tries to bail himself out of a jam by giving a speech. In 1952, the media accused Nixon of accepting illegal reimbursements for his political expenses. Eisenhower was even considering dumping him from the ticket as VP. Nixon gave the speech of his life, viewed by sixty-million people on TV. He claimed that the only gift he ever received from the fund was a cocker spaniel puppy his children named Checkers. The speech saved Nixon's political career and made his family's black and white mutt an overnight sensation.

"Maybe Checkers ate the tapes," Kennedy suggests, tongue planted firmly in cheek.

Beasley laughs. "I don't think it really matters WHAT he says this time. When the media starts cataloging your screw-ups by name, you're toast."

"Firing the Special Prosecutor WAS a colossal screw-up," Kennedy says, looking back at the TV. "The 'Saturday Night Massacre' – sounds like a damn horror movie."

"He HAD to know the Attorney General and his Deputy would quit in protest," Beasley replies.

"Whoever's advising him is either an idiot of epic proportions committing political malpractice, or he is sabotaging Nixon's presidency intentionally," Kennedy declares. "Firing the prosecutor who is investigating you is asinine. Doing it on a Saturday night is so transparently stupid it reeks of masochism. Moreover, refusing the Committee's subpoena is always a losing proposition. It attracts attention and makes the President look like he's hiding something."

"The tapes will end up in litigation," Beasley predicts. "Probably the Supreme Court."

"Of course they will," Kennedy agrees. "And he'll lose."

"You mentioned his advisors," Beasley says after a brief silence. "The White House has a bunker mentality. The staff has taken on Nixon's personality. It does not trust anybody. It has Nixon pitted against the Justice Department, Congress, and now the Supreme Court. There's nobody left. The Nixon White House is literally at war with the entire government."

"After all these years, you SHOULD know him better than anybody," sneers Kennedy. "Why the hell didn't he just destroy the tapes?"

"That's the million-dollar question, isn't it?" Beasley agrees. "He did order the taping system be disconnected after Butterfield spilled the beans. I cannot figure out why he did not just load up all the tapes, head out to Camp David for the weekend, and have a big bonfire. It is too late now though. His favorability ratings are in the mid-to-low thirties."

"Which is probably why he's speaking tonight," Kennedy concludes.

"A Nixon crisis equals a national crisis," Beasley agrees.

Kennedy looks at his watch. It shows 7:58 pm. The TV above the bar is promoting the upcoming speech, volume turned down low. "Could you turn it up?" he yells at the bartender. A couple of commercials later, a beleaguered-looking President appears on the screen. Kennedy slides from the booth, accompanied by Beasley. Together, they join the other patrons crowded around the bar, straining to hear.

After a few defensive – and worthless – minutes, Nixon finally comes to the point. "People need to know whether or not their President is a crook," he says, pausing. "Well, I am not a crook."

"Jesus..." the bartender mutters under his breath.

***

Washington D.C.

July 26, 1974

Kennedy often wonders why they call it the "Express" Bus Service. There is nothing fast or direct about the meandering route the service takes, traipsing from the Washington Mall to Arlington National Cemetery. *I could probably run there faster*, he thinks.

He watches the eager tourists boarding with their cameras and sun visors. *Like sheep*, he mumbles contemptuously under his breath, laughing out loud as the college-age tour guide pretends this is the first time she's explained the significance of the fifty-eight steps leading up to the Lincoln Memorial. Bored, he finds himself observing the Japanese couple next to his seat, fascinated by their rapid-fire pointing and incoherent babbling.

After a few minutes, he grows tired of that scene too and looks at his watch. He sighs and pulls his hat down, covering his eyes. *Might as well get some sleep*, he thinks, doing his best to shut out the exuberance around him.

An hour later, Kennedy observes the newly confirmed CIA Director perched on a stone pergola. He groans, watching Arrowhead check his watch as he approaches. "Sasha was right," he says aloud. "And I'm late too. Shit. I SHOULD have run here instead."

Not surprisingly, the President's "I am not a crook" speech last November 18 did NOT have the desired effect. In fact, it backfired. Polls are now showing President Nixon to be upside-down on the "Do you believe the President did anything illegal" question.

Three days later – on November 21 – Nixon played the Checkers card again, just as Kennedy had jokingly predicted he might. In a national "dog-ate-my-homework" moment, the White House first claimed two of the tapes subpoenaed by the Committee were missing. Next, after Congress informed the Administration the third tape had a mysterious eighteen-and-a-half minute erasure in it, the White House Chief of Staff testified with a straight face in federal court that "some sinister force" must be at work in the West Wing, causing a gap in the tape. Later, Nixon's secretary – Rose Mary Woods – testified she re-recorded or in her words, "dubbed over" five-and-a-half minutes of the tape by accident. When one of the members asked her about the remaining thirteen minutes, Miss Woods just shrugged, acting mystified. The members of the Committee were not amused. They smelled a rat.

On February 6, the House Judiciary Committee opened its investigation into whether Nixon's actions rose to the level of "high crimes and misdemeanors." Its first action was to subpoena nineteen recordings of Presidential conversations and seven-hundred documents.

On April 11, it subpoenaed forty-two additional tapes. Five days later, Special Prosecutor Leon Jaworski subpoenaed sixty-four more tapes. On April 30, under white-hot public pressure, the White House released edited transcripts of the tapes, hoping they would appease the Special Prosecutor and the Committee. They did not.

On May 9, the House Judiciary Committee opened impeachment hearings against the President. By then, the Committee was convinced Nixon was playing a game, gambling that Congress would not dare impeach a sitting President with so little hard evidence.

On July 24, the Supreme Court called Nixon's bluff. In a unanimous decision, the Court rejected his claim of executive privilege. Nixon would have to turn over the actual tapes. Finally.

It did not take members of the Committee long to understand why Nixon did not want to release the tapes in the first place. Paranoid, vindictive, and bigoted comments spilled bitterly from his lips. The edited transcripts tried to sanitize President Nixon's profanity with "expletive deleted" insertions but the voice on the tapes was unmistakably Nixon's. The words were also his – raw and uncensored. That was BEFORE he said a word on the tapes about Watergate.

When the topic DID come up in one conversation, Nixon plotted with Bob Haldeman – his Chief of Staff – on how to coerce the CIA into convincing the FBI to "back off" the investigation. Haldeman did most of the talking in the beginning.

> *The Democratic break-in thing, we are back in a problem area because the FBI is not under control. Gray (FBI) does not know exactly know how to control them and their investigation is leading into some productive areas. It is going in some directions we do not want it to go. I think the way for us to handle this is to have Walters (CIA) call Gray and say, "Stay the hell out of this...this is ah, business we don't want you to go any further on."*

Then Haldeman spent the next few minutes explaining to the President the campaign's role in the break-in, including the involvement of CREEP chairman and former Attorney General John Mitchell, after which he laid out a plan to "deny, deny, deny" and use every Machiavellian tool in their toolbox to derail the investigations.

Finally, Nixon approved Haldeman's plan.

> *All right, fine, I understand it all. We will not second-guess Mitchell and the rest. You call them in. Good deal. Play it tough. That is how they play it...then that is how we play it too.*

A prosecutor could not have laid out the case any better. The President of the United States was attempting to obstruct justice.

Kennedy meets Arrowhead on Roosevelt Drive and they begin walking in the direction of the Arlington Memorial Amphitheater.

"What, you can't run in the daytime, only at midnight?" Arrowhead asks sarcastically.

"Believe me, I wish I had," Kennedy replies, rolling his eyes and thinking about the fast-talking tour guide and the jabbering Japanese tourists.

"Lazy ass," Arrowhead chides him.

"Will the President...?" Kennedy tries redirecting the topic, humorless as usual.

"...The President is fucked," Arrowhead interrupts bluntly. "He deserves it for being so stupid."

"You know what's on the tapes?" Kennedy questions, skeptical.

Arrowhead nods. "Everybody knows how these things work. Small fish commit crimes like Watergate – carrying out orders passed down to them through multiple layers. The big fish never risk exposure. They always get away – if they are smart. Nixon might as well have taken out a full-page ad in the Post. His own words, his own voice, all on his own secret taping system..." his voice trails off.

"His political cover will scurry for cover like rats on a ship," Kennedy predicts.

"It's already happening," Arrowhead agrees. "Tomorrow, the House Judiciary Committee will charge Nixon with obstruction of justice, abuse of power, and contempt of Congress. It WILL impeach him. The one question on everybody's mind is who will he take down with him?"

"He could scorch this whole town," Kennedy guesses.

"Oh man, could he ever," Arrowhead declares. "In one of the tapes, he is heard saying –

> *...If this gets out, it will make the CIA look bad and it's likely to blow the whole Bay of Pigs thing, which I think would be very bad for both the CIA and the country...and for American foreign policy."*

"Jesus. Everybody who matters in this town is connected to intelligence – or was," Kennedy says. "He's warning all of them that he can burn the whole house down if he has to. I don't understand the Bay of Pigs reference though," he admits, surprising Arrowhead.

"The Agency knows EXACTLY what he means," Arrowhead explains. "John Dean testified that whenever Nixon spoke of the Kennedy assassination, he coded it as the 'Bay of Pigs.' What he is really saying is Watergate is part of a black-ops lineage that goes back to the late fifties. The assets involved in the Watergate break-in are the same ones involved in Bay of Pigs, Operation Mongoose, TWEP, the Kennedy assassination – and now CREEP."

"Different branches, same tree," Kennedy muses, putting the pieces together in his mind.

Arrowhead nods. "Intelligence KNOWS that Watergate leads right back to Kennedy and Dallas. And we ALL know what that means."

"There absolutely can't be a trial of Nixon," Kennedy concludes. "Impeachment OR criminal."

"Exactly," Arrowhead agrees. "Like he said, it would take the whole country back to 1963."

"1963 means Oswald and New Orleans," Kennedy says. "Advantage Nixon."

"And New Orleans means Medical Manhattan," Arrowhead continues. "Again, advantage Nixon."

"But Medical Manhattan means SV-40 and SIV," Kennedy counters. "Advantage Agency."

A thought stops Arrowhead in his tracks. He turns and looks at Kennedy with eyebrows raised. "And who's the son-of-a-bitch that decided inoculating two-hundred million Americans with a contaminated polio vaccine was a good idea?"

"Richard Nixon," Kennedy answers him. "Advantage Agency."

"More like game, set, match," Arrowhead declares gruffly.

***

Washington D.C.

September 8, 1974

The American people are reeling, pummeled by the corruption of their leaders. Like a punch-drunk gladiator, they are exhausted by the never-ending legal process and delirious from the unrelenting bedlam of the media circus.

Scandal has made a wreck of the executive branch. It is as if the '72 election never happened. The popularly elected ticket of Richard Nixon and Spiro Agnew has been hauled away kicking and screaming to the boneyard, forever disgraced.

First, the Vice President resigned, agreeing to the generous plea deal offered by the federal prosecutor. In exchange for his resignation from office, the state reduced felony charges of bribery, tax fraud, and conspiracy to a single charge of failing to report income. Restitution payments to the state of Maryland provided a soft landing, beating the alternative – federal prison. However, his resignation did leave behind a vacancy.

Most Americans had no idea who Gerald Ford was

when Nixon announced him as Agnew's replacement. The twenty-five year veteran of Congress was only one heartbeat away from the most powerful position in the world, and everybody was asking, "Who?"

Now, he is their President.

After hearing the tapes, all ten Republicans on the House Judiciary Committee who originally voted against articles of impeachment announced they would vote to impeach the President when the matter came to a vote before the full House. Republican Senators could only count fifteen votes to acquit in a trial to follow. After more than two years of lying, obstructing, and covering up, President Nixon was finally out of options.

And so on August 8, President Nixon also resigned, foreclosing on an impeachment trial in the Senate. That same day, in his swearing-in remarks to the nation, President Gerald Ford tried reassuring the country, saying, "My fellow Americans, our long national nightmare is over."

But yours is just beginning, hotshot, thought Sasha, one of the few people in the world aware the new President has a debt to pay. Sure enough, thirty days later to the day, ABC, CBS, and NBC announced

President Ford had asked for time on a Sunday evening to address the nation. The fast-spreading rumor is he will pardon now-private citizen Richard Nixon.

This morning, the *New York Times* published a story on the front page with the headline, “FORD THE RESULT OF A CORRUPT BARGAIN?” On the back page, the Times editorial staff is branding a potential Ford pardon as a “profoundly unwise, divisive, and unjust act" that will undermine the President's "credibility as a man of judgment, candor and competence.”

Whatever history Ford plans to make tonight, Kennedy and Sasha will be witnessing it together, having met at the bookstore for the momentous occasion.

“Public opinion is definitely in favor of a criminal trial,” Kennedy says, reacting to the interviews on TV. “Especially since Nixon’s resignation got him off the hook in the Senate. Folks want his head on a spit.”

“They can have his head anyway they want it,” Sasha replies, chuckling. “But they can’t have a trial. People forget. Ford has skin in this game too,” he adds. “It’s not just the CIA and Nixon.”

"He WAS on the Warren Commission," Kennedy recalls.

"NOBODY has vouched for the Warren Report more than he has," Sasha declares. "He won't allow it to be re-litigated." Both men turn their attention to the TV screen. President Ford is visibly sweating.

The rumors are correct. President Ford issues a "full and unconditional pardon," permanently immunizing Nixon from criminal prosecution. He explains that he believes the pardon is in the best interests of the country. Then he calls the Nixon family's situation a "tragedy in which we all have played a part. It could go on and on and on, or someone could write the end to it." He pauses before continuing. "I have concluded that only I can do that, and if I can, I must."

The firewall holds. As Arrowhead predicted, Nixon's choice was not a gamble after all. Ford has paid off. There will be no trial.

***

Chapter Eighteen

***

Operation Reciprocity

Washington D.C.

November 18, 1975

"But how does making this report public serve the national good?" the reporter questions the Chairman on live television.

"It's a good question," he responds patiently. "Despite the temporary injury to our reputation, the Committee believes foreign peoples will respect us more for keeping faith with democratic ideals than they will condemn us for the misconduct revealed. In fact, we doubt other countries would have the courage to make such disclosures."

Not courage, Sasha thinks, watching the exchange, *just plain dumb.*

Senator Frank Church is no shrinking violet. In 1956, he ran for the Senate at the tender age of thirty-two.

Upon winning the seat, Senator-elect Church became the fifth-youngest member in the history of the U.S. Senate. Remarkably, he served as a Democrat in the very Republican state of Idaho. Even more remarkably, Senator Church won re-election three times, an unimaginable achievement in the conservative state.

Not many Democrat Senators dared challenge Majority Leader Lyndon Johnson at the height of his power. Frank Church did, defying the Senate intimidator THREE times. The first time, the young Senator voted "no" on a bill Johnson wanted passed, earning the transgressor six months of silent treatment from the seething Texan. One year later, Church redeemed himself, winning back the Majority Leader's favor by supporting a second Johnson project – the Civil Rights Act of 1957. For a brief period, Church became Lyndon Johnson's protégé, landing a coveted seat on the Senate Foreign Relations Committee.

The second time happened in 1964 after the Gulf of Tonkin Incident. In a private meeting, he warned then-President Johnson, "In a democracy, you cannot expect people whose sons are being killed to exercise judgment if the truth is concealed from them." The President ignored the advice, continuing his lies to the American people about the events in Southeast Asia.

The third time, Church became one of the first Senators to publicly oppose the Vietnam War, putting him at odds with the Johnson Administration again. The antiwar movement was not quite as easy to delegitimize when key members of the Senate Foreign Relations Committee like Frank Church and Chairman J. William Fulbright were part of it.

Clashing with Lyndon Baines Johnson is one thing. Unmasking the US intelligence community and laying bare its iniquities for the entire civilized world to see is quite another.

Americans were shocked when former CIA Director James Schlesinger published the infamous "family jewels," exposing decades of illegal activities at The Agency. The ensuing public outcry has triggered this Congressional inquiry. At the beginning of the Congressional session in January, the United States Senate formed a Select Committee – with Senator Church named chairman. The "Church Committee" has been investigating the full range of intelligence activities to determine if they were "illegal, improper, or unethical." More specifically, the Committee is examining the CIA's intelligence-gathering and covert operations. As was the case earlier with Schlesinger's revelations, Langley is not the least bit happy about it.

Just this morning, the Church Committee released its preliminary findings. The Interim Report on Intelligence Activities is the latest proof that Senator Church either is the most courageous politician in all of Washington – or as Sasha believes, the dumbest. According to the Chairman, four questions are guiding the Committee.

First, did the US participate in plots to assassinate foreign leaders? Second, did the US assist dissidents who were trying to assassinate foreign leaders? Third, if so, what level of government was involved? Finally, did higher authorities exercise too little control over the agencies involved?

In a section titled "ASSASSINATION PLOTS INVOLVING FOREIGN LEADERS," the Committee has produced almost three-hundred-and-fifty pages of answers to those four questions. Each page practically explodes with damaging testimony and incriminating documentation.

Sasha is sitting in his bookstore office, thumbing through his copy of the report, more stunned that he CAN read it than by WHAT he is reading. *We would never allow the public to read this*, he thinks. *America and its constant crises of conscience – always confessing their sins.*

The report lists five foreign leaders targeted by the CIA for assassination during the '60s. Four of the plots succeeded, though not always at the hand of The Agency directly.

Patrice Lumumba from the Congo, Rafael Trujillo from the Dominican Republic, General Rene Schneider from Chile, and Ngo Dinh Diem from South Vietnam were all leaders of Third World countries, none of which posed any threat to the United States but all of whom were opposed – and later deposed – by the American government. Whether the plots were to kill or overthrow, they were disposed of the same in all four cases – death by gunshot to the head.

Sasha is more interested in the one that got away. According to the report, the American government was actively engaged in a plot to kill Cuban dictator Fidel Castro during the years 1960-1965. *No shit*, Sasha thinks, chuckling. During those years, the CIA coordinated with organized crime figures and anti-Castroite Cuban refugees by providing money and materials for the hit.

Furthermore, the Committee continues, evidence suggests "ranking government officials authorized the establishment of a generalized assassination capability within the CIA referred to as Executive Action."

Jesus, Stalin WAS right, Sasha realizes, remembering a conversation he'd had with NKVD boss Lavrentiy Beria decades ago in which Beria recounted Stalin's prediction in 1945 how the Soviets would ultimately defeat the Americans in the Cold War.

> *War is a desperate death match. There are no rules except one. WIN. We do not mind so much how we win the victory, only that Mother Russia survives and its enemies do not. Americans have to win with righteousness and virtue, honorable traits in peacetime but calamitous in war. Let them wear their moral superiority like a bandana in one of their cowboy movies. We will tighten it around their necks like a noose and destroy them with it.* –Joseph Stalin

We don't even really have to spy on the Americans, Sasha thinks, amazed. *Eventually, they feel the need to tell us everything – like Stalin said – their moral high horse will be the death of them.*

***

Moscow, Russia

December 1, 1975

"How in the hell do you plan to run a Polish Jew for public office in America?" Brezhnev asks, thunderously loud as usual. The General-Secretary tosses the file on his desk, staring hard at Father over his thick glasses. "His legend better be ironclad."

"He survived Auschwitz, didn't he? The 12th Congressional District in Manhattan should be a breeze," Father responds. "There are close to 2 million Jews on the Lower East Side, most of whom are immigrants from Eastern Europe. He IS New York, which is why we chose him."

"Working in Nixon's office for the last twenty-five years won't hurt him?" Brezhnev wonders.

"Hell no," Father declares. "Nixon could run for office and STILL win the Jewish vote because of Henry Kissinger. Beasley is a Nazi death camp survivor. Lower Manhattan will love him. We can only HOPE our opponent brings up Nixon during the campaign. It would mean he's desperate."

"Operation Reciprocity..." Brezhnev mumbles, reading the file again. He shakes his head. "He's not a natural born citizen…," he says, thinking ahead.

"…No, but his mother was," Father interjects, anticipating Brezhnev's question. "According to the legal scholars we've consulted, a natural-born citizen is not just someone born in America. It also includes people who meet the legal requirements for US citizenship at birth, like a child of an American citizen."

"His mother was born in America?" Brezhnev asks, surprised.

Father nods. "New York City, born and raised," he declares. "She met her future husband on a family trip to Poland in 1933. They married and she never returned to the states."

Brezhnev is quiet for a moment. "Is the swallow in place?"

"We're saving Anna for the kill shot," Father explains. "It shouldn't be hard. Sasha reports that the Delilah Unit has already primed the pump." Brezhnev's head jerks up, an evil grin on his face. Both men laugh.

"You are confident, no?" Brezhnev asks.

Father shrugs. "Confident enough to predict the state

of New York will have an open Senate seat in '78," he says matter-of-factly. "Has Anna EVER failed us before?"

***

New York City, New York

October 29, 1976

"What did Jakub Berman know and when did he know it? That is the question the voters of the 12th Congressional District deserve to have answered," the young man loudly declares, a group of supporters raucously cheering him on.

It is the candidates' final debate before the upcoming election. Surprisingly, the issue has yet to come up. However, the polls are showing Berman ahead by eight points entering the final weekend of the campaign. As Father predicted, Berman's opponent IS desperate. All eyes in the room turn toward Richard Nixon's former staffer.

This is it – don't fuck it up, thinks Kennedy, standing by himself in the back of the hall, surveying the crowd. *Just as we rehearsed*, he coaches Berman silently.

"As many of you know," the older candidate begins quietly, "I lost my entire family at Auschwitz in 1941. In the years afterward, a savage root of bitterness began to take hold in my heart – planted like a seed during those dark days. I nursed my grudge – growing it into a full-fledged hatred toward anyone I thought could have prevented Hitler and the Nazis from executing their evil, but did nothing. For those years, I was in my own living hell, no better than the ones who gassed my father and mother. When I began working for Senator Nixon in 1947, he started challenging me to forgive – to live again. The healing process began when I finally accepted that challenge." Berman pauses, the once-boisterous crowd hushed by his transparency. "I recently learned that my opponent's father, while serving as Representative of this same district before the war, was a close friend and confidante to Ambassador Joe Kennedy. This, despite the Ambassador's anti-Semitic and pro-Nazi public statements before and during the war." Berman turns his head and faces his opponent. "When I was young, I might have asked you the same question, 'How much did YOU know about your father and when did you know it?' Asking a son to dishonor his father is reprehensible, no matter the human failing. So too is forcing a man to disavow the second father who gave him back his life. Would that neither of us ever be that treacherous and disloyal." Berman finishes speaking and turns back toward the crowd.

The debate moderators are speechless. The crowd is silent. The only sound is the humming of the heating units blowing warm air into the large hall. Berman's opponent at least has enough sense to keep his mouth shut. He shifts his weight nervously from one leg to the other while pretending to scribble something important on a pad of paper.

Finally, from the middle of the crowd, an old woman stands to her feet and begins clapping. Another woman in the back of the auditorium joins her. Then another. People are jumping up all over applauding respectfully. There are no whistles, no cheers. Just clapping. Some are dabbing their eyes with handkerchiefs. After a few moments, the crowd begins exiting quietly. Everybody who is present and heard Berman speak agrees. This election is over.

***

New York City, New York

November 2, 1976

The election-night victory party is just getting started. As predicted, candidate Jakub Berman is now Representative-elect Berman. Supporters, friends, family, and most importantly in politics – contributors – are gathering for a night of celebration. Berman looks on, astonished. *Who in the hell hired this band?* he wonders, surveying the long hair and tattoos gyrating on the stage. *My god, this is awful!* Even though the night is young, the bartenders are already struggling to keep pace with their patrons. On a positive note, the dancing is off to a promising start.

Election-night parties in Manhattan are legendary. Party donors come to gloat. The ladies come to see and be seen. Everyone comes to participate. The Big Apple is a kinesthetic experience. Its social functions are hands-on events. Participants expect debauchery. The more the better.

“Congratulations!” the Senator booms, slapping Berman on the back with a loud thud. He raises his glass, toasting the man of the hour. “Terrific party!” he lies, bloodshot eyes flashing hungrily as he scans the scene in front of him. Like a predator stalking his prey, the Senator focuses most of his attention on the brunette bombshell posing seductively by the bar. Representative-elect Berman watches him watching her.

Her long red gown clings to every curve. Two small butterflies, beautifully tattooed on the small of her back, play a tantalizing game of peek-a-boo every time she moves. The waist-high slit uncovers enough thigh to make any red-blooded man have heart palpitations.

"You'll have to excuse me Congressman," the Senator apologizes, holding high his empty glass, "time for a fill-up." Berman nods, smiling. *The bait is set*, he thinks. *Here comes the very big fish.* Walking away, the Senator looks back over his shoulder, gesturing and barking loudly, "I'll meet you in DC for your orientation." Berman gives him a thumbs-up. "Can't wait!" he replies, giving him his best smile. *Can't wait my ass,* he says under his breath.

Right on cue, the woman turns and faces the Senator as he approaches the bar. Berman smiles as she gives him the full treatment. The innocent smile. The enormous eyelashes, batting shyly. The brown eyes, sparkling like gemstones. The head tilted downward, drawing the carnal man's eyes in the direction of her well-formed breasts straining against her gown.

"Are you a friend of the Congressman?" Berman hears her inquire of the Senator. *Jesus, Anna is going to take that poor son-of-a-bitch apart piece-by-piece,* he thinks, chuckling.

Berman's eyes find Kennedy standing alone on the far side of the room. He nods; *it is your turn now.* Minutes later, the bartender motions for the Senator, holding up the phone, interrupting his dalliance. Annoyed, he carries the phone to the far end of the bar, loudly pretending to give the caller a piece of his mind. Every few seconds, he looks back at the woman who acts as if she does not notice. Berman watches with admiration, thinking, *Anna's so good he thinks HE IS stalking HER.*

A minute later, the Senator hands the phone back to the bartender and empties his glass. Then he approaches the woman, whispering in her ear. He reaches behind the bar for his coat, lifting the collar to protect against the freezing rain. Berman smiles as he watches the Senator hurriedly make his exit, not even bothering to say good-bye.

"Speech, speech!" the assembled crowd is chanting. "Speech, speech!" Everybody is looking at New York City's newly elected Congressman and clapping. His attentiveness to the Senator has almost caused him to forget why he is here.

The embarrassed Berman smiles and waves at the crowd, taking the microphone as the room hushes. "Thank you for coming tonight," he begins slowly. "My heart is full. I am honored and grateful for the opportunity you've given me to serve the twelfth congressional district of this great state." He pauses, pointing out different people in the crowd. "Many of you are now my constituents. My hope is that one day you will all look back at this night and say this was your best vote. That is down the road. Tonight is a celebration. Eat, drink, dance – have a great time! Thank you."

Hesitating, he relinquishes the microphone to the bandleader, dreading more noise pollution. As people rush to congratulate him, he sees Kennedy across the room, checking out the action at the front door. Berman's eyes trace Kennedy's, catching the backside of Anna disappearing into a waiting limousine. He laughs, knowing that somewhere in the night, a libidinous Senator is waiting for her.

***

New York City, New York

November 2, 1977

“Fundraising is a bitch,” Beasley complains, slamming the hotel room door shut behind him. He finds the nearest chair and throws himself into it with a loud sigh. Then he looks at his watch. “I’m late.”

“Money talks,” Kennedy tells him, paying no attention to the time. He is preoccupied, standing by the window overlooking a subway station. Crowds of impatient people are scurrying up and down the stairs, jockeying over taxis and racing the time clock. He watches as two men on the street below start pushing and shoving, fighting over the last cab in line.

After the skirmish ends, Kennedy turns his attention to Beasley, settling into a chair next to him. “I hope so,” Beasley grumbles. “I feel like I’ve eaten enough rubber chicken this year to choke a Billy goat,” he adds, rubbing his expanded midsection.

“Quit bitching and do something about it,” Kennedy says bluntly. “I was stressed out and thirty-five pounds overweight when I left The Center and came to America so I took up running again. Look at me now.”

What a pompous ass, Beasley is thinking. “Running won’t raise one damn nickel for the party,” he counters, rolling his eyes.

Kennedy sniffs. "You've raised a lot of nickels, it's true," he concedes, glancing down at a report sitting on his lap. New York Republicans will owe you big time next election cycle. Officially, you have worked more than three-hundred events and raised over fifty-five million dollars for the New York Republican Party since your election – in ONE year."

"Politicians are such whores," Beasley claims. "You wouldn't believe the shit I've promised to get that money," he mumbles, his voice trailing off.

"The groundwork is laid," Kennedy declares. "After tomorrow, you won't be working for them as much as they'll be working for you," he predicts.

"But the field isn't clear yet," Beasley counters.

"It WILL be," reveals Kennedy. "The Senator doesn't know it yet but his ass is grass."

"How?" Beasley asks, curious.

"Just make sure you buy a paper tomorrow," Kennedy answers. "The Times," he adds, referring to *The New York Times.*

Beasley pauses for a moment. "What's the timetable?" he asks finally.

“The fall-out will be swift,” says Kennedy, confident in Anna’s work. “The Party will NOT be able to save him. In fact, it will have to move quickly. Your fundraising efforts alone have placed you in the on-deck circle. My hunch is that someone will back-channel word to you within twenty-four hours.”

“What if the media...” Beasley starts but is not able to finish his question.

“...Don’t you dare!” Kennedy interjects forcefully, sitting up straight in his chair. “The press will try to get you to go on-the-record before you or anyone else is ready. Don’t you do it! Let the Republican Party officials help you with the announcement and the timing.”

Beasley stands to his feet. “You make it sound like a done deal,” he comments.

“It’s NOT yet. Just keep your eye on the ball ‘Senator’ Berman,” Kennedy lectures. “The mission is a long ways from being a done deal but we ARE on schedule. It’s my responsibility to Sasha to make sure we STAY on schedule.”

***

Moscow, Russia

November 5, 1977

General-Secretary Leonid Brezhnev pours himself another drink. It is still morning, but that has never stopped him before. He swivels in his chair and stares out the window. It is Moscow in November. The snow is falling. With a sigh, he leans back, propping his feet up on the sill. A moment later, the Soviet leader is snoring, still holding the half-empty glass in his hand. The loud knocking startles him.

"Mr. Secretary?" Father calls out, cracking the office door open.

Brezhnev jerks and spills his remaining drink on his lap. "Goddammit!" he growls. "What the fuck?"

"Mr. Secretary?" Father repeats, aware it is too late to bail out now.

"Who is it?" Brezhnev sputters. "What the hell do you want?" He turns and faces the door, still wiping the whiskey and ice from his pants. He looks up. "Oh, it's you. Come in." He motions for Father to have a seat. "Son-of-a-bitch, I had a bit of an accident," he explains. Father nods, keeping his silence.

"Well, what is it?" Brezhnev asks impatiently.

Father reaches out and hands the General-Secretary a newspaper. "Operation Reciprocity," he tells him. "It's moving along nicely."

Brezhnev pulls out his glasses, wiping the lenses with his shirt. "Why the hell am I looking at the god-damn *New York Times*?" he asks gruffly. Then he sees the photo. "Jesus, what a dumbass," he says, coughing all over the front page. "Is this the guy?" he asks, pointing at the naked man snorting cocaine on a bed. "And these ARE ours, no?" Father nods.

"The Senator must have enemies at the *Times*," Father tells him. "Anonymous deliveries went out all across the city of New York – every media outlet. This story appeared the NEXT day."

The story continues on page four of section A. Brezhnev turns the pages, finding the other photos. "That bitch is the best..." he mutters under his breath. "The best," he repeats.

Brezhnev looks over the paper at Father. "When does this cocksucker's Senate term end?"

"Next November," Father replies. "But he's not going to make it to the election. He is damaged goods. The

Republicans will ease him out before then."

"Married?" Brezhnev asks.

Father nods. "And Catholic too..."

"...Shit, none of that means anything," the General-Secretary interrupts. "Kennedy was married and Catholic, too. He screwed half the Eastern seaboard," Brezhnev says, settling back in his chair again.

Father laughs. "Maybe so, but photos of him banging a Russian prostitute and snorting cocaine never made it onto the front page of the *New York Times* either," he adds, still chuckling.

"Point taken," Brezhnev replies, putting down the newspaper.

"Berman hasn't been in Congress long but he's raised a ton of cash this year," Father declares. "The Party WILL reward him."

"Are you sure we're not moving TOO soon?" the General-Secretary asks, skeptical.

"The sooner the better," claims Father, shaking his head. "Berman is hot right now, coming off a big win a year ago. He has a lot of momentum."

"Anything can happen in a special election," Brezhnev cautions, standing to his feet. "Let's not fuck this up. We need that Senate seat."

"That's what Sasha is for," Father explains confidently.

***

Chapter Nineteen

***

Manchurian Candidate

Washington D.C.

January 2, 1979

"The dictabelt changed everything," Arrowhead declares, handing Kennedy a copy of the House Select Committee on Assassinations Report. "The Committee's preliminary report was ready for the printer, completely finished. The members had made their minds up, doubling-down on the Warren Report, pinning it all on Oswald again."

"The dictabelt?" Kennedy asks, settling himself on the sidewalk bench near Ford's Theater. The street in front of the famous landmark is almost deserted, tourism in the capital city sustaining its annual cold-weather slump in the wintertime.

"One of the motorcycle cops with the Dallas Police mistakenly keyed his microphone open for eight minutes during the motorcade," Arrowhead answers.

"An acoustics firm tested the tape and confirmed a minimum of four shots from two locations, one of which was from the grassy knoll area..."

Kennedy tries saying something but Arrowhead is not finished. "That's not all," he says, gesturing with his hand for Kennedy to hold his thought. "The Warren Report also concluded Oswald's Mannlicher-Carcanos required 2.3 seconds per shot, which is how it came up with a 6.9 second time frame for three shots. But the dictabelt recording picked up four shots in 5.6 seconds, with the first and second shots only separated by 1.6 seconds."

"That means a second shooter," Kennedy concludes.

Arrowhead nods at the thick book Kennedy is holding. "Yup. The Committee had to tear up its report. It now says the assassination was the result of a conspiracy but it is unable to identify the other gunman or the extent of the conspiracy," Arrowhead explains.

"Unable or unwilling?" Kennedy half-asks, knowing the answer.

"Probably both," Arrowhead responds. "Thanks to us, nobody even knows the real Oswald yet. This is the third time The Agency has succeeded in withholding evidence of CIA links to Oswald from Congress. The last thing we need now are enterprising congressional investigators intent on identifying the other gunman or the extent of the conspiracy."

"Looks like the Committee is talking out of both sides of its mouth," Kennedy says, looking at the page labeled, "CONCLUSIONS REGARDING THE KENNEDY ASSASSINATION."

"I'm not sure I follow you," Arrowhead replies, appearing unsure.

Kennedy begins reading alou*e Committee believes, based on the evidence available to it, that the Soviet and Cuban governments, anti-Castro Cuban groups, the national syndicate of organized crime, the Secret Service, the FBI, and the CIA were NOT involved in the assassination of Kennedy.*

He stops reading, looking up at Arrowhead.

"They don't have a damn clue," Arrowhead responds, shaking his head. "It's the Committee's way of blaming it all on Oswald again, even though the evidence – and their report – both say otherwise."

"The Committee CAN'T say who was part of the conspiracy but it CAN exonerate two foreign governments, an entire refugee population and half of the intelligence community," Kennedy says, rolling his eyes. "Hear no evil, see no evil."

Arrowhead shrugs. "Notice who ISN'T cleared?"

"Oswald," Kennedy replies.

"Right," Arrowhead agrees. "It's a conspiracy of one." Both men laugh.

By the mid-1970s, polls showed that eighty percent of the American people did not believe the Warren Report. The deaths of Martin Luther King, Jr. and Robert Kennedy in 1968 at the hands of "lone assassins" only added to the suspicions that government conspiracies had silenced the three loudest anti-Vietnam War voices in America. Trust in government was at an all-time low. Something dramatic was necessary to restore that trust.

Under public pressure, the United States House of Representatives established a Select Committee on Assassinations in 1976 to investigate the deaths of John F. Kennedy, Martin Luther King, Jr., Robert Kennedy, and the attempted assassination of Alabama Governor and presidential candidate George Wallace. A little over two years and five million dollars later, the

Committee has finally issued its report.

“Two government investigations, two different conclusions,” Kennedy concludes. “The Warren Report said lone assassin and the House Select Committee says conspiracy.”

“But both implicate Oswald…” Arrowhead points out.

“…And both clear the CIA,” Kennedy interjects forcefully.

“Like I said, a conspiracy of one,” Arrowhead responds.

“That’s one of the main differences between our countries,” Kennedy says finally. “We Soviets KNOW we are beasts. We do not operate under illusions. Americans THINK the west is superior, making them and their leaders noble savages, incapable of succumbing to their most primitive and depraved urges. In the end, Soviets are at least honest. Americans are up to their necks in lies, trying to perpetuate their myth.”

“America’s full of humanists, the easiest people in the world to fool,” Arrowhead growls. “They HAVE to believe the best about themselves and people like them. It is why Oswald is the perfect scapegoat. He was a Communist. He tried to renounce his American citizenship. He married the Russian woman. He tried to go to Cuba..."

"...He's not one of them," Kennedy agrees. "Ergo he's an assassin."

***

New York City, New York

May 24, 1980

The hotel room door opens. This time, it is Kennedy arriving late. Beasley is lying sprawled out on the bed, napping. Kennedy slams the door, startling Beasley. He sits up, rubbing his eyes drowsily.

"How's the speech coming along Senator?" Kennedy barks, coming right to the point.

"You're not going to like it," Beasley responds. "It's pretty hard-hitting."

"Good," replies Kennedy. "The Republican Party is your audience, not me. Reagan wants to select a likeminded partner. You only have one bite at this apple."

Ronald Reagan has been running for President since 1968. Since losing the nomination narrowly to Gerald Ford at the '76 convention, he has been crisscrossing the nation speaking about the evils of communism, departing from establishment orthodoxy by provocatively labeling the USSR the "Evil Empire." When he was asked what a Reagan Presidency's Cold War strategy would be, his blunt response was, "That's simple. We win, they lose." Clearly, candidate Reagan is not a disciple of the containment policy.

With the 1980 Presidential election approaching, the Soviets are keeping a close eye on Reagan. The incumbent Democrat is, in Brezhnev's words, a "total fuck-up." His four years in office back up Brezhnev's words.

The American economy is in a freefall. Rising oil prices have caused an energy crisis, resulting in long lines and short tempers at the gas pumps, panics over heating oil shortages, and an overall frustration with inefficient, gas-guzzling, American-made cars. This "oil shock" is affecting prices of everything from groceries to consumer goods.

Runaway inflation and stagnant wages, or "stagflation," are crushing Americans like a vise-grip.

Compounding these problems are skyrocketing interest rates. Economists have invented a new indicator, consolidating all of the grim statistics into a single "Misery Index."

Normally, the American people are some of the most optimistic people on earth. Not anymore. A melancholy depression has settled over the land like a thick fog. The President, in an effort to encourage the American people, called it a "crisis of confidence" in his recent televised address. The people disagree. They blame the malaise on him.

Foreign countries sense weakness. Last November, Iran seized fifty-two Americans from the US Embassy in Tehran. Since then, the President has failed in his efforts to negotiate their release. A Special Forces mission to rescue them ended with eight US servicemen dead and no hostages rescued – the collision of a retreating helicopter with a C-130 transport plane over a desert in the Middle East reflecting the ineptitude of this American government.

Less than one month after Iran stuck its finger in America's eye, the Soviets sent fifty-thousand troops into Afghanistan, ignoring America's warnings to abide by international law and the UN charter. The west views the invasion as a Soviet provocation – an attempt to dominate the region and most important, strong-arm much of the world's oil supplies.

Ever since, the world has been holding its breath, anticipating a muscular US counter. Instead, the only response so far from the American President has been to announce a boycott of the 1980 Summer Olympics in Moscow.

Embarrassed by the whole spectacle and infuriated by their President's limp-wristed weakness, the American people are not their usual confident selves. None of this is good for an incumbent President seeking a second term.

Soviet intelligence believes the mood in America is ripe for a candidate like Reagan. If so, thirty-five years of Soviet strategy will have to change. The Russians will not be the only ones playing on offense anymore. More importantly, the Soviets know this new President will need a "minder."

Before, Reagan's cowboy diplomacy seemed reckless and confrontational. Now, it makes sense to the people. Still, politicians have been slow to embrace such an adversarial foreign policy. Until now.

Senator Berman is in Highland Falls to deliver the commencement address at the United States Military Academy at West Point. After the speech, candidate Ronald Reagan will not be a voice crying in the wilderness anymore.

"How hard-hitting?" Kennedy asks, curious.

The Senator reaches down and opens his briefcase, retrieving a copy of the speech. He coughs, clearing his throat.

> *The Soviet invasion of Afghanistan is a naked act of aggression...it is communism's attempt to forcefully subjugate a free and independent country...and to impose atheism on a traditionally Islamic people. The US cannot allow the Soviets to dominate a region that contains more than half of the world's oil supply...*

Kennedy holds up his hand, stopping Beasley in mid-sentence. "...Okay, I get it. Is there anything about US intervention in there?"

"Money and weapons for the freedom fighters," Beasley replies.

"You mean the Mujahedeen?" Kennedy asks.

“WE call them freedom fighters,” Beasley clarifies. “In America, anybody resisting the Red Army is a freedom fighter.”

“The Mujahedeen is a nasty bunch,” Kennedy argues, playing devil’s advocate.

“The enemy of my enemy is my friend,” Beasley counters.

“Good,” Kennedy agrees. “Very good. Reagan is calling for the same. This puts you on the same page as the presumptive Republican nominee for President. Let’s hope it’s enough.”

***

Elmhurst, New York

July 13, 1980

“Drop me off here,” Senator Berman instructs his driver. “I will walk the rest of the way.” The instructions he was given were clear – he could NOT be followed. The press has staked out the campaign manager’s home, waiting for an act of carelessness. If the media does sniff out this encounter, it will not be his doing.

The Senator has dressed down for the occasion. One does not normally walk through a Queens, New York neighborhood wearing a business suit anyway. Especially on a hot Sunday afternoon in July.

The ethnic diversity of the borough is unmistakable. Latin music is coming from the storefront with the "El Patron Mexican and Latin Cuisine" sign hanging above the door. The windows are open. He can hear the patrons speaking in Spanish as he passes. He cannot believe how much of Queens the subcontinent owns and operates. *I hope the last person to leave India and Pakistan remembered to turn out the lights*, he thinks. Everywhere he looks, the Senator sees Asian people milling around. Whether they are Japanese, Chinese, or Korean, he is not sure. *Maybe they are Filipinos*, he thinks, laughing under his breath.

He pulls the slip of paper from his pocket and checks the address again. *There it is*, he says to himself, seeing the yellow house with the white shutters. He turns in the alleyway and enters the fenced-in backyard through an unlocked gate. *Just as he said*, he thinks. As he nears the house, he sees the back door open, signaling him to enter.

An older gentleman is waiting for him as he enters the

kitchen. "Sorry for the subterfuge," he says. "Mr. Casey's house would have been too obvious. We had to improvise." He extends his hand. "Mr. Casey's father," he says, introducing himself. "I was watching you. You were good, like a pro," he adds, pointing outside.

"It was nothing," Senator Berman responds. *It really WAS nothing*, he thinks.

Mr. Casey's father leads him through the main rooms of the house to a back office. Three men sit around a large table in the middle of the sunlit room. They jump out of their chairs, all smiles, welcoming the Senator. After some small talk and a few stiff drinks, the four men get down to business.

"Together, we represent the two largest states in the US," Republican nominee Ronald Reagan begins, beginning the confab.

"Eighty-six electoral votes banked," Republican National Committee Chairman Bill Brock states, doing the electoral math for the candidate. "Also, more than six-hundred thousand Jews live in Miami-Dade, Broward and Palm Beach counties in Florida. That three-county region is the third-largest Jewish metro area in the United States, behind only New York City and Los Angeles. If you add in the smaller Jewish communities that are sprinkled around the state, one out of every ten American Jews calls the Sunshine State home."

"Average age – sixty-eight," blurts William Casey, Reagan's brilliant campaign manager.

Senator Berman smiles knowingly. "Retired Jews vote," he acknowledges. "I know. They're my base."

"Your childhood story is gold," says Casey. "Jewish boy survives Auschwitz, loses his family during the war, comes to America as a refugee and makes it big."

"And in case you're counting..." Brock begins saying.

"...We're ALWAYS counting," Casey interjects, chuckling.

"Florida means seventeen more electoral votes," Brock finishes, nodding at Casey.

"Electoral numbers aside," Reagan says, the recruiting pitch coming full circle. "Your speech at West Point impressed me. It took guts. I am planning a more aggressive policy position toward the Soviet problem and I need a partner in that effort. Will you join me?" Senator Berman pretends to be surprised.

"Your life story – how big do you want to make it?"

Casey asks, applying the pressure.

“Are you asking me to be your Vice President?” Senator Berman asks, genuinely flattered.

“I am,” Reagan responds. “I want you in Detroit next week at the Convention. I want you to give your West Point speech after your nomination on Wednesday night,” he says firmly.

“Tell us we won’t have to vet anyone else,” urges Casey.

“You won’t. I accept,” Senator Berman declares, beaming.

***

Washington D.C.

November 4, 1980

“Sir, it’s becoming more and more apparent that you are going to win a huge victory tonight,” the journalist begins. “What do you think Americans see in you?”

Mr. Reagan smiles. "Would you laugh if I told you that I think, maybe, they see themselves and that I'm one of them? I've never been able to detach myself or think that I, somehow, am apart from them."

Sasha watches, shaking his head. In his line of work, he is not supposed to feel anything but he cannot help himself. *Who CAN'T like this guy?* he thinks. "And I REALLY like his running mate," he says, laughing loudly.

Dismissed by the liberal intelligentsia as an intellectual lightweight, accused by the alarmists of being a dangerous cowboy, denounced by the left as a heartless right-winger, and mocked by a media establishment for being a B-movie actor, Ronald Reagan has survived all the epithets and insults hurled his way.

Rather than becoming bitter or growing frustrated, "The Gipper" – a familiar Reagan nickname given him after he played George Gipp in the film *Knute Rockne, All-American* – never seemed to care, pursuing the presidency with a special brand of good cheer and optimism. Reagan's trademark slogan, "Win one for the Gipper," typifies the happy warrior's fighting spirit and plucky attitude during a heated and often brutal campaign, greatly impressing the American people. Reagan is giving conservatism a pleasant voice and an appealing face, charming voters who never before voted Republican.

Just as Sasha and the Soviets suspected, the American people are searching for an antidote to the dark days of Jimmy Carter. Candidate Reagan, urging Americans to believe in themselves again and declaring the United States to be a "shining city on a hill" whose best days are ahead, is their choice. Though many have accused his campaign of being too extreme and simplistic, the desire for change is running so deep it does not matter.

The journalist was right. Tonight, the numbers are all on Reagan's side, winning the election in a landslide. After all the counting is finished, the Reagan-Berman Republican ticket will have won 44 million votes, or 50.7 percent, and 489 electoral votes to Carter's 35.5 million votes, or 41 percent, and only 44 electoral votes.

For the first time since Franklin Delano Roosevelt, the American people have chosen a President who campaigned against ever-bigger government, shattering the New Deal coalition that has so dominated American politics for most of the pervious half-century. The irony is that Reagan had been a Democrat and a fan of Roosevelt in his younger days.

However, as he grew older – studying politics and government – he became more conservative, eventually switching parties.

Never given the credit for his pragmatic skills as a two-term Republican governor of California, during which he was more conciliatory than his adversaries are willing to acknowledge, Ronald Reagan's critics constantly underestimate him. His mellifluous voice, his reassuring manner, and the skills he learned as an actor have helped him become "The Great Communicator" – another Reagan nickname – using television, the dominant medium of the age.

He is also old. At sixty-eight, Reagan is the oldest person ever elected President, but the American people do not seem to mind because he is in such good health and looks much younger. Even though he has many candles on his cake, his political approach is fresh and new. President Reagan will now be setting a new direction for the country – rolling back Communism, strengthening national defense, cutting taxes, and stopping or slowing the growth of government.

By his side will be Vice President Jakub Berman, the Soviet Union's NOC inside the White House, Sasha's crowning achievement. Operation Reciprocity – one huge step closer to fulfillment.

***

Chapter Twenty

***

Bloodless Coup

Moscow, Russia

March 23, 1983

"What if free people could live secure in the knowledge that their security did not rest upon a threat of instant US retaliation to deter a Soviet strike?" President Reagan begins. "What if we could intercept and destroy strategic ballistic missiles before they reached our own soil or that of our allies?"

General-Secretary Yuri Andropov, Leonid Brezhnev's successor, looks confused. "What the hell is he talking about?" he asks Father.

"Star Wars," Father replies. "We've spent over one-trillion dollars building the world's biggest land-based nuclear missile arsenal and Reagan wants to make it into a pile of scrap metal," he explains.

Reagan continues his speech.

> *Since the 1950s, the Americans and the Soviets have employed the strategic offensive doctrine of Mutual Assured Destruction. Both countries have stockpiled enough ballistic nuclear weapons to destroy the world many times over. The Strategic Defense Initiative renders even the most advanced offensive weapons useless, impotent.*

"Impotent?" Andropov yells angrily at the television. "Impotent?" He thunders. "The world is going to see which of us is impotent!"

The "Butcher of Budapest" has a long history of doing whatever is necessary to protect Soviet interests. As Soviet Ambassador to Hungary in 1954, he convinced Premier Khrushchev to use the Red Army to crush the Hungarian uprising ruthlessly. Andropov's strategy proved so successful it the Soviets employed "Yuri's Revenge" repeatedly in future rebellions.

In 1967, Andropov became head of the KGB. His idea to create a network of psychiatric hospitals as a means of punishing dissidents and would-be defectors became operational in 1969. He ordered people maimed, killed, and worse.

It was also Andropov's idea to invade Afghanistan in 1979. Brezhnev was hesitant, afraid of the international backlash, but Andropov and the KGB overruled him. In 1982, Brezhnev died and Andropov succeeded him. In the year since, Yuri Andropov keeps trying to break Kabul. Ronald Reagan on the other hand keeps making him buy it. "Payback is a bitch," President Reagan likes to say. "Afghanistan will be the Soviets' Vietnam," he promises anyone who will listen.

Just as the Russians backed the Viet Cong against the Americans, the US is backing the Mujahedeen against the USSR. Operation Cyclone is the codename for the CIA program to arm and finance the Afghan resistance.

Soviet pilots and tank commanders report Afghan "holy warriors" smiling and aiming highly sophisticated shoulder-launched Stinger heat-seeking anti-aircraft missiles at them from their caves. The Mujahedeen uses the CIA-supplied weapons to shoot at the MiG-21 fighter jets and Mil Mi-24 helicopter gunships – knocking scores of them right out of the Afghan sky. On the ground, the Soviet T-55 tank has come under withering assault from shoulder-launched anti-tank missiles (ATM's).

At the beginning, Red Army soldiers were shooting at poppy farmers and goat herders armed with outdated

Kalashnikov rifles. Now the rebels have brand-new AK-47 automatic rifles with armor-piercing ammunition.

According to Arrowhead, funding for Operation Cyclone in 1980 was twenty-million dollars. In less than three years, it has reached six-hundred million dollars and is continuing to rise.

“How much money is Reagan asking for now – for this Star Wars program?” Andropov asks.

“According to Beasley, he is asking Congress for two-hundred billion dollars,” replies Father. “That’s just a marker though. The Administration expects the total cost to be more than one-Trillion dollars,” he says, adding extra emphasis to the “T” in “Trillion.”

“Jesus! Where do the Americans get the money?” Andropov exclaims, frustrated. “They’re bleeding us. First Reagan’s military build-up, then Afghanistan, and now this – son-of-a-bitch!”

Meanwhile, the President is still speaking.

> *In 1961, President Kennedy issued a challenge. Putting men in space and on the moon seemed impossible at the time. Some criticized the space program for throwing good money after bad. Yet, eight years later, America did the unfathomable.*

Today, I am issuing a new challenge. It will not happen suddenly. It cannot succeed without failure, and it will not be cheap. However, it will be worth all the time, the toil, and the treasure. The future of America and its allies depends on what we do today.

General-Secretary Andropov reaches over and turns off the television. “We can’t keep up,” he says, shaking his head. “The President thinks he can bankrupt the Soviet Union with economic warfare.”

“He might be right,” Father declares abruptly.

“This is why we launched Operation Reciprocity, no?” Andropov asks. “For such a time as this?”

Father half-nods his head. “Well, the plan WAS to win the election in ’88, actually,” he reminds the General-Secretary.

“We can’t wait,” Andropov says firmly. “By then, it will be too late.” He pauses, considering his options one last time. “I can’t take that chance.”

***

Washington D.C.

March 24, 1983

Sasha leaves the path, descending the bank, climbing through the weeds to the culvert below. The grass is drenched from the early-morning dew, soaking through the bottoms of both pant legs and waterlogging his shoes and socks. Sticky web-silk, spun by an enterprising spider covers the opening of the pipe. *Must have been hard at work all night*, Sasha thinks, aware that Arrowhead loaded the dead drop less than eight hours ago.

He clears the web with a stick and reaches inside, feeling nervously with his hand, searching for the familiar metal box. After locating it, he pulls the box carefully from its hiding spot, brushing away the dirt. The box is heavier than he expected. *Must be the whole bag*, he guesses.

He opens the box, retrieving a brown paper bag. Inside the bag is another bag – this one packed with colorful gourmet jellybeans. Sasha examines the candy, not entirely sure what he is trying to find. Taped to the inside of the box lid is Arrowhead's note. It reads, "As requested – only the black beans are loaded. The other colors are placebos."

Sasha carefully places the bag of jellybeans inside the brown paper bag, securing it tightly and inserting the package into his jacket pocket. He quietly fastens the lid in place and bends down, reattaching the magnetic box in its hiding spot, inside the metal culvert.

He waits a few minutes before climbing back up the bank. It is early morning and the trail is still quiet but in an hour when the sky brightens, the park will be swarming with people jogging and walking their dogs.

Satisfied that he is alone, Sasha steps from the weeds and back onto the trail, walking away quickly. His heart is pounding in rhythm with his squishy shoes. *We are SO close*, he thinks, adding up in his mind all the times Operation Reciprocity could have gone off the rails. *But it didn't. We are SO damn close...*

***

Washington D.C.

March 25, 1983

"It's been a long time," says Caleb as Sasha takes the seat across from him at the diner. He sips his coffee, taken back by Sasha's weathered appearance. He cannot help wondering about the lines on Sasha's face, as if time has been marching an entire division of

Russian infantry troops over it.

Physically, Sasha still looks like he could wrestle or outrun a bear. Still fit and trim. Still the jet-black hair, just a little less of it. His eyes, ever piercing. The lenses on his glasses are thicker, but Caleb can still see Sasha's eyes flashing – just as they did when he was younger. The laser-beam focus is still evident – age has not diminished Sasha's trademark intensity. *If his mind is still sharp, why is The Center recalling him?* Caleb wonders.

"Yes, too long," Sasha agrees. "Joshua?"

Caleb shakes his head sadly. "It won't be long. Huntington's disease is hereditary. His father and brother both died of it years ago. Now the family is worried about Joshua's kids."

"They can be tested..." Sasha says, stopping short when he realizes he is talking to a doctor.

"...Right," Caleb interjects. "But they're afraid to. And after watching what it's done to Joshua, I can't say I blame them," he adds. Both men grow quiet.

"Coffee?" asks the waitress, handing Sasha a menu.

"Yes, black," he replies, declining the menu.

"I was surprised to hear from you," Caleb says finally, changing the subject.

"I've been going over forty years of notes for my final report," Sasha replies. "Lots of history we've lived. Important, too."

"Interesting times," Caleb agrees, folding his hands in front of him.

"My file indicates 'PENDING' on the matter of monkey viruses," Sasha says, remembering the purpose of the meeting. "I'm hoping you can help bring some closure."

"I can try," Caleb replies, shrugging.

"Last we spoke," Sasha begins, reviewing the file, "SV-40 and SIV were epidemics waiting to happen. Incubation period for both was thirty years. The contaminated doses were between 1955 and 1963." Sasha looks up, removing his glasses. "You're the medical expert. Were we right?"

Caleb nods. "It's worse than we thought," he reports. "Since 1973 when the incubation period first expired, soft-tissue cancer rates have skyrocketed. Skin cancer is up over seventy percent. Lymphomas and prostate cancers are up sixty percent, and breast cancer has gone up thirty-five percent. And it's only the beginning."

"Sounds like an epidemic to me," Sasha notes. "What about research and development for a cancer vaccine?"

"Nothing," Caleb replies, shaking his head. "We stopped trying. Treating cancer is more profitable than curing it..."

"...HOW profitable?" Sasha asks, taking notes.

"Understand, these are projections," Caleb cautions. "But our actuaries are usually dead-on. By 2015, the US will spend one-hundred and thirty-seven million dollars a DAY to treat the various cancers. And it will spend three-billion dollars per YEAR treating the one-and-a-half million new diagnoses at two-hundred thousand dollars per patient." Sasha whistles as he scribbles the figures in his notebook.

"All that money, all those treatments, and the sad truth is most cancer patients die anyway," Caleb adds. "Slow, excruciatingly painful deaths."

Caleb pauses for effect before continuing. "And when I say excruciating, I really mean it. The CIA weaponized cancer by roasting macerated tumors with a high-intensity radiation beam. Those galloping cancer cells are so lethal they kill human beings in twenty-eight days. Guess what we use to treat cancer with now?" Sasha looks up, shrugging.

"Radiation!" Caleb declares.

"What about chemotherapy?" Sasha asks, incredulous.

"Worse. Chemotherapy is an intravenously administered poison that is so toxic it kills ALL living matter. Have you ever seen the hazmat suit doctors have to wear when they administer chemo treatments?" Sasha asks rhetorically. "The point is repeated chemo and radiation treatments kill the whole body by degrees."

"But people pay big money..." Sasha protests.

"...Because their doctors tell them to," interjects Caleb. "And when you're desperate to live, you listen to the so-called experts. It is a toxic triangle. Pharmaceuticals manufacture the drugs, the government approves them, and doctors prescribe the treatments that use them."

"The healthcare INDUSTRY," Sasha concludes. "What about SIV?" he asks.

“The first reported case of Simian Immunodeficiency Virus was in 1981,” answers Caleb. “Since then, ‘human’ has replaced ‘simian’. We call it HIV now. You’ve heard of AIDS?”

Sasha nods. “Of course. It’s a death sentence, isn’t it?”

“It’s terminal, yes,” answers Caleb. “Best estimates are that millions of Americans are carriers of the virus. They do not know it yet. Because it transmits sexually, we do not know how big this epidemic will be. Conservatively, probably fifty-thousand diagnoses a year and by 2015, two-million total diagnoses and six-hundred and fifty-thousand deaths.”

“Son-of-a-bitch,” Sasha exclaims under his breath. “I’ll bet that treatment is expensive too…” Sasha guesses.

“Using the same 2015 projections,” Caleb says, “one-million dollars a case MIGHT buy patients an extra twenty years of life. They WILL die of the disease though; it’s a matter of when, not if.”

“SV-40 and SIV – a double-whammy,” Sasha declares.

“It’s safe to say the cure for polio was the worst thing to ever happen to the public health of the American population,” Caleb replies.

"Or the best thing to happen to government planners," Sasha counters. "In that case, Thomas Malthus would be proud..."

"...Population control?" Caleb interjects. "That's pretty cynical, even for you."

Sasha sighs. "It's a fact. War is the single-greatest stimulus program any government has in its arsenal. The Vietnam War would not have happened in a Kennedy second term – seven-hundred billion dollars that would not have been funneled into the military-industrial complex. The Cold War would have ended – that's another ten-trillion dollar hit. Epidemics thin the herd, maximizing resources. Cancer and AIDS – epidemics with no expiration dates."

"Millions dead. Trillions spent," agrees Caleb. "Christ almighty..."

***

Washington D.C.

April 2, 1983

"Ronald Reagan was rushed to Bethesda Naval Hospital late last night. Early reports indicate the

President was experiencing shortness of breath and chest pain," the breathless reporter begins. "No new information is available at this time," she adds, standing in front of the entrance to the famous hospital.

The National Naval Medical Center is most often associated with its location in the affluent and highly educated community of Bethesda, Maryland. Dedicated in 1940, its original purpose was to take care of the medical needs of military personnel only. However, keeping Franklin Delano Roosevelt physically fit for office became a full-time job. His lower-body paralysis required a lot of care. The medical center volunteered to provide FDR with all the medicine and treatment he might need. Ever since, "Bethesda" Naval Hospital has been the primary medical care facility of American Presidents and their families.

Sasha listens as experts speculate on-air about the President's symptoms. Their consensus view is that it's heart-related. Possibly a blockage or a mild heart attack. "It can't be too serious," one of them says confidently. "He aced his physical exam in January. For two days, an entire team of the best doctors in the world screened and tested the President. He even underwent a whole-body CT scan. Believe me, if he had anything, they would have found it."

"It's probably just stress," they eventually conclude. *It is NOT his heart and it is definitely NOT stress*, Sasha thinks.

Twelve hours after his arrival at Bethesda, the President is still there. Meanwhile, there is nothing new to report. The story is getting bigger by the hour. The gaggle of reporters and cameras stationed outside the hospital keeps growing larger. When the President's health is in question, no news is bad news. A hastily called press conference with White House Press Secretary Larry Speakes is about to begin.

On the other side of Rockville Pike, well-wishers with handmade signs are assembling. A prayer vigil with lighted candles is underway. It started with just a handful of people early this morning. The number is in the hundreds now. Some of them are holding hands and singing quietly. No one is a Republican or Democrat right now. Everybody is an American.

"This is where we stand," Mr. Speakes begins, clearing his throat nervously. It has obviously been a long night. Normally sharp as a tack, this afternoon he is a rumpled mess. His thick uncombed hair betrays him – the left side pointing randomly in opposite directions and the right side flattened against his sweaty head. His once-creased pants – now wrinkled like a thrift-store bargain rack. His shirt collar has either a coffee or tobacco stain on it. His tie is loosened and flopping out over his buttoned-up suit coat. Worried-looking and bleary-eyed, the normally unflappable White House spokesman struggles to read his own prepared statement, giving away the seriousness of the situation.

"Yesterday morning, the President complained of shortness of breath and chest pain," he says, looking up briefly. "The White House Medical Unit arrived on the scene after receiving the call from the Secret Service. The White House doctor ruled out a heart attack, prescribing bed-rest and observation for twenty-four hours." He clears his throat again and swallows hard.

"During the day, the President's condition gradually worsened," Mr. Speakes continues. "New symptoms such as wheezing, difficulty swallowing, and a loss of appetite appeared. "Then last night, the President began coughing up blood. White House doctors had President Reagan admitted at that time to Bethesda Naval Hospital for further testing."

The Press Secretary pauses. “The President is currently undergoing a battery of tests, some of which are not very comfortable. But he IS in stable condition,” he clarifies. Mr. Speakes closes his briefing book and looks out at the reporters.

“The next statement you receive will be from the medical professionals after they have arrived at a diagnosis. I understand there are many questions that need answers. Please save them for the doctors. Thank you.” He turns to leave, ignoring the shouted questions from the White House press corps.

“Has the twenty-fifth amendment been invoked?” a loud voice calls out, piercing the din.

Mr. Speakes freezes in mid-stride. He is aware the cameras are rolling. Americans are watching. Foreign governments are waiting. The ruckus dies down when he raises his hand for quiet.

“Vice President Berman is meeting with the Cabinet members as we speak,” he says. Reporters are scribbling the news furiously. “In the event it should become necessary, a Section-four draft of Amendment twenty-five is being prepared. We’re just waiting to hear from the doctors.”

There is an audible gasp throughout the room. In American history, the invoking of Section-four has NEVER happened. There has never been a need for it. *Holy shit*, Sasha thinks, watching the press conference. *He is already incapacitated. Operation Reciprocity has definitely crossed the Rubicon now.*

Three hours later, the whole world hears from the doctors. “The President has been diagnosed with stage-four lung cancer,” the oncologist begins stiffly. An aide places a display on the easel next to the podium, handing the doctor a pointer. “These x-rays show cancerous tumors in one lung and cancerous cells in the fluid around the other lung. Unfortunately, this is an aggressive, fast-moving cancer. And as you can see in these next x-rays, it has already metastasized to the patient’s brain and kidneys.”

“The President receives the best medical care in the world. How could...?” a reporter begins to ask.

“...I know what you are going to say,” the doctor interjects. “The truth is, about forty-percent of all patients diagnosed with non-small-cell lung cancer are diagnosed at stage-four. Because lung cancer does not have a distinct group of symptoms, patients often mistake symptoms for other, less-serious illnesses.

And of course, doctors rely on patients to disclose their symptoms…"

"…But this isn't some macho tough-guy who refuses to acknowledge his symptoms or go to the doctor," a second reporter protests. "This is the President of the United States. A diagnosis this catastrophic – shouldn't it have been detected earlier during one of his annual checkups?"

"It should, yes." The doctor agrees. "This is a highly unusual case. It is as if we are examining test results from two different patients – only we are not. In January, this hospital gave the President a clean bill of health. Since then, clearly, something very sinister has invaded his body. With regard to lung cancer in particular, the patient is not a smoker nor is there a familial predisposition. He has demonstrated no individual genetic susceptibility to the disease. None of us have ever seen anything like this before…"

"…What is the survival rate for patients diagnosed with this kind of cancer?" the first reporter blurts.

"The five-year relative survival rate is two-percent," the doctor states matter-of-factly.

"Oh my god!" someone in the hushed throng cries out.

There is a long pause. For once, the press corps is silent. Finally, an emotional voice penetrates the stillness. “What treatment are you prescribing?”

“The patient’s cancer is too advanced for chemotherapy to serve any useful purpose,” explains the doctor. “I am therefore recommending radiation therapy.”

“What’s the difference between chemotherapy and radiation therapy?” She presses him.

“Chemotherapy is a treatment to cure,” he answers, gulping. “Radiation therapy is a treatment to comfort.”

***

Washington D.C.

April 30, 1983

It happened faster than most thought imaginable. “We interrupt this program to bring you the following important news bulletin,” the anchorman begins somberly. “This morning, at six-thirty eastern time, President Reagan died of lung cancer at the Naval Medical Center in Bethesda, Maryland. He was seventy-two.” A magnificent Saturday morning in

America – interrupted by the tragic news. Just twenty-eight days after his diagnosis with terminal lung cancer, the President is dead.

Immediately, a pall settles over the land. It does not matter that forty-one million Americans had voted against him in the 1980 election. After the debacle that was Jimmy Carter, Ronald Reagan and his sunny optimism and staunch faith in America had restored the American people's hopes for better days and happier times. Those hopes were only just beginning to come true.

Reagan's tax cuts in 1981 had put extra money in consumers' pockets, which in turn, put income in small businesses' cash registers. Factories had begun hiring again and builders started putting up new houses as fast as they could. Gone were the long gas lines caused by the oil shock of the 1979 energy crisis. Gone was the American people's "crisis of confidence."

The economic indicators that matter most – unemployment, inflation, and interest rates – began going down and just kept going. The curses of stagflation and the misery index had become not-so-distant memories. The Carter malaise was gone – replaced by the Reagan confidence and can-do enthusiasm.

The Americans were even standing up to the Soviets again – in Afghanistan AND outer space. On the day of Mr. Reagan's inauguration, the Ayatollah released the fifty-two hostages held by Iran. Four-hundred-and-forty-four days of humiliation ended. What Carter could not do in a year, Reagan did in twenty minutes. America was back. Now the author of this comeback story is gone.

"Acting President Jakub Berman was sworn in at seven-fifteen eastern time this morning, the oath being administered by the hastily-called Supreme Court Chief Justice Warren Burger in a chapel at the Bethesda Naval Hospital," the reporter continues. "The new President plans to address the nation this evening at eight-o-clock, eastern-time."

Sasha looks at his watch and sits back in his chair. *There will be books written about this if it works;* Father's words keep going through his mind. *It worked,* he thinks. *It really worked.* Operation Reciprocity had been his idea. The mission of a lifetime. With each successful step in the plan, Father had delayed Sasha's recall. Now the hard part – his part – is finished. His successor will take it from here.

What a way to go out, Sasha thinks, a look of satisfaction on his face.

The voices on the television drone on. Dignitaries remember Reagan the politician. A seemingly endless parade of former neighbors, boyhood friends, and grammar-school classmates tell and retell his life story. Funny anecdotes displaying Reagan's fabulous sense of humor abound. *Poor President Berman,* Sasha thinks, chuckling. *Who can follow this guy?*

Finally, some actual news. "The First Family has declined the formal state funeral," the reporter announces. "Instead, the President's coffin will lie in state at the Capitol Rotunda next Monday and Tuesday," she reads from a prepared statement. "Wednesday morning, Ronald Reagan will travel by train on his final journey back to California. The private funeral service will be a family-only ceremony at Rancho del Cielo, the Reagans' vacation home atop the Santa Ynez Mountain range outside Santa Barbara, California. The President will be buried in Simi Valley, future home of the Ronald Reagan Presidential Library."

The camera turns back toward the anchorman, still sitting at the news desk. He is holding a piece of paper, just handed to him. He clears his throat and begins reading. “By order of the President, I hereby declare next Saturday, the seventh day of May, to be a national day of mourning for the passing of President Ronald Reagan. I hereby order all flags on federal and state buildings to be flown at half-staff for the entire month of May.” *Nice touch Beasley*, thinks Sasha, nodding his head. *A good beginning...*

“Fellow citizens,” announces the reenergized anchorman, directing their attention to an image of the White House on the screen. “From our nation’s capital in Washington D.C., President Berman speaking to the nation from the Oval Office.”

Americans do not like to admit it but physical appearance matters a great deal when they choose a President. Whether he was standing behind a podium or sitting behind his desk, Reagan looked like the leader of the free world. Sasha knows the American people need reassurance tonight. He breathes a sigh of relief when the new President appears on the screen. *Damn*, he whispers to himself. *Beasley looks like he is straight out of central casting...*

“My fellow Americans,” begins the President. “Today, our nation has suffered a grievous loss...” *They have*

NO idea, laughs Sasha.

***

Chapter Twenty-One

***

End of the Cold War

Moscow, Russia

May 1, 1983

"The proletariat revolution is coming to bourgeois America," Yuri Andropov declares boldly. The General-Secretary is standing in front of the window that overlooks Red Square, nursing a drink. He pulls back the heavy curtain and peeks outside.

Today is International Workers' Day. Most of the world recognizes "Labor Day" as a celebration of the working class but May Day in the Soviet Union is an important national holiday honoring the success of the Bolshevik Revolution in 1917. It is normal to see fifty-thousand people gather in Red Square for the annual parade. *If they only knew*, Andropov thinks between sips, watching the unknowing throngs below. He looks back over his shoulder at Father. "This May Day will be one for the ages," he predicts, walking away from the window.

Father nods. “If anyone ever deserved the ‘Hero of the Soviet Union’ award, it’s Sasha,” he says, giving credit where credit is due. “Karl Marx would be proud. Operation Reciprocity will finally allow workers in America to gain a class consciousness and mount a revolution against the capitalists...”

“...Workers of the world, UNITE!” Andropov interjects loudly from across the room, standing before his most prized possession – his liquor cabinet. His back is to him but Father knows the General-Secretary is refilling his glass – again.

Like his predecessor Brezhnev, Yuri Andropov is a “functional alcoholic.” Father used to think it was the job, but he knows now that both were heavy drinkers BEFORE their promotions. He cannot remember a time he has seen Andropov WITHOUT a drink in his hand. He does not know when the General-Secretary is drunk because he has never seen him NOT drinking. Yet, he functions normally – in a relative sense anyway.

Of course, he has heard the whispers. Some think Andropov’s volume button would not always be on “high” if he drank less. Others believe the General-

Secretary's harsh profanity might be less mean-spirited absent the booze. And his legendary temper tantrums – Andropov's fits of anger are scary. No one in Moscow has escaped his wrath. In fact, even Politburo members say Andropov is not happy unless he is mad. Most people suspect the alcohol unhinges him. Father disagrees. He thinks Andropov would be a much bigger asshole if he DID NOT drink.

He waits for the General-Secretary to lift his glass. "As for the timeline," he begins, "we have to win the election in '84 first," reminds Father. "When we do, we'll have the next eight years to work with," he adds.

"Ah, but that's your job, no?" Andropov responds, waving his hand dismissively. "This," he says picking up the folder on his desk, "is a ten-item agenda Sasha's replacement will help Beasley implement in a Berman Administration."

"Out of curiosity," Father says, "what are the broad strokes of that agenda?"

"The goal is to fundamentally weaken America in every way – economically, militarily, culturally, socially, religiously, and constitutionally," Andropov begins. "First, Americans will be dissuaded of their notion of individual rights. They must learn to value the common good above all else."

"Guns and religion?" Father asks.

"And a free press," the General-Secretary adds. "We can't control a population if it's criticizing us. We sure do not need the people trusting in their gods, and firearms. The people must be encouraged to trust the central planners instead – by force, if necessary."

"We must make the American people wholly dependent on government," Andropov continues. "Their rugged individualism will not be tolerated. We will accomplish this by increasing poverty and expanding the welfare state from cradle-to-grave."

"Poverty equals dependence on the government," Father agrees.

"Which translates into what?" Andropov asks rhetorically.

"Government control over the people," Father answers dutifully. "What about people who are insulated from poverty?" he asks.

"That's easy," the General-Secretary boasts. "Class warfare. Proletariats vs. the bourgeoisie. It makes it easier for the government to confiscate wealth..."

"...For the common good," Father says, familiar with the argument. "Then what?"

"The American currency must be undermined," Andropov goes on. "The expansion of welfare will help with that. Also, the takeover of healthcare and education – both are very expensive."

"Deficit spending?" Father guesses.

"Exactly," the General-Secretary declares. "All of that new government spending will raise the national debt to unsustainable levels – downgrading America's credit rating. Then it will default."

"What about population control?" Father asks.

"The Americans already abort two-million babies per year," Andropov tells Father. "That's an impressive number. Over time, we'll substitute an alien population for an indigenous one."

"It will take an entire generation to dismantle the American identity that way," claims Father. "It's brilliant but slow."

The General-Secretary smiles. "That's why we open the borders," he tells Father. "The white population will shrink. It already is. Latin American immigrants will flood across the southern border, none of whom gives two shits about American exceptionalism. They'll come for work and send their earnings back home..."

"...Taking jobs and draining even more wealth out of America," Father predicts.

Andropov laughs. "Some of this will be hard. But some will be easy because they are already doing it to themselves," he brags.

"You're going to be a busy man..." Father claims.

"...I'm busy already, no?" the General-Secretary responds, shrugging.

Father disagrees. "No. Busy is running TWO hemispheres."

The End

***

Epilogue

***

The United States government pronounced the Salk polio vaccine safe. This, despite Dr. Eddy's warning that it was not. Less than two weeks later, that same government withdrew the Salk vaccine from the market after forty-thousand children who received the inoculations contracted polio, almost two-hundred were left paralyzed, and ten died.

The United States government mandated two-hundred million American citizens receive the subsequent Sabin polio vaccine in 1955-1963. This, despite Dr. Eddy's warning that it contained the monkey viruses SV-40 and SIV. That same government assured the American people the Sabin polio vaccine was safe but now concedes it was contaminated.

The United States government claimed SV-40 would not cause a cancer epidemic but now acknowledges that it has. That same government vehemently denied any connections between SIV and HIV but now admits that AIDS is a direct descendant of SIV.

The United States government worked secretly – albeit half-heartedly – to develop a cancer vaccine for the beginning of the cancer epidemic it denied publicly, but privately knew was coming – playing Russian roulette with American lives.

The United States government used cancer research as cover for a covert Medical Manhattan Project in New Orleans to weaponize SV-40, converting galloping cancer cells into a lethal bio-weapon to assassinate foreign heads-of-state.

The United States government exploited human beings, utilizing them as unsuspecting lab rats in its final step in the testing ladder for its new bio-weapon.

The United States government's "cure" for ONE epidemic (polio) has produced TWO catastrophic epidemics – cancer and AIDS – both of which are ongoing and seemingly incurable.

Now the United States government claims children's vaccines do not cause autism.

Pregnant women know not to consume fish and shellfish due to dangerously high levels of mercury. Research has shown the adverse effects mercury has on brain and nervous system development in a fetus. Symptoms observed in children exposed to the high levels of mercury as a fetus include impairments of their cognitive thinking, memory, fine motor skills, attention, language, and visual spatial skills.

Yet, the government-mandated vaccines are pumping massive amounts of mercury into children's brains before age three – the age of brain development.

In 1986, Congress passed the National Childhood Vaccine Injury Act, forever immunizing the pharmaceutical companies from financial liability related to vaccine injury claims. The line of demarcation was 1991 when the number of vaccinations for children doubled. In 2002, CDC's own baseline numbers showed 1 in 150 children diagnosed with autism. In 2004, the numbers bumped to 1 in 125 8-year olds diagnosed with autism. In 2006, the numbers bumped again to 1 in 110. By 2008, the numbers had virtually doubled to 1 in 88 diagnosed with autism. Indeed, since 1991, the CDC reports that the number of autism cases in the US has risen by 2700%.

Like cancer treatments, there is big money in the manufacturing of children's vaccines. In 2011, the World Health Organization estimated the income of the top six children's vaccine manufacturers to be an absurd $5.7 billion per year. The companies claimed

90% of that total goes to pay costs – only leaving them a 10% profit. Assuming that is true, that still leaves one-hundred million dollars in profit per company per year!

It is a win-win for the pharmaceuticals. The money they make manufacturing and selling the vaccines on the front end multiplied by the profits they rake in treating the symptoms on the back end – symptoms caused by their own vaccines – is staggering. How can they lose? Especially since the law exempts them from lawsuits!

Like the cancer industry's toxic triangle, Big Pharma and government lock themselves in a vaccination tango of money and power. Big Pharma wines and dines the political classes with contributions, junkets, six-figure speaking fees, lucrative board appointments, and lobbying positions.

In return, the politicians grease the gears of Washington D.C.'s regulatory machine. FDA approvals of Big Pharma's experimental new drugs are fast-tracked. The government awards fat contracts to manufacture new drugs and passes new laws mandating the vaccination of the nation's children.

Batting cleanup is the corporate media, fearmongering

the society at-large with unvaccinated horror stories and browbeating anti-vaccination parents – labeling them "anti-science" – and tagging them with vulgar epithets like "negligent" and "child abusers".

It is a zero-sum game. There is no second place, only winners and losers. In this rigged game, Big Pharma pays-to-play and Washington D.C. plays-for-pay. Media conglomerates get their advertising dollars and political access. Meanwhile, the American people are not even in the game. And the beat goes on...

"Those who don't know history are destined to repeat it" —Edmund Burke

***

About the Author

Barry Jones is a high school history teacher at Franklin High School in Williamson County, Tennessee – near Nashville. Other titles authored by Mr. Jones include – *Flagrant Foul* (2008), *Letters to Toby* (2012), *Coup d' Etat* (2014), and *Treasonous Cabal* (2018).

Without exception, in his twenty years in the classroom, the JFK assassination, the Watergate Scandal, and the CIA's "Medical Manhattan" Project have generated more student interest than any other topic. This novel, *Wilderness of Mirrors,* is more-or-less a literary interpretation of his years teaching these subjects.

Mr. Jones is a family man. He and Katrina have been married twenty-eight years. Together, they have four children – daughters Shelby and Casey, and sons Toby and Sammy. The Jones's make their home in Fairview,

Tennessee.

A public speaker, Mr. Jones is available upon request. For information, feel free to contact the author at 931-494-0070 or at the following e-mail address: Blj34_37146@yahoo.com

Made in the USA
Monee, IL
14 June 2021